WINGS OVER MALTA

RON POWELL

This book is dedicated to
the people of Malta
and the pilots from all over the world
who fought to protect them.

Table of Contents

Chapter 1 – Welcome to Malta

Jack pulled the reflector sight ahead of the 88's nose and squeezed the bottom of the rocker switch. His Spitfire shuddered as cannon tracer raced away and smashed into the bomber's wing root.

He hesitated, Messerschmitt 109Fs bearing down, anti-aircraft shells bursting ever closer. Then, as if torn along a serrated edge, the 88's port wing peeled away.

'Yes.'

Wing and bomber began to tumble as he dived past. Moments later, he cleared the barrage. He looked back, hoping...

But no. Alongside the debris of the bomber, emerged two 109s. They turned onto his tail, noses flashing. Jack's stomach tightened as glowing rods of tracer arced toward him. A thud and his Spitfire rocked.

'Damn!'

He rolled upside down. Four thousand feet below lay the golden rock and soil of Malta. Hiding among its folds and jagged outcrops offered his best, perhaps his only chance of survival. He pulled.

By the time he reached the vertical, the air tore past at 420 miles an hour. Behind, both 109s arced down in pursuit. Ahead, the ground rushed up.

Jack heaved on the stick, straining to overcome the airflow buffeting the elevators. The g mounted until his weight quintupled. Blood drained from his head and upper body, dimming his vision to a grey mist. And still he pulled, groaning with the struggle to remain conscious and keep his head up.

At last, the nose of the Spitfire began to respond. But the rocky terrain raced ever closer. Sweat coated his body, yet his mouth was dry. With one final effort, he yanked the nose above the horizon. Still the aircraft sank, heading for a towering rock wall.

A gap!

Arms aching, Jack rolled right, wingtip almost clipping the dusty scrubland. Within a narrow canyon, he snapped to wings level. Limestone walls flashed past. The rough ground climbed, but so did his Spitfire - until it shot out of the gulley.

With a surge of relief, he eased the back pressure, feeling light-headed as blood returned to his cheeks and stars sparkled before his eyes. At little more than 50 feet, he levelled and looked around.

To his rear right, a black dart dived behind a squat tower atop a small hill. A bubbling cloud of orange and black rose up, expanding to envelop the sunlit stone.

Jack winced. But it was one down.

Bulbs of hot metal flashed overhead.

'Bugger!'

He eased lower, hugging the terrain, no higher than the tops of the stunted trees. Zigzagging, but always easing left, roughly west, the ground racing past in a blur. No sight of his pursuer, just the odd glint of tracer. Cresting a small rise, he shot out over the Mediterranean, turned hard left and pulled down. A swift look back revealed a 109 bursting over the same cliff.

Breathing hard, Jack rolled out just above the water, the craggy coast to his left. Blue waves turned turquoise then sparkling white as they crashed against the base of sandy yellow cliffs.

No time to admire the beauty.

He flew south, jinking, sweeping as close to the rock wall as he dared. The cliffs climbed and he climbed with them, staying 50 feet below the lip. He was sodden in sweat, twisting in his seat.

Was this how a hunted animal felt?

At the cliffs' highest point, he pulled up and with a clearance of no more than 20 feet rolled left onto a north-easterly heading.

Every instinct told him to stay low. But this was his first sortie over Malta, and...

'You're gonna have to climb, Jack.'

The airfield was no more than three or four miles away, but he'd never find it at this height. And he daren't surprise its gunners by blundering in at zero feet unannounced.

Still no sign of the 109. He eased back on the stick.

A series of thudding impacts. His canopy shattered. Vapour belched from the engine cowling. A dark shape shot behind.

He froze, memories flooding in.

Come on, Jack. This is different. No blood. No pain. No fire. Yet!

Screwing his eyes, he fought the fear. It had paralysed him then, and threatened to do so now.

'Not this time,' he screamed, manoeuvring to look for an assailant that seemed to have vanished.

Oily vapour streamed back from the spinner, spattering the windscreen. The oil temperature was rising, the pressure falling.

How long before the engine gave out?

He raised the nose, converting speed to height, making the most of what power he had. The terrain below was awful.

Then, the landmark he'd hoped to see. The citadel perched on its hill.

'Ye...'

The muted whoop of triumph was drowned by an ear-splitting graunch. The propeller stopped, one of its three blades just beyond the vertical. Jack pushed the nose forward to enter a glide, the only sound the airflow whistling through the jagged holes in the canopy.

The airfield was just beyond the hill, about two miles away. Could he make it? Wind light, so no help or hindrance from that quarter.

'Wheels and flaps up, canopy open.'

Much to his relief, despite the damage, the hood slid back and locked.

He wasn't used to straight approaches. What wasn't

hidden beneath the long nose was distorted by the oil mist on the perspex. But weaving for a peek would lose precious height; so, sweaty palms twitching on stick and throttle, he thrust his head left into the airflow and peered along the engine cowling.

All too soon, he slid to the right of the citadel, sinking beneath its creamy stone bastions toward tiny fields guarded by dry stone walls.

At no more than 20 feet, he passed over coils of barbed wire, a gun emplacement and a line of aircraft pens. Startled faces looked up.

He raised the nose to reduce the rate of descent. Raised it again.

The Spitfire touched down amid loud scrapes, thuds and bangs. Jack was buffeted from side to side, instrument panel and world beyond the cockpit a juddering blur. Then, a resounding clang and sudden stop.

Thrown forward, his head...

Chapter 2 – Three Days Earlier

At the end of the flight deck, Jack lunged against his shoulder straps like a ski jumper leaping into the void. Despite the encouragement, he and his Spitfire sank toward the waves. Spray lashed the canopy. His heart pounded. He played the stick, trying to coax the nose up without pulling into a stall.

But it was no good. He was going in.

Then the propeller seemed to bite on thicker air. As the tallest white caps reached up to lick at its belly, the fighter levelled.

A glimmer of hope.

Jack pushed his left hand against the throttle and eased the stick back with his right. Finally, the Spitfire responded, drawing away from the ocean - and the towering bows of the carrier.

He took a deep breath, blew out his cheeks and patted the top of the instrument panel.

'Well done, old girl.'

Satisfied with the acceleration and rate of climb, he raised the undercarriage and lowered the wing flaps to drop the wooden wedges holding them at 15 degrees. Unconventional, but it had seemed to work, giving extra lift without too much drag. He brought the flaps up again, and the Spitfire skipped ahead.

Climbing through 250 feet, his heartbeat slowing, he entered a gentle left turn and looked over his shoulder. For the first time in nearly a month, he was in his element, in an environment he understood, and over which he could exercise at least some control. The feeling of relief bordered on elation, but only until he refocused on the carrier. At that point, it melted into concern for those about to follow him.

HMS Eagle was bigger than anything he'd seen in Barry Docks; and yet, when he and his fellow pilots had boarded her back in Gibraltar, they'd soon concluded that her 667-foot flight deck was nowhere near long enough for a fully laden Spitfire.

Since then, the Navy had done all they could to boost their confidence, emphasising that they wouldn't consider launching unless the carrier was going full bore into wind, which would give them at least 30 knots airspeed before they even released their brakes.

It would be a piece of cake.

Jack had almost believed them, right up to the point where he'd strapped in and watched the first section of five struggle into the air. His own narrow margin of success had merely confirmed their original assessment.

The floating runway was too bloody short.

And he was an experienced operator, whereas all bar one of his section were relative novices.

The first was lining up.

Jack dragged his eyes away to quarter the sky.

The shadowing Junkers Ju88s seemed to have disappeared for the time being, chased away by Argus's Fulmars. Two Blenheims orbited above, waiting to lead him to Malta. Three others were already lost to sight, shepherding the first section toward the Island.

Relying on bombers for navigational assistance stuck in Jack's gullet, but one of the early Hurricane missions had lost eight aircraft, and their pilots, when they'd run out of fuel short of their destination. So perhaps the Blenheims were a necessary evil.

He returned his gaze to the carrier. A sandy brown Spitfire was nearing the end of the flight deck. It was crawling, moving far too slowly to get airborne. And when it finally inched ahead of the deck, Jack sensed it dropping.

'Ohh my God!'

He held his breath, waiting for a splash as the Spitfire sank onto the water to be run over and cut in half by the carrier, just like another of the Hurricane pioneers.

But no, it edged away from the great grey airfield and started its own gentle turn.

Jack breathed again. 'Well done, Kibec.'

He throttled back to give the young French Canadian a better chance of catching up.

The third aircraft was already in position, its occupant no doubt dreading the next 30 seconds, and hoping he'd never have to do anything like it again.

You had to admire the Navy fliers who did it for a living, not only taking off and flying away from their floating airfield, but having to find the bloody thing again when it was doing all it could not to be found in thousands of square miles of featureless ocean. And then, they had to land on a deck that could be pitching and rolling all over the shop.

He shuddered at the thought, and looked up to where the two Blenheims were still orbiting. No sign of a third section of bombers yet. Turning his attention to the sea, he scanned methodically out to the distant horizon.

He'd done his fair share of convoy patrols over the Channel, but then, enemy air activity had been the major concern. Over the last few weeks in the Atlantic and Mediterranean, he'd become more attuned to potential surface and sub-surface threats.

Below decks, with no idea of what was out there, you felt incredibly vulnerable, awake to every bang and scrape, of which there were many. Things became a little clearer when you were allowed topside, but even then, the sight of destroyers dashing this way and that could be profoundly unsettling.

Were they in pursuit of definite sightings, or off chasing phantoms? No-one ever saw fit to tell them. It had made him a very nervous sailor.

Much better off up here, he thought.

Beneath him, against all their inclination and training, the 13 ships of Force H, two carriers, a battleship, a cruiser and nine destroyers, steamed steadily into the southerly wind. Foaming wakes trailed for miles, a godsend for German or Italian recce aircraft, and the ships and bombers they'd summon up. For the time being, though, no enemy was in sight; not that Jack was likely to spot the vessels they feared most: U-boats.

The third Spitfire narrowly avoided a watery grave and the fourth lined up.

Approaching 2,000 feet, Jack steeled himself for an operation he'd been quietly dreading. He was about to find out whether the engineers had fixed a snag that had foiled their first attempt to reach Malta, and caused a frustrating, week-long, delay.

On 22nd February 1942, Jack and 15 other pilots of various nationalities had arrived at Gibraltar on the 5,000-ton freighter, Cape Hawke. Below decks were the first 16 Spitfire fighters destined to operate outside the UK. While Force H gathered around the Rock, the brand new MkVBs were removed from their crates, partially rebuilt and craned onto the Eagle.

For the carrier and its escorts to sail as far as Malta would be suicide, not only exposing them to prolonged attack from the Italian navy and German U-Boats, but also putting them in range of Axis bombers in Sardinia, Sicily, southern Italy and North Africa. So, for Operation Spotter to succeed, the Spitfires had to launch from south of the Balearics, a little over 300 miles east of Gibraltar, but 700 miles west of their island destination.

Spitfires had been fitted with auxiliary fuel tanks before, but, unlike Hurricanes, never ones large enough to allow them to reach Malta. That was about to change. As they sailed on 26th February, down in Eagle's hangar deck, brand new 90-gallon tanks were being attached beneath the engine cowling of each Spitfire.

When Jack saw the result, he was appalled. It was as if the curving grass box from a large lawnmower had been tacked between the undercarriage legs of his favourite machine. And to add insult to injury, when the aircraft were brought on deck for engine runs, some of the tanks refused to feed their precious cargo into the re-designed fuel systems, while others siphoned it into the airflow.

Nothing the RAF groundcrew tried was to any avail. With the deadline for flying from the carrier approaching, the pilots watched their engineering officer head for the bridge. Their lives were in his hands.

The squadron leader received the full blast of the captain's fury, but he refused to declare the aircraft serviceable, for which Jack and his fellow pilots were eternally grateful. Without his moral courage, they had no doubt they'd have been sent off to *give it a go*.

Instead, they sailed back to Gibraltar, powered by the steam issuing from under the old man's hat.

It didn't take much imagination to guess the tone of signals whistling between the Admiralty and Air Ministry, especially when it was discovered that the tanks hadn't even been tested prior to delivery.

The RAF contingent braced themselves for a rough time from the crew of Eagle. But relations remained cordial, if full of venomous banter. After all, the Navy had always called the RAF 'penguins' – all flap and no fly. And on this occasion, they were right.

An expert arrived in Gib armed with information that could have saved a lot of pain and inconvenience.

Firstly, when fitting a tank, if the seal between it and the aircraft was even slightly damaged, it would admit air and cause siphoning. And secondly, if the bulbous sump at the bottom of a tank was dented, it could block the pipe feeding fuel to the aircraft.

On closer inspection, the seals on several tanks were malformed, while some of the sumps had been damaged, either in transit, or when being fitted.

The Navy drummed their fingers, and the RAF groundcrew worked round the clock to put things right.

Finally, on Thursday 5th March, with repairs and testing complete, and much humble pie consumed, Force H set sail for a second attempt. En route, one of the Spitfires had to be cannibalised to fix further problems with the others.

So, when they launched a few minutes after dawn on Saturday 7th, they were down to 15.

Not the RAF's finest hour.

Jack looked to the heavens and placed his right hand on the fuel selector. If the overload tank failed to feed, his options were limited.

Fearing for their precious flight deck, the Navy had forbidden the RAF pilots to return to the carrier. The ban wounded Jack's pride, but, with the experience of taking off fresh in his mind, he had to concede that they had a point. The chances of pulling off a successful landing on your first ever attempt were pretty slim.

Unfortunately, the alternatives, flying south to land in North Africa, heading back to Gibraltar, or ditching next to one of the ships and hoping to survive and be picked up, were none-too attractive either.

He took a deep breath and turned the selector from Main to Auxiliary, alert for the merest glint from the fuel pressure warning light, or the tiniest stutter from the Merlin. After what seemed a sensible delay, with no red light and no change in engine note, he relinquished his grip.

So far, so good.

The fifth Spitfire had lined up. Its pilot was the only member of his section Jack had met before. Sergeant, now Flight Sergeant, Johnathan Charles, had been at Biggin Hill in September 1940, arriving a few days before…

He reached down and ran his fingers along the deep gouge in his right calf, then shook himself free of an all-too-familiar memory.

No time for that now.

He was less worried for JC than those preceding him. But frankly, his friend's take off looked no less frightening. Headwind or not, he seemed to have nothing like flying speed when he reached the end of the flight deck. Nonetheless, after giving Jack an anxious few moments, the Yorkshireman climbed away and turned to join up as quickly as possible.

Two Spitfires had already positioned themselves wide to either side of Jack's tailplane, and the third was cutting the corner to pass behind and take up echelon on the right, beyond Kibec. They were climbing through a haze layer with a ruddy tinge. To the east south-east, into sun, glare reduced the visibility to no more than a few miles.

Jack reached for his sunglasses.

About 60 miles into that shimmering haze lay the coast of North Africa. The distance made him uneasy. Like all single-engine pilots, he disliked being out of sight of land. But he positively hated being out of gliding range, even when it was Vichy Algeria, hostile territory.

Before he could reflect further, he noticed the Blenheims setting off on an easterly heading.

'What the..?'

The twin-engined aircraft were meant to wait until the fighters joined them at 10,000 feet.

Despite the initial shock, Jack could understand why the bomber pilots were so eager to set off. They'd arrived late and if, as he suspected, it was because they'd had trouble finding the carrier group, they'd have eaten into their fuel margins, so they couldn't afford to hang around.

'Bugger off, then,' he said. 'See if we care.'

He still talked to himself. It took the edge off his loneliness and helped pass the time, and there'd be plenty of that to wile away this morning.

Anyway, he wasn't worried. Other than the haze, the weather was good, and even if he lost his guides, he'd prepared his own map. He set off in pursuit though, lowering the nose a smidgen to strike a compromise between maintaining a climb and having sufficient speed to overhaul the bombers.

Until they reached their destination, strict radio silence was the order of the day. None of his section had waggled their wings, so it was safe to assume they were all taking fuel from their overload tanks, a belated tribute to the efforts of the groundcrew back on the carrier.

He looked down at the ships, still sailing south, awaiting the third section of Blenheims. They'd be itching to launch the last five Spitfires, turn about and head back to Gibraltar.

Jack touched his forelock in salute.

'Thank you, and good luck.'

He took out his map.

The plan was to stay north of the Algerian and Tunisian coasts, aiming just seaward of Bizerta, then Cape Bon, before turning south-east to give the island of Pantelleria and its enemy fighters a wide berth. Once past, they'd turn east for the final leg, hoping to sneak in between raids and land at Takali in about three and a half hours.

As long as the bombers flew smoothly, minimising the need for the Spitfires to pump their throttles, they should have more than enough fuel to reach Malta.

The major concern was meeting enemy aircraft. Their ammunition boxes had few shells and bullets, the bulk of the space being given over to pipe tobacco and cigarettes. Jack sympathised with the shortages on the Island, but even so...

At least the other reason given – reduced weight and improved take off performance - made more sense now. A few more cannon shells might have had him dipping into the ocean!

Jack put the map away and looked back to see that he was now the point of a neat arrowhead, two aircraft in echelon to either side of him at 50 yards spacing. The pilots exchanged cordial waves.

Beyond Kibec, with his matinee-idol good looks, was Mal Cotrell, a baby-faced Australian with about 25 hours on Spitfires. To the left, inside JC, was an American, Pat Olsen, another youngster, but one who'd at least flown a few sorties over France.

During the Battle of Britain, Fighter Command had been a pretty cosmopolitan outfit, but as time had passed, many more pilots had appeared from overseas, and not just from the Empire. So many Americans had joined the RAF that they'd been given their own, Eagle, squadrons. Pearl Harbour had slowed the flow, but they were still well-represented on this operation, with three in total, alongside two each from Australia and Canada, and one from New Zealand. Most, like the British pilots, were no more than 20, and low on experience, especially of the type of ops to be flown over Malta.

At 24, Jack was an old-timer, and commissioned to boot. Flying Officer Jack Williams. Who'd have thought it? Certainly not him. The commission had come through with his posting, so his experience as an officer was minimal.

Passing 7,000 feet, they emerged above the haze. All around, a crisp brown horizon line separated the rusty layer of North African dust and sand from the blue of the sky. To the north, a few brilliant white cumulus clouds thrust up, while to the south, there was a hint of distant mountains, their snowy peaks glinting in the rays of the early morning sun.

Jack had flown many hours since the Battle of Britain, but he'd never lost his wonder at the beauty of days like this, or his delight at the sight of a Spitfire.

Pat Olsen's machine was low in his eight o'clock, standing out above the haze. The overload tank was out of sight, if not out of mind, and only the dark letter-box opening of the Vokes tropical air filter showed beneath the front of the engine cowling. Otherwise, with the exception of the barrel of the Hispano 20mm cannon thrusting a couple of feet forward of each wing, he could have been looking at one of the old Mk1s climbing out of Biggin Hill in the summer of 1940.

He scanned back from the spinner and shimmering propeller disc, along the engine cowling concealing the Merlin 45, to the glinting canopy, and on to the tapering rear fuselage and curving tailplane.

As if realising the effect it would have, the young

13

American chose that moment to roll his Spitfire briefly to 45 degrees.

Bloody marvellous. The elliptical wings, subtly re-profiled since 1940, were still unmatched in aerodynamic efficiency and visual impact.

Jack felt a catch in his throat and found himself patting the instrument panel again, like a jockey patting a favourite racehorse.

But he was also struck by the unsuitability of the desert camouflage. No doubt it could be effective over the sand and rock of North Africa, but over the Mediterranean it made the aircraft all-too visible. He couldn't believe they'd be wearing it when they flew over the seas around Malta.

Not there yet, though, Jack.

Above the haze, visibility was limited only by the curvature of the Earth, but down through the swirling layer, he could see no more than a few miles of featureless ocean.

Just have to trust the Blenheims.

He was still overhauling them, but put his hand down to his map to reassure himself it was still there.

After one and a half hours out of sight of land, he spotted a darkening on the horizon, below and to the right of the widely-spaced pair of Blenheims.

'Thank goodness for that.'

He had no complaints about the bombers' stewardship. Once he'd caught them, he'd throttled back to a comfortable 1950 revs, and, after a few minor adjustments to match their speed, he'd hardly touched the throttle. With the other Spitfires spaced a few hundred yards apart to minimise their own throttle movements, they'd pootled along at 180 mph.

The major problem had been boredom.

He'd allowed himself a couple of daydreams about Caroline.

He still couldn't believe such a clever, beautiful, woman wanted to be with him. But, apparently, she did. And he certainly wanted to be with her.

14

He already longed to hear her voice, to feel her softness against his skin, to watch her standing, naked, at the side of the bed in the mornings, drying her dark brown hair. It was a picture he hoped would sustain him over the coming months. He wondered if there was some image of him she'd cherish. He hoped so.

Apart from his sojourn in hospital with his calf, and the odd weekend when he'd been unable to get away from Heston, they'd been very lucky. Even when he'd returned to operational flying, it had been from Biggin Hill, so they'd been able to live together again - unofficially.

Neither had mentioned marriage. He often wondered if he should, but sensed that Caroline wouldn't want the subject raised. And if she preferred to risk the opprobrium of living in sin to being widowed a second time, who was he to argue?

Anyway, nothing, not even a wedding ring, could improve her in his eyes. After the war, maybe, but who knew when that might be?

He looked down to the right at the northern tip of Tunisia, Cape Blanc, and the city of Bizerta. They'd soon be easing right for just shy of 30 minutes.

None of the 16 pilots who'd arrived on Cape Hawke had ever been to Malta, although they all knew something about it from newspaper articles and cinema newsreels. These showed some destruction, but tended to be upbeat, emphasising the bravery of the defenders and the fortitude of the Islanders.

Their first briefing on HMS Eagle had painted an altogether darker picture.

They'd gathered in the wardroom. With its battleship grey metal walls, floor and low ceiling, and dark mahogany furniture, it made even Jack feel claustrophobic. He and his fellow pilots sat around the walls, peering through a thickening cloud of cigarette and pipe smoke at a slim, moustachioed, man of medium height in his late 20s, standing with his back to the bar.

Wing Commander MacLean, the officer on Gibraltar responsible for operations such as theirs, spoke in the clipped tones of an experienced, Cranwell-trained, staff officer.

'For most of the second half of last year, the Italian Air Force was running the show, and, frankly, making a pretty poor fist of it. Little more than nuisance value really, which allowed us to wreak havoc on Rommel's supply lines.

'However, since Christmas, the Luftwaffe's returned from Russia - hundreds of the blighters. Probably won't bugger off again until late spring, if at all.

'And unfortunately, they've come back with the 109F. The Hurricanes are no match. They barely make 15,000 feet in the time it takes the Friedrichs to reach Malta. So, they're always on the back foot.'

He hesitated, as if deciding how to continue.

'And as for the pilots, well, a lot of our chaps are fairly green around the gills, while the Hun is fresh from the Eastern Front, which is a pretty bloody business, by all accounts.

'The upshot is that the 88s have had it pretty much their own way, plastering the airfields and harbour until our offensive ops have all but ceased. Worse than that, there are precious few Hurris left, hardly a dozen serviceable yesterday, I understand. Probably even fewer by now.'

In a habit they grew to recognise, he smoothed his thin moustache with thumb and forefinger, before continuing.

'So, not a healthy state of affairs, then. Added to which, it's become almost impossible to mount a convoy from here or Alexandria. Apart from the odd submarine and fast minelayer, hardly anything gets through.

'As you'll find out in a couple of days, the Island is beginning to run short of just about everything; not only military supplies, but basics, like food and heating oil.'

'And cigarettes,' Harv Johnson, one of the Americans, butted in, provoking a round of general laughter.

16

The wing commander winced in acknowledgement of their concern. But if he considered expanding on the issue of ammunition versus tobacco, he decided against it. Instead, he straightened, stepped away from the bar and stroked his features into a youthful picture of Churchillian determination.

'Yes, they're short of cigarettes, but also just about everything else that makes life worth living. And this is where you chaps come in. Operation Spotter is the first step on the way to redressing the balance, regaining the upper hand. You and your Spitfires will give Malta a chance to match the 109Fs and see off the bombers, something the Islanders have been waiting for for a very long time.

'A great deal is resting on your shoulders, and I know you won't disappoint.'

Jack shook his head at the memory, lips creasing into a rueful smile. The wing commander had done his best, but the little speech and the subsequent delay in flying to the rescue had left them feeling more daunted than inspired.

If the five Spitfires ahead were on course, and the five behind set out as planned, that still made only 15 against the 400-odd German aircraft on Sicily. Not to mention the many more the Italians held in reserve. And most were barely 60 miles from Malta, a flying time of 20 minutes, 15 for the 109Fs.

Unless they were followed by many more Spitfires, the chances of changing the reality on the ground – or in the air - seemed pretty remote.

To make matters worse, few of his fellow pilots had ever been in combat. And most of those had only been on offensive sweeps over France, nothing like scrambling to meet raiders over your own territory. Only the small number of Battle of Britain veterans among them had experience of this.

After his briefing, Wing Commander MacLean had opened up to a more select group.

'Why does Fighter Command insist on sending inexperienced and, in some cases, frankly unsuitable, pilots to Malta? Why doesn't someone force them to send more of their best?'

Jack knew why – so as not to weaken their own squadrons more than they had to – but he decided not to offer an opinion. Neither did Squadron Leader Stan Grant, their youthful leader, or Pete Brown, a short flight lieutenant with prematurely receding grey hair and a manner that conspired to make him seem much older than his 22 years.

The wing commander hadn't finished. 'It was the same with the bloody Hurricane pilots!'

He slammed his hand on a bulkhead.

They flinched at the unexpected clang.

'Sorry, didn't mean to startle you. And they are sending some good eggs,' he said, indicating that he included present company.

'But Malta's no place to send novices, as you're about to find out.'

Jack looked to his right at Kibec and Mal, and then at Pat, close on his left. It seemed grossly unfair that these youngsters had the whiff of failure about them just for being sent to Malta. You could only hope they were merely inexperienced, and not 'unsuitable', as the wing commander had put it.

Feeling a sudden surge of resolve, he stiffened in his seat.

'Well, we'll just have to prove the bastards wrong, won't we?'

At least JC was a known quantity, a solid hand. The wiry Englishman had fulfilled his early promise, scoring steadily throughout the Battle of Britain and cementing his reputation on subsequent operations over France.

Jack glanced at the Blenheims just as they began their turn round Cape Blanc.

He added a smidgen of throttle and moved the stick to the right. The other four followed. After a turn of little more than 15 degrees, the bombers rolled wings level again. He matched their roll rate and reset the power.

Not much in the way of excitement, but it was good to do something after 90-odd minutes of straight and level flight.

In some ways, this wasn't all that different from the various operations Fighter Command had been flying over France and the Low Countries for the last year or so, often with 30 or 45-gallon overload tanks to extend range. Many of these had also involved long periods of inactivity, flying straight and level in large formations. If you encountered enemy fighters, and especially the new Focke Wulf 190s, there'd be a brief period of intense excitement, terror even, then the boredom of the return leg, if you survived to make it.

There'd been Rhubarbs – dashes across the Channel by a few aircraft to attack airfields or targets of opportunity; Rodeos – similar, but involving sweeps by whole squadrons; Jim Crows – regular patrols on set routes; Ramrods – providing fighter cover for genuine bombing raids; and Circuses – designed to look like Ramrods, but with the bombers merely decoys for layers of fighters, hoping to draw up and destroy the 109s and 190s.

When the winter weather had permitted over the last 6 months, Circuses had been the usual fare for the Biggin Hill Wing. They seemed a costly way of taking the fight to the enemy, with few gains and many losses, often of inexperienced pilots who, for one reason or another, fell behind and were picked off. Not only the inexperienced, though. Even the likes of Douglas Bader had been shot down and captured.

In many ways, it was the Battle of Britain in reverse, the Luftwaffe having all the advantages of fighting over its own territory, Fighter Command all the disadvantages, including losing pilots and aircraft that failed to make it back across the Channel.

And all to keep the Luftwaffe on its toes.

The only other offering had been convoy patrols, another mind-numbing exercise most of the time. Jack had begun to feel as if he was merely helping to make up the numbers, lost in a large machine where his talents, such as they were, seemed to add little.

So, for reasons he still found hard to explain, he'd decided to volunteer for Malta; although, the more he heard, the more he doubted the wisdom of the decision. At least at home he'd been able to spend most nights with Caroline, surely enough to make up for any amount of boredom.

The Blenheims moved up his windscreen, beginning the climb to 15,000 feet well before the leg on which they'd pass abeam Pantelleria. He added a growl of power and raised the nose to follow.

The slant visibility improved with height until Jack could see the Gulf of Tunis and the ruddy Tunisian coast to his right. Hostile territory again, but it gave his spirits a lift. Cape Bon was in view by the time the Blenheims levelled. He eased the throttle back to hold position behind them.

As planned before departure, he waited a few moments, then switched fuel from Auxiliary to Main. Once again, he stayed alert for the tell-tale signs of fuel starvation. Content with the performance of his own engine, he looked to either side, acknowledging a thumbs-up from each of the other four.

Again, so far so good.

The empty tanks could be jettisoned, but they wanted them in Malta, so unless they were attacked and had to lose them to improve performance, they'd be taking them all the way.

A sudden glint in the haze caused his pulse to quicken. Sunlight on something near Cape Bon. And was that a dark shape, or shapes, climbing through the murk?

He shifted in his seat, his skin prickling as if suddenly charged with static electricity. But hard as he looked, he failed to spot anything concrete, just swirling patterns of dark and light, spectres playing on his imagination.

Just as well, really. If a squadron of 109s attacked, the Spitfires would soon run out of ammo and have to scatter, or rely on the Blenheims for protection. Now that really would be a turn up for the books.

A few minutes later they turned right onto 170 degrees to skirt Pantelleria, another leg of about 30 minutes.

After ten minutes, Jack could just make out the ghost of an island in the haze to the left, 20 miles away. Until they reached Malta, this was the leg on which they were most likely to meet trouble, so he redoubled his lookout.

A couple of times, he saw flashes in the distance. But, whether sun on a canopy, the portholes of a ship, or anything else, he never found out. Either way, no aircraft threatened.

Way beyond Pantelleria, a thin trail of dark smoke appeared above the horizon. A few minutes later, the snow-capped summit from which it issued thrust above the haze.

Mount Etna. Sicily.

Perhaps because Axis aircraft covered the airfields beneath it, the volcano had an evil look, like some infernal foundry. And although, as the southerly leg continued, it diminished in size, it never disappeared completely, remaining a brooding presence, lowering his mood.

His calf ached, as it often did on long sorties. No matter how much he rubbed or tried to flex it, the cramped conditions caused it to throb. This time, he let his mind wonder back to the day he'd received the wound.

On 6th September, 1940, a 109's cannon shells had done for his engine, his canopy, his calf and, something that still pained him more than the wound itself, his confidence and self-esteem. He'd frozen with terror, staring at his blood-soaked hands, aware of the 110 growing to fill his rear-view mirror, but unable to act.

And then, in a flash of black and orange, the 110 had disappeared.

The sudden, inexplicable, reprieve should have restored at least some composure, but it didn't. Another orange glow had appeared, out there, beyond his hands.

Fire!

Flames reached back to lick round the edges of his shattered canopy. But still he sat there, unable to think clearly, unable to move. Slowly, he became aware of a voice.

'Get out of there, Jack!'

It was familiar, belonging to someone he trusted, and it was commanding.

'Get out of there!'

It must have galvanised him into action, because he'd managed to take to his parachute and land without breaking anything.

The next day, he'd woken up in hospital, free of burns, but having lost buckets of blood.

The orange flash in his rear-view mirror had been Alex Lowe colliding with the 110.

Some thought the young officer had misjudged his attack on the twin-engined fighter, but Piers White, the owner of the warning voice, was sure that Alex's action had been deliberate.

Jack believed him. And of course he could never be anything other than eternally grateful to Alex for making the ultimate sacrifice. He thought of it often, and often when he was having the most fun, flying on a beautiful day like today, or in the afterglow of making love to Caroline. At such times, he was painfully aware that his friend had forfeited his own young life to allow such moments.

Apart from a spectacular scar and an almost imperceptible limp, he'd made a full physical recovery. But, his mental state had been – remained - more fragile.

He'd railed against the move to an Operational Training Unit, but, in hindsight, it had allowed him to get back in the air without the threat of immediate death, at least not at the hands of the enemy. His students were always trying to kill him in one way or another, but their inexperience allowed him to reassert his skill as a pilot, to regain his confidence.

And he thought it had worked. Right up to the point when he returned to the reality of the front line. He soon discovered that the prospect of combat filled him with dread - and that the fear followed him into the cockpit.

He'd even developed a tic in the corner of his left eye during periods of stress. As yet, it was invisible – he'd checked – and he was sure the crewroom remained oblivious to his inner turmoil. But turmoil there was.

All that said, he'd weathered the strain of missions over France, and combat. He'd even added a couple to his score, regaining his reputation as a solid hand. But it wasn't enough to restore him to his Battle of Britain best, or make him feel his presence was worthwhile - not by a long way. And the fear remained, gnawing away.

So why Malta? What on Earth was he trying to prove? And to who?

Caroline? But she'd never given the slightest indication that she doubted him, or his courage.

Alex or Binky, or any of the others that had died or been maimed during the Battle of Britain? Perhaps, but he didn't think so.

Well, whatever the reason, there was no pulling out now. Whether he'd be able to contain his fear in Malta, only time would tell.

The one thing he could never overcome was his guilt.

If only he hadn't frozen when the shells had hit. If only he'd reacted instantly, turned, or pulled up and away from the 110, as he had so many times before. Alex could still have been alive, or at least have lived to fight another day, lived to spend more time with his young lady, Sophie.

She was another reason for guilt. He'd intended to seek her out, but while he'd been in hospital, she too had been posted. Deterred partly by their difference in rank - she was a WAAF officer – he'd failed to track her down, or even to write. He'd been a coward in that too.

A cannon shell ripping through his flesh was no excuse for any of it.

By the time they turned left onto 105 degrees for the final leg, Jack had managed to shake off the malaise and was in a better frame of mind, once again admiring the blue of the sky and the Spitfires dancing in the sunlight.

His bladder and the imprint of the dinghy bottle on his backside were of more concern than his calf. Perhaps he should have refused that last cup of tea. But, unless their arrival proved overly-exciting, he was sure he could hold on. It was either that, or pee in his new officer's hat!

Etna, now in his 11 o'clock, began to grow again.

To his right, Kibec and Mal Cotrell suddenly turned away from him, but with no more than about five degrees of bank. After a few seconds, they rolled left and turned gently toward him. He tensed, puzzled, making ready to turn away.

They were too low for lack of oxygen to warrant unconsciousness, but had they fallen asleep? Both of them!

He was wondering what to do, when the French Canadian waved and rolled right again. The penny dropped.

'Silly buggers.' he smiled.

At least they'd found a way to relieve the boredom. For a fleeting moment, he considered joining in and seeing if Pat and JC did the same. But, no, someone had to play the adult.

Not that he was grumpy. Their antics weren't ideal fuel management, but he was happy for them to have their fun as long as they didn't become over-exuberant.

'A joke's a joke, but keep your arse off the pillow,' as one of his instructors at Halton had been fond of saying when Jack and his fellow apprentices were being too boisterous in class. The phrase had bemused them at first, but had become clear enough with repetition.

Kibec and Mal's jolly little jape was nowhere near the

threshold for such an admonition. But then, out to his left, Pat and JC began gently descending and climbing, like porpoise playing in the surf.

Very funny, but it raised the spectre of them trying to outdo each other. Jack allowed a few more repetitions before making an exaggerated yawning motion.

To their credit, they knocked it off immediately. Just as well, because he wasn't sure how he could have stopped them if they'd been determined to continue.

Anyway, the tom-foolery had filled a few minutes, and Etna had grown some more and moved into the 10 o'clock, a welcome indication of progress. It shouldn't be too long before Malta itself became visible.

'Exile One, f...ow the Hur..... and the ....ield will be... your tw...........ock, fifteen miles.'

'Exile One, roger.'

Great. The leading section was in contact with the Island. What's more, the exchange sounded pretty relaxed, with no hint of anxiety or impending danger. No guarantee that their own arrival would be without incident, of course, but hopeful nonetheless.

Nods to either side indicated that they'd all heard the transmissions. But Jack was sure it was Stan Grant that had spoken, rather than one of the bomber captains. What had happened to the Blenheims?

A few minutes later, it was the squadron leader that spoke again. 'Gondar, this is Exile One, field in sight.'

'Roger, Exile One, clear in and watch out for 109s. Woody out.'

'Exile One, roger and out.'

This time, Jack could hear Malta loud and clear. He waited for his own lead bomber to chirp up. Nothing. The silence became deafening. They must have the wrong frequency. If not, surely they'd have tried to establish contact by now.

He pressed the transmit button. 'Gondar, this is Exile Two.'

'Hello, Exile Two, Woody here, good to hear you. Trust all is well?'

Woody could only be Group Captain Woody Woodhall, the controller about whom Wing Commander MacLean had eulogised. His R/T was said to be non-standard, and it was certainly less formal than that over southern England. Jack didn't feel qualified to relax into a similar style just yet.

'Gondar, this is Exile Two, section complete, including escorts.'

'Good show, Exile Two. You're clear in, with Hurris coming to meet you.'

'Exile Two, roger.'

'The big jobs seem reluctant to speak, but they'll peel off when the Hurris pick you up. And just be aware, a plot is leaving Sicily. Looks like little jobs. Hope to have you down before they arrive, but can't promise.'

'Exile Two, roger.'

Well, that all seemed clear enough, assuming little jobs were fighters. The group captain's voice still carried no hint of anxiety, but the thought of 109s pouncing when the Spitfires were short of fuel and ammunition had raised Jack's heartbeat.

For some time, he'd been watching a small patch of cumulus clouds in the distance. Now, with about 50 miles to go, a hint of land appeared beneath them. A few miles later, the Blenheims began a gentle descent and he followed. Unbidden, his section closed to a spacing of 20 yards.

A little later, with the cloud thinning, he could make out four islands. The most northerly, Gozo, was about a third the size of the southerly, Malta. Nestled in a narrow channel between them was a much smaller island. Must be Comino. And off the south-west coast of Malta was a tiny smudge that had to be Filfla, a favourite for bomb and gunnery practice, apparently. Which presumably meant it was uninhabited.

The evidence of his eyes seemed to mesh with what they'd been told.

'Malta is roughly the shape of a rugby ball or beech leaf, about 17 miles by nine, with the long axis running from north-west to south-east.'

Mention of the Island invariably seemed to be followed by, 'smaller than the Isle of Wight.' Well, they were certainly right about that. He was used to seeing the island south of the English coast from a similar distance, and Malta looked much smaller.

Tiny.

And as their briefer had said, 'All the targets – harbours, airfields and barracks - are crammed into the southern two thirds, no more than a few miles apart.'

Jack almost wished he was a bomber pilot.

And yet, here he was, riding to the rescue. More like flying into the lion's den. He looked to either side, trying to imagine how the others might feel.

'Exile Two, Hurris twelve miles low in your eleven o'clock, report when sighted.'

'Gondar, this is Exile Two, roger.'

A minute or so later, he spotted them, a couple of Hurricane IIs, silhouetted above the haze layer, climbing in line abreast. Having expected a larger reception committee, he searched for more, but to no avail. Oh, well, two it was.

As he transmitted, the Hurricanes began a turn.

'Gondar, this is Exile Two, escort sighted.'

'Roger, Exile Two, follow them in.'

'Exile Two, roger.'

Jack pushed throttle and stick forward and they soon passed down the left hand side of the Blenheims. He gave them a wave and the two bombers eased right, bound, he guessed, for one of the two surfaced runways on the main airfield, Luqa.

Exile Two closed on the Hurricanes.

The Controller spoke to Exile Three, a little edge to his voice. 'We've lost the formation of little jobs for the moment, so keep your eyes peeled.'

'Roger Gondar.' It was Pete Brown's voice.

At 3,000 feet, they caught the Hurricanes just as they sank below the base of the lowest cumulus clouds and passed over steep cliffs roughly midway along the south-west coast.

The ground was greener than expected, but scarred by frequent ravines and outcrops of weathered limestone. A scattering of hilltop villages, all built of the same creamy material, were surrounded by cascading terraces or walled enclosures, too small to be labelled fields. Most seemed to contain crops or trees rather than livestock, while a few bore evidence of recent ploughing.

A very inhospitable place for a forced landing, Jack thought.

Even from 2,000 feet, he could see the whole island clearly. The dominant feature, on the far coast just to the right of the nose, was a large town. Shining in the sunlight, its central spike of densely packed cream buildings thrust between two narrow inlets of shimmering blue water fringed with more densely packed buildings.

Valletta, the capital, and home to most of the Island's quarter of a million inhabitants. The inlets would be its two harbours.

Just inland was a racecourse, and a little to the south of that, an airfield with metalled runways that could only be Luqa.

Then, much closer, sitting in a valley beyond a walled town perched on a hill, he spotted what must be their airfield, Takali. It had been built on a dry lake bed, which Wing Commander MacLean said reverted to type very quickly when the heavens opened, as they had for much of January and February.

Jack waited a couple of seconds, before transmitting. 'Gondar, this is Exile Two, airfield in sight.'

'Roger Exile Two, cleared in with a southerly wind. See you later. Woody out.'

The Hurricanes began a descending right turn and Jack followed. Below, an airfield he'd have described as dusty with tinges of green was ringed by tracks and a few clusters of buildings. It was bisected by one definite dirt strip, running east-west, and the hint of three more, the faintest running north-south, the others diagonally from roughly north-west and north-east.

The most striking thing, even from this height, was the number of bomb craters.

The Hurricanes suddenly pulled up and away and Jack assumed the lead. None of the landing strips seemed totally free of craters, or obstructions, but given the wind direction, he set them up for the southerly strip.

He cleared Kibec and Mal into echelon left, continued the right turn onto a downwind leg, did his landing checks and, as he entered his curving finals turn, looked back to see the others strung out at a sensible spacing.

A green flare rose from a wreck of a bus to the right of the runway. Cleared to land.

Crossing over the northern airfield boundary, the level of destruction became more apparent. Nearby buildings all had shattered roofs and gaping windows. Skeletons of aircraft and vehicles lay everywhere.

More worryingly, the strip crossed several circles of newly laid earth, and was bordered by numerous red flags. These would mark unexploded or delayed action bombs that could blow at any time, or at any disturbance, such as a passing aircraft.

Jack closed the throttle and raised the nose gradually into the landing position. After a short float and a bounce, his Spitfire settled onto the dusty earth. The surface could have been smoother, but it wasn't bad considering how much was newly restored.

Laying off the brakes, he trundled forward to leave space for those landing behind him, then turned right between two circles of newly packed earth and a few red flags.

'What the fuck?'

Black balls of smoke expanded to his front right. Through them, at no more than 50 feet, shot four

Messerschmitts, noses flashing.

Over Jack's shoulder, Pat Olsen and JC were on the ground, Kibec was about to touch down and Mal Cotrell was 100 yards behind the Canadian on short finals.

Fountains of dirt raced across the airfield toward them…

Chapter 3 – The Shock of the New

'Bandits right, nine o'clock,' Jack shouted.

Even if Pat, JC and Kibec had seen the dust-spouts, there was little they could do about them. But Mal Cotrell reacted immediately. Black smoke spat from the stub exhausts of his Spitfire, its nose reared up and its landing gear began to retract.

The Messerschmitts flashed past, followed by a couple of Hurricanes. These passed over Mal with no more than feet to spare and raced after the swiftly-climbing 109Fs.

Kibec touched down, seemingly unharmed, and Mal roared overhead.

Jack fast-taxied forward a short distance to leave room for the others to clear the landing run. His headset was filled with the sound of his own rapid breathing. Sweat prickled his body.

'Better than last time though, Butt.'

Attacked on the ground at Biggin Hill, he'd finished upside down in a flaming wreck.

What to do now? Hit the throttle and race into the expanse of bomb craters and red flags; jump out and run into the same landscape; or wait for the truck that seemed to be weaving and bouncing in their direction?

Much as he itched for decisive action, he decided to sit on his hands, waiting for Kibec to turn off to join Pat and JC behind him. For the moment, he couldn't see the 109s or Hurricanes, and Mal's Spitfire was scuttling downwind, its wheels lowering again.

He hoped the young Australian hadn't been too distracted. It would be all-too-easy for someone of his experience to screw up an approach to a strange and less-than-ideal runway, especially with enemy fighters in the vicinity.

The battered old Bedford stopped by Jack's wingtip, but only briefly. With a shudder and belch of exhaust fumes, it rumbled off, turning and heading back in the direction from which it had arrived.

It had dropped off a lone airman.

Dressed in khaki short-sleeve shirt and shorts, rolled-down socks and dusty boots, the young man ran behind the wing and in next to no time appeared, kneeling, at Jack's side. Beneath a mop of unruly black hair, his deeply tanned face broke into a smile.

'Hello, sir. Welcome to Malta.'

Without waiting for a reply, he pointed and shouted, 'Straight ahead, sir. I'll direct you.'

Jack was glad to open the throttle. He taxied as fast as he dared whilst weaving from side to side to see down the side of his Spitfire's high nose. The last thing he wanted was to drop into a crater, or run down a red flag – and over the unexploded bomb it marked.

He made to look back.

The airman hanging onto the canopy arch anticipated his concern. 'It's okay, sir, they're following.'

Jack smiled and gave a thumbs-up, before they both glanced upward.

The 109s were at about 500 feet, still being harried by the gunners and the Hurricanes. Although they offered no immediate danger – except perhaps to Mal - that was no reason to hang about, so Jack added a smidge of throttle. The Spitfire bounced ahead, the airman hanging on gamely.

A couple of times, they passed closer to red flags than ideal, and there was the odd lurch as a wheel sank into the surface of a recently filled bomb crater. On these occasions, they exchanged resigned grimaces.

As they trundled past a burned-out Hurricane, Jack raised an eyebrow. The airman merely shrugged, as if it to say, 'what can you expect'.

Otherwise, their communication was restricted to a thrusting arm to indicate a change of direction, and raised thumbs when Mal Cotrell landed safely, followed, a few minutes later, by the two Hurricanes.

Jack took the latter as a signal that the 109s had been

seen off. He decided to slow down a little, striking a balance between not hanging about, and getting them to wherever they were to park in one piece.

He also took a moment to appraise his chaperone, who seemed grateful for the change in pace.

He was probably no more than 20, and yet, above pinched features and prominent cheekbones, his eyes were those of a pensioner, sunk into wrinkled, grey-brown, sockets, the likes of which Jack hadn't seen since looking in the mirror at the height of the Battle of Britain. Even more striking was his physique. Although muscular, his painfully thin arms and torso made his shirt seem several sizes too big.

It all seemed to bear out stories of food shortages and lack of sleep they thought might have been exaggerated.

They were nearing a couple of low buildings and a few olive green tents toward the western perimeter of the airfield. The buildings were little more than shells, canvas awnings hanging from their low facades. Men stepped from the shadows or rose from the grass to wave.

They passed the openings of a line of aircraft blast pens, square enclosures with side and back walls of stone, sandbags and, more surprisingly, what looked like four-gallon fuel cans. The first couple of pens contained Hurricanes, or the wrecks of Hurricanes, and the next five, Spitfires, with attendant groundcrew. The four beyond were empty, but each had a small group of airmen standing outside, dressed in a mixture of khaki dress and blue uniform.

As they neared the fifth pen, several airmen, all as thin as his guide, ran to meet them. The young man indicated a sharp left turn and made a chopping motion across his throat.

Jack slowed to allow two of the airmen to grab a wingtip each, then, with a roar of throttle, began his turn. After 90 degrees, he straightened, closed the throttle, pulled the engine cut out and leaned back, breathing in clouds of exhaust fumes as the propeller wound down and stopped.

Silence. The first for nearly four hours.

It didn't last long.

'Brakes off!'

'Brakes off,' he replied, before turning off the mag switches and fuel.

As the others leaned against the leading edge of the wings, his guide jumped down to throw his weight against the tailplane. They pushed the Spitfire back into the relative safety of the ten-foot high walls.

'Brakes on!'

Jack applied the brakes. 'Brakes on.'

Airmen with triangular wooden chocks ducked under each wing.

A few moments later, he echoed the call of 'Brakes off.'

The aircraft rocked as tradesmen set to work. He leaned back and closed his eyes, content to wait for someone to help him unstrap. After a lengthy pause, sensing no-one had appeared at his side, he opened his eyes. Those groundcrew he could see were on the wings, screwdrivers in hand, undoing panels. Others were no doubt underneath, doing the same.

Jack smiled and shook his head. Their sole interest seemed to be the cigarettes and tobacco. He rolled off his flying helmet and ran a gloved hand through his wavy black hair, then undid his Sutton harness and parachute, unplugged his R/T and oxygen and slowly unfolded his wiry frame to its full five feet ten inches.

A squadron leader of similar height and build stood at the pen entrance. His welcoming party, Jack presumed.

He stepped out of the cockpit door, limped down the wing, jumped to the ground and rounded the tailplane, by which time he was moving more freely. The squadron leader came forward and stopped in front of him.

'Hello, Jack, Squadron Leader Turner. Glad to have you aboard.'

Jack was impressed at the use of his name. Must be on

some manifest. He was pretty sure he was meeting Bull Turner, who'd served at Duxford and Tangmere under Douglas Bader, earning two DFCs, and his own squadron.

'How was it?' the man asked, his Canadian accent seeming to confirm Jack's tentative identification.

Beneath a high forehead topped with wavy hair the colour of dark copper, there was a jaw-clenching tension in the Bull's face that Jack recognised only too well.

'Fine, sir, that is, until we touched down here. Quite a welcoming committee.'

'Yes, all too frequent, I'm afraid. Let's hope the next section manage to avoid them.'

The words were light-hearted, but the squadron leader's expression remained severe, and his limbs seemed all a-twitch, keen to be doing anything other than make small talk. He looked at his watch.

'Look, sorry to rush, but I've a few loose ends to tie up. Catch up with you later, and apologise to the others for not meeting them.'

Jack clicked to attention and watched him go. 'Wilco, sir.'

Seemed a bit uptight, but they couldn't ask for a more experienced CO, if that's what he was. In which case, where did Stan Grant fit in? Oh well, no doubt they'd find out in due course.

He glanced back.

The cigarette and tobacco boxes were just beginning to appear. Looked like he'd have to remove his own kit. Not that it took long; his new hat, a change of shirt, socks and underwear, and his wash kit. They'd been assured that the rest, what little there was, would arrive from Gib, somehow, sometime.

The third section landed without incident. About 50 minutes later, Jack and most of his fellow newcomers were sitting with a group of Malta veterans outside one of the olive green tents. Several things set the two groups apart.

King's Regulations stated that khaki dress was not to be worn in Malta until April 1st. So, Jack and his fellow newcomers were clad as they would have been in Kent: light blue long-sleeve shirts, long blue-grey trousers and black shoes or flying boots. A few even wore their blue-grey jackets, although most had now hung them over the backs of their chairs.

Like their groundcrew, the resident pilots had obviously decided to ignore dress regulations, favouring a bewildering hotchpotch of blue and khaki uniform, clashing ensembles, such as blue jackets and khaki shorts. Few had the suntans sported by the groundcrew, but they were just as gaunt, their skin and clothing coated in a layer of grey dust that looked as if it had been building up for days, weeks even.

Jack glanced down at the pristine cuffs of his new barathea jacket, each with its one medium rank ring of light blue.

How long before he looked as careworn?

Not long he guessed, now that he'd gained a new understanding of the severity of their predicament. And the catalyst hadn't been the greeting from the Messerschmitts, or the distant sound of aero engines, explosions and anti-aircraft fire.

No. It had been lunch.

They'd just eaten two rounds of gritty, greyish, bread, daubed with a foul-smelling spread and filled with...well, some form of equally foul pressed meat. It had arrived on a two-wheeled wooden cart, pulled by a small horse, its ribs sticking out of shivering flanks. The poor animal's eyes moved Jack close to tears, although the Maltese carter looked in little better shape.

The 'meal' had been washed down with what they were told was tea. He was sure no-one would have called it that back in Blighty.

Now, much to the amusement of the old hands, the newcomers were sucking their teeth, crinkling their noses and grimacing in various displays of disgust and discomfort.

An English voice with no discernable trace of regional accent broke the silence. 'Welcome to Malta'.

Jack had already grown to dislike the phrase. Invariably, it seemed to be associated with some unpleasant experience.

He turned to look at a slim, dark-haired, flight lieutenant, a few years older than the rest. The man sported a bright blue cravat, a sartorial flourish often favoured by the regulars trained at the RAF College, Cranwell. Like most, Jack still favoured his trusty silk scarf.

Rocking his chair onto its rear legs, the flight lieutenant continued. 'I'd like to say you get used to bully beef sandwiches, but you don't. And yet, I can also guarantee you'll spend the whole morning looking forward to them. Because, unfortunately, that's all there is.'

JC, who'd always looked undernourished, was the first to respond. 'That's all very well, sir, but what about the tea?'

'Ah,' said the flight lieutenant, as if about to reveal some particularly unpleasant snippet. 'That'll be the goats' milk.'

While the newcomers stared into their mugs and grimaced afresh, the old hands looked at one another and laughed.

The sound of engines had been getting louder, and Jack scanned the sky. Most of his erstwhile shipmates did the same, but, once again, the veterans seemed unperturbed.

The newcomers were still smarting from another unexpected development.

Four of their number had been driven off to fly Hurricanes. It seemed there were too many Spitfire pilots and not enough airframes. And Squadron Leader Grant wasn't their CO. He was staying with them, but in what was termed a supernumerary position. Not unprecedented, but unusual.

There seemed to be quite a bit about Malta that was unusual.

It hadn't all been bad news, though. They were now members of Number 249 (Gold Coast) Squadron, Royal Air

Force, an outfit Jack knew had performed well in the Battle of Britain. They'd been flying Hurricanes on Malta since the previous spring.

Jack looked up to see three twin-engined aircraft no more than a few miles from the overhead at about 15,000 feet. From the engines thrusting forward of each square-ended wing, and the slim fuselages tapering back to angular tailplanes, he identified them as Junkers Ju88s. Above them, sat about ten smaller dots – 109s.

A few of the veterans now began to take an interest. Not the flight lieutenant, though. He spoke again.

'Some of you have already met the CO, Squadron Leader Turner. I'm Laddie Lucas, Flight Commander A for my sins.'

Jack recognised the name, one on a small list of relatively experienced Spitfire pilots sent out about a month earlier.

Laddie pointed into the shade of the tent's awning. 'Buck McNair, here, is Flight Commander B.'

A tall, sandy-haired, flying officer smiled and waved. But before he had a chance to say anything, nearby guns crashed out, their reports all but drowning out the rising wail of a siren. Finally galvanised into action, the veterans jumped up and charged toward a couple of nearby slit trenches. After a brief hesitation, the newcomers followed.

Jack limped for a couple of paces, then got into his stride, dodging or hurdling a trail of overturned chairs, before leaping into the left hand trench. No sooner had he landed than an explosion shook the ground.

From his Biggin Hill experience, he knew three things. First, the bomb hadn't been too close; second, it would be followed by others that might be; and third, much as he now feared combat, he'd much rather be up there chasing bombers than down here among their bombs.

More explosions, each closer than the last, the thundering whoomph of their impacts rising in volume to challenge the staccato thump of the guns. The tremors, bangs and pressure waves were regularly spaced. Only one bomber, he thought - so far.

He raised his head just enough to see over the lip of the trench. To his right, a Lewis gun clattered, fired by a determined-looking member of the groundcrew. The airman was firing at an 88 levelling no more than 4,000 feet above. Another bomber, a few thousand feet higher, was still in its dive. The machine gunner seemed unlikely to bother either, but the Bofors gunners might. Their shells burst in black puffs around both aircraft.

JC tapped Jack on the shoulder and mouthed, '88s,' into the din. Jack nodded.

The first line of explosions stopped several hundred yards short. Showers of dirt cascaded around mid airfield, leaving clouds of smoke and dust to drift north on the breeze. Jack hadn't realised how much his stomach had tightened until it eased.

Everyone now seemed to be peering over the edge of the trench. About half - the veterans - wore tin hats.

This time, Jack could pick out the whine of bombs. Then another tremor and pressure wave, followed by another. A muffled crump, then more, the rhythm regular again, the volume rising. Initially, the explosions were cloaked by the billowing smoke. But then, they burst out, sending earth, dust and mushroom clouds of smoke into the air. The explosions marched to within a few hundred yards, then stopped, the sound of falling debris drowned out by the clatter of Lewis and Bofors guns.

Jack looked up. A third 88 was pulling from its dive.

The shocks began again, followed by booms. Closer this time. Pressure waves assailed his whole body. Dust, stones and furniture bounced to the rhythm of the explosions.

Worried faces dipped beneath the parapet. Some sank to the duckboards on the trench floor and covered their heads with their hands. As the ground shook more violently, Jack did the same, flinching as debris spattered his hands and back.

A terrific tremor, then the loudest bang yet, followed by more debris, some of it large enough to sting as it fell on him.

The next bomb would bury them alive. He curled into a tight ball. Waiting. Afraid to breathe. But there was only silence. Even the guns had stopped. He uncurled. Others did the same. JC made to climb from the trench. A hand appeared on his forearm.

The hand belonged to the second flight commander, Buck McNair. He was shouting, but Jack heard the words as if through several layers of cotton wool.

'I should hang on here for while.'

JC turned toward him, and Buck shouted again, the words still barely audible. 'The show may not be over.'

The accent was Canadian.

They stood around, the veterans looking pensive, the newcomers shaken and self-conscious, until...The machine and anti-aircraft guns opened up again.

Jack peered over the rim of the trench. A fighter burst from the smoke to the north-east, no more than 50 feet above the ground. Others appeared, but the first flew straight towards their trench. Its nose sparked.

Fountains of dirt, coming their way.

Jack ducked and covered up. The knot of fear tightened. Bullets and cannon shells fizzed, filling the air with whining screams, metallic clatters, dull thuds and the smell of cordite.

Long after the Messerschmitts roared overhead, the Lewis gunner fired, providing a rattling accompaniment to, and then outlasting, the Bofors barrage. But eventually, even the machine gun fell silent, either for lack of targets or ammunition.

Distant, muffled, voices shouted inaudible orders.

Jack unfurled again. At his side, JC looked scared, his eyes wide, lips thin. Jack had seen the expression before, when they'd been stuck on the ground during a raid on Biggin.

The difference between veterans and newcomers was less evident now. All had a coating of dust, and all, to a greater or lesser extent, looked stunned. From the tic pulsing in the corner of his eye, Jack guessed he looked the same.

It was soon clear that none of the bullets or shells had hit the trench. And despite the apparent violence of the onslaught, most of the nearby damage seemed fairly insubstantial. A few shattered chairs and tables, shredded tents and awnings. Further away, though, it looked more serious.

Black smoke and orange flame bubbled above one of the furthest blast pens, one that hadn't long received its Spitfire. Khaki-clad figures raced towards it.

Too late, Jack thought.

Within an hour or so of their arrival, they were one down, and without even getting airborne.

Taking their lead from the veterans, they climbed out of the trench. Jack was still shaky, but he was distracted from close analysis of his own mental state, or anyone else's. As far as the eye could see, figures rose out of the ground of the airfield perimeter, many armed with picks and shovels. There must have been hundreds.

'First Dorsets and The Buffs,' Laddie said, his voice sounding much clearer.

The other old hands drifted away, but Laddie and Buck stayed in attendance, looking set to be their guides for the time being.

'When they're not filling in craters, they're usually building blast pens, or digging trenches and shelters. And just be prepared, we sometimes get roped in as well, especially when they're working on pens.'

'Yes,' Buck took over, 'the sooner we have enough aircraft to keep us all occupied at our day jobs, the better.'

Laddie looked to be mid-20s, erect and relatively smartly dressed in KD, with neatly parted hair, waved as if tended

41

with a brush – and then there was the cravat, of course. His manner was assured and friendly, a bit like a respected senior prefect. Buck was several years younger, less formal in attire and manner, full of nervous energy, long hair swept back.

An airman bounded up and, seeing Laddie, confirmed that one of the Spitfires was a write-off. His choice of words was an eye-opener.

'Spitchered, sir. Completely fuckin' spitchered.'

Buck McNair laughed at their quizzical expressions. 'No. I'd never heard it before I came here, either. But believe me, it seems to fit the bill, and you're gonna hear it a lot from now on.'

Much of the next two hours was filled with sights that emphasised how different life on Malta would be from anything the majority had ever experienced.

Apparently, the pattern of a bombing raid followed by strafing was fairly standard.

'Happens at all the airfields at least once a day, often more,' Buck explained. 'And as you discovered earlier, the 109s tend to hang around to try and pick us off when we come back to land.'

Laddie jumped in. 'Yes. They seem to regard the airspace over Malta as their own, and unfortunately, to date, we haven't been able to disabuse them of the idea.'

They decided to wander over to the blast pen from which smoke was still rising. On the way, they passed a line of evenly spaced craters, the result of the third bomber's handiwork. Tons of earth and rock had been thrown out to ring each deep hole. A few emitted wisps of smoke, like mini volcanoes. But one crater seemed to be missing, replaced by a small disturbance in the surface.

'Either unexploded or delayed action,' Buck explained as they hurried past. 'We all hate them.'

The last bomb, the one that had made the loudest report, had landed right on top of a newly-delivered Spitfire, sitting in the centre of its pen. Impressively, the three blast walls, although scarred and minus a few stone blocks and sandbags, were still standing. Of the aircraft, though, little remained.

The smoking hole was surrounded by pieces of wreckage: a wingtip, spar or rib here, a mangled propeller blade or cannon barrel there. Only the engine block was relatively intact, sitting on the lip of the crater, stripped of its ancillary components. Half a dozen groundcrew moved about, picking up scraps of metal and putting them into piles.

Well and truly spitchered, Jack thought.

They walked back along the line of pens. A couple of Spits had superficial shrapnel damage, but nothing that couldn't be fixed during the couple of days it would take to prepare them for the skies over Malta.

Jack hadn't been able to hide his surprise when the diminutive flight sergeant in charge of the groundcrew mentioned the timescale.

Forage cap perched to the side of a head of slick, brylcreemed, black hair, pencil moustache twitching, the senior NCO explained that as well as resetting radios, removing overload tanks and harmonising guns and cannon – which hadn't been tested prior to delivery - they had to apply a more appropriate colour scheme: maritime blue/grey.

Jack wasn't going to argue about the paint job, but shouldn't some or all of the other tasks have been done before they'd arrived?

It wouldn't be the last time he'd feel sympathy for the undernourished groundcrew.

Seated back outside the tent, they waited for transport to *the other side* to pick up kit, such as their tin hats.

Laddie leaned his chair back. 'Fraid there aren't many vehicles left. We seem to lose them at the same rate as aircraft, and, with no convoys making it through, they're even less easy to replace.'

'You can't fly them in,' Buck added helpfully.

'So, as you've already seen, no fire engines, just a few hand pumps or buckets, and only a couple of bowsers. The groundcrew often have to fill the kites by hand from four gallon cans. Takes an age - although, on the plus side, filled with earth or sand, the empty cans make bloody good building bricks.'

Buck took over. 'There aren't many trucks or buses either, and that's a regular pain in the ass. It means everything takes twice as long as it should, because you spend so much time hanging around waiting. And when it comes to getting a lift on days off, forget it. Some days, we can't even get a bus to and from the messes.'

They followed Buck's gaze to the town Jack had seen as they flew in. Shining in the glare of direct sunlight, a high defensive wall of golden limestone ran round the summit of a tall hill a mile or so to the south-west. Above the wall rose impressive buildings of the same material. Front and centre, above a jutting, triangular, bastion, a large basilica flanked by towers was topped with a dome of red tiles that positively glowed.

'Just in case you haven't been told, the town's Mdina. Some of the officers live to the left of the cathedral there, in the Shara Palace...'

Later, Jack discovered that the spelling was Xara, but that x, or xx, on Malta were pronounced sh, as in should.

'Oh, a friggin' *palace*, ay,' Mal Cotrell broke in, Australian accent making the most of the word palace.

Amid general laughter, Kibec kicked Mal's chair.

Jack was glad to see the exchange. There may not have been much to laugh at since their arrival, but the mood had been too subdued, lacking in banter.

But the jibe also reminded him again of his new status. It didn't seem that long since he'd been taking the mick out of the officers at Biggin Hill for living the high life in Sambrook House. Even they hadn't lived in a palace.

'Yes, sorry.' Buck paused for a name.

'Sergeant Cotrell, sir, Mal Cotrell.'

'Well, yes, Mal, some of us do live in a palace. But don't worry, your accommodation isn't too bad either, and it's only a few hundred yards further on.

'The only problem is, no matter where you live, on days when there's no transport, you have to climb that bloody hill.'

Beneath the walls of the citadel, terraced fields and vineyards fell several hundred feet in every direction. The nearest steep slope petered out about half a mile from the airfield.

Laddie took over. 'Not a very endearing prospect at any time of day, I can tell you. And the temperature isn't too bad at the moment. We've been told it's twice as hot in summer, which makes the hill twice as steep.'

'Anything else to cheer us up, chief?'

This time it was a New York accent.

Laddie looked at a young, fair-haired, pilot officer at the back of the group. 'Eh, yes. Sorry about that' – he paused.

'Harv Johnson.'

'Sorry, Harv. Perhaps we have laid it on a bit thick. But I suppose the bottom line is that you'll have to get used to doing without some of the things you've taken for granted back in Blighty.'

'I'd only just stopped missing the things I could only get back in the States,' Harv batted straight back.

Amid the laughter, Laddie maintained the bantering tone. 'Well, Harv, that sounds to me like an own goal. You chose to come and join us.'

They were all impressed at how many Americans had taken up a fight that, until a few months ago, could be said to have had little to do with them. That didn't mean they were going to tell them, though.

When their bus arrived, it was ancient, a 20-seater with battered purple and cream bodywork, missing windows and

45

green leather seats, worn, cracked and minus most of their stuffing. The flat-capped Maltese driver, 60 if he was a day, was short and skeletal, with skin like wrinkled leather.

After his experience of lunch, Jack wondered what the locals were living on.

And there was no doubting where the driver placed his trust. He was surrounded by tens of crosses and religious statues dangling on short pieces of string or chain. It was a wonder he could see past them and out of a front windscreen hazed with spider-web cracks.

Laddie and Buck greeted the driver with handshakes and smiles, then settled on the front seat as the bus set off amid a cacophony of crashing gears and backfires.

Bouncing round the airfield, Jack and the other nine newcomers – Stan Grant was presumably with Bull Turner – soon found their attention drifting from the inadequacies of the bus to the numerous working parties filling in craters in the centre of the airfield. There seemed to be a distinct absence of mechanical assistance, most of the work being done with shovels and wheelbarrows.

The lack of vehicles was partly explained by the number of burnt-out wrecks they passed, tens of them, from Bedford trucks to steamrollers, or at least the rollers from steamrollers. They spotted only one working example, trundling back and forward over circles of newly laid earth.

Jack noticed two lonely figures, kneeling by a red flag. He shivered.

It was difficult to imagine anything more cold-blooded than walking up to and dealing with something that could blow you to smithereens at any moment. He was pretty sure he wouldn't have had the courage.

Looking outwards at the northern perimeter, not a building seemed undamaged. Most were obviously abandoned, their roofs smashed and windows gaping.

Some looked like old accommodation blocks.

'Laddie?' he shouted over the noise of the rattling bus. 'Where do the groundcrew live?'

Laddie turned in his seat and pointed at the shattered buildings. 'In those until late last year, when they were bombed out. Then they moved to an area known as the The Pottery, but that was bombed out too, about the same time as the officers' mess on the airfield. So then, they went to a place called the Madhouse'

He pointed to the south, where a three-storey building stood in glorious isolation. Only, even from this distance, you could tell there was nothing glorious about it. It was a shell, or more accurately, without its shell, most of the outer walls missing, revealing the ravaged innards.

'Apparently, the owner stabled his horses on the first floor so they could enjoy the view. Hence the name. But guess what..?'

There was a none-too-enthusiastic chorus of, 'It was bombed out.'

'Yep. So now they live up the hill in Rabat, or in Nashar, a few miles to the north; the groundcrew that is, not the horses.'

Buck also turned round. 'And they're even less likely to get transport, so they usually end up walking. It's about 45 minutes each way to Rabat, even more to Nashar, really rough when you consider that they often run just the one shift, which means they start at about four in the morning and finish around midnight.'

Laddie took over again. 'Yes, among the many things that rankle is the fact that there are less groundcrew on the whole of this island than there are on most RAF stations back home.'

Guns suddenly crashed out and the bus jerked to a halt. Laddie and Buck led them from the battered vehicle and they gathered in front of the dented radiator grill. There were no sirens, but between the reports of their own guns, they could hear a heavier flak barrage to the south, where black circles erupted in the sky, like fistfuls of soot spattering a huge blue canvas.

'Luqa,' Laddie shouted, just as the sound of aero engines

made them turn.

Two Messerschmitts dived from the north. They crossed the airfield boundary at about 250 feet, noses sparking.

Buck and Laddie ran down the side of the bus and crouched. The others darted after them. As he passed the door, Jack noticed the driver, still seated at the wheel, head bowed, lips moving.

The air fizzed as spurts of dust passed either side of the bus and raced toward the troops in the centre of the airfield. The 109s roared overhead.

Slowly, the airmen unwound. Laddie and Buck looked little more than resigned. The rest looked ashen, their eyes full of the same unspoken thought: what sort of hell is this?

Chapter 4 – Champing At The Bit

That evening in the Xara Palace, Jack and the other pilots sat out on a second floor terrace awaiting a series of briefings to mark their arrival. Mdina was some 600 feet above the plain and, sitting above its perimeter wall, the terrace offered unrestricted views over the eastern half of the island and the sea beyond. You could see why, over a thousand years earlier, Arab invaders had built their fortified capital on the hilltop.

The senior officers stood with their backs to their audience, looking out over a low wall topped with an ornate, wrought iron railing. They'd all watched a large formation of Ju88s approach the overhead of Luqa at about 15,000 feet. One by one, they'd dived, disappearing into a ferocious ack-ack barrage from which it was difficult to imagine anything emerging unscathed.

But now, 5,000 feet lower, they'd begun to appear, pulling from their dives and turning to climb above the Palace. The ground beneath the barrage was peppered with tens of short-lived orange flashes that sent up great clouds of smoke, dust and debris. A succession of muffled booms and cracks reached the terrace.

Eventually, the senior officers turned toward the pilots, presumably having decided they had to crack on. They'd been told the Air Officer Commanding Malta, Air Vice-Marshal Hugh Pughe Lloyd, had a dinner date with the Governor.

The AOC was twice as old and much stouter than most of those on the terrace, but he looked resplendent in his best blues, one thick and one medium stripe of light blue adorning each cuff of a jacket also bearing a set of pilot wings and an impressive selection of medals, including the Military Cross and the DFC. He had a pedigree running back to the First World War and the Royal Flying Corps, and had been a bomber squadron and station commander before arriving in Malta.

With the light just beginning to fade over the battle raging behind him, he stood, whisky and soda in one hand, cigarette in the other.

'I don't need to tell you,' he began, in a booming, authoritative, voice, 'that you arrive at a very difficult time. Far from here, we've suffered the setbacks of Singapore and Hong Kong, not to mention Pearl Harbour' - he nodded at a couple of the Americans - 'while closer to home, we've had the reverses in the Balkans, and the loss of Greece and Crete.

'And then, with the arrival of Kesselring's air fleet in Sicily, things have become increasingly dire here. So dire that we're no longer able to prevent Rommel's supplies crossing the Mediterranean to North Africa.'

Jack and the others had already discussed the significance of facing their old Battle of Britain adversary, Albert Kesselring. Should they be full of confidence, knowing they'd beaten him before, or fearful of a man who wouldn't be caught out again?

Given the odds, fear seemed the most appropriate reaction.

'And make no mistake,' the air marshal continued, 'Malta is the key to North Africa, perhaps the whole bally war. We simply have to regain control of the skies around this island. Only then can our own bombers go out and stop Rommel getting his supplies. But, and here's the nub of the matter, of the 370 Hurricanes delivered to Malta, only 28 are left.'

After that startling statistic, the AOC looked at his watch. He polished off the whisky and soda and, in words similar to those used by Wing Commander MacLean on the night before they'd left Eagle, exhorted them to superhuman efforts. Stirring stuff, but as they stood for him to leave the terrace, Jack was no wiser as to how their 14 Spitfires were going to achieve the turnaround required.

Group Captain Woodhall spoke next. A short, slim, man in his mid-40s, with grey-flecked dark hair and matching moustache, he'd earned an outstanding reputation as a controller and station commander at Duxford.

He stood waiting for them to settle back into their chairs, then leaned back on the rail and took the pipe from his mouth.

'Look, as the AOC says, it's very good to see you all. But I'm not going to lie to you, until more Spitfires arrive, we, or,' - he pointed at them with the stem of his pipe - 'should I say, *you*, are still very much up against it.'

Jack sensed that they were about to receive a more realistic and helpful insight.

'Even after the kites you've delivered are prepped, there just won't be enough to go round, and you're likely to be doing a lot of sitting about. Not that all of you will mind that.'

While people smiled and shifted in their seats, he took a draw on his pipe, before continuing.

'But let's look on the bright side. Ideally, we spot the raids forming up and leaving Sicily, at which point, we scramble you and what Hurris are available to climb as high as possible to the south. No matter how imaginative the Hun is in varying his direction of attack, let's face it, he has to end up above the same ten by ten square of the Island, because that's where all the targets are. Usually, the bombers will be at around fifteen thousand and the 109s no more than a couple of thousand feet higher.'

He reached for a glass on the table to his left and took a sip of gin. Behind him, the gathering dusk revealed frequent flashes, some brighter and longer lasting than others. Attention had shifted from Luqa, now dark and silent, to Valletta. Muffled booms and the crack of anti-aircraft fire still accompanied the light show.

Jack thought it an amazing backdrop. It emphasised the vulnerability of the Island, and their responsibility to defend it, if they could.

The group captain continued. 'Again, ideally, we'll have worked out which target or targets they're actually after before we turn you in to approach - out of the sun. Then, if you can keep the 109s occupied for a while, it should allow the Hurris to get among the bombers before they start their dives, or at least before they drop their bombs.

'That said, if the 109s aren't about, feel free to join the Hurris. But the little blighters usually appear at some point. And when they do, they're likely to chase you all over the Island, before making a nuisance of themselves back at the airfield.'

He paused to take a long draw on his pipe.

Jack wondered if some of the less experienced pilots were able to imagine what the combat behind the group captain's words might be like. He doubted it. He'd had no idea what to expect before his first sortie over Dunkirk. But after that, before every flight over the beaches and on into the Battle of Britain, he'd tried to imagine what might unfold. Things rarely worked out as he'd envisaged, of course, but he'd always found the process useful, and unaccompanied by fear.

Right up until Alex's death.

Since then, all his scenarios had effectively been nightmares that ended with some form of grisly death. And he couldn't stop his imaginings, even though they did nothing but stoke his anxiety.

His tic began to pulse. He hoped no-one could sense his discomfort.

The group captain began again.

'Just one more thing. I understand you've also experienced strafing by the 109s.'

Jack pictured the fighters bursting through the smoke over the airfield.

'Well, I'm afraid we find it much harder to give adequate warning of that particular nuisance, because they tend to fly most, if not all of the way, at low level. All I can say is that we'll do our best.'

With that, he handed over to the station commander and OC Takali Wing, Wing Commanders Jack Satchell and

Sandy 'Ragbags' Rabagliati respectively.

After they'd had their three-ha'pence, much of it administrative detail, their new CO, Bull Turner, another pipe smoker, honed in on the practical again.

Twitching like a thoroughbred mare at the starting line, he set off at a gallop.

'The first thing we saw when we got off the Sunderland a month ago was a flight of Hurris going off in vic.'

Some whistled in disbelief, while others looked as if they didn't understand the problem. The vic formation was still seen as the height of skill and good discipline in some quarters, and the tighter flown the better.

The Canadian addressed the whistlers. 'Yes, and you don't need me to tell you how it ended. Most of them probably never even saw the 109s, and they paid a high price for their stupidity.'

A few people shifted uncomfortably in their seats, but Bull wasn't in a mood to let anyone down gently. Without raising his voice unduly, but with evident emotion, he prodded the stem of his pipe at them and said, 'There'll be none of that vic or line astern crap on my watch, certainly not on 249 Squadron, and hopefully not on the rest of the Island either.'

At this, he glowered at Woody and the two wing commanders, who stiffened under his gaze and nodded their approval.

Using his pipe for emphasis again, he continued. 'We're gonna fly as pairs within whatever formation we happen to launch, be it sections of four, flights of eight or, God willing at some point, squadrons of twelve.

'Laddie and Buck will dig into the detail, but for those of you that were still flying vics or line astern back in Blighty, the principle is,' – he put the bowl of his pipe in the adjacent ashtray and held his hands out at shoulder height, a couple of feet apart, palms down – 'you fly a widely spaced line abreast, each of you looking inward to quarter the sky *all* around the other.'

While his right hand drew a circle round his left, his head and eyes moved as if he was sitting in an aircraft, something they'd noticed he seemed to do every so often anyway, even when standing in the bar.

'When you turn, you cross over' – again, the CO demonstrated, tilting both hands left wing down, and sliding the right hand, on the outside of the turn, behind and below to sit on the left.

'And no, for those of you looking for a round of beer, I didn't exceed thirty degrees of bank in the bar.'

Amid the general laughter, he lowered his hands.

'Suffice to say, it's what the Germans have been doing since the Spanish Civil War, and believe me, it works.

So that was the theory, but the prepping of the kites meant a two day delay before they could put it into practice.

They tried to rationalise that time on the ground would be useful, allowing them to gain their bearings and settle in. But, having come such a long way at more than a little hazard, they were soon fed up with inactivity. They hadn't even been asked to build shelters, nor do anything else come to that. Soon, they were itching to play their part.

There was plenty of evidence they were needed.

Although there were only a couple of raids on Takali itself – somehow, the Germans seemed to have overlooked their arrival – the area to the south was alive with the sights and sounds of battle. The old hands said the targets were Luqa and a line of blast pens and taxyways stretching south towards a new strip being constructed at Safi.

By day, they saw tens, if not hundreds, of 88s and 109s, and they heard them all night, when a few Italians were rumoured to join in. What with the whoomph of exploding bombs, and the crack of Bofors and 3.7-inch anti-aircraft guns, Jack hardly slept a wink during his first three nights in the Xara Palace.

Takali's few remaining Hurricanes scrambled a few times. Once, they managed to put up eight. But, although they made several claims, it was hard to see what real impact they could have. And inevitably, a few more of the precious fighters were lost and damaged, with one pilot killed and one in hospital.

Because personnel from the various bases tended to be billeted in the same towns and meet in the same venues when off-duty, news travelled quickly.

They heard that several Wellingtons, Blenheims and a Maryland had been destroyed at Luqa and the Safi strip, most burnt out on the ground. And during a raid on Sunday night, a taxying Wellington hit another taking off. Only a couple of aircrew survived, and they were badly burned. And finally, a bus full of groundcrew from Luqa was hit on the Naxxar road. No fatalities, but nine severely injured.

In the light of such stories, walking over to watch their Spitfires being prepared only added to their frustration.

Jack had been allocated to A Flight. Starting Tuesday, they were to spend the remainder of the week on earlies, pitching in at 5.30 in the morning and being relieved by B Flight at one o'clock in the afternoon.

Chapter 5 – Tuesday 10th March 1942 – Into Battle

It was still dark when they boarded the bus. As the vehicle rattled down Rabat hill, Jack, sitting at the back, wiped the sleep from his eyes and looked at the bobbing heads and shoulders of his new companions.

At the front, sat the CO and Laddie. Behind them, whether by accident or design, were the other Malta veterans: South African, Pilot Officer Danie Du Toite, known as Zulu; New Zealander, Pilot Officer Mike Daly; and American, Flight Sergeant Kim Kaminski.

Further back, seated in ones or twos were his shipmates from Eagle: Englishmen, JC and the prematurely aged, Pete Brown; Scot, Pilot Officer Dave Campbell, a diffident youngster with strawberry blond hair and freckles; sparky American, Pilot Officer Harv Johnson; Canadian, Sergeant Kibec Fournier, whose nickname was based on his angry correction of anyone mispronouncing the name of his home province as Kweebeck; and another live-wire, Australian, Sergeant Mal Cotrell.

Apart from the CO and Laddie, who leaned toward one another to talk on occasion, most spent the short journey in silence. Even when the bus deposited them in the cool, pre-dawn, gloom of the airfield and the CO and Laddie disappeared into the ops tent, there was little chatter. Mostly, they hovered around, yawning and drinking tea.

Jack rubbed his chilled hands and tried to quell his grumbling bowels. Fear rather than the debilitating diarrhoea they'd all heard about. After about half an hour Laddie emerged and paired some of the new boys with Malta veterans, in Jack's case, Kim Kaminski.

Jack and the dapper, dark-haired, American found somewhere to sit and talk. They soon agreed that over the last few days they'd exhausted the theory of flying over Malta. They just needed to go and do it. So, after a brief exchange of truncated life histories – the NCO had spent many hairy months flying over Malta with 126 – they drifted back to sit on the edge of the group re-forming outside the ops tent.

The sun came up and the morning progressed. They witnessed plenty of enemy activity overhead, as well as evidence of raids on Luqa. But the phone lines from the Lascaris ops room buried beneath Valletta remained silent. Until 10 o'clock, when the flap of the tent flipped back and the CO and Laddie emerged.

Jack tensed.

The CO gestured to Pete Brown. The flight lieutenant jumped to his feet, picked up his helmet and, without a glance at the others, set off after the squadron leader, already heading for the blast pens.

Jack hoped his relief wasn't too evident. Not that it lasted long. Laddie nodded at Kim, 'Red Three,' then at him, 'and Four. Cockpit readiness. Pens fifty eight and fifty nine. Good luck.'

Oh well. Time to learn the Malta form, Jack.

He stood and walked off alongside Kim. After a few yards, they glanced at one another, shrugged and smiled. Jack wondered if the American would feel the need to give a few final words of advice.

But no, he merely fixed Jack with piercing blue eyes, touched his forelock, and said, 'Good luck, sir,' before turning off towards a pen with the number 58 on a piece of wood leaning against the foot of its sandbag wall.

Jack walked on and turned into pen 59. From the front, he couldn't really see the full effect of the Spitfire's new paint scheme. But, for the moment, there were more pressing things to worry about, like meeting the groundcrew.

He nodded a greeting at an airman standing behind the right wing, and turned to the other, who hopped up from his seat on the two-wheeled accumulator trolley by the right wing tip. His face, beneath a mop of sandy hair, was familiar. Changed, but familiar.

And then the penny dropped. Jack's heart leapt and he shouted in joyful surprise, 'Smudger!'

Smudger Smith had been Jack's rigger for his last few days at Biggin in 1940. The airman stepped forward, thin face wreathed in a broad smile. 'Flight...I mean, sir. Good to see you, and congratulations.'

They shook hands and stood back to look at one another.

Jack noted that Smudger's shoulder still bore the two-bladed propeller badge of a Leading Aircraftman.

While the war had meant sometimes meteoric promotion for aircrew – partly because of the death rate - the groundcrew still had to wait years before receiving any form of advancement or recognition, no matter how well they performed. It was a sad matter of fact rather than a point for discussion though.

And anyway, the next few minutes left little room for further small talk, just long enough, as he was strapped in, for Jack to find out that Smudger had been on the Island since early 1941, over a year.

It showed. No longer a baby-faced boy, beneath the smiles and the banter, he had the same haggard look as the rest of the groundcrew.

By the time Jack had set up the aircraft to his satisfaction, Smudger had taken up position by the trolleyac, its batteries trickling electrical power into the aircraft via a black lead connected under the nose. They continued to exchange glances and smiles as Jack drummed his hands on the canopy arch, waiting.

He suddenly realised that his tic, a near constant companion since the AOC's briefing, had disappeared. Meeting Smudger had given him a real lift, but he also sensed another, more unexpected, reason.

Pride.

He seemed destined to be part of the first Spitfire formation to take off in the defence of Malta.

At 10.15, two red flares arced into the sky to the south-east.

Jack's start-up signal was greeted by a thumbs-up from the engine fitter to his front left. He lifted the magneto and fuel switches, pumped the primer with his left hand, then pressed the starter and booster coil buttons with his right. When the engine coughed into life, he released the start button, locked the primer pump, released the booster coil and breathed in the fumes belching from the stub exhausts.

By this time, Smudger had removed the power lead from beneath the cowling and thrown it clear. Jack waved away the chocks, added a growl of power and released the brakes. Smudger and the fitter walked alongside his wingtips until he cleared the pen. He waved them off and turned.

Three Spitfires weaved ahead of him. He followed them the short distance to the threshold of the westerly strip, from where eight Hurricanes had just departed.

The CO's Spitfire halted on the centreline, and Pete and Kim tucked their machines to either side of his tailplane. Jack slotted to the right of Kim's tailplane.

As he applied the brakes, three more red flares shot into the sky from across the airfield. A second section of Spitfires must be about to follow them. There was no time for further conjecture. An airman thrust his head and shoulders above the glass cupola of the battered bus to the left of the strip. He raised a Very pistol in his right hand and fired a green flare into the sky.

Jack breathed in deeply, flexed his hands, then opened the throttle to keep pace with the others, now leaving a trail of dust behind them. His Spitfire rumbled over the rough surface, accelerating rapidly. The growl of the Merlin and the air and exhaust fumes streaming through the open canopy gave him another lift, as if they were a drug he'd been denied, if only for a few days.

His body tingled with excitement rather than fear.

The flying controls gained authority and his rudder inputs diminished, as did those of the aircraft to his left. When their tailwheels rose, he eased the stick forward to raise his own. A few seconds later, he applied a light backward pressure to follow them into the air, the ride suddenly smooth, as if rolling off cobbles onto polished metal.

Once safely clear of the ground, he swapped hands to rotate the chassis lever forward to raise the undercarriage – no need to pump any more – and eased right.

The CO transmitted, 'Woody, this is Tiger Red, airborne.'

'Roger, Bull, climb vector one three zero. Numerous big and little jobs on their way, angels one five.'

Jack closed his canopy, shaking his head at the strange informality of the R/T.

'Wilco, Woody.'

Extraordinary, a group captain and a squadron leader using first names!

Pete and Kim positioned their Spitfires 100 yards to either side and raked slightly back from the CO. Jack adopted a similar position to the right of Kim. In this wide finger 4 formation, they climbed into a clear blue sky.

Despite his sunglasses, Jack found himself squinting as he quartered the airspace around the other three Spitfires, admiring their elegant lines, if not the hastily applied paintwork. The blue/grey borders surrounding squadron letters, numbers and roundels were uncharacteristically tatty, but who cared? The colour looked much better suited to operations over Malta.

Out to the left, about two miles away, he caught sight of the eight Hurricane IICs.

'Tiger Red Lead from Red 4, friendlies left ten o'clock, slightly high, two miles.'

'Roger, Jack, visual.'

First name again. No doubt he'd get used to it in time. And it wasn't as if there were another ten Jacks airborne, as there might have been during the Battle of Britain.

They were soon climbing above the 126 Squadron Hurricanes, which drifted right to pass behind. The ease with which they'd been overhauled only emphasised what the Hurri pilots were up against when confronting the new generation of 109s. They must struggle to keep up with the bombers, Jack thought.

In an effort to reduce weight and close the performance gap, the newly-delivered IICs had had two of their four cannon removed, but the gains had been only marginal, while, of course, they'd lost some of their firepower.

And finally, with the incessant bombing and lack of spare parts, they'd become increasingly difficult to keep airworthy. Only cannibalization of wrecks, or even other serviceable kites, allowed them to fix, not only battle damage, but also more routine snags. One of the Hurricane pilots said he'd suffered five engine failures in as many weeks.

To take off against an enemy flying superior aircraft was one thing; to do it in something you feared would fall apart around you, quite another. And yet, there they were, clawing for height yet again.

The climb was uneventful, although it sounded as if the Spitfires following them had been harassed by 109s on departure. Only three had made it into the air and Jack hoped that wasn't because of enemy action.

Four 185 Squadron Hurricanes had also been launched from Hal Far, a grass strip toward the very south of the Island. So now four formations were climbing to the south-east.

After passing over the east of the south coast above a large horseshoe bay, there was nothing to see but sky and ocean. The nearest land was Libya, 200 miles to the south.

'Bull, Woody here, three sections of three 88s and thirty 109s approaching Gozo at between 15 and 17,000 feet.'

For such a specific identification, they must have come within range of the binoculars of Malta's Observer Corps.

A few minutes later, the controller turned all but the Hal Far Hurricanes left about. The choreography of turning 180 degrees in finger 4 still didn't come naturally, but Jack worked it out, passing behind and beneath everyone else to end up on the left of Red Section, with Kim, then the CO, then Pete to his right.

Nothing said more about the size of Malta than that it disappeared under the nose of his Spitfire as soon as he was pointing at it.

'Now you see it, now you don't.'

Sicily and Mount Etna, on the other hand, were only too visible, 100 miles or so to the north.

'Bull, Woody here, vector three four zero. I think your bandits are going for Takali. They're at angels one five, twenty miles.'

'Wilco, Woody.'

From subsequent radio calls, it became apparent that two sections of bombers were heading for Luqa. Woody directed the Takali Hurricanes and the second Spitfire section toward those. The Hal Far Hurricanes, still struggling to make 15,000 feet, were turned back toward Takali.

Red Section continued to climb through 21,000 feet. Within a few minutes, they coasted in. To their left, the air above Luqa was dotted with puffs of black, but no bandits were in sight.

Jack took a deep breath, set max boost, switched his reflector sight on, released the gun safety catch, lowered his seat a notch and tightened his straps.

'Bull, this is Woody. Should be in your twelve o'clock, about five miles.'

As he replied, 'Roger, Woody,' the CO eased them right then left, giving them a better view down toward Takali.

The air above the airfield was pock-marked with black smoke, but Jack couldn't see what the anti-aircraft gunners were shooting at.

An American voice chimed in. 'Left ten o'clock low.'

Jack spotted them. Above the flak barrage, three Ju 88s, turning right through south to the east of Takali. At least ten 109s shadowed them in loose pairs at various heights, the nearest about 5,000 feet below.

His stomach tightened and, when he tried to swallow, his mouth was dry, as if suddenly lined with felt. The tic had returned.

'Woody, Tiger Red, tally-ho, three big, ten little jobs.'

'Roger, Bull, good luck.'

'Escorts first, Tiger Red. In we go.'

The noses of the three Spitfires to his right dipped and, after the merest hesitation, Jack pushed stick and throttle to stay abreast Kim.

Diving out of the sun, they were, as yet, unseen. Jack hoped it would stay that way until they were among the 109s, giving the Hurricanes a shot at the bombers, unmolested.

That was the theory anyway.

Kim eased left, splitting Red Section into two pairs, each spearing towards a pair of 109s.

The Hurricanes called tally-ho on the bombers. Six of the German fighters increased their roll rate and pulled down, but the two highest pairs rolled out and raised their noses, heading for Red Section.

They'd been rumbled.

Still got height and speed, though, Jack tried to convince himself as his pulse raced.

The last vestiges of optimism melted as the noses of the 109s heading for him and Kim sparked. Tracer set out from the twin machine guns atop their engine cowlings and the cannon barrels bored through their propeller spinners.

They'd fired far too early, but Jack still flinched as the pinpricks of light elongated and rushed up to race past his canopy as bulbs of blue-white and red. Picturing the shower of equally deadly, but invisible, metal accompanying the tracer, he resisted the temptation to duck or, even worse, turn away.

Sweat prickled his upper lip and forehead, and his heart thumped, but he set his jaw and watched the fighter ahead of him approach. The closing speed was over 600 miles an hour.

'Hold it, Jack. Hold it…Now!'

At 1,000 yards, he pressed the centre of the rocker switch to fire his .303in machine guns and 20mm cannons. The clatter was deafening. His nostrils filled with the smell of cordite, and the thumping recoil of the cannons seemed likely to slow his Spitfire to a halt, or rip its wings off.

He fought the vibration to keep the aircraft pointing at the target, which rushed onward, firing in its turn. With impact imminent, he prayed the German wouldn't do as he did and pushed. The Messerschmitt darkened the sky, passing no more than a couple of feet above his head.

The contents of Jack's stomach and all the dust in the cockpit had floated up with the negative g. But the Merlin 45 hadn't even coughed, another improvement from Battle of Britain days.

With no idea whether he'd inflicted damage, he swallowed the bitter bile and glanced right. No sign of Kim. A more comprehensive scan also failed to spot the American, or the CO and Pete.

For the first time, he noticed the shouts in his headset. The Hurricanes were engaging the bombers, and warning of diving 109s. Aware of the need to find a companion, he glanced about, feeling the fluttering signs of panic.

'Stop it, Jack.'

At that moment, his airframe rocked and the radio went dead.

'Shit!'

He'd dithered too long. In his eight o'clock, a 109 turning in. Probably one of those they'd just passed. After an instant of wavering indecision, he pulled up and barrel-rolled left. Straining, he fought to keep his head erect and his eyes following his adversary. Inverted as the 109 dived past beneath him, he pulled into the second half of the roll.

For some reason, the Messerschmitt didn't counter as expected. It merely levelled and turned right towards Grand Harbour. Jack frowned, but reduced the back pressure and eased right to dive on the rear right quarter of the German.

He'd heard so much about the skill of the Eastern Front veterans. But this one seemed to be sightseeing rather than fighting. Perhaps they'd become complacent after weeks of facing only Hurricanes.

Whatever the reason, the German's lack of action banished at least some of Jack's fear. But it also made him uneasy. He scanned for a wingman. Nothing close, but more 109s several thousand feet above.

Ignoring them, Jack closed to within 200 yards and pressed the top of the rocker switch. The first tracer rounds from the wing-mounted machine guns weaved behind the 109. He adjusted, using stick and rudder to roll and pull the reflector sight over the German aircraft. The tracer trail followed drunkenly, intercepting the fighter to the rear right of its cockpit, raking over its fuselage and along its left wing, bisecting the black cross.

Bits flew off as Jack flashed overhead.

What now?

The silence in his headset was deafening. There'd been so many warnings about the dangers of remaining airborne without a serviceable radio. But the fighters above seemed to have disappeared. Surely he ought to finish off the 109?

And what about the bombers?

A compromise. Leave the 109 to crash or limp home, but have a go at any 88s he encountered during his recovery.

Descending through 15,000 feet, he pulled round to the left for Takali. The airfield was easy to spot, as was Luqa, a few miles to the south. The sky above both was dotted with ack-ack, black puffs spreading and dissipating to form a canopy of dark mist. The combats he'd heard before his radio went dead must be somewhere near the smoke, but he was damned if he could see them.

He'd just resolved to ease right and circle round to the north of the anti aircraft barrage when, two miles to his left and 2,000 feet below, he saw movement. It was an 88, heading roughly north in a 40 degree dive toward Takali. A bombing run.

He doubted he'd reach it before it dropped its bombs, and certainly not before it entered the barrage. So why not just ignore it and head for home? But no, even with his tic pulsing and his stomach churning, he couldn't do it.

'Got to give it a go, Jack.'

Passing 12,000 feet, he lowered the nose, eased right and pushed on the throttle. The best he could hope was to chase down for an intercept from the rear right quarter.

By 8,000 feet, the distance was closing, the bomber close enough for Jack to pick out the machine gun barrels thrusting from the perspex of its bulbous crew compartment. Shortly afterwards, it entered the barrage.

He was still in clear air, but close enough to see the short-lived, fiery, cores of bursting shells. He swallowed, wiping sweat from his brow.

Over France, he'd generally been part of the high escort, flying well above the flak. You often saw bombers enter it though, and then a fireball, out of which flaming debris would flutter earthwards; or worse, a fuselage, largely intact. You waited, usually in vain, for parachutes, imagining what it was like to be in there, burning, or just trapped by the forces in the tumbling hulk, seeing the ground rushing up, until...

He'd always felt cowardly for watching from a safe distance, ghoulish for watching at all. And on the few occasions he'd been close escort... The images lived with him for days afterwards.

So, why enter a barrage now? Why not sneak round it?

Railing against whatever sense of loyalty or responsibility drove him, he pushed on the throttle and dived into the mist.

It was another world. From below, ack-ack tracer climbed. The shells glowed red, growing to the size of fire extinguishers, before bursting, like huge black and orange fireworks. Shock waves rent the air. It crackled with a sense of danger.

Ahead, the bomber bounced, its wings rocking as shells burst nearby. Jack closed, his Spitfire lurching more wildly, the crack of explosions audible over the roar of his Merlin.

'No!'

A stick of bombs fell from the bomber's belly.

Amid the disappointment, a sudden unease made Jack look back. A pair of 109s, diving into his 5 o'clock, more further back.

'Bugger!'

Things were going from bad to worse.

At least he was now within range of the bomber, pulling out of its dive to present an almost perfect plan view. The crew, the tops of their brown leather flying helmets visible through the perspex, still seemed oblivious to his presence.

Jack pulled the reflector sight ahead of the 88's nose and squeezed the bottom of the rocker switch. His cannon tracer raced away and smashed into its wing root.

He hesitated, 109's bearing down, anti-aircraft shells bursting ever closer. Then, as if torn along a serrated edge, the 88's port wing peeled away…

Chapter 6 - Crisp White Sheets

Jack struggled to free himself.

'It's alright, sir. You're all right!'

He registered the voice, but all he could see were machine gun bullets kicking up the dust as they raced towards him.

Why couldn't he undo his harness?

'It's all right, sir. We've got you.'

How could it be all right? Was that fuel he could smell?

He opened his eyes and tried to locate the harness pin.

Two hands grasped his. A head bobbed before him. He stopped struggling and leaned back, still confused, but less scared. The airframe was ticking and someone nearby was shouting, but he couldn't see anything beyond the head and the instrument panel.

'That's better, sir. We'll have you out in a jiffy. Just stay still and we'll see if you're all right.'

He felt drunk, and his head hurt like the blazes.

'Well, everything looks to be in one piece, sir. But you've had a nasty bump on the head.'

That explained the headache. He reached up, but a hand intercepted his.

'Shouldn't poke at it for the moment, sir. We'll get the MO to have a look.'

Things finally started to clear. This wasn't the aftermath of strafing Messerschmitts. That had been three days ago, the day of their arrival. But why was he here now?

'What happened?' His voice sounded weak and distant.

'You just scraped in over the fence, sir. Went along all right at first, but then you hit the roller off that burnt out steamroller. Pulled you up short, as it were.'

Engine failure. Sinking below Mdina. Fear of landing short. The return of memory brought with it a tingling surge of relief. He'd survived.

Despite the headache, he could see some humour in the turn of events. They'd been saying for days that someone would crash into one of the rollers.

'Have I shifted it?'

'Unfortunately not, sir. You tried, but your kite wasn't quite up to it.'

'And me?'

'I've seen worse, sir.'

Jack's nose crinkled, but his aching head couldn't place the distinctive smell beyond a vague association with unpleasant memories. He opened his eyes. A dim lamp above his head lit a small space surrounded by curtains below a high white ceiling. He lay in a bed with crisp white sheets. Beyond the curtains, he sensed a larger space.

'Hello, sir.'

A female voice. He looked left. A short dark-haired woman in a white uniform stepped out of the shadows and took his wrist in her soft warm hand. She smiled down.

'Welcome back, Flying Officer Williams.'

He remembered being lifted from his battered Spitfire and put in the back of an ambulance. The ambulance had rocked gently and, well, here he was.

'How long..?' he ventured.

'You've been asleep for the last 15 hours.'

Her voice had a trace of accent, Maltese he guessed. She was very young and slightly plump, with a pretty, dimpled, face and dark eyes. Or dark in the subdued lighting of what he now guessed was a hospital ward. She let go of his wrist and lifted her eyes from the watch on her uniform.

'If you didn't know, you had a nasty bang on the head,' she whispered.

As he lifted a hand, she continued. 'You've had a few stitches.'

Great. A scar to go along with his broken nose. He winced as he touched bandages, covering what seemed to be a fair old lump.

'Where am I?'

'Imtarfa.'

69

The hospital just across the valley to the north of Mdina. He still felt groggy, but he also wanted to piece things together.

'Sorry to bang on…' He left a space for her to fill.

'Nurse Dingli,' she said. Then, mirroring his thoughts, 'Like the cliffs.'

The ones he'd flown over prior to being hit. Unknowingly, she'd slotted another piece into the jigsaw.

'Thank you,' he smiled. 'I saw them this morning, or yesterday, whenever it was.'

'Yesterday. It's three in the morning,' she smiled back.

'Right. But, Nurse Dingli, why am I in hospital rather than sick quarters?'

She leaned a little closer and spoke even more softly. 'Because you were unconscious. The doctor wants to see you in the morning, just to make sure you're all right.'

With his immediate questions answered, he suddenly felt very tired.

'Thank you.'

'That's all right. You get some rest now. I'll pull back the screens and I'll be just at the end of the ward if you need me.'

He hardly noticed her slide the curtains and go. Nor did he feel any further curiosity for his surroundings.

Caroline stepped into his embrace. Her body, soft and curvaceous, nestled into his lean angularity. Her dark, wavy, hair was still damp against his face, filling his nostrils with the scent of fresh soap. Their lips met and he stroked a hand down the smooth skin of her back.

'Mmm,' she teased.

Giggling, they parted briefly to drape themselves on the bed, Jack resting on one elbow to look down on her, smiling up at him. He leaned into another kiss, stroking the back of his fingers from under her chin, down onto a breast, circling…

He leaned back against primped up pillows, no longer fighting to work out where he was and what had happened.

He'd had a good night's sleep and a breakfast of bread and jam, and despite a residual headache, felt fit and ready to leave the hospital. All he had to do was convince a doctor, although no-one seemed to know when one would appear.

He watched the activity on the ward – nurses moving between a couple of dozen beds containing the genuinely sick and wounded. The odd groan or retching sound issued from behind a screen.

Despite the surroundings, dreams of Caroline had restored his spirits. If he'd been the whistling type – and not in a hospital ward – he might have whistled.

His optimism was premature. A weasel-faced doctor appeared just before lunch, looked at his wound, then into his eyes, and decided to keep him in for another night. The only thing that relieved the ensuing boredom was a surprise visit from several of his flight.

Out here, it seemed 249 had a tradition of visiting, not only their own sick and wounded, but also Italian and German pilots they'd put in the hospital. He doubted they'd have done it back home. It was another Malta oddity.

Anyway, Laddie had appeared with Kibec, JC and the young Scot, Dave Campbell. They'd done their best to cheer him up, although there seemed to be precious little good news. Kibec and Dave already looked to be suffering, their faces tight with tension and lack of sleep. It couldn't be the stress of flying, because lack of airframes meant neither had flown.

'I think it's going to be one of our biggest problems, Jack,' Laddie confided while the others were lost in their own banter.

'Yes, the less they fly, the less they'll want to, and the more it'll play on their minds.'

'I know, but it's not an easy one to solve at the moment.

If you have any brainwaves while you're skiving in here, let me know.'

Jack smiled at the playful slight. 'I'll give the problem some thought.'

Laddie's recognition that his experience might be of use to his new squadron had already given him a lift.

'Ooh, and by the way,' Laddie continued, changing the subject and indicating that the others should listen. 'You might want to claim at least a share in an 88. The gunners have been crowing, but a few of us thought it was you that nailed it.'

'Yes,' JC chipped in, his Yorkshire accent contrasting with Laddie's more neutral tones. 'We were watching from dispersal, and we're pretty sure it was you.'

So was Jack, although he couldn't totally discount the possibility that the gunners had contributed, even severed the bomber's wing.

'Well, yes, I think I may have had a hand in it, if nothing else. I'll see the IntO when I get back.'

He decided not to mention the Messerschmitt he'd at least damaged a few minutes before entering the barrage.

From behind screens a few bed spaces down on the opposite side of the ward, came the unmistakable sound of vomiting. They all grimaced as the retching went on much longer than seemed possible.

Jack had been listening to similar noises all morning, and from more than one bedspace. A nurse had confirmed that it was the unpleasant form of dysentery known as the Malta Dog. The veterans had been full of black humour on the subject since their arrival.

Kibec was the first to speak, his Gallic features crumpled in disgust. 'Sounds like the Dog?'

'Yes,' Laddie said. 'This is where you end up if you get a particularly bad attack.'

Kibec tapped Jack on the arm. 'And apparently, Jacques,' he said, his transatlantic and French accents mixing in a cocktail that Jack never tired of hearing, 'if you haven't had it, you soon will.'

'Bloody marvellous,' Dave Campbell said mournfully. 'Something else to look forward to.'

Jack was just about to thank them for cheering him up, when the sounds of an evacuation of a different kind issued from the same bedspace.

Laddie stood up, hands clasped over his mouth and nose. 'Well, nice to see you, Jack, but I think we'll be off.'

The others positively shot out of their seats.

'See you tomorrow, hopefully.'

As they backed away, waving sheepishly, Jack tutted, 'Cowards'.

He wished he could go with them, and preferably before the smells reached his bedspace.

As the four pilots approached the screens, a nurse appeared, holding something under a white cloth at arms' length. Even she looked as if she'd rather be somewhere else.

The pilots veered away and increased their pace.

For obvious reasons, Jack hadn't noticed the bombing during his first night in Imtarfa. But during the day and his second night, the explosions sounded as loud as from his bed in Mdina. The hope that being in hospital offered some form of divine protection hadn't lasted long.

By breakfast on Thursday, he'd had little sleep and felt worse than the previous day. Nonetheless, later in the morning, following the most peremptory of examinations, the weasel-faced doctor discharged him.

Before he left just after lunch, a nurse changed his dressing and returned his uniform, freshly laundered and pressed. Another battered bus – was there any other sort on Malta - collected him and several other servicemen from the hospital entrance. It set off to deposit them at various locations around the Island. The lurching progress did nothing for Jack's headache, so he was relieved to find that Rabat was to be the first drop-off point.

During the drive, he was shocked at the devastation.

Along the road between villages, even single dwellings had been hit, their walls demolished, contents - furniture, ornaments and clothes - either spewed out onto the street, or on display within the shattered husks of what had become life-sized dolls' houses. And in the villages themselves, whole streets had been reduced to rubble.

It was hard to believe that destruction on such a scale wasn't deliberate. Italian radio said only military targets were being hit, but Nurse Dingli said the bombers seemed to delight in hitting civilian targets, especially churches. And the 109s attacked anything that moved, from the Gozo ferry, to buses and cars, even cyclists and pedestrians.

The Maltese were paying a high price for their unstinting support of the Allied cause.

The bus dropped Jack in a square on the eastern edge of Rabat, near one of the entrances to Mdina. After the journey, he was relieved that the golden blocks of this stretch of the town's defensive wall remained untouched. How long could it last, though?

He walked over a bridge spanning a wide ditch, and under an impressive arched gateway emblazoned with coats of arms. Once within the walls, large limestone houses, monasteries and palaces towered above main thoroughfares no more than a couple of yards wide, barely wide enough for a horse and cart. Many of the side streets were too narrow for vehicles of any sort, and curved in a way Jack had never seen before. Apparently, in a different era of warfare, this had reduced the range of arrows. Now, it meant he could see no more than a few of the buildings in each alley, so perhaps there was plenty of destruction, but hidden from view.

He weaved his way to a shaded courtyard, crossed and entered the Xara Palace, sitting above the eastern wall of the town. He'd already experienced the views its stunning location afforded, but the destruction he'd witnessed emphasised just how exposed and vulnerable it was.

He made for his room. On the way, he ducked into the ablutions and had a look at himself in a mirror. His black hair stood up in comical clumps above the bandage wound round his head. Where the temple above his right eye had impacted the reflector sight, the dressing still bowed out a good inch or so. The last time he'd looked in a mirror, the black eyes had been a surprise, but they'd lightened a little, and the scratches around his pinched cheeks and square jaw were almost healed.

'Still not a pretty sight, though, Jack.'

It was a good job Caroline couldn't see him.

No sooner had he reached his room than the boom of explosions began. It helped solve one quandary – where he should go next. He rushed to the terrace, finding the majority of his flight, including Laddie, there.

After a few nods of recognition, everyone turned away from him to look back over the plain. Three 88's were swooping into the barrage above Takali, while others emerged from the smoke lower down. These headed straight for the terrace.

There was something epic about the scene, the bombers' approach framed by a backdrop of explosions that threw huge plumes of debris several hundred feet into the air.

Jack tensed. If the 88s had any bombs left or their gunners fired, they could wipe out half a Spitfire squadron in one pass. Most of those around him wore tin hats, but no-one ran for cover. The bombers came on to roar a few hundred feet overhead and turn right for Sicily. They left the plain covered in billowing clouds of smoke and dust.

No Spitfires or Hurricanes were evident, but several 109s raced around the smoke, noses flashing, before they too climbed away towards Sicily. The airfield gunners had fired throughout, but seemingly without success.

Excitement over, Laddie walked across and gave Jack an appraising look.

'Bugger off,' he said. 'I don't want to see you before Monday morning.'

Jack was relieved. The lump was unlikely to react well to being squeezed into a tight flying helmet. And as for flinging his head around in the heat of combat, forget it. The ride on the bus had been bad enough.

In the air, he'd have been dead meat.

They arranged a car, and he was driven five miles north to the aircrew rest facility at St Paul's Bay on the north-east coast of the Island. There, he spent most of his time relaxing in a comfortable villa, overlooking the small island on which St Paul had been shipwrecked on his way to eventual martyrdom in Rome.

The Bay wasn't totally divorced from sight and sound of the war, but most of the bombing was far enough away to allow sleep, and there seemed to be few limits on diet, as long as you liked fish.

By Sunday night, he was feeling a fraud. His temple no longer throbbed, the swelling was subsiding and he'd removed the bandage. The four stitches were unsightly, and the bruise, becoming more lurid by the day, was now bright purple with tinges of yellow, like oil on a puddle.

On Monday morning, he returned to the Xara Palace to find he was sharing a room.

Mike Daly, the New Zealander that had flown out with Bull Turner and Laddie was tall and well built. Although they'd met before Jack's crash, they hadn't spoken much. Now, they hit it off immediately.

Mike had travelled to Britain in 1937 and joined the Volunteer Reserve. Like Jack, he'd finished flying training in time for Dunkirk, and he'd spent much of the Battle of Britain and beyond at Hornchurch, before being sent to an instructor post in mid–41. To escape that, he'd jumped at the chance of a Middle East tour, only to end up among the vanguard of Spitfire pilots bound for Malta.

Like Jack, he was newly commissioned, but lacking his room-mate's years of airman service, he wore the thin rank ring of a pilot officer. They joked that if no-one else would speak to them because of their recent elevation from the lower decks, at least they'd have each other. Not that either had met with any snobbery. In fact, just the opposite. So far, their operational pedigree seemed to have gained them a surprising level of respect and deference.

Before lunch, Mike brought Jack up to speed with events.

'Luqa and Grand Harbour are still copping most of the daylight raids, but we get a few, usually around the same time every morning, afternoon and evening. Woody doesn't launch us against everything, and when he does, it's usually as a four-ship, with anything up to a dozen Hurris from here and Hal Far.'

He nodded at Jack's head. 'Don't know how you found it, but when I've flown, there's been so many 109s about that even if you manage to hit the first without being seen, the rest are all over you. We've been lucky to lose only one so far.'

Jack did his best to raise an eyebrow and Mike gave a name.

'Pat Olsen.'

Jack winced, picturing the young American messing about on their flight to Malta.

'Came with you on the Eagle, didn't he?' Mike asked.

'Yes. I didn't know him that well, but he seemed a really nice lad.'

They were both experienced enough to know there was no mileage in dwelling on such things, and the Kiwi moved on.

'Not sure how,' he said, pushing a wave of dark hair off his forehead,' but we've only had three badly damaged, yours and a couple of others on the ground. The Hurris haven't done so well, though. We try to keep the 109s off them, but there's just so many of the bastards.

'And finally, there's been a command re-shuffle. Ragbags left for Egypt on Saturday and Bull took over as

OC Takali Wing, so Stan Grant's our new Boss.'

'Ah. That explains the supernumerary bit,' Jack said. 'And I know he doesn't look as fierce as the Bull, but, as we found out on Eagle, he knows what he wants, and isn't afraid to bash heads to get it.'

'Yeh, we've already found that out,' Mike replied with a smile. 'And the Bull was all in, not that that's stopped him trying to convince Woody to let him fly.'

They seemed to have reached a natural break. Mike looked at his watch.

'Ready for lunch?'

Jack wasn't sure he was. Fresh fish was unlikely to be on the menu.

It wasn't, and bully beef sandwiches seemed a poor substitute. Thirty minutes after the meal, hat raked back clear of his stitches, he joined the other members of A Flight for the bus ride to the airfield.

Cloud on the deck meant they were unlikely to fly, but the weather on Sicily must have been better. No sooner had they waved farewell to B Flight, than the drone of aero engines began. Soon after, distant anti-aircraft fire and explosions crashed out. Luqa or Valletta again, Jack guessed. There were lulls, but never for long, and it seemed only a matter of time before they were targeted.

Such was the ramshackle state of their stone buildings that they chose to use tents in preference. Jack ducked through the canvas door of one with a piece of paper bearing the word Ops tacked to a wooden pole supporting its awning. Inside, an airman sat behind a trestle table bearing a couple of telephones of the wind-up variety.

Laddie stood before a couple of boards hanging from the tent frame.

'No flying for you until those stitches are out,' he said, without looking up.

Jack could have remonstrated but, once again, he was grateful. Wearing a helmet over the still substantial bump and threads would have been neither pleasant, nor sensible.

'Okay, Laddie, thanks. But they should be coming out tomorrow afternoon.'

'Right. We'll think about it then, shall we? Doesn't mean you can't fill sandbags, though,' the flight commander said with a grin.

So, Jack mucked in to help build aircraft pens, taking it in turns, either to fill sandbags and fuel cans, or to cart them over to the soldiers and civilian labourers doing most of the building.

Many more folk seemed to be involved in construction than when he'd last been on the airfield. Perhaps it was just that fewer were needed to fill in craters, and they'd all disappear again if there was a heavy raid.

He wouldn't have called the work fulfilling and his soft, pilot's, hands were soon sprouting blisters. But there was some satisfaction in seeing the walls grow in height, and in knowing they were increasing the odds of their kites surviving anything other than a direct hit.

The sound of bombers was incessant, and when they passed close to or through the overhead, the tension palpable. Everyone stopped work and looked up at the cloud, straining for the whine of bombs.

In the end, only two small raids hit Takali, the explosions far enough away for Jack to watch in relative calm, but also some admiration for the accuracy of crews dropping their ordnance on or remarkably close to the airfield, despite total cloud cover.

During one of the lulls, Jack went to the engineering tent to see if he could find the whereabouts of Smudger.

He missed having his own rigger and fitter, tradesmen you grew to know well, men with whom you could chew the fat and get a different perspective on events. But there just weren't enough kites for them to have their own airframe and groundcrew. Seemed unlikely there ever would be.

And there was another dimension, harder to quantify, but real nonetheless. Until four years earlier, Jack had been an airframe fitter himself. Speaking to the groundcrew, taking an interest in their work, seemed somehow to keep him in touch with his roots in the Service.

Directed to an isolated pen, he found a person he assumed to be Smudger kneeling under the tailplane of the resident Spitfire. He rounded the wing and waited for an opportune moment to interrupt what looked like a delicate operation.

It was Smudger all right, squinting into a small rectangular hole that swallowed his left arm up to the shoulder. His right hand held a torch, the beam directed into what space was left. His face was contorted into a one-eyed grimace.

Just as Jack made to speak, there was a metallic clang.

'Shit!' The cry was loud and heartfelt.

'Not disturbing anything am I, Smudger?' Jack ventured, wincing in sympathy.

The young man extricated his arm, backed out and stood up. He raised a hand to shield his eyes and squinted, then smiled in recognition.

'No, sir. Just discussing whether this bloody machine wants its trim fixed or not.'

He gave the Spitfire a playful kick.

Jack marvelled at the state of his erstwhile rigger. The ribs stuck out of his bare torso, his arms and legs were painfully thin and his eyes grey and sunken. But it was Smudger who looked the more concerned. He'd noticed Jack's head.

'How is it, sir?'

'Oh, not too bad now. I've had worse.'

They exchanged a knowing glance and Smudger said, 'Yes. I remember, sir. Seems a lifetime ago.'

Jack could well imagine that a year on Malta would seem like a lifetime, several lifetimes. As a pilot, he expected to spend no more than six months on the Island,

and there was a rumour this might even be reduced to three. But Smudger was likely to be there for the duration, facing excessive hours, incessant bombing and short rations.

He decided to avoid such topics in the short time they had for a natter.

'Glad to see a Spitfire again?' he enquired.

The question seemed to take the airman by surprise. But after a few moments' contemplation, he said, 'Yes. Yes I am. Although the blokes that haven't worked on them before are less keen.'

Jack raised an eyebrow.

'Compared to the Hurricane, sir. Too much metal. Too many panels and fastenings, and' - he nodded down at the opening into which he'd been reaching – 'too many nooks and crannies. And the leckies haven't stopped whinging since they found they have to take the seats out to get at the batteries.'

'Serves 'em right for being leckies, then, doesn't it?' Jack took the cheap shot his friend had offered.

'Too bloody true, sir. Should have studied for a real trade, shouldn't they?'

They both laughed, and it seemed a good note on which to end.

'Well, Smudger, I'll leave you to it. Look after yourself.'

'Thanks, sir. You too.'

Jack walked away, glad he'd made the effort to seek the tradesman out, but worried at his appearance. It put his own difficulties in perspective.

Shortly after rejoining his colleagues to fill more sandbags, Jack had his first experience of another source of fear and uncertainty: delayed action bombs.

The first exploded in the middle of the airfield. A working party had been toiling nearby. When the smoke cleared, they watched a limp figure being lifted into the back of a truck. Some time later, a second exploded, much closer. The earth shook and they flinched as great clods of earth and dust shot upwards.

They didn't know whether the first had been marked by a red flag, but the second hadn't. So X didn't always mark the spot. The devices could be almost anywhere, just waiting to go off. It wasn't a consoling thought, and it reinforced Jack's respect for the men he'd seen taking the lonely walk onto the airfield to deal with such things.

Although the cloudbase on Tuesday morning was little more than 500 feet, there were breaks, and they'd already witnessed raids on Luqa and the launch of fighters from Takali. There was, therefore, every reason to anticipate flying, which made the jolting bus journey down to the airfield a sober affair.

As Jack looked at the faces, he thought back to the brief conversation with Laddie in Imtarfa. The less they flew, the more daunting the prospect seemed, especially given the odds.

On arrival at the airfield, the mood was darkened further by news from B Flight of heavy patrolling by 109s, and the loss of another of their pilots. Flight Sergeant Ian Cormack, one of the Eagle group, had crashed near Filfla, the island to the south-west of the Dingli cliffs. His loss seemed especially tragic for not being the direct result of enemy action.

Confronted with overwhelming numbers of fighters and no bombers, his section of four had decided discretion was the better part of valour and dived away. To the dismay of the rest, he'd just flown into the sea. The fact that he was relatively experienced added to their sense of bewilderment.

Leaving the others still discussing the mystery, Jack set off for the Medical Centre, this time in a battered Austin, rather than a battered bus. The southern perimeter seemed no less of a mess than the northern, and the airman driver pointed out a few more landmarks, or rather, the piles of rubble where landmarks such as hangars and messes had stood before the bombing.

At one point, he stopped and pointed at four shelters cut into the rock.

'They tried to use 'em for Hurricanes,' he said in a broad Cockney accent, 'but chunks kept falling off the roofs. So now they're used as offices and workshops. Although why the fuck it's all right for rocks to fall on people and not on a bleeding Hurricane, only the plonker who came up with the idea could tell yah.'

Jack laughed at the blunt assessment, and they drove on.

The majority of station facilities were now in rows of large Nissen huts the driver called Elephant huts on the eastern side of the airfield. He dropped Jack outside one marked, Medical Centre, and promised to pick him up 30 minutes later.

In the interim, Jack bore the ministrations of a none-too-sympathetic male nurse who snipped and tugged at his stitches, ignoring his wincing grunts of pain. Inspected in a mirror afterwards, the bloody wound looked like something from a Frankenstein movie, complete with little holes where the stitches had been. He couldn't believe it wouldn't leave a scar. But at least the bruise was now little darker than the bags taking shape under his eyes. The black eyes were no longer in evidence.

When he arrived back at the squadron, whistles and grimaces confirmed that he wasn't the only one to find his appearance gruesome. He went to seek out Laddie.

The flight commander took one look at him and said, 'No way, Jack. I know what I said, but I've changed my mind. We'll have another look tomorrow.'

Jack decided not to feign disappointment.

That evening, he sat alone in his room in the Xara Palace. The power was out, so a single candle provided the only light. Its flame smoked and sputtered in the draughty air, throwing shadows on the wall next to his bed.

In other circumstances, he might have seen beauty in the dancing patterns. But tonight, his thoughts were coloured by fear of a return to combat. His mind conjured a sinister, hooded, figure that advanced and retreated as the candle flickered. With every approach, the spectre's billowing cape threatened to engulf him.

The sound of raucous laughter from the terrace bar broke the spell for a while. But it failed to lighten a mood darkened by the exchange of gossip with that evening's visitors.

Luqa had lost four Wellingtons, with a further three damaged, alongside a PR Spit, a Mosquito, and another bowser. And there were now so few Hurricanes that two squadrons had been disbanded, their pilots spread amongst the others, their groundcrew sent to Egypt.

The light rations didn't help. This evening's dinner of Maconachie's stew and a few soggy vegetables had left him with a gnawing hunger that breakfast was unlikely to satisfy.

He'd been trying to put at least some of his thoughts and experiences in his daily letters to Caroline. But he didn't want to alarm her unduly, so he hadn't been totally honest. Not that the censors would allow anything sensitive to be passed on anyway.

It was probably Laddie that censored his letters, although he couldn't be sure, because the form was to black things out and send the correspondence on, rather than discuss issues with the writer and request changes. Jack tried not to let the fact that his words would be seen by a third party prevent him expressing the depth of his feelings for Caroline, or his longing for her. But he sometimes wondered what the censor would make of his more passionate jottings.

He, in his turn, had to censor some of the groundcrews' letters, a job he hated, but also found fascinating. Some obviously weren't bothered that someone else was going to read their innermost desires, or perhaps the knowledge added to their excitement. Luckily, he still couldn't put faces to many of the correspondents' names, so there'd been no embarrassment at meeting someone whose florid letter he'd just read.

Not that any of them knew whether their letters would get through. Although he handed his in every morning, he had no idea whether they'd get off the Island, or how and when Caroline's would reach him.

Their kit still hadn't arrived, and probably never would.

How he missed her.

Like his fear, he tried not to show it, but he was homesick. Not for the fields and lanes of South Wales or Kent. But for Caroline. Only for Caroline. He'd give anything to have her in his arms, to smell her scent, hear her voice – share her bed. She was never far from his thoughts.

One surprise was that his daydreams were remarkably chaste, not at all the steamy affairs he'd assumed. He wasn't sure why, it was just the way it was.

It had been confirmed that three months was considered more than enough for fighter pilots to serve on Malta. But who was to say the policy would be implemented, or that he wouldn't then be posted elsewhere.

The prospect of three months' separation was bad enough; Smudger hadn't seen his fiancé for a year, and who knew when they'd meet again, or if she'd wait for his return? Others had already endured longer separations with little, if any, news.

And letters could be a mixed blessing.

Inevitably, some held bad tidings: the death of friends or relatives, or the devastating news that a wife was seeing someone else. Even the casual mention of another man in a letter could send the recipient into a frenzy of fevered imaginings. At least Jack didn't feel he needed to worry in that regard. Not yet, anyway.

The candle sputtered. Gnarled fingers crept along the wall toward him.

Chapter 7 – Wednesday 18th March - Back In Harness

It had all started so well, a timely scramble, one of four climbing to the south-west into clear skies, top cover for about a dozen Hurricanes preparing to intercept a large formation approaching from Sicily.

Then, shortly after passing over the south coast at 12,500 feet, they were bounced.

Fighting a surge of panic, Jack reacted to the first shout and flash of tracer by pushing to gain speed. He scanned above, glimpsing a couple of dark shapes. They flashed behind before he could identify them.

Kibec was no longer to his right, so he pulled that way, passing ahead of and beneath a Spitfire climbing straight ahead. It must be the young Canadian.

Had he been hit?

If not, he was flying far too timidly; although, as Jack knew only too well, understanding the need for action was one thing, doing something when frozen with shock and fear, quite another, especially if you were wounded.

Breathing heavily, he pulled up and left, and grunted into the radio, 'Get weaving, Kibec.'

After 90 degrees of a gut-wrenching turn, he could see that his words had had little effect. The Spitfire had levelled, but was still flying straight, a sitting duck. As if to emphasise the point, a 109 appeared, zooming up on his friend from behind and beneath.

Jack pulled until his Spitfire shuddered. Only then did he reduce the back pressure to maintain a slight judder through stick and airframe. He was turning at the maximum rate, struggling to keep his head up, looking through the top of the canopy.

'Break left, Kibec, break left.'

Kibec flew straight on, the 109 closing to within 200 yards.

Jack could pull no harder. To do so would put him into a

stall or a spin, neither of which would help the Canadian. He could only watch as the German closed to within 100 yards and fired. The rounds hit home and the Spitfire belched black smoke from beneath the front of the cockpit and rolled left onto its back.

Jack was still pulling round as the 109 turned hard right, disappearing beneath his engine cowling, giving no chance for an exchange of fire. He snapped to wings level and looked for the other Spitfire. It was spiralling earthward.

'Come on, Kibec, get out of there!'

To his surprise and joy, a parachute blossomed.

'Yes!'

It shone white against the blue sea and Jack watched it for a few seconds before jinking to quarter the sky. Low to his left, two further 109s were all over a Spitfire.

Either the CO or Mal Cotrell, he thought.

But Kibec's nemesis was still out there somewhere, maybe creeping up from behind. The fear he'd suppressed returned, raising the hairs on the back of his neck.

Time to turn away and head for home?

Fuck that!

He rolled hard left and pulled, grunting again as the g forced him into his seat.

'Woody, Kibec's under his brolly three miles south of Delimara.'

He could only hope the controller picked up the message and sent a launch. If there was a reply, he failed to pick it out among the other noise in his headset. Anyway, by this time, his mind was focussed elsewhere.

Half a mile below, a lone Spitfire corkscrewed madly. One hundred yards behind it, a Messerschmitt 109F countered every move, squirting frequent bursts of tracer. A second 109 sat a little back to the left, its pilot waiting for their prey to turn or loop into his own arc of fire.

It seemed only a matter of time before one of the 109s succeeded.

Jack rolled into the inverted and pulled, allowing himself

to lose sight of the trio as he arced into a vertical dive. Stars sparkled and his eyes bulged as he unloaded to hold negative g. Using his favourite TLAR – that looks about right – method, he counted, 'One, and two, and three, and...' He rolled hard right and pulled, grunting and straining at the renewed onset of positive g.

Not bad. He'd put the rearmost Messerschmitt high in his one o'clock about five hundred yards ahead. If, as he suspected, its pilot was mesmerised by the fight ahead of him, he might just get a surprise.

Drenched in sweat, Jack relaxed the back pressure to zoom up and then pull right. Beyond the 109, tracer still flashed between the Rotte leader and the jinking Spitfire. Perversely, he needed the RAF pilot to avoid doing anything too dramatic.

As the range closed, he set the safety off. At 200 yards, with the wingman still oblivious to his presence, he pressed the centre of the rocker switch, bracing against the vibration and recoil of his cannon and machine guns. He revelled in the sound, smell and sight of the fury he'd unleashed.

Tracer sparked on the rear fuselage of the Messerschmitt. Bits flew off. Then, a sudden, intense, jet of yellow flame beneath the cockpit erupted into an explosion. The centre section disappeared in a blossoming cloud of orange and black. The engine and propeller shot forward, while the rear fuselage and tail assembly seemed to stop in mid air, then fall slowly away.

The cockpit was in the fiery cloud.

Jack pulled hard right away from the debris, then reversed his turn. Five thousand feet.

His breath came in gasps, his body ached and he felt sick. Not from fear – there hadn't been time for that - or from the carnage of the last few minutes. He rarely felt compassion for the men he maimed and killed now. No, his nausea was a result of the constant manoeuvring and extremes of g.

He spotted the Spitfire, diving away towards Malta. But

where was the other Messerschmitt?

And then he saw it, diving north-east over the ocean.

This time, he decided not to push his luck. It was no good even thinking of helping the Hurricanes. Their battle had been – was – being fought miles away above the airfields. He had neither the time, the fuel, nor the ammunition to join in.

There was something he could do, though.

'Woody, Jack here,' – he'd decided to go along with everyone else's method of addressing the group captain over the R/T –'heading to look for Kibec off Delimara.'

The over-worked controller found time for a reply. 'Roger, Jack, launch on its way. Give top cover.'

Jack felt a little lift in his spirits and some of his tiredness fell away.

The wind was a light south-westerly at the surface, so Kibec should have been blown a bit east of north during his 8,000 feet or so of descent - if a 109 hadn't shot him as he dangled there, or deflated his canopy with a close fly-by.

Dispelling such thoughts, Jack headed for a point two miles off Delimara Point, the rocky south-eastern tip of the Island, and spiralled down. Passing 1,000 feet, he spotted one of the powerful rescue launches approaching, black bow high out of the water, white wake fanning out behind.

The vessels had transformed the survival chances of aircrew ending up in the sea, at least those that could get into their dinghies, or stay afloat and stave off the cold. The thought brought his focus back to Kibec.

Jack levelled at 250 feet and began to circle, scanning the waves for a hint of his friend's upturned face, or more likely, his dinghy, parachute or Mae West. Even with the light wind throwing up few white caps, the disturbances of swell and current produced swirls of white everywhere. Each of these prospective sightings raised Jack's pulse rate, but there were just so many, they soon swamped his senses.

It was worse than looking for a needle in a haystack, because he had no idea where the haystack was in the first place. The launch seemed to trust his judgement, though, setting up its search pattern beneath him.

Despite his own difficulties, Jack felt for the crew. How much trickier it must be spotting someone when you were only a couple of feet above the water yourself? The slightest swell must hide anything more than a few yards away. Even so, he soon found his early excitement giving way to disillusionment at the futility of the task.

He'd moved to a new area about half a mile from the launch when he spotted activity on its light grey deck. Arms were raised and he scanned the sea where they seemed to be pointing. Seeing nothing, he raised his eyes and re-focused.

Two aircraft. They turned and, as one crossed behind the other, the size and wing shape left no doubt.

'Shit!'

The 109s rolled out, but heading for the launch not him.

Another chance to sneak away? How many more would he get?

The Germans entered a shallow dive.

Jack turned hard right, determined not to be late again. He pulled to the buffet, relaxed to maintain it and grunted into the radio.

'Woody, Jack here, two little jobs attacking the launch.'

There was no reply and, at this height, he doubted he'd been heard.

He rattled round the turn, arms aching, vision greying. Through the self-induced mist, the launch came into sight, bows high, water boiling astern as it began to accelerate from a near-standing start. A few degrees further round and the 109s appeared, still intent on their strafing run.

Jack snapped to wings level, heading into the gap between launch and attackers. He pressed the top of the firing button, sending out a stream of machine gun tracer. The reaction was immediate. Both 109s jerked left, heading straight for him from no more than half a mile away.

Well, you've certainly distracted them, Jack. Now what?

Their noses flashed. He returned fire with gun and

cannon and sped between them.

The launch was heading back for the coast ahead of a maelstrom of white water. Hoping the 109s would stay with him, Jack turned hard right, away from the vessel. His best chance was to hug the water, but it was easy to over-cook a tight descending turn from a couple of hundred feet, especially with g dulling your vision.

Sweat pouring, heart racing, he arced down until he felt he was about to dip a wingtip in the waves, then rolled to wings level and looked for his assailants.

They were sky-lined, rolling out of their own turns to point at him, not the launch. He was tired and scared, but it was a minor victory, even if it added immeasurably to his personal danger.

Head-on again, although one Messerschmitt had eased wide right, no doubt to pull onto Jack's tail if he survived the next pass. They were closing fast, the 109s in a shallow descent. Jack raised the nose a smidge to point at the Rotte leader and fired.

Their tracer crossed. Hot metal flashed all around. Jack flinched. No impacts, but a collision imminent. He pushed, squeezing between Messerschmitt and water, then pulled right, wingtip dipping toward the sea. The other German was already turning.

Jack levelled his wings and eased even lower, so low the rearing swell seemed destined to splash if not swallow him. It was desperate stuff. His only chance now was to run away. But only if the 109s were following him, not the launch.

He eased up and right. The launch was little more than a speck in the distance. Perhaps it would return to its search when the immediate danger was passed, but he sensed it could already be too late for Kibec. Both 109s, sky-lined again, rolled out to follow him.

And then, between him and the launch, two other aircraft. Spitfires diving towards the Messerschmitts. These turned away to face the new threat.

The surge of relief coursing through Jack's body threatened to overwhelm him. Salt water pricked his eyes. He hadn't expected to survive. The sudden reprieve left him feeling utterly drained, listless to the point of giving in to sleep.

With a struggle, he recovered at least some of his composure and climbed to fly round the south-west coast to the Dingli cliffs, all the time watching an ugly pillar of black smoke.

Did it mark Takali?

It did. He joined the circuit to the north of the cloud, low on fuel after so much time at high boost. Suddenly, the air around him erupted with tracer and flak. His heart raced. Panic bubbled as he cast his eyes about.

'Come on, Jack, pull yourself together.'

Raid or no raid, he had to get down. He dived for a curving approach to the south-westerly runway.

Above, a pair of Hurricanes appeared, firing at something lost in drifting smoke and blossoming bursts of flak. From below, it was clear the cloud was made up of plumes from several fires, the darkest rising from close to their dispersal.

On short finals, with canopy open and gear and flaps down, Jack had the feeling he was being stalked again, but the Bofors guns were putting up a shield of fire and he decided to continue his approach. He doubted he had the fuel for any other option.

Despite his fevered state and the many distractions of the unfolding drama, his body seemed automatically to produce the actions required for a perfectly respectable landing. How the less experienced coped was beyond him.

Wheels safely down, he took a deep breath and blew out slowly, like a deflating balloon. As he turned right to clear the strip and raised the flaps, two Messerschmitts shot through the black smoke to his front.

'Shit!'

He pulled the engine cut-out, released his seat and parachute harnesses, removed his helmet, opened the door and launched himself from the cockpit. Ignoring the tightness in his calf, he leapt from the wing and ran for an adjacent bomb crater. Shells whined and clattered. He vaulted the crater rim and landed on his backside. The 109s roared overhead.

Apart from sore buttocks, he was unhurt. But his hands wouldn't stop shaking; in fact, his whole body shivered. He was sweating profusely, yet it was as if he'd been dumped in freezing water.

He'd thought nothing would ever compare with the intensity of the Battle of Britain. And yet, he'd just had the most hair-raising hour of his life. Not only that, but from the stories he'd heard since his discharge from hospital, it was the norm, the reality of being a fighter pilot on Malta. He'd either have to come to terms with it, or...

Or what?

There was no alternative. Like everyone else, he'd just have to get on with it.

During the short period of contemplation, his heart rate slowed and the shaking subsided. Perhaps it had been as much physical exertion as fear. He hoped so.

He also noticed his tic. It had probably been pulsing since they'd been bounced, masked by the pace and intensity of unfolding events. Now, it seemed like an old friend, a welcome sign that his mental state was no worse than before.

He smiled and washed his face in his hands. Here he was, rationalising something that up till then he'd perceived as a weakness. The world was turning upside down.

Hearing a revving engine, he rolled over, crawled up and looked out of the crater. Against the dramatic backdrop of the bubbling black plume, a rubble-stone camouflaged Bedford was driving towards him, or at least towards his Spitfire. The latter had a jagged tear in the wingtip. Otherwise, it looked intact.

He climbed out of the hole and, dusting himself down, walked toward the cockpit. By the time the Bedford appeared alongside, he'd put the mag switches and fuel off, retrieved his parachute and headset and was standing by the damaged wingtip.

Smudger Smith leaned from the driver's window. 'Shouldn't hang around here, sir, it's not healthy.' He nodded at the Spitfire. 'We'll pick it up later.'

Jack walked round and climbed into the passenger seat. After the briefest of smiles, Smudger looked ahead, smashed the gear lever into first and played the clutch and accelerator. They lurched away, the engine and gearbox emitting tortured howls.

Jack made to shout something, but decided against it as the young driver grimaced in concentration, his sinewy left arm and leg co-ordinating to double de-clutch into second gear and accelerate away amid more mechanical grating. They still had much to catch up on, but the cab of the Bedford was no place to do it.

The truck bounced over the uneven surface, Smudger weaving it around the numerous obstacles. Jack looked out at the airfield. Most of the smoke pillars were decaying, including one rising from a pen, but the worst still rose, thick and black. At its base, the ghost of a vehicle cab and chassis, glimpsed through a crackling inferno of orange and black.

'Bowser, sir,' Smudger shouted. 'Eight hundred fucking gallons.'

Given the shortage of aviation fuel on the Island, it was an enormous loss. And another bowser gone. More refuelling by hand, up to 22 tins for a Spitfire, many tens more for something like a Wellington.

No sooner had they reached the ops tent than sirens sounded and guns crashed out. Jack jumped from the cab and joined the stream of people heading for the slit trenches. He looked back, expecting Smudger to be behind him, but the young SAC was driving the Bedford away.

Jack stopped, turned and shouted. His words were lost in the cacophony. After a moment's indecision, he dropped his parachute and made for the nearest trench. Just as he reached the lip, the tremors began. He looked back.

The Bedford was turning into the nearest blast pen as flashes of flame, mushrooms of smoke and fountains of dirt began to erupt just beyond it. Jack jumped into the trench and covered his head with his hands.

The tremors and crashes rose in frequency and intensity, each successive shock wave and heave of the earth seeming closer than the last. The ground shook and the blasts coalesced into one continuous, crashing, boom.

Jack huddled and squirmed, his body bouncing with the impacts, his face contorted into a frantic grimace. Debris dropped onto his back and hands. It could only be a matter of time before something crushed or tore into his body, or he was buried alive.

Of all the unpleasant things he'd experienced in the war to date, being bombed was the worst. You were impotent, totally vulnerable, nothing but luck between you and oblivion. The only saving grace was that everyone else was huddled up in a similar manner.

Not everyone of course. The gunners and those groundcrew with weapons would still be at their posts, blasting away at the enemy. And others, such as Smudger, would be driving vehicles, fighting fires or continuing to refuel and service aircraft.

He had nothing but admiration for their courage and devotion to duty. They all deserved medals. It made him feel small and cowardly in comparison.

After what seemed an eternity, the bombardment stopped. The clatter of anti-aircraft and machine gun fire continued for a while, but then, even that petered out.

Silence, or an absence of any noise loud enough to penetrate Jack's ringing ears.

Thirty minutes later, with the light beginning to fade, the

two Spits that had come to Jack's rescue returned. Soon after they'd been pushed back into their pens, Laddie and Pilot Officer Zulu du Toit, one of a couple of South Africans on 249, walked towards him.

'No sign of Kibec, I'm afraid, Jack,' Zulu said as Laddie swept past into the ops tent.

'What about the 109s?' Jack asked.

Although sunk into the deep sockets that marked him out as a Malta veteran, Zulu's blue eyes sparkled.

'Didn't seem quite as keen to hang around when we arrived. In fact, they couldn't wait to get away. We chased 'em for a while, and I think Laddie clipped one, but he decided looking after the launch was more important than going halfway to Sicily - just in case there were more 109s stooging about.'

He ran a hand through his jet black hair and suddenly looked very tired.

'Sorry about Kibec. The launch was still looking when we came away, so you never know.'

Before Jack had time to express disappointment or make comment, the sirens began their wail. He looked around. A red flag was being raised over the ops tent and the Bofors guns began to crash out. Zulu and he ran hell for leather and were in the slit trench before Jack looked up.

Most of the dark cloud that had covered the airfield had dispersed to reveal 88s circling at about 15,000 feet, fighters above. From the unhurried way the bombers and their escorts were manoeuvring, they were unopposed.

Jack counted seven 88s. One by one, they began to dive, a few of the fighters doing the same. He'd met a gunner at St Paul's Bay who'd explained what he and his colleagues tried to achieve as a raid came in. Jack now tried to relate what he saw to the young officer's description.

While the attackers were above 10,000 feet, the gunner had explained that the Bofors gunners would try individual, aimed, shots. Above Jack, a small number of shells were exploding around the bombers, some quite close, but none close enough to cause much damage.

As the raiders approached 10,000 feet, the gunfire became more intense. Jack now knew that each gun was firing at a different, pre-determined, point in space. The aim was to put as much lead as possible into an imaginary box between about 3,000 and 10,000 feet.

Jack watched the barrage intensify, but only until bombs fell from the first bomber. At this point, reason gave way to fear. He sank to his knees and lowered his head.

Fear turned to terror as he heard the whine of the first bomb rising in volume to a frantic screech. It was going to be close. Very close. The noise, ground heave and pressure wave all arrived at once. Subsequent bursts were equally forceful, accompanied by waves of heat and the strong smell of explosives and burning. Jack was thrown to the ground. He curled up, hoping for the best as the earth shook and debris bounced off him and his tin hat.

The unholy, thunderous, racket went on for what seemed several minutes with no reduction in intensity. Jack's senses – sight, hearing, smell, touch – were all swamped as his body was buffeted this way and that. Such was the force of the tremors that, even if his mind had found the clarity to order such an action, he could not have risen to his feet.

He was like a pebble in an earthquake, totally at the mercy of the forces around him.

And then, the heaving stopped. Unable to hear anything, he assumed the sound had also ceased. He lay still, hoping his bowels and bladder hadn't betrayed him. It had happened to others, always being ignored as neither a subject for pity nor banter, something that could happen to any of them.

It was the most intense barrage he'd yet experienced. Surely, anything worse really would signal the end.

He opened his eyes.

Close at hand through the gathering gloom, almost every tent had been flattened, every awning torn away. Chairs and trestle tables, or their remains, either carpeted the ground or were piled against the walls of the gaping one-storey buildings.

Further afield, the base of several dark pillars glowed orange in the dusk.

That night's post-mortem on the terrace was a solemn affair. The few positives - a couple of confirmed and probable 109s and 88s - were far outweighed by the negatives.

By some miracle, the raid on Takali had left no fatalities, but the airfield was out of action until the army could fill the holes scarring the operating surfaces. In the blast pens, two Hurricanes had been destroyed and one damaged.

Elsewhere, a further two Hurricanes from Hal Far had been lost into the sea. One pilot had been rescued, albeit with both legs shattered, and the other, like Kibec, was still missing. This left the Hurricane force in a parlous state.

The consensus among the Spitfire pilots was that they were in little better shape. Since the one spitchered on the ground the night they'd arrived, they'd lost three in the air, while Jack's one-sided tussle with a roller had left one seriously damaged. A further two had been damaged in that evening's raid. With other snags and battle damage, such as Jack's shredded wingtip, serviceability was reduced to low single figures.

But the Wellington force had fared even worse; in fact, it had ceased to exist. Out of 17 twin-engined bombers flown to the Island, 13 had been destroyed and three damaged. The sole survivor was on its way to Egypt, taking with it any hope of a swift return to offensive operations against Rommel's supply lines to North Africa.

And on Sicily, one of the photographic reconnaissance pilots had shot forces, including gliders, massing on and around airfields. The news seemed to solidify rumours of invasion. It was hard to see how a determined assault could be resisted; certainly not by a handful of Spitfires and a few creaking Hurricanes!

Even the silver lining, news that Eagle was to make a second delivery of Spitfires came with its own cloud. Everyone on the Island seemed to know, so the Germans must know too. The carrier and the aircraft flying from it were likely to have a very hot reception.

Chapter 8 – Thursday 19th March – Valletta

After a fitful night listening to sporadic raids and anti-aircraft fire, Jack woke to another clear day and a breakfast of two thin rashers of fatty bacon and one round of toast coated in cart grease. The accompanying mug of urn-stewed, goats' milk, tea added its own unpleasant aftertaste. He was still smacking his lips in disgust when he joined most of A Flight on the terrace.

Laddie motioned him over to join Pete Brown, Harv Johnson, Dave Campbell and Mike Daly.

'Right, you lot, I've had enough moaning about your kit not turning up. I've organised a bus to take you into Valletta. Should be able to get anything you need there. Mike's going to nursemaid those that haven't been before.'

Unlike Jack, some had already explored the city, or at least its fleshpots, if their stories were to be believed.

The view from the terrace to the east made the prospect of a trip to the capital less attractive than it should have been. Smoke marked it as the target of at least one of the early morning raids. And on the airfield, a black pillar still rose over the remains of the precious bowser.

When it arrived, the bus, complete with cracked and missing windows, already had the NCOs new to A Flight – JC and Mal - aboard. They were billeted in a requisitioned hotel a few hundred yards outside Mdina's walls in Rabat.

The bus was driven by another painfully thin Maltese man three times their age. Surrounded by the usual religious art and statuary, he set off down the hill, driving impossibly fast on the narrow, dusty, tracks. Every few hundred yards, he shot his passengers a manic, gap-toothed, grin, as if seeking recognition of his skill and daring.

Jack for one refused to establish eye contact. He just gritted his teeth and hung on.

Approaching the first small settlement, the driver looked back and shouted, 'Attard,' as if he expected someone to jump up and get off. Even if anyone had been foolhardy enough to take up the offer, there was no way they could have kept their feet as the bus lurched around potholes and piles of rubble, forcing the few pedestrians into ditches or up against dry-stone walls and buildings.

Apart from the feeling of jeopardy, Jack's overriding impression of the journey was of grinding poverty. Although only five miles from the capital, Attard seemed to lack any amenities, even drainage, if the stuff oozing down the centre of the roads was anything to go by.

And most of the Maltese he saw were bent double, working tiny fields within dry-stone walls. The men were dressed in collarless shirts, grubby jackets, trousers and boots, the ensemble topped with flat caps, while the women all wore long black dresses and tent-like hats of black cloth. Groups of children and some of the younger men and women were quick to wave and smile, but most adults were more neutral, their deeply wrinkled and careworn faces displaying neither friendliness nor hostility.

There seemed to be no intermediate stage between youth and old age, perhaps because most of the men of military age were serving elsewhere on the Island, or overseas.

Fuel shortages meant they met few other vehicles, and even the small number of donkey carts and gharries – horse drawn traps – were pulled by skeletally thin animals.

'You might not believe it looking at that poor thing,' Mike shouted, pointing at a horse with its ribs sticking from its scraggy flanks, 'but there's a thriving market in horse meat.'

The Maltese, human and animal, were obviously starving. They desperately needed a convoy, and you had to wonder how long they could hold out without one, whether invaded or not.

As they neared the capital, the size of the settlements and the buildings increased, but so did the level of destruction, with many large structures reduced to rubble.

Just after 10am, having driven up a slight incline out of

Floriana, the bus dropped them by an ornate fountain in front two large triangular bastions jutting from Valletta's high walls. The fortifications were on a much grander scale than Mdina's, but built of the same creamy limestone blocks.

Mike gathered them in the shadow of the bus.

'Before you all disappear,' he said, 'transport's at midday. And for those of you that haven't already sampled the delights of Valletta...' He shot a knowing glance at Harv Johnson.

'Why pick on me?' the New Yorker retorted. 'It was dark. I never saw nothin'.'

'That's not what you told me,' Mal said, giving his friend a playful push. 'You said you saw *everything*.'

When the laughter had subsided, Mike continued. 'Okay, then, for anybody that's interested in seeing another side of the place, I thought I'd give you a quick tour. Feel free to do your own thing, though.

'Straight over the bridge,' he pointed between the bastions, 'you come into Kingsway. If there are any shops left standing, that's where they'll be, and the tailors all carry KD, or make it to measure. Straight on and you reach the sea in about fifteen minutes. Side to side, it takes about five, so you can't really get lost.

'And if you want to see The Gut...' He shot another look at Harv, who shrugged as if resigned to his new reputation. 'It's a couple of streets down on the left – Strait Street, although I doubt anything's open at this hour.'

'Not what the sailors told me,' Harv interrupted.

Again, Mike waited for the laughter to subside.

'Finally, if there's a raid, just follow everyone else. The place is undercut like a Swiss cheese.

'Okay?' he said. When no-one came back with any questions, he turned and set off.

They followed his sturdy frame across a bridge over a deep dry moat, through the walls and into the city. The first thing Jack noticed was the smell. To the odour of sewage that had wafted around at various times during the bus journey was added a much more pungent and deeply unpleasant aroma. Other noses crinkled.

'Bodies,' Mike said, nodding at a pile of huge blocks to their left. 'Some may have been there for months, apparently.'

To Jack, the walls of the Xara Palace, built from similar materials, had always felt solid and dependable. But if the place was hit, and collapsed…He looked at the jumble of stone and shuddered.

Mike waved an arm over Kingsway. 'With so many buildings in the same state, there's just not enough time or heavy machinery to get at them, so there they lie.'

Jack looked along the thoroughfare, sloping gently down towards the sea, just visible at its eastern end. No more than 20 yards wide, it was lined with three and four storey buildings, the upper floors sprouting enclosed wooden balconies, the ground floors mainly given over to shop frontages, shading under awnings. But every few yards, rubble had tumbled across from left or right out of gaps that must have contained similar buildings. Few of the shops that had survived had any glass in their windows.

Close on their right, though, stood an impressive building of tall columns and sweeping stone staircases. Apart from a few shrapnel scars, it seemed untouched.

'And that?' Jack asked.

'The Opera House,' Mike replied. 'Their pride and joy.'

He clapped his hands. 'Right, those that want the tour, this way.' He set off to the left.

Everyone followed.

After a couple of minutes walking through untended gardens, they stopped atop a bastion. A hundred feet or so below was a body of water several hundred yards wide.

'Marsamxett Harbour,' Mike said.

Its rippling blue surface was smeared with dark streaks of oil, and dotted with all manner of flotsam. To his left,

Jack noted a couple of medium-sized freighters and corvettes sporting jagged holes, dents and scrapes that could only have been the result of enemy action. But these were of no more than passing interest, because the harbour also contained an upturned, rusting, hull, a couple of part-submerged, listing, superstructures, and several jutting masts and funnels.

Most striking of all, near the far shore beneath a distinctive, arched, façade, the conning tower of a submarine rose from the water at 45 degrees.

'And that,' Mike said, pointing at the arched building and its grizzly companion, 'is Lazzaretto, where the submariner's hang out. Believe it or not, there are probably three or four operational submarines over there, but they spend most of the time submerged, trying not to end up like that.'

'You mean,' JC said, incredulously, 'that when they're not underwater out there' – he pointed at the ocean beyond the harbour entrance - 'they're underwater in here?'

'That seems to be the flavour of it,' Mike replied.

Jack decided his bed in Mdina wasn't so bad after all. At least it wasn't under water.

He was pretty sure he spoke for all of them, when he said, 'I always knew they were mad, but I didn't know they were that mad.'

There were nods and grunts of agreement.

'Well, if you think this is bad,' Mike said, 'let's go and have a look over the other side.'

Intrigued, they retraced their steps past the Opera House. The Maltese they passed were dressed for the office rather than the fields, and most acknowledged them with a nod or a smile. At one point, a group of children ran alongside, arms outstretched, laughing and shouting, 'Peelot, peelot.'

Eventually, they passed through a large set of wrought iron gates into a garden, at the end of which was a paved terrace, hundreds of feet above the water.

Harv gave voice to Jack's immediate impression. 'Wow!

Would ya look at that?'

'Yep. Grand Harbour.' Mike stood back to let them take in the scene.

In the bright sunshine, the panorama of shimmering water and golden stone was breathtaking. Opposite were several deep inlets, their entrances guarded by large fortresses whose high walls fell to the water's edge. Otherwise, the shore was lined with wharves and warehouses, beyond which densely packed buildings ran away to the horizon.

But it was the level of destruction that was most striking.

Once again, the water was awash with oil and debris, and evidence of more, and larger, wrecks. All around the harbour's edge, masonry, dockyard machinery and cranes tumbled into the water. Nothing seemed to have escaped damage, and that included the adjacent residential areas.

And yet, there were signs of activity, normality even. Several large merchantmen and a couple of careworn destroyers were moored beneath them, and tens of small boats plied across the harbour and between the various inlets.

When he thought they'd had enough time, Mike stepped forward again.

'This is the Upper Barrakka Gardens,' he began. 'Over there is what they call The Three Cities. I'm afraid I only know the names of two of the creeks. The one straight ahead is Dockyard, and the one to the right is French Creek. That's where Illustrious was moored just over a year ago.'

Jack guessed most of them had seen the newsreels of the Luftwaffe attempting to destroy the aircraft carrier sheltering in the heart of the harbour. In the most famous shot, it was totally enveloped in the smoke and dust of a fierce bombardment, just the odd crane jib poking above the swirling miasma. Miraculously, the ship had survived to sneak away, but it was all-too-evident that the Maltese had paid a heavy price.

Nowhere was the damage more eye-popping than around

French Creek. Faced with such destruction, there was little appetite for banter.

Mike must have sensed it. 'Okay, twelve o'clock at the bus. See you then.'

Jack shook his head and smiled. Once again, although given the opportunity to disperse, they'd stuck together, like a small flock of sheep. Mike duly shepherded them down Kingsway to a tailor, from which they emerged with, or had put in an order for, khaki uniform.

On the way, the New Zealander had pointed out megaphone-like speakers attached to walls or atop posts.

'It's called the Rediffusion system,' he'd explained. 'The authorities use it to pass on important messages and warnings. I heard the tail end of a pep talk from the Governor last time I was here. Very stirring it was too.'

On their way back up Kingsway, these same speakers began to emit a persistent wail.

'Three guesses,' Mike said.

Jack and the others followed him as he crossed the street and joined a line of men and women filing through a double doorway beneath the overhanging wooden balcony of a townhouse. Once inside, they passed under an arch and into a small, rectangular, courtyard, flanked with citrus trees and overlooked by three storeys of windows. Adorning the centre was an ornate, but dry, fountain, complete with trumpet-blowing cherub.

It would have been an idyllic place to sit in the shade with a cold drink, Jack thought. If it wasn't for the sirens and the now audible beat of aero engines.

Mike led them to the far corner, down a flight of stone steps and into a whitewashed basement room. There, someone in an Air Raid Precaution arm band counted them off as they filed through another doorway and descended a rough-walled, spiralling, stone staircase, little wider than Jack's shoulders. It was lit by bare light bulbs dangling, a yard or so apart from a line of black electrical cord tacked to the spiralling roof.

They'd descended about 20 feet, when Jack stepped into an underground chamber, passing a niche in the wall containing a brightly painted Madonna and Child and a flickering candle. The white-washed chamber was the size of a small, low-roofed, village hall. Perhaps as many as 50 people stood in groups or sat on wooden benches lining the walls. Mike made for the far corner by a hessian screen and the pilots followed.

Although it was obviously a shelter that opened to the public, it didn't look like a public shelter, and Jack couldn't help feeling like a stranger that unexpectedly finds himself in someone's front room. As they formed a defensive circle, only Mike looked anything like comfortable.

And yet, as more people stepped into the space, there was no hint of hostility. Just the opposite, in fact. Admiring looks and smiles made it plain that the airmen were welcome, the centre of attention even, although no-one tried to engage them in conversation. Rather, each group struck up its own murmur of animated chatter.

The Maltese spoke in their own language, an idiosyncratic mixture of Arabic and southern European unique to the Island. Jack doubted he'd ever learn much of it, not least because all Maltese had at least a smattering of English, and most, especially in the towns, were completely bilingual.

'The majority head for the large public shelters they've built over the last 18 months or so,' Mike whispered. 'Some even live in them. But nearly all the bigger houses and shops in Valletta have cellars that are also open to anybody. Bloody good job too,' he said, as the first rumbling boom reached them.

'Sliema,' a confident voice announced, setting off a chorus of sage nods. The rumbling continued, but seemed, for the moment, to come no closer.

The ARP warden stepped into the cellar. This seemed to be a signal for people to make themselves comfortable, spreading out to occupy the space they'd provisionally reserved. Mike sat and they followed suit, sinking to the stone floor, knees drawn up within folded arms.

The murmur of conversation subsided into a wary silence. Where heads weren't actually cocked to one side, you sensed that everyone was listening for the next reports. When they came, all Jack could tell was that they were far enough away to be no immediate danger.

The crack of anti-aircraft fire was also audible. Not too close as yet. Another source of comfort, perhaps.

Not that he was enjoying the experience. Although the raids at Takali had been much more violent and threatening than this one, he wasn't sure he didn't prefer the slit trench to this cave. He couldn't help thinking back to Biggin Hill, and the aftermath of the direct hit on a shelter that had killed Brummie and so many more of 246 Squadron's groundcrew.

The bulbs dimmed and went out. The only light was from the flickering candle. Another boom. Closer this time. Sweat began to prickle his upper lip.

What was it like to be buried alive?

When the lights came back on, everyone looked pensive, but no more than that.

How did they stay so calm?

This was his first experience of sheltering beneath a shattered city with the stench of death all around. They must have done it hundreds of times. It made him feel very humble.

And surely, shouldn't they be resentful that these pilots weren't up there driving the bombers back? But no, they seemed to sense that they would be if they could. Jack would certainly have preferred to be anywhere other than down this hole.

He realised that the rumbling had stopped. As one, the occupants seemed to breathe again. Their shoulders relaxed and the murmur of conversation began again.

After a lengthy pause, Jack noticed Mike raise his

eyebrows toward the ARP Warden. The man nodded back.

'I think we can go,' the New Zealander said, standing up.

Once again, they followed him across the floor, smiling and nodding at the locals, who also made to rouse themselves.

At first, the street was deserted. But as they walked uphill towards the Opera House, people filed out of houses, often many more than the house itself could possibly accommodate. After a brief moment blinking into the light, they set about their business.

Must have been like it in London during the Blitz, Jack thought, although the bombing here was confined to such a small area, and had lasted twice as long.

The bus had just entered Floriana when the Rediffusion speakers wailed again, followed by the crash of anti-aircraft fire.

The bus pulled over and they disembarked to join another line of people disappearing through a low doorway. This time, they descended deep into a much larger complex of tunnels. In contrast to the bright whitewash of the shelter they'd just been in, the rough-hewn walls here were grimy and damp. The air was fetid, thick with the pungent aroma of stale sweat and, well, there was no other way to put it, human waste, liquid and solid.

When the pilots were eventually able to stop, the press of people had forced them much further in than they'd have liked. Jack thought it had probably been a vast underground warehouse, although, apart from a few barrel-sized rings ground into the walls, there was no evidence of such use now.

To either side of the main tunnels, were chambers of varying size, some looking freshly-hewn, many little more than office-sized, others much larger and divided into cubicles, either by pre-existing low walls, or more recent partitions of wood or fabric. The air of permanence came as a surprise. Mike had said people lived in the public shelters, but Jack hadn't thought what it might mean in practice.

Most cubicles seemed to be about ten foot by ten. Those he could see into were pictures of constrained domesticity – carpets, kerosene stoves, bedding, usually on the ground, the odd low stool holding a mother with babe in arms. In and around, a constant hubbub of squealing infants, shrieking children and admonishing mothers. There were few men.

The remaining chambers were set up as dormitories. Again, there was some evidence of long term occupation – top or bottom bunks made up and topped with a few possessions – but most had nothing but a mattress, presumably awaiting a transient visitor, staying only for the duration of a raid.

Each chamber had a hessian screen in one corner, the source of the overpowering smell, Jack guessed, his nose crinkling. He wasn't proud of his squeamishness. After all, these people hadn't chosen to live in such extremity. That said, he just wanted to get out. The faces of the others betrayed the same thoughts. Even Mike looked less assured than before.

Thankfully, they didn't have long to wait. Just as Jack realised that he'd heard or felt no evidence of bombing, the line of people began to backtrack. When they re-emerged into the light - to find the bus driver still sitting behind the wheel – Jack realised that no-one had spoken since the burst of excited chatter that had greeted the Rediffusion alarm.

The rest of the return journey was completed in silence. The scenes of poverty and destruction were becoming more familiar, but the short visit had wrought a change in Jack. The day to day reality of the Islanders' existence had vastly increased his respect for them.

How on earth were they coping so well when faced with such privations?

But also, he realised his own fears were petty in comparison. They needed him and he was going to do his damndest to come up to scratch.

Jack arrived at the airfield, fired up and ready for action. But it was a frustrating afternoon. Although the sky was clear and there was evidence of enemy air activity in the boom of distant explosions and the crash of guns, the Takali Wing remained on the ground.

'Woody's keeping us back for something,' Pete Brown said, running a hand over his thinning hair.

Since their arrival, Jack couldn't help thinking the deputy flight commander had begun to look more and more strained.

'Keeping us back for what?' Harv asked, the frustration evident in his tone.

'How should I know?' Pete retorted, sounding tetchier than the rhetorical question warranted.

'Well,' Harv said, refusing to let the matter rest, 'I can't help thinking we're letting the folks we saw in Valletta down. No matter how few kites are available, we should be up there.'

'But given that you're not,' a new voice cut in, 'perhaps you'd like to go and help build another shelter.'

They turned to look at Laddie.

'What? With these hands,' Harv remonstrated jokily, showing off his blisters.

'Fraid so, old boy,' the flight commander said, ushering them out of their chairs. 'I'll see if I can rustle up some hand cream. In the meantime, get over there.'

It was just after five when Jack looked at his own calloused hands, then pushed them into his aching back. Lugging rocks and sandbags wasn't the job he'd have chosen, but at least it felt as if he was contributing.

For the first time that afternoon, the sirens wailed and the guns crashed out. They ran for a slit trench adjacent to their half-constructed shelter, several hundred yards from the ops tent.

The raid was the longest Jack had witnessed, with at least ten 88s and a dozen 109s diving over the airfield. The ground shook and the dust flew, but mercifully, the action stayed well away from them. As the raiders departed, relief at their own good fortune gave way to concern for those around the south-east perimeter, from where several clouds of smoke rose.

It wasn't until that night in the Mess that they heard the extent of the damage. There'd been no casualties, but two Hurricanes and a Beaufighter under repair had been written off, and another Spitfire damaged.

They also heard two major snippets of news. First, a convoy was due to leave Alexandria the next day, and second, the balance of Spitfires was due to arrive in a couple of days.

Perhaps it was for these events that Woody was trying to preserve his meagre forces.

Chapter 9 – 20th/21st March - Days of Thunder

'He never stood a chance.' Laddie said, pushing his fingertips against his eyes, then washing his palms down his cheeks.

The flight commander looked all-in. He'd just informed them that Dougie Leggo, a larger than life Rhodesian on B Flight, had bought it.

'D'you know what happened?' Mike Daly asked.

He and Dougie had been good friends.

'Only too well. I saw it, or the aftermath,' Laddie said, his eyes taking on a far-away look.

The A Flight pilots had only just arrived at the airfield, but Laddie had been there all morning. He said it was the only way he was likely to get any flying, and he was probably right. There seemed to have been precious little chance during the afternoons.

'Dougie was over the moon,' Laddie began, as they gathered round, just outside the ops tent. 'Said he'd spent most of the night in the company of a young lady in Valletta. Hadn't got back until the wee small hours. And frankly, it looked like it.

'Johnny Plagis offered to take his slot, but of course, Dougie was having none of it, and – well – I'm afraid we let him have his way.'

It would be hard to imagine anyone looking more contrite than Laddie at that moment. He cleared his throat and, with a mighty sigh, carried on.

'Anyway, I don't know whether you saw the big raid on Valletta?'

'Yes. We watched it from the terrace,' Jack said.

Most of A Flight had gathered there after breakfast. It had become the norm after every meal, drinking tea, smoking and, often as not, watching raids in progress. Less often, they also watched the Takali Wing take off in response.

'Saw you scramble as well,' Jack continued.

'Yes, Woody decided to use us for a change, and Buck, Raoul, Dougie and I set off for the 109s, while the Hurris went after the bombers. We were never going to get to height, but we managed to catch a few of them unawares, and Buck bagged one.

'But when we tried to regroup, Dougie had slipped back. Raoul spotted him a few thousand feet below, with a 109 creeping up. He tried to warn him, but he just didn't respond, and the bastard nailed him.

'I didn't see the attack, but I spotted a smoke trail, and then a Spit at the head of it, spiralling down, minus its tail. I thought that was that. But somehow, Dougie managed to get out. Then, as his brolly was deploying, a 109 flashed by and it candled. Just trailed behind him as he fell.'

Jack wondered how high the Rhodesian had been, but decided not to ask. High enough to make for a grisly death, if he'd been conscious.

'Can't be certain, but I think the bastard shot up Dougie's chute, if not Dougie himself,' Laddie concluded.

'Wouldn't be the first time,' JC said. 'They did the same to Pat.'

It was only a rumour, but a very persistent one. This seemed a more definite example of the practice. There was nothing constructive to be gained from another rant against it, though, especially as Jack knew some of his fellow pilots were prepared to do the same. It was even sanctioned by the powers that be.

Despite everything he'd seen, and the friends he'd lost, he still didn't have the stomach to shoot another human being dangling from a parachute, or to collapse a billowing canopy with a close fly-by; even though he was pretty sure a 109 had tried to do it to him in the summer of 1940.

They settled down outside the ops tent to wait, either for the call to scramble, or, more likely, until they were sent to lug rocks.

The morning's raid had been the largest Jack had seen: about twenty 88s and upwards of fifty 109s. If the Hun continued to send such numbers, surely they'd have to confront them. But then again, perhaps the increased odds were what deterred Woody from risking them, especially as they might be needed if and when the promised convoy came within range.

As Jack, by now dressed in khaki like the rest, settled back to wait, he mused on another element of the Dougie Leggo affair.

During the summer of 1940, alcohol had been a constant companion. He knew very few pilots that hadn't used it as a pressure release valve, or a crutch. And he couldn't pretend there weren't mornings when he'd been on something less than top form because of the amount he'd consumed the night before.

At dawn some mornings it had seemed as if every aircraft on the airfield contained a pilot breathing deeply of 100% oxygen in an effort to clear his drink-befuddled brain.

But now, on Malta, stories like Dougie's were the exception rather than the rule. Very few of them seemed to get plastered before they flew. He certainly didn't – or hadn't yet. And it wasn't due to a shortage of alcohol. That, at least, still seemed to be available. Okay, the beer, his tipple of choice, was an acquired taste, but there was every spirit you could imagine, and at knock-down prices.

No, the truth was, or at least, the way he saw it was, that in 1940, although they'd flown off in their flights or squadrons against overwhelmingly superior numbers, they'd always felt in the ascendancy, supremely confident in their aircraft and their tactics. And the contact with the enemy had been likely to last no more than a few minutes up at 20,000 feet. They hadn't even considered the slight edge that might be lost through over-imbibing the night before.

The same reasoning had followed through to operations over France. Although they were up against the Focke Wulf

190 and more capable variants of the 109, engagements were usually short-lived, and they almost always had superior numbers. Enjoying a drink, even to excess, didn't seem that big a deal.

But over Malta, not only did the Hun have numerical advantage, but the Spitfires had only a slight edge over the 109F, if any, while Hurricane pilots were up against far superior machines. And the 109s had the numbers and the fuel to harry them from the moment they took off to the moment they landed, if they could evade long enough to land at all.

Reducing your ability to perform by flying with a hangover suddenly seemed madness. They needed to be on their mettle the whole time.

The other exceptional thing about Dougie's story was that he'd found a girl. Apart from the professionals in the clubs on the Gut, they were in very short supply. Not that there weren't girls on the Island – there had to be – but in a deeply conservative Catholic country, those that were let out at all were very closely chaperoned.

Parents knew that pilots, no matter how attractive they might be to their daughters, were only on Malta for a brief period, and so were not strong marriage material. The groundcrew and the army, on the other hand, were likely to be around for the duration, so they were a much better bet, especially if they were Catholic. The Irish regiments seemed to benefit most from this logic.

Hard to believe that any parent would favour a Pongo over an airman, but there it was.

There were a few British girls in Valletta. Warby, the recently-departed reconnaissance pilot had bagged one, but they were even scarcer.

Apparently, the best a love-starved young pilot could hope for was an invite to dinner or a party at one of the local palaces, where they might meet the daughters of the local nobility. It seemed a few relationships had been struck up in this way, but they rarely, if ever, exceeded the bounds of friendship.

Not that Jack was interested anyway, although he did feel sorry for the younger hot-bloods.

'All right, you 'orrible lot!'

The words had broken into a very pleasant reverie. Jack squinted in the direction of the voice.

'Get off yer backsides and over to them shelters. At the double!'

The none-too-impressive impersonation of a drill instructor was greeted with all manner of two-word abuse.

Shielding his eyes, Jack looked up at Laddie, silhouetted against the bright sky.

'Sorry, chaps, but your presence is requested at the building site,' the flight commander said, reverting to his normal polite tone.

The odds of them flying had obviously lengthened.

Jack looked at his watch. Three thirty. He'd had about an hour's undisturbed sleep, more than he seemed to get in his bed in the mess most nights. And, almost inevitably, he'd dreamed of Caroline.

He groaned as he pushed himself out of his chair and stretched.

'Sorry to disturb your beauty sleep, Jack,' Laddie said, 'especially as you had such a smile on your face.'

Several of the others were looking at him and laughing.

Jack blushed.

'Well come on then,' Laddie hustled.

Reluctantly, amid another torrent of swear words, they began to rouse themselves. Jack picked up his tin hat and led the group toward the soldiers and civilian labourers toiling a few hundred yards away. The temperature was now in the mid-70s, pleasant for lolling about, and still not too hot for physical labour.

As he walked, he tried to hang on to the image of Caroline climbing onto the bottom of the bed, breasts swaying as she crawled towards him, smiling a lascivious little smile. But the image faded as the reality of his surroundings sank in: a dust bowl, pitted with craters and covered in burnt out vehicles and aircraft.

It was just shy of 6pm and they were about to down tools when four 109s swept over the north-western boundary at about 50 feet. The fighters were over the centre of the airfield before red flags appeared and the sirens began to wail. And they'd fired into the buildings in the south-east quadrant and started a climbing left turn before the guns started to fire.

By this time, Jack and the rest were haring for the nearest slit trench. Just as well. The 109s completed their wingovers and ran in from north-east to south-west. Straight for them.

Jack peered over the lip. The last few bodies were disappearing into trenches or behind shelter walls when the noses of the 109s sparked. In what seemed to have become the normal run of things, spurts of dust raced towards their trench.

Jack watched for as long as he dared, then ducked down. Almost immediately, the air was full of the whoosh and whine of cannon shells and machine gun bullets, closely followed by all manner of thuds and pings as the projectiles smashed into the ground and any objects in their way. His nose twitched at the whiff of cordite.

The sound of aero engines and shells receded, but he kept his head down and looked around the trench. No-one seemed to have been hit, but faces were unable to conceal the fear of being strafed. Pete Brown and, next to him, Dave Campbell were visibly shaking.

Sure that no-one was looking, Jack placed a hand on Dave's arm. The young Scot offered a weak, embarrassed, smile, then closed his eyes and took a deep breath. As he blew out, the shaking stopped. Jack turned away.

Rottes and Schwarms of 109s appeared over the airfield on and off for the next 30 minutes. In the quieter periods, the pilots leapfrogged between shelters and trenches, making for the ops tent, just in case they were needed. But neither Hurricanes nor Spitfires were launched, and no Hurricanes from Hal Far arrived to contest the airspace over Takali.

If the strafing runs were meant to draw them into the air, they'd been unsuccessful.

Just before 6.30pm, with dusk falling, they were preparing to pack up and leave, when Jack sensed something at the limit of his hearing. Before he could work out quite why, he felt a deep unease.

Other heads turned to the west, where the orange disc of the sun was disappearing behind the bastions of Mdina. Above the stone, purple in shadow, the sky darkened with height, from salmon pink to a deep blue-black in the overhead. But the first words uttered were not in praise of the beauty of the sunset.

'Bloody hell!'

JC had only just beaten Jack to the punch, and with a much milder expletive than had been about to leave his lips.

At an elevation of about 45 degrees, a huge formation of aircraft had come into view. It stretched back for miles, the six leaders climbing into the darker blue, the rearguard still appearing.

'Must be hundreds of the bastards,' Harv said.

Jack hadn't seen anything like it since the Battle of Britain, when raids of this size had been commonplace. By contrast, their own incursions over France and the Low Countries rarely contained more than a dozen bombers, a pattern the Luftwaffe had seemed to follow on Malta since his arrival.

But not tonight. This might be as many as 100 bombers at around 15,000 feet.

'Some are 110s,' JC shouted.

'Oh good, at least they're not all bombers, then,' Harv responded, with more than a hint of irony.

The words rippled over Jack. He was transfixed. The

light was fading, but the whole formation was now visible, 110s to either side of a core of tightly packed bombers, 109s buzzing around above. The leaders were probably no more than five miles away.

Loudspeakers blared and red flags were raised over the ops tent and gun emplacements, but the pilots held their ground. Jack resolved to dash for the nearest trench at the merest hint of noses dipping into the customary dive. But, as they came on, it began to look as if they were going to overfly Takali on the way to Valletta or Luqa. Even the anti-aircraft guns held their fire.

What was that?

A whistling screech – screeches - rising in volume. The hair on the back of his neck stood up.

'Bombs!' someone shouted.

He'd known that. Of course he had. And yet, none of them had moved until the word was uttered. Now, though, with the guns crashing out, they charged for the shelter of the trenches. They'd run no more than a few yards before the ground began to shake and explosions rang out behind them.

Either aircraft had dived in unseen, or the 88s were forfeiting the accuracy of dive-bombing to bomb from on high. Not that accuracy seemed a problem. They were hitting the airfield, albeit several hundred yards away - for the moment.

Breathing heavily, Jack was one of the last to reach the trench. He held onto his tin hat, jumped in and turned to peek out. No more than 1,000 yards to the north-east, the air pulsed with orange-yellow sunbursts, producing a strobe affect on shockwaves rippling through the smoke, and dust and rocks bouncing into the air. Fearsome booms took only moments to reach them. Some of the explosions were huge, overlaying the almost incessant mayhem with noticeably fiercer flashes, more violent tremors, ear-popping shockwaves, and thunderous reports.

At first, the bombardment seemed confined to the same

small area. But then, flashes within the smoke moved ever closer to their trench.

Jack peered up. The bombers were increasingly lost in the gathering gloom, but one was suddenly illuminated by a shell burst. Before he could tell whether it had been hit, the ground heaved. He found himself on the floor, nursing a painful elbow. His ears had popped again, and this time he was deaf. Small stones rained down.

He looked about. The other occupants of the trench, mainly fellow pilots, were either curled on the ground, or rising to their knees, brushing themselves down. No-one was standing. Mal had a cut on his cheek, bleeding freely. They struck eye contact and Jack pointed. Mal wiped a hand down his face, looked at the blood, nodded and reached into a pocket.

There was another flash and violent tremor. Jack decided to stay down and curled into a ball. More debris fell. He could hear nothing, but orange flashes penetrated his tightly shut eyelids. Pressure waves rocked him and the ground shook with an incessant background rumble, felt rather than heard. Some of the flashes, shocks and tremors were more intense than others, as were the accompanying showers of dirt.

He lost track of time. Beyond maintaining a tight ball, he also lost control of his body. It bounced around as the bombardment dictated. With the expectation that every moment would be his last, his fear was also uncontrollable. He so wanted to live, but couldn't think why. The pounding had knocked all sense, all reasoning, out of him.

At times, he thought he might be screaming, crying even, but he couldn't really tell. All that existed were the flashes and the shaking.

He had no idea when the bombardment stopped. It just dawned on him that the ground was no longer heaving and debris no longer falling. Every muscle, every fibre of his being, had been clenched tightly, waiting for death – either through the instant oblivion of a direct hit, or the lingering torture of burial alive.

He unclenched his jaw and flexed his hands and feet. At least he was in control of something. Next, he opened his eyes. It was dark, or too dark to pick out anything other than shadows. His ears registered nothing, not even ringing, and his mouth was full of grit. He spat, a dry, unproductive spit, so he puckered to salivate and spat again. After a brief coughing fit and another spit that removed at least some of the grit, he flexed his neck and shoulders. Again, it felt good to move – to be able to move.

He sat up, knowing that he was groaning, but unable to hear any sound; although, somehow, he sensed raised voices.

In the trench, others were stirring. Tentatively, like him, but stirring nonetheless. There was a hint of light, low in the sky to his front, just enough to silhouette the unfurling figures. He stretched his arms and legs. Miraculously, he seemed to be in one piece. The only pain was from his left elbow, and that was unlikely to merit a mention given what they'd just been through.

As his eyes became accustomed to the dusk, he was pleased to see Laddie, JC, Mike, Harv, Dave, Pete and Mal standing or getting to their feet. They all looked dazed, shaking their heads, feeling their limbs, grimacing and poking at their ears. Mal dabbed at his cheek. Their faces were grubby, their eyes wide and surrounded by rings of cleaner skin that gave them the look of startled Pandas.

Jack wasn't in the mood to smile, and no-one would have reciprocated. They were looking through him, their eyes and cheeks reflecting a flickering orange glow. He turned round.

Toward the Elephant huts, flames danced tens of feet into the night sky, illuminating dense columns of smoke that rose into the darkness. Similar fires burned at several locations round the perimeter. The blazes in the centre of the airfield were small in comparison, incendiary bombs burning themselves out for lack of a fuel source.

There was a sudden flash to Jack's left. About 100 yards away, beyond the debris of upturned tables and shredded tents, clouds of black and orange bubbled above a shelter. It contained, or had contained, a Blenheim that had landed earlier, en route for Egypt. The ferocity of the fire must mean it was fully fuelled, if not fully armed.

No fire appliance was going to turn up. They knew that. And yet, caught in the light of the flames, a valiant battle was being fought. NCOs pointed and mouthed orders, and a stream of khaki-clad figures rushed in and out of the shelter carrying buckets. It had to be pointless, but they were still giving it a go, despite the danger.

The scene pricked Jack's conscience. He looked at the others. It had had the same effect on them. Gone were the looks of helpless bemusement, replaced by a determination to do something.

But what?

They walked toward the ops tent. On their side of the airfield, only the pen containing the Blenheim seemed to have suffered a direct hit. But over the other side, several similar blazes raged. Viewed in near silence, the scene had a dreamlike quality.

The ops tent itself had disappeared, its tables overturned, contents scattered across the ground. Laddie and Pete stooped to pick up telephones, put the hand-pieces to their ears and tapped at the cradles. They listened for a while then shook their heads. Laddie placed his back on the ground, while Pete merely dropped his. He looked awful, ashen-faced and dead-eyed, exhausted.

Laddie signalled and they gathered round him.

'Pointless to launch into the dark.'

He was shouting, but Jack could only just hear. The posture of the others indicated that they too were struggling to catch the flight commander's words.

Laddie worked his lips, spat to the side and continued.

'Even if we found a clear take off run, the chances of catching any of the bastards are next to zero.'

He waved an arm over the scene. 'And we certainly couldn't land back here.'

And if we can't, Jack thought, the new Spitfires - it had been confirmed they were arriving the following morning - might not be able to either. It was too difficult to engage in small talk, so he kept his thoughts to himself. But perhaps Laddie was thinking along the same lines.

'Let's walk out to the nearest hole and start filling it in,' he shouted.

Their individual effort seemed pretty futile. But soon, the rest of the flight, who'd been stood down for lack of airframes, turned up and pitched in, followed by the CO and most of B Flight.

They worked until about 9 o'clock, by which time many more soldiers had arrived, their faces and metal tools glinting in the firelight as they threw earth and rocks into tens, maybe hundreds, of craters.

There were no buses, so the pilots walked back to the Xara Palace and Jack fell straight into bed. For once, he heard none of the nuisance raids that continued into the small hours.

He woke at about 7am, feeling grubby and dishevelled, which he was, but also better rested than for days, probably ten days – since his first night in hospital. His elbow was swollen and when he came to move, it stuck to his bedclothes. He sat up and peeled the sheet away, wincing as the graze began to weep tiny bubbles of blood. His ears still buzzed and everyday sounds were muffled.

He padded to the ablutions and found enough water for a decent strip wash. Baths were rationed and he'd got used to the smell of stale sweat, his own and other peoples. At least his laundry was done for him by local mess staff, so he was able to put on fresh uniform, a luxury he was all too aware was denied their NCO pilots and groundcrew.

Feeling marginally more human, he sought out breakfast. The thin rashers of bacon and toast failed to satisfy the hunger that now seemed a constant companion.

If you spoke to the right people, you could get extra on the black market, anything from biscuits to horse meat. But so far he'd had neither the opportunity nor the will to join in the trade. Anyway, he couldn't help feeling that the spivs and those that bought from them were taking food from the mouths of the locals, who didn't have the funds to pay the inflated prices.

He poured a mug of tea from the urn, ladled in four teaspoons of sugar to try and mask the taste and walked out onto the terrace. Mike and Pete were sitting in wicker chairs near the railings, their own mugs of tea on a small round table in front of them. Much like Jack, any flesh not hidden by their KD uniforms was covered in scratches and welts.

It emphasised that though his elbow might be painful, it was nothing out of the ordinary. He stood to one side and looked out over the plain.

Below three quarter high cloud cover, the visibility was good, except over Takali, which was shrouded by a cloak of shifting grey mist. Several smoke pillars still rose, joining into a single funnel that drifted up and away to the north-west and disappeared into the cloudbase towards St Paul's Bay. Smaller pillars of grey climbed above some of the surrounding villages.

'Over a hundred tons, apparently,' Pete said, brow furrowed. He seemed to have recovered some of his composure. 'But only two casualties. On the airfield, that is. Not sure about the villages.'

With so much smoke rising, it was hard to believe there hadn't been considerable loss of life.

'Laddie says to stay here for now,' Pete continued. 'If the CO wants us, he'll send a message. It'll only be to fill in holes anyway. Even if any kites are left, it's hard to believe we could get airborne.'

Looking down at the smoke-shrouded airfield, it was difficult to disagree.

Jack pulled a chair alongside Mike's and rested his tea on his knee. There the three of them sat in a silence broken only briefly as they were joined by, first, Dave Campbell, then Zulu du Toit - who'd been out of action with a bad case of The Dog. Each received the same short update, after which they too settled back to look out over the plain.

They might have sat like it all morning, but, just after 8.45, the hair on the back of Jack's neck stood up.

An unwelcome, if familiar, sound had intruded. Aero engines! He turned to try and look back through the roof of the palace.

'Oh, no, not again,' Dave Campbell said, his doleful Aberdeen burr expressing a trepidation they all seemed to feel.

Jack rose with a groan and moved forward to the railings, leaning out to look up and as far back into the north-west as he could.

''Fraid so,' he said.

They all stood up and joined him.

'Eighty eights again,' Mike said, as rank after rank of bombers appeared above the roof of the adjacent building.

Up at around 15,000 feet were tens of them, escorted by an equal number of 109s. And they were heading straight for Takali.

Pete returned to his chair, grabbed the tin hat hanging by its strap and put it on. The others followed suit.

By the time they turned round, the first bombs were exploding. Shockwaves pulsed through the smoke like ripples on a puddle. Great fountains of red earth shot out of the mist, carrying on upward for hundreds of feet. Larger objects also appeared, seeming to hang for a while, then fall slowly back.

Rocks? The shattered remains of vehicles? Bodies?

Jack grimaced. Even from the safety of their eyrie, they

were flinching and hunching their shoulders at the louder reports. How much worse to be down there, sheltering in a slit trench or blast pen, or, even worse, caught in the open.

Luqa had large underground shelters. Surely more effort should have gone into providing the same level of protection at Takali? Too late now, though.

The 88s were bombing from height again, and, while hating them for it, Jack had to admire their accuracy. As far as he could tell, nearly all the bombs were landing within the airfield perimeter.

After about 25 bombers and their escorts had passed over, there was a brief lull.

Laddie joined them. 'I think we're better off here for now,' he said, in reply to the question written on all their faces.

Jack let the statement kill off the feeling that they should have been running down the hill to help in some way. What could they have achieved? Marching down when the raids were still on would merely risk pilots that would be needed if and when they had the means to fight back.

The first formation had been out of earshot for only a short while, when the beat of more engines had them looking at one another.

Here we go again.

This time, a greater proportion of bombs fell on the surrounding settlements. At first, Jack thought it might just be uncharacteristic inaccuracy. But then he noticed small sections of aircraft diving in to bomb and strafe the villages.

You could almost forgive them for hitting military airfields. How else were they to attack the air assets on Malta? But what could possibly be gained by targeting innocent civilians?

He struck eye contact with Mike.

'Murdering bastards,' the New Zealander spat, his jaw set in a manner that said, equally clearly, just you wait.

Jack nodded. He shared the sentiment, but doubted their ability to gain retribution, at least in the short term. Their

Spitfires seemed unlikely to survive, so the new delivery, if it made it, would only put them back at square one.

Mike must have read Jack's mind, or come to the same realization.

Eyes blazing, he turned away and roared, 'Fuck!'

They spent the next hour watching raid after raid.

By 10.30, when the latest lull seemed to have been long enough to indicate a genuine break, more than 200 aircraft must have passed through the overhead. The anti-aircraft guns had been crashing away throughout, their shells bursting around the massed formations of bombers and fighters, but not one seemed to have been hit. Not one seemed to have given the guns the slightest heed and deviated from its route.

Was this the precursor to invasion? Who knew?

They stood, lining the railings, recharged mugs of tea in hand. The horizon had disappeared, obscured behind a great arc of smoke, rising above fires in villages from Mosta in the north, to Zebbug in the south. In the centre was Takali, or what was left of it, hidden under a huge dome of smoke, tinged red by dust caught in the billowing up-currents. Here and there, the smoke glowed orange, and there were frequent booms, presumably delayed action bombs, or exploding ammunition and fuel.

The tiny airfield, nowhere more than a thousand yards in diameter, must have been hit with at least as many bombs as the previous night: hundreds, if not thousands.

And what about those down on the airfield, not only the pilots, but the groundcrew? How had Smudger fared?

Just before 11, they heard more engines. The hair on back of Jack's neck stood again. Only this time, not in trepidation, but in hope. They were Merlins, too many to be Hurricanes from Hal Far. They leaned out, craning their necks.

First a Blenheim, then a Hurricane, and then three vics of three Spitfires. They cheered and waved tin hats in the air as another couple of Blenheims came over. Unsurprisingly, the aircraft by-passed Takali, flying through the thinner wisps of smoke to head south, the sound of their engines disappearing towards Luqa.

Very sensible, but disappointing.

A few minutes later, the decision to shun Takali was more than vindicated. About ten 110s bombed the airfield from shallow dives, while a similar number of 109s flew into the smoke, the sound of their cannon and machine guns reaching up to the terrace as a pernicious, staccato, whisper.

Six Hurricanes appeared from the south-west. For once, they had the advantage of height, and they chased the Germans toward St Paul's Bay. Any ensuing battle was hidden behind a veil of smoke.

They waited for more Spitfires. Surely, there should be another seven? But no more came.

Lunch – a bully-beef sandwich – had been a subdued affair, each lost in their thoughts; in Jack's case, dreading a return to the airfield. He almost wished he had the Dog, like Zulu, whose pained expression and frequent absences from the terrace had led Laddie to stand him down once again.

When the flight commander eventually led them down the hill toward the smoke, they passed tens of traumatised figures caked in dust trudging in the opposite direction. Jack began to wish he had the courage to turn about and follow them.

How many felt the same?

He simply dreaded sitting under another raid. His tic pulsed and he began to realise what it meant to feel weak at the knees.

The airfield was a complete shambles. Smoke and flames still rose from buildings and pens round the perimeter, and hundreds of troops wielding shovels dotted the operating surfaces. The smoke was blowing north-east away from them, but the air was full of its smell – a mixture of aviation fuel, oil, cordite and rubber.

Squadron accommodation comprised a few tables in the open, surrounded by splintered tent poles, shredded canvas and scraps of paper. Perhaps some of the ghostly figures trudging up the hill had been the pilots of B Flight, because none of them were in sight.

Amid much arm-waving and pointing, Laddie and the CO joined in an earnest conversation. After a few minutes, they walked over.

Perhaps it was Laddie's relative experience that led Squadron Leader Grant to spend most of his time with B Flight, but this, and the days Jack had been absent after his crash landing, meant that he'd seen little of the CO. He'd heard much, though, and all of it good.

Now, the man stood before them, slim, youthful, erect, and as smart as could be expected when coated in dust following an air raid.

'Sorry, chaps, but as you might have guessed, the airfield's u/s at the moment. The station commander hopes they'll manage to clear enough for us to nip over to Luqa before dark, but we'll see.

'Damage reports are still coming in, but it seems we've been remarkably lucky. One destroyed and a couple with blast damage. And, by some miracle, no casualties beyond the two airmen injured last night. In the meantime, it's more of the same, I'm afraid.'

He looked from face to face. 'Any questions?'

Jack wondered whether more of the same meant craters or blast pens, but otherwise, there really wasn't anything to query.

Faced with a deafening silence, the CO smiled and said, 'Okay, then, let's see how the rest of the day unfolds.'

It was blast pens. But, before he set to with the others, Jack excused himself and went to seek out Smudger. He found him in a pen, under the wing of a Spitfire raised on jacks and minus a wheel.

Jack recognised the airframe and walked straight over to the starboard wingtip. Smudger joined him.

'Had to rob it off of the one you hit with the roller, sir.' The airframe fitter patted his handiwork.

'Okay, no need to rub it in,' Jack said with a smile.

He wasn't sure why speaking to his old rigger cheered him up. Perhaps it was the link with Biggin Hill and, more loosely, Caroline. And the sense of perspective was there again. It was only four years since he'd been an airframe fitter himself, although under nothing like the same circumstances.

'At least I'm not responsible for all the wrecks on the airfield now,' he said.

'No, I think the Gerries are a few up on you after the last 12 hours, sir.'

Jack ran his hand over the wingtip. 'You've made a fine job of it, Smudger.'

'Thanks, sir, but we were lucky we robbed it yesterday afternoon. When they went back for more bits this morning, she was spitchered.'

So that was the one destroyed. It had been a bit of a wreck, anyway, so perhaps, in a perverse sort of way, they'd been lucky. He wondered if the groundcrew knew more than the CO. They often did.

'What was the final score?'

'Including last night, sir?'

Jack nodded.

'Well, we didn't lose any, just a couple damaged. Gerry seemed to buy the ruse that there's an underground hangar over there.' He pointed to the north-east. 'We've been laying wrecks out for weeks, making it look as if they were on a pan.'

Jack hadn't heard that one before, and hadn't noticed the subterfuge from the air, probably because he hadn't had time to admire the airfield. But the story would explain why the south and west of the airfield had escaped relatively lightly.

Smudger continued. 'Meant 126 and the visiting aircraft got hit hard, though. Not sure how many they lost. And they spitchered another bowser.'

It was obvious from the airframe fitter's pained expression that this hurt more than the loss of the odd aircraft.

'And this morning?' Jack enquired.

'Well, they must think the underground hangar is toast, because we all copped it.'

Jack dabbed at his tic and marvelled that the rigger seemed outwardly unaffected by the bombing, or by fear at what the next few hours might hold. Or was he just a good actor, like the rest of them.

'Only one lost, and that was your roller kite, sir.'

Jack smiled. At least now *his roller kite* was gone he probably wouldn't have to hear the term again.

'This one picked up some shrapnel.' Smudger waved a hand over the wing, where there was evidence of recent filing and patching. 'Gouged a few nicks and shredded a tyre.'

He ducked under the wing, manoeuvring past the jack to where he'd been kneeling when Jack arrived. There, he knelt down before a wheel leaning against the starboard main undercarriage olio. He grasped the edges of its new tyre, grunted as he strained to lift and offer it up to the stub axle, and then pushed. The old wheel, its tyre shredded, lay to one side.

'Seems another minor miracle, really, but there were only another couple with similar,' he said, grimacing as he jiggled the tyre from side to side and pushed against it.

Then he sat on the ground, leant back on his arms, raised his feet and kicked the soles of his boots against either side of the new wheel.

'I think they got a few more Hurris though, sir,' he said, the effort now evident in his voice.

Jack decided it was time to leave the rigger to get on with his work, and return to his own, before they accused him of shirking.

'Okay, Smudger, I'll get out of your hair. Take care, now.'

'Thanks, sir. You too.'

Smudger smiled, then lay back and gave the wheel another almighty kick.

Jack joined in the task of rebuilding a damaged pen a couple of hundred yards from what had been the ops tent. They cleared the debris of blown in parapets and set about restoring them, ideally with the blocks, sandbags or cans that had been blown out in the first place. His elbow twinged every time he bent or straightened it, but it still didn't merit a mention when everyone was suffering to a greater or lesser extent.

At 2.15, the CO appeared in the opening and waved them toward him. They gathered round, glad of the breather.

'I thought you'd be interested in the latest on the reinforcements from Eagle,' he began.

'The weather over the carrier and most of the western Mediterranean was smeggy, and the second section of Blenheims didn't arrive. So, the nine you saw this morning are it.'

There were a few groans.

'I know, but there it is. Force H sailed back to Gibraltar with the final seven still on board. Whether they'll mount another operation for so few, who knows? I'm not sure the Admiralty'll be too keen.

'Anyway, Squadron Leader Gracie led them in, and he's the new CO of 126 *Spitfire* Squadron.'

There were a few more groans. The new kites hardly replaced their losses to date; so, instead of one squadron with no aircraft, there were now two.

The fresh-faced squadron leader held up a hand. 'I know what you're thinking, but we'll just have to make the best of it and come up with some sort of plan for sharing

133

airframes.'

The CO stayed and mucked in.

At around 2.30, the sirens began to wail. They crowded into the nearest slit trench, peering up and listening intently. As the sirens fell silent, Jack heard the drone of engines.

He looked at Mike, whose pained expression belied a state of apprehension similar to his own.

Above a gap in what was now little more than a thin layer of scattered cumulus, Jack spotted dark shapes.

'There!' he pointed.

A formation of 88s surrounded by 109s approached from the north-west at around 15,000 feet. They disappeared behind a white floret of cloud just as the anti-aircraft guns opened up.

Jack's stomach knotted and his mouth became dry. Sweat began to prickle his upper lip and forehead.

The question of whether the formation would bomb from level, enter a dive, or overfly the airfield altogether was answered when the screech of bombs joined the crack of the guns. Both sounds were soon drowned out by the thunderous roar of the first explosions. The ground heaved and Jack's ears popped. It wasn't long before a violent tremor threw him to the ground. The sound wave deafened him and dirt and small rocks showered down. He didn't attempt to rise, but curled into a ball and gritted his teeth.

Shouldn't familiarity make the experience easier to bear?

He flinched at every new tremor and fall of stones, waiting for the ordeal to end or his life to be extinguished.

The bombardment was much shorter than the previous evening's, or the one witnessed that morning. It had seemed as unpleasant, though, reducing Jack to a cringing wretch, a condition he hated but, much to his shame, was unable to control.

When the ground had remained still long enough to make it reasonable to assume the raid had ended, he went through a recovery process that was also becoming familiar: flexing his extremities, then his limbs and, eventually, climbing to his feet and trying to clear his eyes, ears and mind.

The lull was all too brief. Even as they were dusting themselves off, the guns crashed out. The sound was muffled and if the sirens were wailing, Jack couldn't hear them. He was also too deaf to hear engines, and no red flags were in sight. But he could see where anti-aircraft shells were bursting.

This time, the bombers were approaching from the north-east, maybe a dozen at about 10,000 feet.

The nose of the lead aircraft dipped. One by one, they dived.

Initially, Jack greeted the reversion in tactics with relief. At least you had some idea of where a diving bomber was aiming, and roughly where its bombs would land. For the moment, the north-eastern perimeter looked the likely target.

The first stick of bombs straddled the centre of the airfield, no more than 500 yards away. Jack's relief turned quickly to fear. So much for his theory, and his judgement.

The explosions marched towards them, sending up great clouds of earth and dust. He tensed, waiting for successive bombers to continue the south-westerly progress. But although the shock waves and tremors could still be seen and felt, no bombs leapfrogged the smoke.

He raised his head another few centimetres, looking over the lip of the trench.

One 88 after another appeared overhead at about 4,000 feet, turned right onto a north easterly heading and raced for home. Each was surrounded by expanding puffs of black smoke. The gunners were getting close, but not close enough.

Suddenly, a tumbling heap of metal burst out of the smoke to their front. No higher than 200 feet and in a shallow descent, the wreck of an 88 was heading straight towards them, wings rotating like the sails of a deranged windmill.

Jack was mesmerised, rooted to the spot.

The right wing beyond the engine was missing, the engine itself on fire. The stricken hulk came on. Even through his deafness, he heard the scream of tortured air, felt the heat. The fuselage flashed no more than 50 feet above, the intact wing sweeping even closer. He imagined a pilot struggling at the controls.

His view of the actual crash was obscured, but orange and black balls of flaming aviation fuel rose only a couple of hundred yards away, near the western perimeter fence.

Troops had been working over there. Jack wondered if they'd been able to get out of the way.

Another two bombers had joined those heading north-west before the ground stopped shaking. Jack waited. The smoke over the airfield remained undisturbed by shockwaves. He shrugged his shoulders, sighing as the tightness in his muscles eased. After a few more seconds, he glanced back at the others.

Laddie was ducking and pointing, his face contorted into a wide-eyed, soundless, shout.

Jack swivelled to see a couple of 109s, noses sparking. Something brushed against him and he turned to see a khaki-clad figure climbing from the trench. It was Squadron Leader Grant. Hunched and weaving, he ran into a sandbag sangar at the rear corner of the pen. The barrels of two Browning machine guns appeared above the low parapet.

Without having made a conscious decision to do so, Jack found himself climbing from the trench. He zig-zagged over the rough ground and turned into the sangar to kneel next to his CO, who acknowledged his presence with a nod of his dust-covered head.

Jack had imagined feeding ammunition belts into the Brownings as the CO fired. But these guns had boxes attached to their outer sides, Heath Robinson fashion. So, while the CO swung the guns and blazed away until his chosen 109 disappeared from view, Jack looked for the next target, tapped him on the shoulder and directed him onto it.

Their main obstacle was the wall of the pen. Most of their targets flashed over it with no notice. Few approached from the west or north-west, their only unrestricted line of fire, and Jack was pretty sure they hadn't hit anything. And yet, it felt really good to be up and doing, rather than languishing in a trench, paralysed with fear.

They hadn't fired for a while when a 109 appeared overhead at about 1500 feet. It climbed away to the south-west, trailing smoke. As they watched, the rear of the engine cowling began to glow. A dark shape appeared alongside, falling quickly.

Jack held his breath. After only a short delay, a parachute blossomed.

For the briefest of moments, he thought of taking up the machine guns and firing on the helpless figure. Then, he wondered whether the CO had had the same thought. Their eyes met and, in what Jack took to be a tacit acknowledgement of a shared sentiment, they exchanged an almost imperceptible shake of the head.

No.

They stood and walked out of the sangar to get a better view of the descending pilot. About a mile beyond him, his Messerschmitt, wreathed in flame, rolled over on its back and pitched into a vertical dive.

One by one, the rest of A Flight climbed out of the nearby slit trench and joined them.

The German was a few hundred feet up, a little to the south of the burning bomber, when his fighter slammed into the high ground in a ball of oily flame.

Jack re-focused on the parachutist. He noticed men running from several directions. Maltese labourers. Each carried, or rather, brandished, some form of farm implement - a spade, scythe, axe or suchlike.

Jack exchanged worried glances with his fellow pilots.

They were too far away to intervene, even if they'd had a mind to – a debate for another time, perhaps.

At first, it looked as if the German might drift over the fence into the relative safety of the airfield. But, the wind near the surface must have dropped. It soon became apparent he was destined to fall outside the wire.

The Maltese were closing.

From behind a blast pen, half a dozen soldiers appeared. Bayonets fixed, they doubled up to the wire, ducked through a gap and ran toward the parachutist. He was about 100 yards beyond the wire, 20 feet up, with a dozen angry Maltese closing from the other side.

The pilot drifted toward the soldiers and disappeared from view, his landing obscured behind running figures. Jack had assumed the troops were rushing out to save the German, but, as the two groups met, he was cast into doubt. A mêlée formed and he began to wonder whether the poor man was being stabbed and hacked by British bayonets as well as the locals' more makeshift weapons.

He winced.

But no, the German suddenly reappeared, held between two soldiers. He looked suitably terrified, but in one piece, being manhandled – dragged - away from the Maltese. The only evidence of the latter was their deadly arsenal, still waving above the heads of the four remaining soldiers.

And then, a tremor. Jack turned to see smoke rising and puffs of black dotting the sky.

He was torn. He wanted to see how the rest of the rescue mission went, but also to seek shelter. The others were caught in the same dilemma, but slowly, with the encouragement of the odd hand on an arm, they turned and made for the trench.

Jack made eye contact with Squadron Leader Grant. Without a word or perceptible gesture, they headed for the sangar.

Once inside, the CO unclipped and discarded the ammunition boxes attached to the Brownings. The arrangement was unfamiliar to Jack, but not, it seemed, to his commanding officer. Acknowledging the squadron leader's hand signals, Jack picked up a new box and offered it up to the right hand machine gun. He was surprised at the deftness with which the first rounds were fed into the gun and the box fixed in place. They repeated the operation for the left gun.

Tremors and pressure waves pulsed around them. Jack picked out the muffled reports of explosions. The improvement in his hearing seemed unlikely to last long.

He half stood and looked up. Another formation of about 20, running in from the south at about 15,000 feet. The walls of the blast pen obscured the impacts of their bombs, which added an unwelcome air of suspense.

There was nothing for them to shoot at, and as the tremors became more violent, Jack doubted the wisdom of remaining above ground surrounded by nothing more than a few sandbags. Larger debris began to fall, shutting out the brief hope that they might make a run for the trench. The CO knelt down and covered up. Jack did the same.

It was another violent, gut-wrenching, experience. The rising intensity of flashes, tremors, pressure waves and debris pointed to bombs dropping ever closer to their inadequate sanctuary. Jack's fear climbed accordingly.

And then, everything went black. Crushed and unable to breathe, Jack panicked.

He scrambled to push up from his squatting position. Whatever was confining him gave a little, but not much. And still he couldn't breathe. He pushed again and the weight shifted some more, but it was still dark and his mouth and nose were blocked.

He was going to asphyxiate!

In what felt like a final effort, he pushed up as hard as he could. The weight fell from his back, allowing him to kneel up and sense light beyond his eyelids. He rubbed at his face, snorting and coughing in an attempt to clear whatever was blocking his airway, then breathed in.

Relief.

He took several gritty, rattling, breaths. His chest heaved. His eyes and nose were streaming, and he washed at both with his fingers, shifting snot and grit in equal measure.

When he opened his eyes, the air was full of dust. The parapet of the adjacent blast pen had collapsed onto their sangar, burying him in shredded sandbags and earth.

The CO was standing, dusting himself off. He looked a fright, coated from head to foot in reddish sand and earth. He managed a smile, though, and extended a hand to help Jack to his feet. Jack winced, noticing his elbow for the first time in several minutes.

It was as if they were in the midst of a violent sandstorm, visibility reduced to a few yards. There were no tremors, but Jack still sensed menace. He couldn't see or hear them, but he just knew 109s were darting about the smoke, adding to the chaos.

They stepped over the remains of the damaged sangar parapet and walked towards the slit trench. Remembering Alex's story of the WAAF trench at Biggin Hill, Jack feared the worst. But the refuge was intact. Grubby, drawn, faces looked up.

Their expressions said, *where have you been?'* or, *what happened to you?*

Jack and the CO reached down and helped their fellow pilots climb up.

The dust was clearing north-east on the breeze, and for once no 109s were in evidence. Jack looked at the blast pen. Thirty feet of its side wall had collapsed. The final ten feet up to the corner had folded onto their sangar.

They'd been lucky. If their shelter had been nearer the centre of the wall, where the parapet consisted of rocks and earth-filled cans rather than sandbags, they'd have been pummelled to death.

The respite was short-lived. Even as they pointed at signs of more destruction across the airfield, a red flag was raised above the nearest Bofors emplacement. The protruding barrel of its gun recoiled, belching out a ball of silver-grey smoke.

Jack's heart sank. Not again?

For the umpteenth time, they jumped down into the trench.

88 after 88 dived down. Sometimes, they seemed to attack from several directions at once, and Jack was never really sure where the next bomb would fall. But most explosions were well to the east of the airfield centreline again, so the pilots spent much of the time with their heads up. Thus, they saw another success for the airfield gunners.

Nearing the end of its dive at about 6,000 feet, an 88 was hit amidships. It shuddered, seeming almost to stop in mid air. The fuselage began to glow and two small shapes fell from beneath it. They were too big to be bombs and Jack guessed what they were. From the expressions about him, others had reached the same conclusion.

As if in slow motion, the bomber split into four sections: fuselage, wings and tail. These seemed to hang for a moment, drifting slowly apart, before the fuselage plummeted like a flaming arrow. The wings and tailplane almost fluttered down, rotating eccentrically about new centres of gravity.

The fuselage chased after the two smaller objects. It was these that held Jack's attention, their shapes unmistakable now.

Limbs flailing, the airmen fell into the smoke covering the centre of the airfield. One by one, the aircraft parts followed, causing wispy disturbances with their passing.

By the time Jack prised his eyes away to look upwards, the raid seemed to be over. Several bombers were climbing into the north-west. Again, the usual follow-on assault by 109s failed to materialise. Perhaps they'd decided there were no targets of consequence left on Takali.

It certainly felt like it.

There were further air raid warnings, and more bombers overhead. Each time, they either took to the shelters, or just stared up, waiting to see if they needed to react. Apart from a throbbing elbow, Jack felt numb, a feeling not helped by the muzziness of his hearing and the grit in his eyes and lungs. Everyone looked the same, dishevelled and shell-shocked.

But no further bombs fell on the airfield. Not that there weren't explosions. Some were UXBs being blown up by the disposal folk, others delayed action bombs. You had to hope none of these caught the brave men trying to defuse them. Or anyone else, come to that.

After patching up minor wounds – miraculously, no-one on 249 had been killed or suffered major injury - they spent the couple of hours until dusk wandering around trying to find little tasks amid the destruction that could make a difference: clearing debris from slit trenches; setting up tables and awnings, even the odd tent; and discovering telephones and phone lines.

With the groundcrew working on the resident aircraft, they began shifting debris from pen entrances, and the taxy routes to the runways, which were being worked on by large numbers of troops. No-one voiced the futility of their actions, although they all knew there was no chance of operating from Takali for some time, not least because of shortage of aircraft.

Another had been destroyed and five damaged. They were down to two serviceable Spitfires.

News trickled in all the time. A few airmen on the other side had been injured, but no fatalities yet. The army had suffered worse, with several deaths where shelters or gun emplacements had been hit. They began to hear of civilian deaths in the local villages. Transiting aircraft, a Beaufighter, Maryland and Wellington had been destroyed, with three more Beaufighters, two Blenheims and a Maryland damaged.

An adjacent reservoir had been breached, flooding the north of the airfield. A million gallons of water had been lost. As if they weren't short enough.

185 Squadron had lost four Hurricanes, with another 15 damaged.

If they'd been hoping for good news, they were sadly disappointed. But how could there be anything but tales of death and destruction.

So many bombs on such a small area!

Soon after 8pm, they trudged their way wearily up the hill to Mdina. Jack's first beer tasted wonderful. It also seemed to defy medical science by washing the grit from his lungs as well as his throat. For the first time in several hours, he breathed easier.

He also felt significantly happier, especially when he and Mike secured their second beers. They clinked glasses and joined the general drift to the terrace. By the time they reached it, Jack was giving Mike a blow-by-blow description of his recent entombment. He was still chatting as they approached a semi-circle of their fellow pilots. A stern-faced Pete Brown turned his head and shoulders and put a finger to his lips.

Jack and Mike looked at one another, eyebrows arched, then tiptoed up to the back of the group. Facing them was Zulu, his face ashen with bad news. They seemed to have missed the start of the story.

'It went off in the entrance. Buck didn't know how, but he ended up at the top of the stairs.'

Entrance to what? And how was Flight Commander B involved?

'Thought he'd had his head caved in. But, he was just shaken. Deaf and covered in dust,' he said, 'but not actually injured. It wasn't 'til he went downstairs that he found them.'

Jack looked from Mike, to Laddie, and on to Dave and Harv. All were listening intently, but in obvious dread of what they were about to hear, their eyes half closed, noses crinkling in anticipation.

'I'll spare you the gory details, but two of B Flight, John Booth and Jimmy Guerin, are dead, along with two from 126, Cecil Baker and Bill Hollis Hallett, plus one of the IntOs – chap called Waterfield.'

Zulu looked at Harv Johnson. 'Eddie Streets was taken to hospital. Bad way, I'm afraid.'

Although on different squadrons, the two Americans, Harv and Eddie, had become partners in crime, their youthful enthusiasm and energy getting them into all sorts of minor scrapes, invariably hilarious in the telling.

Jack couldn't pretend he'd known any of them very well, not least because they lived in the Point de Vue, a requisitioned hotel just outside the walls in Rabat. Was that the building that had been hit? If so, it was a long way from the airfield.

Zulu looked all in. Jack felt sorry for him, having to be the bearer of such bad news, and at second hand.

Laddie was the first to speak. 'And Buck?'

'He's okay, Laddie. Drunk as a skunk. But okay.'

Zulu looked as if he was going to add something, but stopped, then grimaced slightly and carried on anyway. 'You might have to play prisoner's friend tomorrow.'

Laddie arched an eyebrow.

'He and Ronnie broke into the bar. Polished off two bottles of whiskey.'

Laddie looked relieved, as Zulu continued.

'The Mess Manager wants his guts for garters.'

'Well,' Laddie said, his face grim and determined, 'the Mess Manager can fuck off.'

Chapter 10 – 22nd March – Goodbye Takali

When they gathered on the terrace after breakfast and heard the grim details – heads split in two, legs blown off, guts spewing out – Jack was glad they hadn't been related the night before. The images would have haunted his sleep, not that he'd had much anyway.

It *had* been the Point de Vue, no more than a few hundred yards away as the crow flew. Whether the bombs had overshot or undershot Takali, or been meant for the town, hardly seemed to matter. It was a reminder that everyone on the Island, combatant or not, was vulnerable to the murderous onslaught.

Once again, the majority stayed on the terrace, drinking tea, chatting quietly and looking out over the plain. Malta was covered in grey cloud, base about 1500 feet, visibility less than five miles. Wisps of smoke rose from the airfield and some of the surrounding villages.

The weather should have provided some respite, but apparently not. 109s had been flashing about, and Takali had been hit again. New smoke pillars meandered up to the cloudbase. Harv must have been up at the crack of sparrows, because he'd already returned from Imtarfa. Eddie Streets had died the previous evening.

Spirits were at a low ebb.

Just before 10am, soon after another small raid on Takali, Laddie appeared. As soon as he strode in, Jack could tell the flight commander had news. He poured a tea from the urn, spooned in a couple of sugars and walked over to a chair, stirring as he came. They turned to face him.

He sat and cleared his throat. 'Well, morning all.' Then he noticed Harv. 'I don't know whether you've heard…'

Harv met his gaze four-square and said, matter-of-factly, 'Yes, thanks Laddie. I managed to get to Imtarfa this morning.'

'Well, sorry, anyway.'

Harv acknowledged another round of sympathetic nods.

Laddie waited patiently before continuing. 'Apart from Eddie, there don't seem to have been any additional casualties, either on the airfield, or at the Point de Vue.'

If the losses of the previous day hadn't been so unusual, they wouldn't have merited mention a day later. You had to move on. Even the brief comment now had made them feel uncomfortable.

Laddie continued, 'I've spoken to the CO, and Buck and Ronne pitched in as normal. I've also had a word with the Mess Manager, and I don't think we'll hear anything more from that quarter. So that's that.'

They all smiled, even Harv.

'Although,' - Laddie adopted an expression of mock sternness – 'I don't want such behaviour to set a precedent.'

More smiles.

'Right. The CO says the AOC visited and seemed genuinely shocked at the state of the airfield. Said it looked like a First World War battlefield – and he should know. But he also said we had to get it up and running as soon as possible.'

He took a sip of tea and leaned forward, as if about to share a confidence.

'That convoy we heard might be coming. Well, it left Alexandria two days ago. Should arrive sometime tomorrow morning. And assuming Kesselring knows as much as we do, if not more, we can expect him to throw everything he's got at it.'

He paused for a moment, sitting upright again, striking eye contact with each in turn.

'And that's where we come in. It's up to us to keep the Luftwaffe off those ships – oh, and defend the Island of course.'

Bloody difficult without an airfield, Jack thought.

'Now, some of you may have spotted a tiny problem. If we can't get off the bloody ground, we can't protect anybody. So the AOC says the Army are giving priority to clearing a strip for us to get over to Luqa as soon as possible.'

Jack doubted Laddie would mention that that would still give them no more than a handful of Spitfires and Hurricanes against 600-odd German machines. He was right.

'We'll go down this afternoon and muck in. The hope is that we can fly out however many kites we've got – four at the last count –this evening or tomorrow morning, when, as you're no doubt aware, we're on earlies again.'

Even Jack let out an audible groan.

'I know. It's a bugger, isn't it?' Laddie said, rubbing his eyes.

'Anyway, in the meantime, the groundcrew at Luqa have been working flat out to get the new kites prepped. So, in the morning, we should have at least nine to share with 126.'

'For Christ's sake, Laddie,' Mike interjected, 'is there any good news?'

'Sorry, Mike,' he looked at the New Zealander. 'But unless I've missed a silver lining, I don't think there is one. The bottom line is that no matter how few kites we have, we've got to protect the convoy on the way in, and while it's being unloaded. And we'll have to do it from Luqa until that place' – he waved a hand over Takali – 'is up and running again.

'One last thing,' Laddie said. 'Bull's decided that until we have more kites we need a shift in tactics. Instead of heading off the fighters while the Hurris go for the 88s, we're all to concentrate on the bombers.'

Same as when the airfields were being hit during the Battle of Britain, Jack thought. 'Makes sense,' he said. 'It's *the big jobs*' – mimicking Woody – 'that're doing the damage, so we need to hit them first, much as we did when the heat was on in 1940.'

'Thanks, Jack, couldn't have put it better myself.'

Before he left the terrace, Laddie called Jack, Mike and Pete aside.

'Look chaps, Jumbo,' – the new OC 126 Squadron was universally known as Jumbo Gracie – 'says most of the pilots he led in are as green round the gills as those that came in with you a fortnight ago. He and the CO have had a confab and decided that although we have to play them in at some time, now is not the time.

'So, I'm afraid the more experienced chaps on both squadrons are going to bear the brunt of ops over the next few days, certainly while the convoy's coming in and unloading.'

It made sense. While the stakes were so high, and there were so few aircraft, they had to maximise their chances, not only of blunting enemy attacks on the convoy, but also of getting their kites back in one piece.

'And it doesn't take a genius to work out that, on A Flight, that means you three and a handful of the NCOs. I'm off to tell them the good news now.'

Jack exchanged a resigned glance with Mike, but when he looked toward Pete, the flight lieutenant was already walking away.

That afternoon, Jack was amazed at the number of troops working on and around the airfield. He'd never seen so many, shovelling dirt into craters and out of trenches, and carrying rocks and sandbags to repair walls and shelters.

B Flight had spent the morning erecting a new complex of tents, only this time, within a blast pen. It was such a simple idea that you had to wonder why it hadn't been done before; although the patch of charred ground in the centre of the walled enclosure dispelled any illusion of invulnerability. They'd still need to take to the slit trenches during a raid.

And they didn't have to wait long for one of those.

Just after 2pm, they were repairing the parapet of a blast shelter when sirens wailed, red flags appeared and the guns barked. They just made the relative safety of a trench before

148

a pair of 109s flashed overhead. Perhaps as many as a dozen of the fighters spent the next ten minutes harrying the poor souls huddled in the middle of the airfield.

The pattern was repeated throughout the afternoon and evening, small raiding parties of 109s appearing to disrupt the repair work. Some were Jabos dropping bombs, just to add variety. Not a single Ju88 was seen.

'Saving them for the convoy,' Mike said when the subject came up as they took a tea break.

'Speaking of which,' Laddie said, appearing from the new ops tent, 'Valletta have just been on. The convoy could be here first thing tomorrow morning, if they survive the attentions of the Italian Navy. They've been making a nuisance of themselves, so Woody's sent a section of Albacores to drop a few torpedoes on the sods. Three of 126 are acting as escort, which means they must have prepped some of the new kites in record time.'

126 wouldn't have to bear the brunt if...

Laddie pre-empted his thoughts. 'Seems there's still a chance we could get out later this evening.'

They did, and with six Spitfires out of a possible eight. Another brilliant performance by the groundcrew, who, Jack knew from a quick chat with Smudger, had spent the previous night on the airfield, snatching a few minutes' sleep on the ground next to their charges when the chance arose.

At 8pm, Jack flew one of the six out. The five minute hop in the dark was much less fraught than the time on the ground at both ends.

At Takali, they took off from a narrow, poorly lit strip. Holes, earth mounds, red flags and the shining faces and accoutrements of soldiers flashed past only a few yards to either side of his wingtips.

And at Luqa, he was met at the end of the runway by a car, which he was told to follow. Hanging on to its dim tail-lights, he taxied for an age, leaving the airfield altogether and winding along narrow dirt tracks flanked by dry stone walls, stunted trees and hills. When he eventually reached his parking bay, it was in the middle of nowhere.

Chapter 11 – 23rd to 26th March – Convoy MW10

Five am. Jack clambered onto the wreck of a bus, found a seat toward the back, leant his head against a window dripping with condensation and closed his eyes. He kept them closed, even when they stopped to pick up the NCOs and he felt someone sit next to him.

The rest of the journey was too cold, bumpy and winding to allow real sleep, but he refused to open his eyes and acknowledge the world until he had to. In between bitter-sweet thoughts of Caroline, he even managed a few naps, but each ended with a neck-jarring jolt into wakefulness.

Only when the engine stopped and there were groans and the tell-tale signs of movement did he give in to the inevitable. He stretched, opened his eyes and nodded at Kim Kaminski, who was getting up from the seat next to him. The NCO smiled and waved Jack into the aisle. Jack smiled his thanks and joined the line of pilots filing off the bus.

He stepped into the dark, one in a crocodile of huddled, silent, figures, their breath steaming in the cold air. After a short distance circumnavigating mounds of rubble, the line began to disappear into a doorway set in a jagged fragment of wall.

Jack was swallowed. He descended dimly lit stone stairwells echoing with the sound of shuffling footfalls. Deep underground, they filed into a large, low-ceilinged, room, the rough-hewn walls of which were lined with benches, some occupied by other groups of hunched figures. A few doors led off, their frosted glass windows emblazoned with black lettering.

This must be G Shelter, Luqa's ops complex. Basic by Fighter Command standards, but positively palatial compared to the tents at Takali. Laddie went through a door marked Ops Room, and they sat on an empty bench, nodding at those they recognised in other groups, but not going over or entering into conversation. The place had the air of a dentist's waiting room, silent and tense.

About five minutes after he'd disappeared, Laddie came out in the company of the CO. It seemed there was to be no grand briefing. Squadron Leader Grant stood before their bench, and they leaned forward to hear an update issued in hushed tones, as if he didn't want to disturb the others in the room.

They were starting the day with 11 Hurricanes, split between Hal Far and Luqa, and 14 Spitfires, to be shared between them and 126. Both types would fly in pairs on 30-minute patrols over either the Island or the various remnants of Convoy MW10: two freighters, Pampas and Talabot, approaching Grand Harbour; HMS Breconshire, an armed supply ship, still a few miles to the south; and their various escorts. There was meant to be a fourth freighter, but, for the moment, nobody seemed to know where it was.

Jack was paired with JC as his wingman. Their acquaintance at Biggin Hill had been all too brief, but on meeting again they'd slipped into an easy relationship based on mutual respect. The differences in experience and age - JC was still only 20 – were tacitly acknowledged, and the new disparity in rank caused no discomfort on either side.

Although, in the main, officer and NCO pilots were billeted separately, as in so many areas on Malta, rank etiquette was more relaxed than anywhere else Jack had served. Many of the officers and NCOs used first names, at least when the adults or groundcrew weren't about, something that caused him no angst whatsoever. He'd always thought it odd that pilots doing the same job should have such different status, and he still dreaded the NCO pilots viewing him as snooty or having ideas above his station.

Despite his commission, he was still the same working class son of a docker from Barry.

For their first sortie, he and JC were tasked with flying

over Luqa to protect returning aircraft. They emerged from G shelter into a grey dawn under a solid cloudbase of 1,000 feet, with tops reported as 5,000, locally higher. Since they'd trooped into the shelter, a stiff south-easterly breeze had picked up, the first hint of a Sirocco, a hot, sandy, wind off the Sahara the old hands said could last a couple of days.

It didn't feel very hot to Jack, but he fancied there was a reddish tinge to the air, like the haze on the day they'd flown off Eagle.

The drive to their aircraft confirmed the impression he'd gained the night before. When they reached the far side of the airfield, they forked off into the countryside, winding down tracks flanked by dry stone walls enclosing fields or orchards. Eventually, they descended into a sheltered valley. All along the route were blast pens, initially walled constructions similar to those at Takali, but increasingly cut into the valley walls. Few contained aircraft, while several held wreckage, or bore signs of damage, an indication that the dispersal plan was no guarantee of safety.

Eventually, JC was dropped by a cutting containing a Spitfire and its groundcrew, and Jack was driven to a similar shelter a few hundred yards further on.

The driver pointed down the track. 'Goes another couple of miles to where they're building a new airfield at Safi.'

So this was the Safi strip.

Jack hoped he could remember the way back to the runway.

That first sortie had been unexpectedly quiet, with no sign of the enemy. Radio chatter indicated that the real action was taking place over the sea.

Their second task, in different airframes, was to relieve a pair of 126 Squadron Spitfires protecting HMS Breconshire, a ship that had made more supply runs to Malta than any other. This promised to be more exciting.

For a start, as they coasted out over the south of the Island at 800 feet, the weather was atrocious, mamma of grey cloud sagging from the cloudbase 200 feet above, visibility a couple of miles, and the Sirocco whipping the sea into a mountainous swell, topped with angry white horses. Fine spray reached high enough to coat their canopies with salt, further reducing visibility from the cockpit.

Five miles south of Delimara Point, Jack looked down to his front left. There, at the limit of visibility, he caught sight of the 10,000-ton supply vessel and her escorts - two destroyers and a much larger anti-aircraft cruiser.

He gestured to JC, holding 100 yards to his right, and pointed. JC nodded and gave a thumbs-up.

'Woody, Tiger Red Three and Four on station.'

'Roger, Jack. Numerous big and little jobs stooging about. Keep your eyes peeled.'

'Wilco, Woody.'

Jack quartered the sky, before returning his gaze to the ships. He was no sailor, but something didn't look right. The Breconshire, some 500 feet long, mast arrays fore and aft, single funnel amidships, looked dead in the water, or rather, was drifting sideways in the heavy seas. At this range, he couldn't see any damage, but either she'd been hit, or she'd suffered a very unfortunate technical problem.

Terrier-like, her escorts darted this way and that, bows diving into and disappearing under waves that obscured their grey superstructures and threatened to top their funnels. Jack couldn't imagine a place he'd less rather be than clinging to their decks, unless it was rattling around below decks.

Despite the conditions, the ships were sending up an erratic anti-aircraft barrage. Their guns, when you could see them, barked grey smoke, peppering the surrounding airspace with balls of black cloud that dispersed quickly on the breeze.

Jack couldn't contact the ships to warn of their approach. He could only hope that someone else had. Naval gunners weren't noted for their forbearance, or their recognition skills. Basically, any hint of an aircraft provided an excuse to fire.

In their position, he'd probably have been the same. Nonetheless, he decided to keep his distance, to try and provide top cover without being seen. A bit like Dunkirk.

Throughout that operation, because the aerial battles rarely took place over the beaches and evacuation fleet, soldiers and sailors had largely been unaware of efforts to protect them. They assumed the RAF had deserted them. Afterwards, they made the point at every opportunity. The list of friends Jack had lost made the animosity hard to bear. He wondered if the sailors below were cursing him now, as they had then.

From his perspective, the Hun held all the cards. They could approach in cloud, dive out to attack, then climb back in to sneak away. Perhaps one had done just that, disabling the Breconshire.

Jack and JC circled the four ships, swapping sides as they turned, straining to see into the mist and the base of the cloud. As they manoeuvred, Jack admired the elegant lines of JC's Spitfire, and the new colour scheme. The blue/grey upper surfaces blended well with the sea, a great improvement on the tropical browns with which they'd arrived.

After a few minutes, one of the destroyers settled close to the Breconshire. Jack guessed it was trying to get a line across. But, as the freighter pitched and rolled, it seemed about to smash its smaller companion. Eventually, the warship moved away, beaten by the high seas.

Every so often, Woody heightened the tension with a warning of bandits in or approaching their area. A couple of times they chased shadows, but found nothing.

Then, Jack spotted a dark shape sliding out of cloud just under a mile to his right, beyond JC.

'JC, Bandit right, nine o'clock, one mile, our level.'

'Roger, Jack, looking.'

'Turning right eighty,' Jack advised.

He rolled to just beyond 90 degrees and pulled to pass behind and below his wingman, now also turning. When he snapped to wings level, the 88 was in his one o'clock, diving toward the ships.

JC snapped out of his own turn and called, 'Got it, Jack.'

Just then, a second 88 appeared, behind and beyond the first. Jack eased right.

'Second, five hundred yards behind. He's mine.'

'Roger, Jack.'

'Woody, Jack, tally-ho, two 88s.'

The reply was lost in static.

Jack divided his attention between the 88 and the airspace around his wingman, quartering it for 109s. JC's head was also in constant motion.

'Good lad.'

They'd be no use to anyone if they were taken out themselves.

With no time to ease behind the bombers, they set up for beam attacks. As they closed to within a few hundred yards, Jack eased further right, adjusting his intercept. The rear 88 suddenly pulled up.

'Shit!' He'd been spotted.

A moment's indecision. Follow JC, or go after the second bomber, already entering cloud?

Stay with JC. His 88 was the greater threat.

Jack eased left and leaned forward, urging his Spitfire to close. JC was about 500 feet above the waves in a shallow dive, the 88, its bomb doors open, no more than a few hundred yards ahead and slightly lower.

For the moment, Jack was a spectator. Flak began to explode. High and short for the moment. Hopefully they'd be able to pull away before the gunners found their range.

JC's Spitfire shivered. Grey smoke streamed back from its wings and tracer arced away. The points of light intercepted the bomber. Angular shards of metal jumped from its fuselage and tail. The Spitfire shook and smoked again. More tracer raced away.

The bomber's left engine exploded. It rolled hard left, right wing rearing up.

Jack flinched, but JC's Spitfire passed a few feet above the wingtip as it continued to roll beyond the vertical.

A pair of anti-aircraft shells exploded a few hundred yards to their left. Jack pulled up and right, then unloaded briefly to drop his left wing. The flaming 88 was spinning toward the sea, chased down by puffs of black smoke from the ships' gunners.

He desperately wanted to watch the bomber's final moments, but not all the shells were aimed at the flaming hulk.

'Hard right, JC.'

Jack rolled and pulled, greying out as the g mounted. Pointing away from the ships, he eased the back pressure and his vision cleared. The second 88 was nowhere to be seen. It could be miles away, heading for Sicily, or close by, hidden in the protective shroud. Who knew? Jack levelled at 800 feet. A few seconds later, JC appeared and took up station 100 yards to his left.

They resumed their patrol, circling the ships. There was no sign of either bomber, and the flak had ceased.

For the next 15 minutes, they chased more phantoms, sometimes in response to Woody's calls, at other times to the firing of the escorts' guns. But they found nothing. Then, shortly before their 30-minute stint was at an end, JC let out an excited cry.

'109s eleven o'clock, slightly low.'

Jack looked down and there they were. Four Messerschmitts, two pairs in loose trail, both in a shallow dive right to left. Showing clearly in silhouette, a 250 kilogram bomb dangled beneath each. His heart raced.

Jabos!

'Okay, JC, let's shake 'em up.'

Not the most precise instructions he'd ever given, but the result couldn't have been more satisfactory if his wingman had been telepathic, or had had time to read and digest a detailed note. As intended, JC rolled 40 left and dived to head off the first pair, while Jack rolled and dived for the second duo, slightly to the right and behind.

'Woody, Jack, tally-ho, four Jabos.'

No reply.

Sweat prickled on Jack's upper lip. Could they cut the corner and hit the fighter bombers before they dropped their bombs?

Two escorts circled the Breconshire, but one of the destroyers sat alongside her again. They made a lovely target.

Puffs of white smoke burst from the cruiser. Jack's stomach tightened and he held his breath.

Who were they shooting at?

Orange fireballs burst around the Jabos.

He exhaled, his relief tinged with the knowledge that he was heading into the same airspace. Had to be done, though, a philosophy obviously shared by the Luftwaffe pilots. They too pressed on, buffeted by nearby explosions.

Jack glanced at the ships. The sea behind the destroyer closest to Breconshire boiled. It began to pull away, turning. All three escorts and the supply ship now spat puffs of smoke. The air around Jack and JC erupted into violence.

A strange time to think it, but Jack realised he hadn't felt fear at any time that morning. And he wasn't as terrified as he might be now.

No time for analysis.

An orange sun burst to his right. He and his aircraft jumped sideways. He winced at another bang to the elbow. To his left, JC's Spitfire bounced, its wings rocking, but still it arrowed toward a rendezvous with the first 109s.

Jack eased a smidge right. He was within 300 yards of the third German. Two hundred yards. He pressed the centre of the rocker switch. Clatter and hiss. Smoke and the whiff of cordite. Tracer. The 109's left wing dipped. It flashed below.

Jack flicked right. The fourth Messerschmitt shed its bomb and turned toward him.

'Yes!'

They passed in the turn. If only the other Jabos had done the same.

He dropped his left wing, but failed to see the enemy fighters, just the ships, still turning and firing. So he rolled and pulled hard right, straining against the onset of about 6g, a product of his high speed. Grunting as he fought to remain conscious, he continued the turn, peering through greying vision.

After about 200 degrees, body aching and covered in sweat, he levelled just below cloud and looked down. JC was half a mile away, in his two o'clock slightly low. The flak was well behind. Jack peered into the barrage. He picked out only one 109, spearing into the cloudbase.

Another scan picked up no enemy. JC's flight path indicated that he too had failed to locate any further threat. It seemed too easy, too good to be true. They'd thwarted the only two attacks they'd seen, and JC could claim at least an 88.

But their time was up. Even if he'd wanted to hang around, Jack's fuel state after 30 minutes of hard manoeuvring at low level dictated a return to Luqa. He rocked his wings. JC eased back until he sat 100 yards to his right.

The benches lining G Shelter still contained a few semi-recumbent figures trying to ignore the world. But around them, things were more hectic. Staff officers and airmen appeared from behind frosted glass doors, dashed to individuals or groups, passed on or received messages, and dashed away again.

Every so often, pilots emerged from the locker room with Mae Wests, helmets and parachutes. The sense of urgency and purpose with which they set out was in stark contrast to those returning, who trudged wearily, coated in dust. Sometimes the two groups met and exchanged a few words; more often, they didn't.

For those that took an interest, the shelter was a hotbed of news, and rumour, although, as usual, it was difficult to tell which was which, even when it came from official sources.

At 1115, Laddie and Kim were airborne, and the remaining A Flight pilots – Jack, Pete, Mike, Dave, Zulu, Harv, JC and Mal – were sitting up and sliding along the benches to face a young intelligence officer positively bubbling with enthusiasm.

Slim, dark-haired, immaculately groomed and wearing a pristine blue uniform, Jack guessed he must be a newcomer. He was, by a long shot, the smartest officer or airman they'd seen since their arrival.

Jack struck eye contact with Mike. They raised eyebrows and smiled.

If the flying officer noticed, it failed to dent his keenness. While the pilots, careworn to say the least, lounged on their bench, he stroked a bum-fluff moustache and set off, the words positively tumbling out of him, accent pure public school.

'Over the weekend, Takali was hit by more than a thousand bombs, just short of three hundred tons of explosives. Pretty impressive in its own right, but even more so when you realise that only two hundred and sixty tons hit Coventry during its blitz.'

If he expected an animated response from his audience, he was disappointed. Jack for one thought the IntO would have been a little less impressed by the statistics if he'd been at Takali during the raids in question. Perhaps the young man had the same thought, because when he resumed, he toned down his delivery.

'Of course, I was forgetting - you know exactly how effective the bombing was.'

He smiled and seemed to lose some of his starchiness. 'So, I don't think it will come as too much of a surprise to

160

learn that, despite the best efforts of the Army, you're unlikely to return to the airfield for several days.'

Jack wondered whether he should express disappointment, but, looking around G Shelter, he decided not. Chaotic and cave-like it may be, but it was a great improvement on their facilities at Takali.

He wondered if Smudger and the groundcrew had a similar refuge. He hadn't recognised the tradesmen on either of his start-ups that morning. Maybe they'd belonged to 126, but it had all been too rushed, too tense, for small talk, so he hadn't found out.

The IntO stroked his near-invisible moustache again. Perhaps he was trying to encourage it into growth.

'Moving on to today's news, I suppose I should start with the bad. It sounds as if we've already lost the Clan Campbell.'

The fourth freighter.

'News came through a few minutes ago that she's been sunk, 20 miles out.'

Jack closed his eyes, imagining the scene, fed by newsreels of the Battle of the Atlantic. A ship, stern high, rudder and screws silhouetted against a grey sky, sliding into the water, oil-coated men trying to swim away on a boiling sea. He hoped escorts would be on hand to pick up survivors, if there were any.

'No news on casualties yet, I'm afraid,' the IntO added, as if reading his mind.

'Thankfully, there is *some* better news. Although Pampas was hit by two bombs earlier this morning, they both failed to explode, and she, Talabot and their escorts are now safely tucked up in Grand Harbour. Unfortunately, damage to the port facilities means they haven't been able to moor alongside, so they're going to have to be unloaded by barge - a slow old process by all accounts.

'The situation with Breconshire is more confusing.'

Jack sat up at this.

'Apparently, she's been hit in the engine room. There

161

was no fire, thank God, but she's lost power and is drifting.'

Jack thought he could usefully add something. 'She was still drifting thirty minutes or so ago, but they seemed to be trying to get a line to her.'

'Yes,' the IntO acknowledged Jack's input with a nod. 'They're still trying. The trouble is she's drifting toward a minefield laid across the approaches to the south of the Island.'

He let that information sink in, before continuing. 'We expect the Hun to do everything they can to hit her, and the two in Grand Harbour, before they can be unloaded.'

They all knew how important the supplies were. Without them, Malta was likely to starve in weeks rather than months, especially as it seemed unlikely that another convoy would be attempted until they'd regained control of the air. Jack wasn't even sure they could protect the few ships that had arrived.

Thankfully, the IntO eschewed a rousing finale, thereby going up several notches in Jack's estimation. Instead, he rather touchingly acknowledged their role in the unfolding drama.

'I think all I can do is wish you all the best out there, unless, of course,' his eyes roved over the group, 'there's anything you'd like to ask me.'

One ship down, three still in need of protection. Nothing more to say really.

Jack shook his head. None of the others spoke.

'Okay then,' the IntO said, stroking his thin moustache. 'Good luck.'

With that he turned his back, walked across to the door marked Ops Room and disappeared inside.

The pilots looked at one another and smiled.

At midday, Jack and JC walked to get airborne for a third time, their task to patrol the eastern approach to Grand Harbour. During the drive out to their dispersals, Jack took in more of his surroundings.

Unlike Takali, which was every inch an outpost, Luqa had the look and feel of a regular RAF station. The airfield was ringed with large hangars and buildings, technical and domestic, *RAF for the use of.*

But, like Takali, it had suffered a dreadful pounding. Not a hangar or building was without signs of damage, and many were totally derelict and unoccupied. There were more intact vehicles, and certainly more aircraft – most of those transiting to and from Egypt passed through Luqa - but also more wrecks. The airfield was covered with burnt-out cars and trucks, and the remains of single and twin-engined aircraft. It was a real mess.

On a better day, their driver said you could see Valletta and Grand Harbour from several points along their route. But although the visibility had improved slightly, the city and its harbour remained stubbornly hidden in the haze. Jack's first view of both came as he and JC flew round to the south of the Three Cities.

Not for the first time, he was grateful for the Spitfire's distinctive wing shape, although even that wouldn't help if the gunners ringing the harbour and its forts didn't make at least some effort to identify them. Little he could do about that though, so he tried not to worry unduly.

He looked past JC to the two merchantmen sitting slap bang in the middle of Grand Harbour. Low in the water, they looked like easy targets. Tens of small ships fussed around them and a couple of destroyers were moored close by. An attacking aircraft was almost bound to hit something. Once again, Jack was glad he was up here looking down, rather than down there looking up.

The sea beyond the breakwaters was less rough than before, more monochrome with fewer white caps. Cloud cover was still complete, and leaden, with a base of 1,000 feet. It was classic goldfish bowl conditions, sea and sky melding into a fuzzy grey bubble that wrapped about them with no discernible horizon. There was nothing to give a point of reference, and it would be all too easy to become disorientated.

They arrived on station four miles to the east of the harbour and settled into a north/south racetrack pattern, scanning for signs of an enemy that Woody said was out there somewhere, in the murk.

A couple of times, Jack's senses tried to deceive him, his eyes and inner ear conspiring to convince him he was pitching or rolling, although the instruments indicated he was flying straight and level. He knew he had to trust the instruments, but it wasn't easy when your whole body was adamant something else was happening.

For one disconcerting period, he was sure he was flying at 90 degrees of left bank, JC hanging, unsupported, just above him, ready to slice down. It took all his willpower to trust the artificial horizon, its bar horizontal, not vertical as his inner ear was screaming.

It was extremely tiresome, and tiring, especially on the third flight of the day. His limbs felt heavy, his mind numb with fatigue, and he began to feel nauseous, mouth dry, cold sweat prickling his upper lip and forehead.

Enemy aircraft weren't the only danger. In these conditions, flying itself could be lethal, as many pilots, young and old - but mainly young - had discovered to their cost.

And so it went on, endlessly staring into the gloom, making frequent reference to the instruments to confirm that he was the right way up, or turning only as intended.

'Four 88s, left ten o'clock, similar level.'

Jack spotted them immediately. Two pairs, both in echelon right, sitting tighter than normal after a formation descent through cloud.

JC began a left turn. Jack rolled and pulled to pass behind and slot into wide line abreast to the left.

He grunted into the R/T, 'Woody, Jack, tally-ho, four big jobs four miles out.'

'Roger, Jack. Good luck.'

The 88s levelled at 800 feet, the second pair drifting

back and right, both wingmen easing out to a wider spacing. They were heading straight for the harbour. They'd probably see it, and its resident ships, in about 30 seconds.

'JC, one two, then three four.'

'Roger, Jack.'

They were within 600 yards, accelerating for a beam attack. Jack released the safety. He watched the bombers' bulbous cockpits and dorsal gondolas, expecting their machine guns to swivel in his direction. But perhaps the crews were all peering into the mist for the harbour entrance.

Four hundred yards.

He pressed the centre of the rocker switch. Any lingering lethargy was banished by the clattering in his ears, the cordite filling his nose, the vibration shaking his whole body and the glowing rods of tracer dancing through the air ahead of him. These passed above the bomber's cockpit and fuselage to cut across the tip of its tailfin above the swastika.

Before he could see any result, Jack flashed above the 88, relishing a brief glimpse of shocked faces. He pulled right, grunting against the g. In his two o'clock, JC turned above the second bomber, tracer filling the air around him.

Jack rolled wings level and speared towards the third 88, no more than 200 yards away. He pressed on the gun switch. His tracer hit the bomber amidships, while its own fire wobbled across the gap between him and JC. Once more, he streaked above the bomber, convinced he'd damaged it, but unable to confirm. JC flashed above the fourth, missing its tailfin by no more than a couple of feet.

'Pulling left, JC.'

Jack rolled and pulled, straining against another 5g turn. His whole body, and especially his neck muscles, ached. But he had to put himself between the bombers and the harbour. He groaned, looking back over his left shoulder.

One 88 was spiralling down, flames wrapped around its left engine. Its roll rate increased as its nose dropped for the final plunge. But Jack drew his eyes away.

He rolled out on south and scanned from sea to cloudbase between the doomed 88 and the harbour entrance, now just visible in the mist. Nothing. The survivors must have pulled up into the grey shroud, no more than 200 feet above them.

The usual dilemma. Chase or stay below?

Jack looked left to where JC was closing on him. He began an orbit to confirm that no other raiders were in sight, and to look for signs of the fourth bomber, or its crew.

'Woody, Jack. One big job down three miles out. The others seem to have called it a day.'

'Roger, Jack, relief on its way. Come on in.'

'Wilco, Woody. Jack out.'

Such a conversation would have been impossible back in the UK, but it seemed natural now.

The fourth 88 had left oil and wreckage on the surface, but no life raft. JC's Spitfire hung in the gloom. The young NCO gave a cheery thumbs-up. Only then did Jack notice that his wingman's tailfin and rudder were peppered with jagged holes, some as big as a fist.

He decided against relaying the information. JC had probably felt the impacts anyway. Better to get them on the ground as soon as possible. He returned the thumbs-up and turned for Luqa.

When they pitched in the next morning, Tuesday the 24th, G Shelter was buzzing again. Despite the early start, Jack felt better rested. He barely noticed his elbow, and, after a relatively successful day and a reasonable night's sleep, some of his personal demons also seemed to have been banished.

Whether it would last, he'd have to see, but he felt closer to the cool, calm and collected image he tried to project than he had for 18 months. Perhaps the very pace of life had made the difference, and the fact that, as a relative veteran of fighter operations, if not Malta, people were relying on him in a way no-one had since the summer of 1940.

Whatever it was, he was glad of the change.

The others who'd flown over the harbour and ships seemed similarly geed up. The disabling hit on Breconshire notwithstanding, they'd kept the Luftwaffe at bay. The other flights of both 126 and 249 had also maintained a clean sheet during the afternoon and evening.

Those that had yet to fly, Dave Campbell, Harv Johnson and Mal Cotrell looked more pensive, as if awaiting some form of initiation, which, in a way, they were. Jack guessed that Laddie would choose to fly one or all of them sooner rather than later. It had to be done, and the longer it was delayed, the harder it would be on them.

The fly in the ointment was serviceability. JC hadn't been the only one to have been on the end of return fire from a bomber and, in the afternoon, 126 had crash landed another kite on the airfield, putting it out of action, maybe for good.

After about ten minutes, Laddie and the young IntO who'd briefed them the previous day came out of the ops room and walked over. The flying officer looked significantly more careworn and tired than the last time they'd seen him.

They huddled up and Laddie stopped to their front. He seemed to sport a different cravat every day, and today's was a rather natty purple polka dot number.

'Okay, the groundcrew have worked bloody miracles. The two kites we left at Takali were flown over yesterday evening and the remaining groundcrew followed them, then set to with 126's. We may get a couple more as the day wears on, but so far, they've managed to give us nine.'

Harv whistled.

'Yes. Bloody impressive, isn't it? Even more so when you know they also spent half the night unloading ships.'

Must be a story behind that, Jack thought, but Laddie moved on.

'Not sure how many Hurris are up yet?' he looked at the

IntO.

'A similar number, I think,' the flying officer said, obviously pleased to be included. 'Nine or ten.'

Thanks, Harry,' Laddie said, before continuing. 'So, between Hal Far and here, we should be able to put up some sort of show. I'll go through the pairings after Harry's given us the general sitrep.'

He stepped back and the IntO took centre stage. 'Morning everyone.'

A few grunts of, 'Morning Harry,' seemed to go down well. The young man smiled and preened his thin moustache.

'Not a lot of change from yesterday, really. Breconshire resisted all efforts to get a line to her, so she's still anchored just outside Marsaxlokk Bay. The Navy hope to get her into Grand Harbour today.

'And as you've already heard, they started unloading Pampas and Talabot yesterday. But it looks as if they're only going to do it by daylight. OC Luqa wasn't best pleased, but none of the high-priced help seemed interested, so he took it on himself and sent half the station down there after dark.'

'Good on him,' Mike said.

'Quite,' Harry agreed. 'Good on him, indeed.'

Jack smiled. How could two renditions of a simple phrase sound so different? He also wondered if the night's activities explained the IntO's slightly dishevelled appearance and tiredness.

'We unloaded all the aircraft spares we could find overnight, and got back about two hours ago.'

'Well done, Harry,' Jack said. And he meant it.

The IntO positively beamed. 'Well, thank you. But it had to be done, because we're expecting the Hun to have another good crack at the ships today.'

Jack expected the same. The wind had gone round and, on the few occasions he'd opened his eyes during the drive from Mdina, he could tell there was better visibility and less cloud. It might make their job a bit easier, but it would also aid the bombers.

'And we think their batting order might include some Stukas transferred from North Africa.'

Harv whistled again.

'Yes, 'fraid so,' Harry responded.

Jack had met Junkers Ju87s over Dunkirk, and knew how effective they could be. They'd also made their mark over the convoys during the early stages of the Battle of Britain. But if you could bypass their escorts and get amongst them, they were vulnerable, so much so that they'd been withdrawn from the Battle by the time 646 moved from Pembrey to Biggin Hill. He never even saw one over Kent.

The question was, would they be able to get amongst them now?

'So,' Harry continued, 'it's likely to be the same as yesterday, protecting the ships, but also the Island.'

He stopped, looking as if he felt he should say more.

But there really wasn't anything else to say. Their task was easy to lay out, if not to accomplish, especially with less than 20 aircraft, only a proportion of which could be airborne at any one time.

JC had a touch of the Dog, and Jack had been right about Laddie blooding the less experienced flight members. He was paired with Mal Cotrell. The Australian was impossibly young and fresh-faced, Jack thought, but he displayed few nerves as they chatted over the possibilities for the morning.

The hands of the shelter clock swept past 7, then 8 o'clock, before they sat back, closed their eyes and tried to rest. It was 9.15 before a hand was laid on Jack's shoulder.

Now, they were flying at 1500 feet in wide line abreast over the south coast toward the Breconshire. The lowest cumulus, bases about 500 feet above, covered around three tenths of the sky, but overlapping stratoform layers a few thousand feet higher meant there was no blue in sight. The cloud structure still favoured the bombers.

Below, the visibility was better – they could already see ships five miles or so ahead – but the sea looked angry, towering white caps driven on by a stiff north easterly wind. The sight of a rotund tug plunging into the swell underlined the difficulty of the conditions.

They'd been told the ships were expecting them, but Jack was still wary as he approached to within a couple of miles. Only when the decks of the cruiser and two destroyers remained free of tell-tale wisps of grey smoke did he relax a little and begin to pay more attention to the airspace around them.

Jack tried to concentrate on sweeping the sky for intruders, but it was hard not to spend at least some time looking at the ships. Breconshire pitched and rolled in the swell, threatening to smash a tug that looked too puny to budge her, even if it succeeded in getting a line across. Meanwhile, with the second tug still a few miles distant, the escorts circled.

For the next 30 minutes, no enemy aircraft appeared, but the tug came perilously close to being stamped on by its larger companion. Eventually, it pulled away. A few minutes later, one of the destroyers approached, circling round to the south.

'What the…'

A circle of sea around the destroyer flattened, then vibrated and boiled white, before jumping into the air, taking the ship with it. The destroyer disappeared behind a white wall that rose about it like a shower curtain. The curtain climbed to several hundred feet before falling slowly back to reveal the ship, sitting on a bubbling, sea.

As his initial horror subsided, Jack's immediate thought was that they'd let a bomber through. He manoeuvred madly, trusting Mal to hang in as he quartered the sky all around the small flotilla. But no, no aircraft were in sight, and he realised such an explosion could not be the result of a bomb.

They'd been told that Breconshire had dropped anchor to avoid drifting into the minefield, but it seemed she'd been closer to it than anyone realised, least of all the captain of the destroyer.

If you live to be a hundred, you'll never see anything like that again, Jack thought.

'At least I hope not,' he said aloud.

Amazingly, as the sea regained its colour and shape, the destroyer looked untouched. But it was no longer underway, and it was hard to believe things were anything other than totally bloody and chaotic on board. As if to emphasise the point, her funnel began belching thick gobbets of ominous black smoke.

They continued their patrol, shifting their focus between looking for enemy raiders and watching the drama unfolding below. By the time the second tug reached the scene, the stricken destroyer had developed a slight list to starboard. Soon, both tugs were braving the minefield in an effort to get lines across.

When the recall came, Jack was reluctant to leave, but he signalled Mal and set heading for Luqa. During the brief transit, he mulled over what he'd just seen, and wondered what would happen next.

G Shelter was full of staff officers and airmen moving this way and that. They all seemed intent on some mission that brooked no interruption. But Jack was determined to find out what had happened to the destroyer, if not the Breconshire. So, when the intelligence officer who'd given their last couple of morning briefings appeared from the ops room door and headed for the executives' offices, he made a bee-line.

'Harry!'

The IntO stopped and turned.

Jack walked up and stretched out an arm. 'Jack Williams – 249.'

They shook hands.

'Hello, Jack. Nice to meet you. Harry Boyd. I remember you, and I've heard your name a couple of times in there.' He gestured at the ops room.

The cultured tones reminded Jack of Binky, and he wondered how his erstwhile friend was doing. He'd heard he was flying Wellingtons, which had come as a surprise, because when he'd last seen him toward the end of his treatment at East Grinstead, his face hadn't been too bad, but his hands had still been a mess, little more than claws.

He shook himself free of the image. 'Look, sorry to ambush you, but have you heard anything more about Breconshire and its escorts.'

Mal had moved up to stand at Jack's shoulder. Jack pointed at his companion. 'We saw the destroyer hit a mine or something.'

'Ah. You were right. It was a mine. And, sorry to say, when they tried to tow her, it broke her back. Then there was a raid and she rolled over, although we're still not sure whether she'd been hit again. The tugs are trying to get a line over to Breconshire now. Anything else?'

Yes, any number of things. How was the battle over Grand Harbour going? Had other ships been hit yet? When would they fly next?

'No. Thanks, Harry.'

'Okay.' The IntO gave a shy smile and resumed his progress across the room.

Jack looked at Mal.

'Poor bastards,' the Australian said, shaking his head. 'Wonder how many were still on board when it rolled over?'

Jack tried to blank out another horrific image.

As midday approached, he began to think they might not fly again, which was fatal. Laddie appeared.

'Jack, Mal, I'd like you to do a stint over Grand Harbour. OC 126 is going to lead a pair looking to catch any Hun sneaking in below, but the cloud seems to have broken up a bit, so I'd like you to provide top cover. Watch out for the harbour barrage. With you about, they shouldn't engage above 10,000 feet without a positive ident, but...'

But indeed.

With more than its share of 4.7 inch guns, the Valletta barrage was an especially impressive sight, a seemingly impenetrable block of sky alive with smoke and flame.

But experience showed that most raiders passed unscathed through even the heaviest barrage. So, if you really wanted to press home an attack, you had to enter the box; and, if you did, the gunners didn't re-aim to discriminate friend from foe.

'Your kites are down the Safi strip again.'

Laddie lowered a chart and pointed at two pens south of the airfield.

'Good luck.'

The Austin was halfway round the airfield when the sirens sounded and red flags began to appear. Their driver made no move to pull over and look for shelter. Sitting in the back, Jack and Mal exchanged resigned glances as the young airman crashed the gears and the engine screamed. Beyond emphasising the driver's bravery and determination, the increase in noise had little effect. Their speed certainly didn't seem to alter much.

Nevertheless, the car bounced over and lurched around obstacles. Jack began to feel like a mobster in a car chase. He turned to peer through the small rear window.

No black and white police cars or Chevies festooned with mobsters firing machine guns, but there were numerous flashes near the centre of the airfield. Geysers of earth and dust rose into the air. The little Austin rocked and Mal and the driver looked over their shoulders.

The sound of the first explosions reached them just as the driver turned hard left. It felt as if they were up on two wheels and about to flip over. But, after an anxious few moments, the little car sank back, wobbling a couple of times before it set off down the Safi strip.

Jack looked across at Mal and they both burst out laughing.

The groundcrew seemed reluctant to leave their machine gun, which was maintaining a ferocious rate of fire. Jack hated not knowing their names or, as in this case, not even recognising their faces.

Scrambles in the Battle of Britain had been no less frantic, with little time to chat to those seeing him off. But there'd been numerous other opportunities to interact with his rigger, fitter and the other tradesmen, not least when setting up his kite first thing in the morning, or on return from a sortie. Here, there was rarely space for such niceties. Different aircraft, different groundcrew every time.

By the time he and Mal taxied back up the strip, the raid was over.

The cloud hadn't cleared as much as they'd been led to believe, but they managed to weave their way up to 14,000 feet before levelling below a layer of altostratus, its uniform grey base 1,000 feet above. Woody had warned of raiders approaching at about their height.

Of course, if they'd had more aircraft, most would have been well forward, above cloud, aiming to intercept before the Island was threatened. But, they'd barely enough kites for point defence, so here they were, tied to the likely targets.

Below them, scattered pillars of cumulus bubbled up through 10,000 feet and marched south west on the prevailing wind. These and numerous thin stratoform layers at various heights tended to overlap and obscure the ground. So far, they'd had no more than the odd glimpse of the blue waters of the harbours and the creamy gold of the settlements surrounding them.

But now, Jack looked down just as a more substantial gap yawned. Clearly visible in Grand Harbour were two dark lenses: Pampas and Talabot. Each was surrounded by smaller vessels, some stationary, others leaving tell-tale wakes as they shuttled to and fro, racing to unload the precious cargoes.

By the harbour entrance, dark grey smoke rose. If it was meant to be a smoke screen, it was dispersing on the breeze far too readily to be effective.

'Jack, Woody here. Bandits still heading your way, angels one five, ten miles, vector three three zero.'

'Wilco, Woody.'

Jack eased round on to a north-westerly heading. They were no more than 90 seconds from the enemy, perhaps a little longer if they were Stukas rather than 88s. He scanned the base of the cloud ahead, while lowering his seat a notch and releasing the safety.

'Five miles, Jack. Maintain vector.'

Must be 88s. They'd have to show their hand soon if they were to dive on the ships. He quartered the sky, paying special attention to the cloudbase. Mal's head was in constant movement, searching just as hard for an enemy that remained stubbornly invisible.

'You should be on them, Jack.'

'Roger, Woody, nothing seen.'

They were about five miles north of the harbour and Jack guessed the bombers and their fighter escort were somewhere in the cloud, waiting for a glimpse of the ground before diving out. He and Mal would have had to pass directly beneath them to stand any chance of a sighting, and although Woody was good, he wasn't that good.

They turned about and began ten minutes of cat and mouse, criss-crossing the harbour, never catching a glimpse of it, or the enemy.

'Right, one o'clock, cloudbase,' Mal shouted.

Jack looked to where two 88s were diving down. He pushed on throttle and stick.

'Here we go, Mal. Eyes peeled for escorts.'

No sooner had he said it than he spotted something in his

peripheral vision. Four smaller shapes.

'Right, two o'clock, four Friedrichs. Stay with the bombers.'

The 109s were turning, but not as if they'd seen them yet. Jack concentrated on the 88s. The twin-engined bombers were diving at a 45 degree angle. They turned right into a gap between two towering cumulus that would funnel them straight down to Grand Harbour, glinting blue ahead of them.

The turn worked in the Spitfires' favour. Without deviating, they were now closing to within 400 yards of the 88s from directly above and behind. Mal was pulling ahead in his eagerness to get at them.

Jack weaved and quartered the sky. Several more of the twin-engined bombers and about ten 109s had appeared.

'Woody, Jack, tally ho, about a dozen big and little jobs, angels one four, diving.'

'Roger, Jack, good luck.'

Thankfully, most of the enemy were still a few thousand feet above, although the first four fighters he'd seen were only half a mile behind.

Tracer flashed overhead, dragging his attention back to the bombers. Below, the barrage had opened up, peppering the sky with shell bursts. Faced with an assault from behind and below, the 88s had split, turning outwards to seek sanctuary in the fluffy white tops of the cumulus to either side.

Mal turned for the right hand bomber and Jack decided to stay with him.

They were closing fast now, Mal, 100 yards ahead, no more than 200 yards from the 88. Its upper gunner squirted him with tracer. Mal returned fire, his rounds sparking on his target's right wing.

Was that a trace of smoke from the engine before the bomber speared into the cloud, followed by Mal?

A few moments later, Jack too was swallowed, finding the interior darker and more turbulent than he'd expected.

Mal appeared only as they passed through lighter patches of mist. Of the bomber, there was no trace.

Suddenly, Jack burst out into clear air, Mal 100 yards ahead. Still no sign of the bomber. If damage hadn't caused an unintentional spiral, it must have rolled and pulled into the heart of the cloud, a desperate manoeuvre for such a large aircraft, and one from which it would be lucky to recover.

'Still with you, Mal.'

'Wilco, Jack.'

Jack eased left and right to level and sit abeam his wingman, all the time scanning the sky. He still hoped to attack further bombers. Below, the barrage was building in intensity, the air bubbling with menace. Not far above, more 88s dived, all attended by at least a couple of 109s.

'Oh-oh!'

Two Rotte appeared to either side of the bright white cumulus. Both seemed to spot the Spitfires and turn in towards them. If there'd ever been a chance to engage the remaining bombers, it had just passed.

The four 109s joined up. Another two appeared, also turning toward them. After all, what other targets were there?

The situation was desperate. A week ago, Jack might have descended into an indecisive panic, but not now. He made another quick scan. Clouds that had seemed only too keen to shroud the bombers had all but vanished.

Sometimes, a fighter pilot had to run away. This was one of those occasions.

'Follow me, Mal.'

He pushed on throttle and stick and rolled toward the heart of the box barrage.

'Roger, Jack.'

He sensed uncertainty in the young Australian's voice. Understandable, but they'd be toast if they flew round the barrage, while the 109s' room for manoeuvre would be restricted if they followed them in, and there was always a chance they'd decide not to risk it.

Fire and smoke wrapped round them. Jack's Spitfire rocked, as did Mal's, its wings twitching as it was buffeted by successive shock waves. The ack-ack intensified. Jack became convinced one or both of them would be hit.

Below 5,000 feet, the ride became a little smoother, and at 4,000 feet, they left the barrage behind, emerging to the south of Grand Harbour and the Three Cities, Luqa to their right.

What now?

Even as the question came to him, Jack realised the answer would depend on the chasing fighters. He hadn't tempted fate by manoeuvring too hard in the heart of the barrage, fearing he'd only pull into a shell burst. But now, he turned right, passing above and behind Mal who turned to sit to his left.

No 109s appeared. Had they even risked the barrage? Perhaps they'd decided not to bother. It was a welcome development, and Jack relaxed a smidgen, turning them right again and descending beneath another layer of cloud.

'Woody, Red 3 and 4, three miles south-west of Valletta, tracking north.'

'Roger, Jack, pancake, I say again, pancake. Raiders heading home.'

Jack was surprised not to be set off in pursuit, but Woody was probably husbanding his resources again. No point in risking them on a wild goose chase.

'Wilco, Woody, Jack out.'

By this time, they were passing abeam the race track at Marsa. Valletta, its harbours and the ships should have been plainly visible, just to their right, no more than a couple of miles away. But the whole area was obscured beneath a billowing grey and black cloud.

They had their smoke screen now, but at what cost?

A Flight were being driven back to Mdina when the Valletta barrage crashed out again. Where the road gave a view to the east, they caught glimpses of Pampas and Talabot. The ships were afloat, but they could tell no more than that. Smoke still rose from the built up areas surrounding both harbours.

Scattered cumulus and overlapping layers of stratus denied a view of the gunners' targets, but that they were firing at a new bombing raid was confirmed when smoke and flame ringed the harbour and great pillars of spray towered above the freighters.

What it was like in one of the smaller ships plying the harbour, Jack dreaded to think.

They ate another meagre lunch of bully beef and gathered on the terrace. The raid was over, but smoke cloaked the harbour, and the ships.

For once, Jack and Mike decided not to sit and brood, but to take themselves off to the Rabat Plaza to catch a film. Mike, especially, felt in need of a break. He and Dave Campbell had had a lucky escape, returning to the airfield short on fuel, only to be harried by 109s that attacked them on short finals.

Mike was able to laugh it off, but Jack couldn't help wondering if the young Scot felt as sanguine. They decided to invite him to the cinema but, having failed to find him, set out alone.

A short documentary about the Battle of the Atlantic was too reminiscent of their last couple of days to provide any form of escape. But the main feature, Pimpernel Smith, proved a more diverting yarn.

Every so often, they heard the distant crump of guns or explosions, but none were close enough to interrupt or end the performance, something they'd been told happened all too frequently. And Leslie Howard made sure the dastardly Nazis lost out in the end, so they left the cinema in relatively high spirits.

Mike had been good company, but oh, how Jack wished it had been Caroline sitting next to him.

When they arrived back on the terrace, it was as if they'd

never been away. To the east came the rumble of explosions and the crack of guns. Events in the air were obscured by cloud, those on the ground, by smoke. Nevertheless, drinks in hand, they stood and watched. As the light faded, the smoke became suffused with an orange glow.

If the pre-dawn gloom was anything to go by, Wednesday 25th March would be as murky, if not murkier than the day before. JC was still hors de combat, so it looked as if Mal would be Jack's wingman again. They sat in G Shelter and waited patiently for someone to tell them what was going on.

Like the terrible twins, Harry Boyd and Laddie appeared from the ops room. The IntO seemed to relish his early morning briefing role, smiling and tweaking his moustache as he crossed the stone floor towards them. Laddie stood to one side and deferred to the younger man.

'Morning, chaps.'

'Morning, Harry.'

The grunted chorus was in danger of becoming a tradition, much enjoyed, at least by Harry.

'Thought I'd start with the airfields, if that's okay.'

More grunts, which Harry interpreted as agreement.

'Well, Takali's still out of action. The Army are doing all they can, but I'm afraid I don't have an estimate for your return.'

'You'll just have to put up with us for a bit longer then, Harry,' Harv interjected.

'My pleasure, Harv,' Harry replied. You sensed that he meant it.

'Hal Far had a torrid time yesterday. Twenty three killed outright in a shelter blast, and another two died in Imtarfa overnight. They also lost their officers' mess, several other buildings and a number of aircraft. No more than a handful serviceable at the moment, although a few more should come up during the day.'

They'd heard about the shelter, but not the casualty

count. Twenty five, although, as Jack knew only too well, it could have been worse.

'As to this place, after the lunchtime raid you experienced, it was hit again later in the afternoon and overnight. Mainly superficial damage, and not enough to affect ops, thank goodness.

'And so to the ships,' he continued. 'In all, the Hun launched two hundred sorties yesterday. And although the harbour and surrounding settlements took a terrible battering, thanks to your good offices, and those of the gunners, they failed to hit any of the freighters.'

Jack suspected the weather had also had something to do with it, but he wasn't going to deflect Harry's praise.

'We expect much the same today. So, I think it's a fair bet you'll be over Grand Harbour and the Breconshire again. But I'll leave Laddie to talk about that side of things. Any questions?'

Harry returned to the ops room and Laddie confirmed their pairings. It was all a bit academic, though. There were only a handful of Spitfires to share between the two squadrons. They'd just have to hope more came on line during the day.

They settled back to await the call to arms. But apart from a few minor incursions, the Luftwaffe failed to appear. So they spent the morning lazing around G Shelter, watching staff officers and airmen hurrying to and fro, seemingly no less busy for the lack of activity overhead.

Jack thought of looking for Smudger, but it was too difficult. The groundcrew were based several hundred yards away, well out of sight or earshot of G Shelter. No good if there was a sudden call to scramble. And Smudger was probably on the airfield anyway, or, more likely, down the strip. Too far to walk, no chance of transport and the same problem if there was a scramble.

Sad as it seemed, unless fate brought them together for a crew-in, they may have to await the return to Takali for another opportunity to chew the fat.

Every so often, Jack felt the need to escape the fug of cigarette and pipe smoke, and the odour of unwashed bodies. Sometimes alone, sometimes in the company of one of the others, he climbed the stairs and breathed deeply of the fresh air.

On one occasion, he was accompanied by Dave Campbell. The young pilot officer looked more than usually pale and on edge, almost furtive. They leaned on the surviving section of wall outside the shelter opening.

'You look as if you need the fresh air, Dave.'

'Aye. It's pretty bloody fetid down there.'

Jack loved the Aberdonian burr, and Dave's wry observations on everything from the weather to the food never failed to raise a laugh, whether intended or not. Today, though Jack sensed that the young man had more than the quality of the air in the shelter on his mind. He decided to dig a little deeper.

'Are you sure there isn't something else, Dave?'

'No, no, I'm fine thanks.'

Jack let the silence linger. Eventually, he heard a little throat-clearing cough.

'Well, actually, there is something.'

Jack shifted to shield them from those hurrying in and out of the shelter. He could sense the turmoil behind the blue eyes looking out from under the mop of strawberry blond hair.

'Do you ever feel scared? I mean really scared.'

Jack had often sensed people grappling with fear. He'd even steered others to help them, either directly or indirectly. But this was the first time he'd known anyone address the issue so boldly.

'Yes, Dave. All the time. Some days worse than others. But the fear's always there.'

'And…and, how do you cope?'

'Truthfully, I'm not sure. When I first started, I was lucky. It didn't get to me too badly, at least, not until the tracer started flying. But then I got wounded, and…well, let's just say I found it much more difficult after that. In fact, I've only just come out of it; in the last few days, or at least I hope I have.'

Well, there. He'd said it. He wasn't as fearful as he was when he arrived in Malta. He hoped he hadn't jinxed the improvement by mentioning it to someone else. And shouldn't the focus be on Dave? Shouldn't he be doing the talking?

'Is there something specific worrying you?' Jack asked.

After a pause, Dave shrugged and smiled weakly. 'Och, just about everything.'

He fidgeted and Jack waited, while the young Scot worked out what to say. When he began speaking, his words were hesitant, hard to find.

'I know none of us knew what it would be like. But I didn't get to fly many ops at home. I thought this would be an adventure, a bit of a game I suppose. But since we got here, sitting under the bombing, seeing the damage...'

He lowered his head and shook it slowly from side to side. When he finally lifted his eyes and turned toward Jack, the older man sensed them looking right through him, reliving some fearful experience.

'And yesterday, with Mike - the cloud, the barrage, the 109s. I didn't have a clue what was going on!'

It went back to what Wing Commander MacLean had said on Eagle: they shouldn't be sending novices like Dave to Malta.

'And when I was attacked on short finals yesterday, I just froze. God knows how I got down in one piece. The kite must have landed itself, because I don't remember doing anything. Just sat there thinking I was about to die, or worse.'

His eyes finally seemed to focus on Jack's. 'Am I making any sense?'

'Perfect sense,' Jack answered softly. 'Couldn't be clearer. Or more familiar.'

He reached down and stroked his calf. That had

heightened his fear. But he delved back in his memory to what it had been like when he started out, a young sergeant lurching into the air bound for the Dunkirk beaches. Then, he searched for the words to express what he found.

'I had no idea what was going on when I first went into combat. In fact, I often had no idea what was going on *without* the complication of combat. Weather, navigation, radio calls - anything, and I'd be in a complete flap.'

He waited for Dave to speak.

'So, how did you cope? How do you cope?'

Jack surprised himself with the certainty of his reply.

'You keep going, and you get better and better with every sortie. And, if you're like me, you keep on because you're more afraid of...' – he was going to say chickening out, but thought better of it – 'of letting everyone down than you are of getting airborne. You face the fear because you're too scared to give in to it.'

Dave leant back against the wall with a heavy sigh.

Jack decided to carry on. He looked around to confirm no-one was in earshot.

'Look, Dave, if you're thinking you're weak, you're wrong. I'd never have had the guts to speak to anyone the way you've just spoken to me. I think it's one of the bravest things I've ever seen.'

The young man took a deep breath, blew out and washed his face with his hands. 'Thanks, J...'

Harv appeared in front of them, panting.

'Sorry, you guys, not interrupting a budding romance am I?'

Dave kicked out playfully. 'Fuck off, knucklehead!'

'Love you too, haggis features. Anyway, wanted downstairs. Things may be on the move.'

The American turned away.

Jack let Dave follow Harv, giving him a pat on the shoulder as he passed. The Scot gave a thin-lipped nod of thanks and entered the shelter.

Just short of 2pm, having eventually sat around all morning, they were on a bus being driven up the hill to Rabat and Mdina. The noise of the engine straining in first gear would have drowned out the sound of all but a direct hit, and conversation was impossible. So Laddie didn't bother shouting when he stood up. He just pointed to the east, where the flash of explosions had begun to pepper the harbour and its surrounds.

B Flight were unlikely to be lounging around for long.

Sure enough, that night, the other half of the squadron returned to the Palace in relatively high spirits. Those that had flown had exacted a heavy toll of Hun aircraft, with the CO himself claiming a 109 and a Stuka. And despite an afternoon and evening of attacks, Pampas and Talabot had survived another day. The strong wind had foiled attempts to tow Breconshire into Grand Harbour, but they'd managed to get her into the shelter of Marsaxlokk Bay.

Buoyed by the news, Jack went to his room, censored a pile of letters and wrote one of his own to Caroline. He tried to ignore the rumbling of his stomach.

The next morning, Thursday 26th March, after an inadequate breakfast, he climbed onto the bus. Dave Campbell gave an imperceptible nod of assurance, and Jack fell into his usual seat. Sporadic raids had disturbed his night and, during the journey, he tried to recoup at least some of the sleep deficit. But thoughts of the day ahead intervened.

If the first sight of stars for several mornings was anything to go by, the weather was breaking. If so, it would, at best, be a mixed blessing: easier for them to intercept the raiders, but easier for the raiders to sight and hit their targets.

For once, Harry's briefing was relatively short and sweet. The airfields had been hit, but apart from another couple of transit aircraft, there'd been little damage of note. Pampas and Talabot were still in one piece and the oiler,

HMS Plumleaf, was alongside Breconshire, planning to spend the day ferrying the freighter's cargo of fuel oil to Grand Harbour. Not hard to guess the targets of the day, then.

While waiting for the dawn, Jack pondered why Dave Campbell had sought him out for advice, rather than one of the other officers.

He understood why he hadn't confided in any of the other young bucks - Harv, Mal and Zulu - and he was unlikely to have approached his flight commander, which ruled out Laddie. Pete Brown wasn't exactly unapproachable, but he was the quiet, introspective type, not a natural source of comfort and advice. Why Mike hadn't passed muster, Jack wasn't sure, but that left only him as a shoulder to cry on.

At the tender age of 24, he'd become a city father!

Just after 7am, he left the shelter for some fresh air. As he'd suspected, the cloud had lifted and the day had dawned crisp and relatively clear, with a light southerly wind.

Ideal for the bombers.

So, where were they?

It was 9.45 before they began to get a sense of something building. The people walking this way and that suddenly seemed more purposeful, and a few of the pilots began to sit up straight, breathing deeply as if preparing themselves for some approaching trial.

Jack looked around, apprising the rest of his flight. They were a great bunch and he was proud to be fighting alongside them. If only they could go into the air in the strength they'd had in the Battle of Britain, as a squadron, or at least a flight. Then they'd show the Hun what they were capable of.

No chance of that now, though. They had six aircraft – between two squadrons!

At 10.15, Jack watched Mike and Dave walk up the steps

behind two pilots from 126. There was no outward sign that the youngster was in any sort of turmoil, but they were all so good at hiding their feelings that this may not mean anything.

Good luck, Dave.

An hour later, Laddie walked over.

Forty minutes after that, Jack and Mal were climbing through 15,000 feet of wispy, red-tinged, haze, heading south, into wind. They levelled at 25,000 feet and set up an orbit to the south of the Island.

After several cloudy days, it was good to fly in clear air. Jack felt his spirits lift, even though the pair of them and a handful of Hurricanes were the only defenders airborne, and Woody had just said a raid of 50 plus was approaching.

Such odds hardly seemed to warrant optimism.

But then he looked at his surroundings. A sharp, undisturbed, horizon line ran all around. Below it, the sea was glimpsed through a rose-tinted veil. Above, the air was unadulterated blue. Mal's Spitfire hung 100 yards to his right, sunlight glinting off its shimmering propeller disc, canopy and curving fuselage. And when it turned or weaved, its elliptical wings held their usual magic. Jack's own aircraft thrummed and vibrated, reacting to the slightest pressure he exerted on the controls.

As he basked in a joy that had been all-too-rare of late, he wondered what Caroline was doing back in Kent.

'Jack, Woody here, two dozen big jobs, twenty Stukas and sundry escorts passing over Gozo, angels one five to one seven. Vector three five zero.'

'Wilco, Woody.'

The Observer Corps on Gozo must also be enjoying the weather. It was the first sighting report giving aircraft types and numbers they'd passed for days.

Jack rolled out to head just west of north. If they had the opportunity to dive on the enemy, they'd have the sun at their backs. He weaved to look under the nose, catching sight of Marsaxlokk Bay a few miles ahead. One of the Hurricane formations was patrolling above it, trying to protect the Breconshire. The other was tucked in close to Grand Harbour.

'Jack, this is Woody, bandits over St Paul's Bay, maintain vector.'

'Wilco, Woody.'

They were approaching the south coast when the air over Grand Harbour erupted with puffs of grey and black, reaching up to about 15,000 feet. Whether the gunners had seen anything, or were just letting the bombers know they were awake, Jack wasn't sure, but he certainly found the barrage a sobering sight. He and Mal would probably have to enter it again if they needed to press home an attack – or escape.

'Jack, Woody here, bandits inside ten miles.'

'Roger, Woody.'

Two minutes or less. Jack went through his pre-combat routine and exchanged a thumbs-up with Mal. His major emotion was excitement, and he hadn't felt his tic pulsing for days.

What had brought the change about?

No time, Jack.

He weaved. Below and a little more than five miles ahead, two formations were silhouetted against the haze, the lead aircraft of the second partially hidden behind and below the tail end of the first. Both phalanxes comprised vics of three, trailing one another by a hundred yards or so. The lead formation was 88s, the following, Stukas. Numerous fighters manoeuvred about both.

'Tally-ho, Woody, bandits as reported, diving in.'

Jack pushed on the throttle and moved the stick forward. Mal followed. No need to tell him to concentrate on the bombers. They'd talked about it often enough.

Although there were only two of them, this felt more like the Battle of Britain. And as in that battle, Jack's excitement had given way to tension, felt in the pit of his stomach.

The Stukas were diving, their vics opening out, the lead elements spearing into the haze just to the north of the shell bursts already darkening the sky over Valletta. The 88s began a lazy right turn above the barrage, presumably awaiting some signal to dive in and join the party. The 109s were harder to spot, but the nearest pairs were high to either side of the 88s.

Diving through 20,000 feet, Jack's airspeed edged past 450 mph, his controls buffeted by the rushing airflow. Mal held rock steady. Jack quartered the airspace around them, then concentrated on the aircraft below.

The nearest 109s were off to their right, half a mile away and no immediate threat. Jack and Mal dived past, unseen, spearing down on the rear of the twin-engined bombers, which were now rolling out on north. Such was the skill of Woody's positioning that they were diving straight out of the sun, unseen by the rear upper gunners, even as they closed to within a few hundred yards.

The first tracer was Mal's, hosing toward an 88 to Jack's right. Jack waited a smidgen longer, looking down on his target's gunner, sensing his fear and confusion as he squinted upwards. At 200 yards, Jack pressed on the centre of the gun button. Tracer smashed into the 88's canopy and raked backward toward its tail, sending debris into the air.

Jack dived behind, buffeted by the bomber's slipstream. He glared at the black crosses on wings and fuselage, the swastika on its tail.

'Bastards!'

The anger dissipated quickly, replaced by concentration on the task in hand. Mal was still to his side, easing right for the Stukas – and the box barrage.

'Good lad,' Jack shouted, forcing his own stick to the right against the airflow.

He looked around. The air was full of peril. Several Stukas and the barrage were dead ahead, and at least two Rotte of 109s seemed to be veering toward them. And yet, although sweat prickled his face, and his mouth was suddenly dry, the tang of fear was absent. He felt in command - for the moment.

Their turn had put them on the tails of two Stukas, no more than 400 yards ahead. Jack found himself staring at another rear gunner. But this one had seen him and a stream of tracer headed his way. Closing fast, with no time to dive more steeply and pull up from the gunner's blind spot, Jack resisted the temptation to duck, or return fire. At 200 yards, tracer rounds whizzing past his ears, he pressed his own gun button.

He fought the controls to keep his Spitfire steady as it bucked and writhed with the recoil. Cannon rounds and machine gun bullets thudded into the Stuka. Its centre section burped grey smoke, which burst into vivid orange flame as the aircraft rolled right.

Jack dived past, into the barrage. Ten thousand feet. He quartered the sky, trying to spot aircraft among the blossoming shell bursts.

What next?

Mal still at his side somehow found time for a thumbs-up. Jack nodded in acknowledgement and pointed down to his left.

He'd failed to spot any 109s, although he sensed they must be near. But he had seen another three Stukas. He turned left to dive into the heart of the barrage after them. The dive-bombers were several hundred yards ahead, but with an overtake of more than 200 mph, the Spitfires were closing fast.

Below was Grand Harbour. At its far, Marsa, end, with no cloud to shroud them, Pampas, Talabot and their attendant ships showed up all too plainly. For the moment, the action was above the vessels, and there was no evidence of bomb bursts. But it couldn't last. Even if he and Mal succeeded in thwarting three bombers each, that still left 40 or so in this raid alone.

'You can only do what you can do, Jack.'

His Spitfire lurched, caught in the shockwave of a nearby shell burst. Then another. A brief glance to his right revealed Mal's wings rocking. The Stukas, now no more than 300 yards ahead, were also bouncing about. Jack eased for the left hand one, leaving Mal a choice of two.

A flash, and the left wing of the right hand dive bomber folded upwards. Fascinating as the sight was, Jack forced himself to concentrate on his own Stuka, just as tracer arced from the rear of its cockpit towards him. This time he returned fire immediately. But the recoil, plus the shock waves and turbulence of nearby explosions sent his tracer wildly awry. In no time, he was abeam his adversary. A bomb fell from each of its wings.

'Bugger!'

Too late to do anything about it. He just hoped they were jettisoned rather than aimed, although that probably meant they'd land on the city. Another quick look round.

'Mal, Jack, turning left and levelling.'

'Roger, Jack, with you.'

The words came as a relief. He'd failed to spot his wingman.

Jack suspected he'd expended most of the fourteen hundred .303 bullets available to his four Browning machine guns, but he should still have plenty of shells for his two Hispano cannon, say half, 60 for each. Enough to justify hanging around for a while, if the situation allowed.

They cleared the barrage and levelled at 2,000 feet to the north east of the Harbour. Once again, the 109s seemed to have been deterred, but no doubt they'd be along soon, if only to escort the bombers home once they'd dropped their bombs.

To enter the barrage again would be foolhardy, but he hoped they might pick off the odd bomber as it emerged.

With that in mind, he climbed to 5,000 feet and positioned them just beyond St Julian's Bay, about five miles north of Valletta. There'd been background chatter on the R/T as they'd passed through the barrage but, not hearing his name, he'd ignored it. Now, he thought he better check in.

'Woody, Jack here, St Julian's, 5,000 feet.'

'Roger, Jack, you may have custom shortly. Break. Jumbo, Woody here, continue climb, more big jobs passing Gozo.'

A gruff voice replied. 'Wilco, Woody.'

So more Spitfires were airborne. Just as well because the Hun really were taking advantage of the better weather. Grand Harbour was ringed by flashes and growing clouds of grey smoke. Then, in his peripheral vision, Jack noted a mighty flash.

He turned in time to see the deck of the freighter tucked furthest into Marsa Creek wreathed in fire. As he watched, horrified, the fire shrank back, to the point where he thought it might have blown itself out. But no, a moment later, it belched horrible bubbles of black and orange. It was a sad and sobering sight, but not unexpected.

After three days of sustained effort, the Luftwaffe had finally hit one of the three survivors of Convoy MW10.

Jack imagined the heat, sound and the smell of the fire. He was sure it was Talabot, the freighter holding the bulk of the ammunition.

Most of Valletta and the Three Cities were little more than a few hundred yards away, but parts of the Corradino Heights, Marsa and Floriana towered over the blazing vessel, their buildings running down to the water's edge.

If the flames reached the explosives…

Tracer flashed over Jack's canopy.

'Shit!'

He'd allowed himself to become mesmerised by the scale of the tragedy. Belatedly, he began manoeuvring, looking for the threat.

Two 109s over his right shoulder. Mal already diving away, two more diving after him.

Jack pulled hard right, straining against the g, praying his assailants would overshoot. More tracer. He reached the buffet and relaxed a smidgen to maintain it.

Mal's pursuers, arcing right to left, were just visible through his greying vision. Worth a try. He pressed the switch to fire guns and cannon. Tracer raced away, but the recoil put him into heavy buffet – and wing drop.

He centralised the controls. The undemanded roll continued. A 109, no more than a few yards above his canopy. His right wing rotated towards it. He held his breath. The fighter disappeared and the roll stopped.

He must have distracted at least one of Mal's pursuers, but where did that leave him?

At 4,000 feet with 60 degrees of left bank, looking down on two 109s pulling back up towards him. No sign of Mal or the other 109s.

'Jumbo, this is…'

Jack blanked out the radio chatter, rolled to 120 degrees of bank and pulled down towards the 109s. He pressed the upper arm of the rocker switch, squirting the remaining second or so of machine gun rounds, more in hope than expectation.

The 109s disappeared. But they'd be back, and probably on his tail. He lacked the speed to dogfight. His only chance was to dive for the ground and try to shake them off.

Then, he remembered one of Jumbo Gracie's pearls of wisdom.

'Head for the nearest airfield at zero feet, orbit in the middle of it and hope the gunners hit the Gerries and not you.'

Thanks, Jumbo.

With St Paul's Bay about five miles ahead, Jack pulled down, playing the buffet again. He rolled out on a south-westerly heading, passing 1500 feet, and pushed on the throttle, trying to eke every last rpm out of the Merlin. The 109s appeared, diving in from high in his 8 o'clock.

He was soaked in sweat, sphincter twitching, but still thinking clearly.

The huge dome of Mosta church was to his front right.

Beyond it sat the ridge, the walls and cathedral of Mdina shining in the sunlight. Beneath them, no more than three miles away, the small barren patch that was Takali.

Malta was such a tiny battle space.

As he neared the ground, tracer flashed around him. He jinked madly, adding enough rudder to make his flight path as eccentric as possible, without losing control. That would be certain death at this height. But so would being hit and attempting a crash landing into the tiny fields careering past no more than 50 feet below.

The airfield was no longer in sight, but Mdina was. He jinked left. The 109s were 100 feet above, 400 yards back.

Mustn't give them a plan view.

To his relief, he shot over the airfield boundary. Below, hundreds of people looked up, some turning and running for cover. He headed for the centre of the airfield, pulled hard right and looked back.

The guns began to belch fire and smoke. The 109s flew straight on as if totally surprised at the new turn of events, exactly what he'd intended.

No time for complacency, though. He continued the right turn, passing over a gun emplacement on the airfield boundary. The gun crew waved their tin hats in the air as he roared past. His heart leapt.

He rolled out pointing at the Mosta dome to have a good look around, then pulled right again. No sign of the 109s, just puffs of black soot over the airfield, rising in height into the north west, like a flight of stairs. They seemed so obviously to mark the retreat of his assailants that he finally relaxed.

But then it took every ounce of composure to prevent relaxation descending into collapse. He was caked in sweat, aching all over and shaking with the exertion and conflicting emotions of the last ten minutes, if not the last hour. He was also worried about Mal. He should have found a way to help his young wingman, although how that could have been achieved, he wasn't sure.

'Come on, Jack!'

He breathed deeply, looked around again and raised the nose, climbing south south-east for Luqa. To his left, Valletta and its harbours were lost under an enormous pall of smoke that billowed up and opened out to darken the sky to the north.

But Luqa was also under a canopy of grey mist dotted with evidence of bursting shells.

Was nowhere safe?

He thought briefly of heading for Hal Far, but would that be any better? Anyway, he hadn't got the fuel, or the energy to mess about. He just wanted to get on the ground.

So, he closed the throttle and, as the speed reduced, lowered gear and flaps for an approach to the south-easterly runway at Luqa, once again trusting the gunners to recognise him as friendly. Passing 400 feet, he advanced the throttle and began a gentle right turn onto the centreline.

A couple of Hurricanes were off to his right, about 500 feet above. As he continued his descent, they turned toward him.

His brow furrowed, then his pulse raced. They were diving.

What was going on?

He waggled his wings. 'I'm a Spitfire, you idiots.'

No sooner had the words left his lips than tracer flashed past. But it hadn't set out from the Hurricanes. It came from behind.

'Idiot!'

He pushed on full throttle and, expecting impacts at any moment, began to weave as much as he dared at low speed. After what seemed an age, he'd accelerated enough to raise gear and flaps, at which point the aircraft skipped ahead and he weaved more extravagantly.

The tracer from the Hurricanes was passing perilously close behind. It soon became apparent why. A 109 raced past to either side. Both began climbing right turns, the left one passing close enough for Jack to see its pilot looking up through the angular canopy. He wasn't looking at Jack, though, but through him.

The Hurricanes sped overhead, pulling for the Messerschmitts.

Jack passed 300 feet above the runway threshold. Making a snap decision, he closed the throttle, rolled to 90 degrees of bank and pulled, holding level as the rubble-strewn ground raced past beneath and the speed decayed. Reducing bank, he lowered gear and flaps, intercepted a normal curving approach path, added a smidge of power, rolled out, closed the throttle and held off for a near-perfect three point touchdown.

Another draining hour of incredible sights and frights.

But it was too soon to relax. If the 109s were still about, he was at his most vulnerable trundling along the ground. So he craned his neck to scan the sky over the airfield. The only aircraft now in sight were the two Hurricanes.

He allowed himself a few deep breaths and taxied as fast as was prudent while weaving to try and avoid unpleasant surprises. At the end of the runway, he turned right and set off down the strip for his pen. Passing Mal's refuge, he was delighted to see the young Australian standing in front of his Spitfire, talking with his groundcrew. His face lit up and he gave an exuberant wave.

Jack finally allowed himself to relax.

When they re-entered G Shelter, Mal dashed over to Zulu, Harv and Dave. The group broke into animated conversation, hand gestures alone giving onlookers the gist from well out of earshot.

Jack was glad to see Dave so engaged. He'd resolved to keep a fatherly eye on the young man, but also to give him space to sort out his own problems, if he could. No doubt he'd seek help or advice if he wanted it.

The others were also in relatively high spirits. And yet, in the few minutes before they handed over to B Flight, the mood changed. Jack's news from the harbour, and the increasingly sombre expressions on the faces of those crossing the floor, added to the feeling that a not-altogether-unexpected tragedy was beginning to unfold.

During the drive to Mdina, the view over Valletta, or of the smoke cloud obscuring it, added to the sense of foreboding.

Unusually, after a lunch of thin Maconachie's stew, rather than disperse to follow their own pursuits until dinner, they moved to the terrace, sitting and peering into the smoke, hoping it would thin and reveal at least some of its secrets. But, over the course of several hours, the cloud merely grew in extent and thickness.

Raids continued throughout the afternoon and evening, some comprising tens of Ju 88s and 87s. Whether the bombers could see their targets or not, most seemed to drop their ordnance into the smoke. Occasionally, it would billow and they'd hear the faint rumble of explosions over the crack of anti-aircraft guns. There were also hints of explosions to the south, in the vicinity of Marsaxlokk Bay. Small numbers of Hurricanes and/or Spitfires attempted to disrupt some of the attacks, but often the raiders seemed to go about their business undisturbed.

There were no visitors to impart the latest gen, although some of the Maltese staff arrived with unsettling rumours. So, the pilots sat around and waited, hoping their colleagues would have more news, at least enough to confirm or counter some of the more outlandish stories.

The sun dropped behind the Palace roof and the raids dried up. But the view to the east still held their attention.

The smoke over Valletta had begun to take on a ruddy glow. At first, the reddish tint seemed uniform, but as darkness fell, hotspots appeared. It was hard to gauge the exact position of the fires beyond in and around Grand Harbour. By 8 o'clock, when it was fully dark, the sinister glow was enough to illuminate the smoke rising into the sky to the north.

There was the odd burst of conversation, laughter even,

but generally, it was a very sober vigil.

It was 9 o'clock before B Flight appeared on the terrace. They looked all in. After a few greetings and some muted banter, the CO, pint in hand, moved forward, standing to one side of the view from the terrace. He placed his beer on the wall, turned to face them and ran a hand through the wave in his dark hair.

'Before I tell you as much as we know about what's been going on, still is going on, by the look of it,' – he gestured over his shoulder – 'I'd just like to say how proud I am of the way you fought today.'

Jack thought the squadron leader looked as if he was struggling to maintain his composure. It was more of a shock than almost anything else in a shocking day. And, in an environment where emotions were kept under tight wraps, it wasn't a comfortable sight, for any of them. The man must be under so much pressure.

'You - and I mean both flights - could not have done more with the resources we were given. But...but, in the end, there were just too many Hun.'

He hesitated, as if wondering whether to continue in the same vein, then took a deep breath and drew himself upright. The emotion dissipated as quickly as it had appeared, replaced with their squadron commander's normal, business-like, demeanour.

'Anyway, I'm afraid the latest news of the freighters is nearly all bad. You'll know that Talabot was hit soon after noon. Fires broke out and they battled to save her, but she was hit again several times during later raids. What you may not have known is that much of her cargo was - is - ammunition. In the end, the fires were just too fierce and the risk of her exploding too great. So, she had to be scuttled. Not that even that stopped all the fires.'

He nodded over his shoulder again.

'They've done their best to evacuate everyone overlooking Marsa Creek but, apparently, most people have refused to leave. Hundreds are lining the harbour, watching the fires. God knows what'll happen if she blows. Wipe out half the bloody city, I should think.'

He gave another nod in the direction of the infernal glow to the east.

'I'm sure you can see that there's more than one fire, though. Pampas had had some close calls, but at about two thirty, a bomb went straight down her funnel into the engine room and exploded. It ripped the heart out of her and she sank, although what's left above the water is still ablaze.'

He sighed and took a long swig of beer. Jack cast a quick glance over the audience. They were transfixed, even Buck and the other members of A Flight, who'd presumably heard most, if not all of it, before.

Squadron Leader Grant put the now half-empty beer down, and ran a hand through his hair again.

'The same raid that hit Pampas hit Plumleaf while she was delivering a load of fuel oil from Breconshire. She ran aground in French Creek. And as for the Navy, they've lost a destroyer and a submarine, and several other ships have been damaged, including the cruiser, Penelope.

'I'll leave you to imagine the effect on the harbour and the cities.'

He leaned forward and picked up his beer again.

'And then, just before we left, news came in that Breconshire had been hit. So, all in all, despite our several successes, a pretty bloody day.'

The squadron leader drained his beer. Jack closed his eyes and shook his head.

A bloody day indeed.

Chapter 12 – The Dog Bites

Jack had a lousy night.

Initially, he couldn't stop thinking about the events of the last few days. But satisfaction at the squadron's achievements, and his own apparent renaissance, quickly dissolved into disappointment at how futile their efforts had turned out to be. All four freighters gone, and only about ten per cent of their vital cargoes saved, barely enough to give the Island a few weeks' grace before the issue of surrender raised its ugly head again.

If they weren't invaded in the interim.

And when these worries eventually subsided, it was only to give way to thoughts of what it must be like overlooking Grand Harbour, watching the fires.

What would happen if the flames reached Talabot's hold?

He lay there, listening to Mike's gentle snores and snuffles, but sure it was only a matter of time before he heard a massive explosion. The more he told himself not to be so stupid, the more intently he listened.

Sometime in the early hours, he began to sweat, and then to feel stomach pains. Soon, he forgot all about Valletta and lay, tossing and turning, hoping he hadn't picked up a stomach bug. Then he began to trot to the toilet at the far end of the corridor. On the third occasion, his groans, liquid bowel movements and the awful smell forced him to admit that he had the Dog.

At 4.30, when one of the mess staff came to wake them, the odour of goats' milk tea precipitated another journey to the cracker box, this time to add vomiting to the list of symptoms.

When he returned to their room, grimacing and holding his stomach, Mike was dressed.

He took one look and said, 'Get back into bed. I'll tell Laddie.'

There was no point in arguing. Jack climbed between the

sheets. His nose crinkled and he made one last request before his friend left the room.

'Mike, please get rid of that bloody tea.'

The MO dropped in on his rounds. Jack expressed surprise at receiving a home visit.

'There are so many of you now,' the ginger-haired squadron leader said, lowering himself and his black bag onto Mike's bed, 'that it's easier to tour the various messes and billets than to try and get you to come to us. Anyway, it'd take a fleet of buses we don't have, so there's no option, really.'

He smiled, his blue eyes twinkling above an impressive handlebar moustache and ruddy cheeks. 'And it gets me out of the medical centre, which is never a bad thing.'

'Glad to be of service, Doc,' Jack said, clutching his stomach.

'From what you've described, I think there's no doubt you have a touch of the Dog, or, with my doctor's hat on, a mild case of dysentery. I'm afraid I can't offer a magic potion, though. If it proves really persistent, or you start to find blood in your stools or vomit, we may have to consider antibiotics and a trip to Imtarfa. But, if it runs it's normal, and, I admit, not very pleasant course, you should start to feel human again in a few days, less if you're really lucky. In the interim, try to eat something.'

Jack pulled a face.

'I know. I realise you might not be able to face solids for a while, *but*,' and he fixed Jack with a steely stare, 'you *must* drink. You have to replace at least some of the fluids you're losing. As to when you can fly again, you can't beat the tried and tested – not before you can fart with confidence.'

Jack smiled. He'd heard the saying before, often, but not from the mouth of a doctor.

The MO smiled back. 'Now, anything else? How's the head for instance?'

Although Jack's scar still had the vivid redness of a recent wound, it seemed to be healing well.

'Fine, Doc. It was no problem after the swelling went down. But I don't remember seeing...?'

'No, you wouldn't. By the time they got you to the med centre, you were away with the fairies. So I sent you straight off to Imtarfa. I'm glad there were no complications, but, if you get any headaches, or there's anything else I can help with...?'

The MO was giving Jack the opportunity to air any concerns beyond his physical health. A few days earlier, he might have taken up the offer, but now...

'No thanks, Doc. Apart from the lousy diet and lack of sleep – oh, and the Dog - I'm fine.'

The MO smiled again.

'Good.' He stood and picked up his unopened bag. 'I'll make sure someone looks in on you at regular intervals with something to drink.'

As he turned to leave, Jack said, 'Thanks, Doc, but could you make sure it's not tea.'

Jack heard laughter as the MO disappeared down the corridor.

The Doc was as good as his word. Every hour, a civilian member of the mess staff appeared with a drink – water or fruit squash, not tea – and once, the flight sergeant Mess Manager dropped in to see how he was.

Not all the drinks were consumed. No sooner had he swallowed them than they came straight back up with small amounts of increasingly acidic bile, all that was left in his stomach. By this time, he had a bowl by the side of his bed, which the mess staff were good enough to empty each time they visited.

No-one was able to relieve the awfulness of the trips to the toilet. At least he seemed to be the only one in their part of the building suffering, so he didn't have to contend with anyone else's smells. He felt sorry for those that would have to contend with his.

Between evacuations, he lay, clutched his stomach and, occasionally, wondered what was happening outside. It was much quieter than the last few days, just the odd beat of aero engines and an even rarer barrage of flak, or a bomb explosion.

His vomiting stopped not long after he became convinced he was turning his stomach inside out with every dry retch. But his cramps and liquid bowel movements persisted.

What the MO only acknowledged on a second visit was how draining the illness could be. Jack felt well and truly dish-ragged, too weak even to visit the terrace. That said, the doc seemed to think he was progressing well enough to avoid a hospital visit. Where such optimism came from, Jack wasn't sure. He still wasn't keeping much down.

For the first couple of nights, Mike moved out, making only the odd visit to keep him up to date with what little news there was.

Partly because of poor weather, there were fewer raids on Friday, and these were mainly concentrated on the airfields. Mid-morning, Breconshire had finally given up the ghost and rolled over onto her side.

Poor weather or not, the bombers returned to the harbours again on Saturday, with one raid lasting most of the afternoon and evening. Even though the ships were under water, the dock workers were still trying to salvage what cargo they could, a dangerous enough business without the incessant bombing. So dangerous had it become that the Navy began evacuating surface ships to Alexandria.

Sunday was another relatively quiet day of poor weather, but it saw the delivery of the final seven Spitfires from Eagle. Until these were prepped, they were down to five kites.

By Monday evening, although still delicate, Jack felt well enough to attempt dinner, followed by a visit to the terrace.

There, he heard that Takali was still out of commission; Hal Far was a mess, its two Navy squadrons amalgamated into one; and Luqa was still suffering damage, with several delivery aircraft either lost en-route, or crashing on landing with the loss of their crews. The only good news was that half a Hurricane squadron, 229, had arrived from North Africa and would operate from Hal Far.

Further rationing – of rice, pasta, flour, bread and kerosene – looked set to make life harder for the civilians. Many more had lost their homes during the raids on the harbour and, with damage to power stations, reservoirs and pumping stations leading to frequent power cuts and water shortages, they now lacked just about every necessity. Starvation was a very real danger.

Jack agreed with Laddie that he should return to work, if not the cockpit, the next day. Their plan lasted no more than 15 minutes, scuppered by a message from Woody.

Despite the latest delivery of Spitfires, there were still far too few airframes for two squadrons. So, the group captain had decided they should work alternate days, ensuring that each squadron had the full complement of aircraft available on the days it flew. In theory, this should give each pilot the maximum opportunity to get airborne.

249s first day under the new arrangements would be Wednesday the 1st of April. Jack's Flight would be on the afternoon shift. That gave them an unexpected full day off, their first for weeks.

The CO secured a bus and the whole squadron headed for Ghajn Tuffieha Bay on the north-west coast, an ideal bathing spot, apparently. Well, almost the whole squadron.

Jack had managed to hang on to both dinner and breakfast, and there'd been no stomach cramps since the previous afternoon. But he wasn't confident enough to fart unless sitting on the toilet, and he still felt pretty washed out, so he decided that no matter how pleasant the prospect, a bus and a beach probably weren't the best places to be.

He spent much of the morning in his room, reading, napping and writing a long letter to Caroline, an activity that led to frequent daydreams. They were a bitter sweet diversion. Sweet as, for the first time in several days, he pictured her in full colour, laughing and swishing her flowered dress as they walked on the South Downs, or smouldering as they made love during a Sunday morning lie-in. Sour, as such thoughts made him pine for her company.

He still hadn't received a letter, and wondered whether she'd received any of his. But he wasn't the only one in the same position, and he refused to worry – yet.

For the first time in many days, he became restless of inactivity and shuffled along the dimly lit stone corridors and stairwells in search of company. None was to be found in the public rooms, or on the terrace, where he settled down to look out over the Island.

The weather was cloudy, but it was noticeably warmer than when they'd arrived three weeks previously. Small pillars of smoke rose above several areas in and around Valletta, but whether sinister, or the result of normal industry or agriculture, he couldn't tell. He heard the odd aircraft above cloud, even the hint of a few distant explosions to the south - Hal Far perhaps - but he saw no fresh smoke.

'How are you feeling?'

He turned to see a broad smile beneath a bristling handlebar moustache.

'Fine, thanks, Doc. Or certainly better than the last few days.'

'Good,' the MO said, moving forward to look over the plain. 'It's very quiet here today.'

'Yes.' Jack rose from his seat and stood next to him. 'They've driven off to Ghajn Tuffieha for the day.'

'Don't blame them,' the squadron leader said, rolling his shoulders and rubbing his neck.

The man looked all in. Jack felt a flash of sympathy.

Couldn't be many days off for a doctor on Malta, service or civilian.

'Another house call, Doc?'

'Yes. Larry Lloyd.' He looked at Jack. 'The Dog. Day one, so not a happy chap.'

Jack smiled.

'But I like to sneak up here when I visit,' the MO said, changing the subject. 'Incredible view.'

'Yes. We spend a lot of time looking at it, watching what's afoot. Not a lot today, though, so far.'

'Don't suppose it'll last,' the MO said, with a heavy sigh. He turned to face Jack. 'Oh well, best be getting on. Glad to see you're better.'

With a, 'Take care,' and a little wave, he made for the stairs in the far corner and left the terrace.

For the first time in a few days, Jack enjoyed a meal – as much as you could enjoy a cold bully beef sandwich, that is. He was also left feeling hungry, which led him to wonder how much the latest reduction in rations would affect them.

There was already little variety – bully beef, hot for breakfast, cold for lunch, Maconachie's pie or stew and the odd vegetable for dinner, and a very occasional biscuit to go with the brackish tea. Perhaps the portion sizes would shrink even further.

He went back to his room, but soon became restless again. On impulse, he dropped in on Larry Lloyd, bearing a glass of orange squash. Larry, who'd flown off Eagle on the 7th of March, was a pilot officer on the other flight. He'd been a lawyer in civilian life; so, although still inexperienced as a pilot, he was slightly older and more assured than many. Jack enjoyed hearing the Englishman's cut-glass, public school, accent, but all he got out of him today as he placed the glass on his bedside table was a listless grunt. Interpreting it as, 'Thanks, but leave me alone,' Jack backed out and closed the door.

Even more at a loss, he decided to go for a walk around

Mdina.

He was standing atop the northern bastion looking across to Imtarfa when he heard the beat of aero engines in the west. The sound increased steadily, until it became clear it was being made by a large formation. Cloud obscured the aircraft themselves, but Jack had no doubt of their nationality, or their intent. In what had become a reflex action, he plonked his tin hat on his head.

Shortly after, the Valletta barrage began to crash out its irregular rhythm. And shortly after that, fresh pillars of dark smoke and dust rose over parts of the city. The dull thud of explosions reached him and he decided to retrace his steps through the narrow streets, past the cathedral and back to the Xara Palace.

Having delivered the NCOs to their various billets, the officers of 249 Squadron returned in high spirits. During dinner – Maconachie's stew – Jack listened to stories of lounging on the beach and swimming in crystal clear water. Smiling and assailing one another with banter, his fellow pilots looked rejuvenated, and he was feeling pretty good himself. Amazing what one complete day of rest could do.

A shame the groundcrew hadn't been afforded the same luxury.

Faced with an early start the next morning, most of B Flight went to bed at a reasonable hour. Most of A Flight, however, stayed late on the terrace, drinking and laughing, despite the backdrop of frequent raids on Valletta.

Jack looked around the happy faces. It had taken three weeks, but most, like him, finally seemed to have accepted that this was their new reality, the life of a pilot on Malta. When they had to, they'd face the bombing and the ludicrous odds in the air, but when they weren't at the heart of the storm, they'd do their best to make the most of it.

Chapter 13 – 1ˢᵗ April – The Blitz Continues

April began as March had ended, with heavy raids, only this time under clear skies. Jack sat on the terrace drinking tea and shielding his eyes from the sun as he watched the action. In the last few days the weather had leapt from spring to summer.

Perhaps the people who set April the first as the date for going into Khaki Dress weren't so dumb after all.

Some of the pilots around him grimaced and groaned, or smacked their lips and clutched their heads. It made him glad he hadn't over-imbibed the previous evening. And the little he had drunk, he'd kept down. He was still a tad short of top form, but he had no doubt he'd beaten off the Dog and was fit for duty.

Most importantly from his point of view, his anxiety and fear of combat hadn't returned.

Just as well, because no sooner had A Flight entered G Shelter than he left it again, a member of the first formation to launch that afternoon. They found their aircraft and taxied out of the Safi strip, the CO leading Kim, Laddie, JC, Jack and Mal. It was the biggest formation Jack had flown in since arriving on the Island.

They were climbing for height to the south when an American accent cut the air. 'Tiger lead, four little jobs, low ten o'clock, three miles, heading north.'

Jack spotted them as the CO transmitted, 'Woody, Stan, tally ho, four little jobs, Delimara, angels five, turning in.'

'Roger Stan, Woody out.'

The nose of the CO's Spitfire dipped and they followed, gaining speed. As the 109s disappeared beneath their wings, they turned left about, rolling out over Delimara Point, 2,000 feet above and behind the enemy fighters.

Jack couldn't believe he was in a formation that outnumbered the enemy. With Mal to his left, he sat a couple of hundred yards behind the CO, Kim, Laddie and JC. He wound the wingspan of the fighters into his reflector sight, set the gun safety off and stroked the rocker switch.

The 109s were still in wide line abreast, flying straight and level with no attempt to manoeuvre for lookout. Air superiority seemed to have led to complacency.

Their speed passing 420 mph, the Spitfires dived behind and beneath the Messerschmitts. Still the Germans flew on, oblivious. Approaching 4,000 feet the CO pulled up. Jack delayed for a couple of seconds then did the same.

The lead pairs closed to within a couple of hundred yards. They shuddered, their wings belching smoke, tracer streaking ahead of them. Only then did the Messerschmitt's split. The one to the right turned hard right, displaying itself in plan view. Jack rolled and pulled, straining against the g to run his gunsight over its tail, along its fuselage, over its canopy and engine cowling to its propeller spinner.

He pressed the gun button. His Spitfire growled and shook. He fought g and vibration to keep guns and cannon on target as tracer snaked over the German fighter. A flash of yellow sparked in front of its cockpit. He grunted, pulling hard in an effort to keep the 109 in sight. Before it disappeared below him, orange flame was playing over his opponent's canopy.

Jack unloaded the g and as his head cleared, manoeuvred to look around. No sign of friend or foe, except for the 109 he'd hit, spiralling down at the head of a trail of black smoke. He watched with a mixture of elation and horror, trying to block images of flaming cockpits he'd seen at closer quarters. He wouldn't wish such a grisly death on anyone. It was a relief when the fighter smashed into the sea a mile to the east of Zonqor Point, the easternmost tip of the Island.

He rolled wings level and Mal appeared to his left. Good job it was Mal. He'd spent far too much time watching the stricken 109. If it hadn't been the young Australian who'd sneaked up, he could have been dead meat. But Mal seemed ecstatic, punching the air with an exuberant thumbs-up, although whether at Jack's victory or one of his own, it was impossible to tell.

'Tiger, this is Woody, pancake, I say again, pancake.'

Jack looked across at Mal, pointed down at the ground and turned for Luqa. Seemed a shame, though. For once, they'd had the upper hand.

As he approached his blast pen, he could tell something was afoot.

The groundcrew were thin-lipped, looking even more eager than usual to get him shut down and pushed back into his pen.

Was a raid imminent?

No sooner had they stopped in the walled enclosure than he felt a rocking as someone jumped onto the wing. Before he could reach down and remove his harness pin, a shadow fell over him and a hand appeared on his right shoulder.

'Don't bother, sir. You're to go straight off again.'

Jack looked up into the tanned face and blue eyes of a corporal about his own age. Beyond him, a couple of tradesmen had jumped onto the wing.

'As soon as they've replenished your ammo, sir, you're to head out after the CO and his wingman.'

Jack looked over his left shoulder at more armourers busy removing panels. The same would be happening beneath the wings. 'Righto, Corporal,' he said, turning back to look up at the man. 'Any idea what the flap is?'

'Sorry, sir, no. We was just told to get you out again, sharpish.'

'Okay, thanks.'

By this time, the trolleyac was plugged in under the nose, and Jack made a quick check of his fuel and oxygen contents, and his brake pressure. Fuel was the most critical. Although he'd been airborne only 25 minutes on the last sortie, he'd spent virtually the whole time at full throttle. He'd used about 30 gallons, so he'd have to keep an eye on things.

In little more than five minutes, the corporal was

checking the gun panels, top and bottom. He emerged from under the left wing and gave a thumbs-up. Jack returned the gesture. But he couldn't afford to start up straight away, and the groundcrew didn't expect him to.

In the air, the wide letter-box opening of the radiator beneath the right wing ingested plenty of cooling airflow. But on the ground, it sat behind the undercarriage leg and outboard of the propeller slipstream. So, if you didn't want the coolant to overheat, you couldn't afford to have the engine running for more than about seven minutes before getting airborne, less in hot weather.

Usually, when pilots walked out together, it wasn't a problem. It was safe to assume they'd start and be ready to taxy at about the same time. But on this occasion, Jack had no idea when the others, parked further down the strip, would appear, and it was a fairly long taxy anyway. He'd have to wait.

The corporal walked out of the pen and stood, looking down the track. Jack drummed his fingers on the canopy arch. The sudden inactivity gave him time to realise just how much the temperature had increased with the clear skies. The perspex and metal were warm to the touch. Sweat trickled down his body.

There were also more flies, something Smudger had mentioned. When they really swarmed, it was said they could drive some people mad. Jack hoped he wasn't one of them.

The corporal turned and walked towards the pen holding both thumbs in the air. Less than a minute later, Jack's engine was purring sweetly as two Spitfires taxied by. He waved away the chocks and taxied after them, waving to Mal, waiting patiently a few yards down the strip.

Once airborne, the CO spoke to Woody and the controller came straight back with the reason for the flap.

'Stan, this is Woody, fifteen big and numerous little jobs approaching Valletta, angels one five.'

211

'Roger, Woody, Tiger passing angels five.'

Well, they weren't going to get above them – or the barrage. That was already popping off, invigorated by the shells delivered by the convoy. Jack wasn't sure he welcomed that particular development.

For the moment though, they continued climbing to the south in finger four, Kim Kaminski to the CO's left, Jack and Mal to his right. At 8,000 feet, they entered a gentle left turn.

'Stan, this is Woody, bandits over Valletta, angels one five, vector three six zero.'

Straight for the barrage!

'Wilco, Woody, tally the bandits.'

Their rate of roll increased as Woody acknowledged the call. Several thousand feet above, a couple of bombers peeled off and descended into the smoke.

Jack admired their courage, but discounted any such label for himself. If he entered the air being ripped apart by gunfire, it was down to a mixture of duty, stupidity and, the main ingredient, a determination not to fail those in the Spitfires to either side of him.

The CO continued the climb and they eased up into wide line abreast. More bombers dived into the smoke, which grew ever darker. Approaching the Three Cities to the south of Grand Harbour, Jack began to pick out the lurid flashes and black splatters of individual shell-bursts. They were a sobering sight.

The four Spitfires levelled at 11,000 feet, but not for long.

'Tiger, diving in. Good luck all.'

Jack pushed throttle and stick to keep up with the CO. He looked right to see Mal's Spitfire following suit. No sooner had they established in the dive than they entered the smoke and the air became turbulent, rocking their wings.

Jack spotted two pairs of 88s diving down, the pair to the right only a few hundred yards ahead. He and Mal eased toward them. The CO and Kim dived steeply for the more distant pair. No words were expected, or necessary.

The air was alive with violence – flashes, jolts, the smell of smoke and cordite, muffled thuds and sharper cracks rising above the sound of the Merlin. But there didn't seem to be any enemy fighters. Once again, their reluctance to enter the barrage was good news.

Jack aimed for the rear left quarter of the nearest 88, itself bucking in the turbulent air. Mal was intent on the bomber a few hundred yards beyond the first.

Jack nodded. The young Australian was good, and getting better with every engagement.

For a moment, time seemed to slow down. Against the background of frequent flashes, the left hand 88 stood out, dark and menacing. Large engines protruded forward of wings that tapered out to square tips. A long fuselage raked back to a conventional tailplane, above which was an elegant, curving tailplane, not unlike the Spitfire's.

Jack's admiration of this feature was fleeting. It bore an emblem that never failed to raise his hackles. The swastika.

Since he'd first seen it over Dunkirk, it had come to symbolise, not only death and destruction, but evil. What had the people of mainland Europe, the British Isles, and now Malta done to deserve the murderous onslaught of machines bearing the hateful device?

Nothing.

A nearby shell-burst set his world rocking and time tumbled forward again. Sparks flashed from the rear of the bomber's perspex canopy and grew into tracer that rushed toward him. The urge to retaliate was overwhelming.

'Hold it, Jack.'

He waited until he was within 100 yards and pressed down on the bottom of the gun switch, revelling in the rhythmic pulse of the two 20mm cannon. His tracer crashed into the bomber's left wing and engine. It flashed flame and rolled left, passing beneath him.

Jack looked right.

Mal and the rear upper gunner of the second bomber

were exchanging fire. Jack pushed on the throttle and eased right after them. The bead of tracer spitting from the 88 ceased briefly. When it recommenced, it made for Jack, the rods of light passing close beneath. He suspected impacts, but it was so difficult to tell against the background buffeting from the barrage.

And then, he was in clear air. Smoke, unnoticed before, streamed back from the 88's lower fuselage. Jack pressed on the centre of the rocker switch and his tracer set out. It smashed into the crew compartment, sending shards of perspex into the air. Return fire from the bomber ceased, flame licked from its cockpit and it rolled right.

Both Spitfires followed, firing into the stricken hulk. Its roll rate continued to increase until it was descending in a tight spiral.

Jack was just about to call them off, when tracer flashed over his left wing. Instinctively, he rolled left and pulled, grunting against the onset of g and straining to look up and left.

Two 109s. Must have been hovering outside the barrage, much as he had a few days before.

'Mal, two 109s,' he grunted.

He continued to pull up and round as the 109s passed down his left hand side.

'Tally, Jack.'

The voice was strained, as if its owner was also suffering the effects of heavy g.

By now, Jack was arcing over the top, searching the sky below for his wingman, and the Messerschmitts. He spotted all three, diving away over the coast to the north of the harbours. Pushing against his fully open throttle, he dived after them.

Mal was jinking madly, the 109s less frantically, having the benefit of both numbers and position. Every so often, tracer sparked from their guns and passed perilously close to his friend's Spitfire. If they were patient..?

But Mal was skilful. He was heading for the ground and

it seemed they had yet to hit him. Jack arrowed straight toward them, but he was gaining only slowly, if at all.

'Come on,' he coaxed, leaning forward, as if to give his Spitfire added impetus.

Then Mel and the 109s eased left over St Julian's Bay, allowing Jack to cut the corner. He bore down on the left hand fighter. Allowing for deflection, he fired ahead of its nose, his tracer setting off drunkenly into space. His machine guns ran out of ammo, but the cannon kept popping and the 109 flew into the path of his shells just as its pilot spotted the threat.

'Too late, Butt,' Jack shouted.

Bits flew off the Messerschmitt and a thin trail of white vapour appeared from its engine cowling. It rolled left and passed beneath Jack, its pilot looking up at him.

Jack switched his attention to the second 109, its pilot now fully alive to the danger. As Mal continued to head inland, his remaining attacker turned right and dived hard for the coast.

Jack looked left but, in the few seconds since he'd last done so, both his wingman and the first 109 had disappeared. It had been damaged, so Mal should be able to get home unmolested. That left the second Messerschmitt.

He decided to go after it.

Even though he'd taken his eyes off the fighter for the briefest of moments, it took a while to pick it out again. The first thing he saw was its shadow, 500 yards ahead and a few hundred feet lower. The angular dark shape was flashing across the rough terrain just inland of the coast. It climbed the flank of a shallow hillside and almost kissed its alter ego.

Jack locked onto the 109, but the shadow vied for his attention, rushing up with every rise in the ground. The German was flying knap of the earth, racing over successive craggy headlands, jinking round creamy stone watchtowers.

Jack closed the distance only slightly as he descended to

about 100 feet. Stumpy trees and dry stone walls flashed by and he found it hard to keep the 109 in sight. Any lower and he'd lose it.

But he wasn't gaining.

Not for the first time he cursed the ungainly Vokes filter. It knocked about 15 knots off the Spitfire's top speed, leaving him with no overtake. His only hope was to cut the corners as the 109 turned. But the German was too clever to deviate through more than a few degrees, enough for Jack to keep pace, but not gain. Nor did he climb and skyline himself to make even a speculative shot worthwhile.

Jack jinked in pursuit, arms aching and sweat running down his face and body. The Dog hadn't raised its ugly head, but it had weakened him. They flashed over St Paul's Bay, passing above small boats whose occupants stared up at them.

More towers. A wider bay. A small peninsula of land. Out over a wider stretch of sea. Islands ahead.

The German seemed more confident now, more certain that the Spitfire lacked the speed to close. In fact, Jack had lost ground. The 109 was jinking less, flying north-west down the western coast of Comino, the small island between Malta and Gozo.

Despite his tiredness, Jack couldn't help but admire the rocky coast and radiant limestone fort. Beyond a headland, smaller islands and stacks rose out of the turquoise sea, their bases pounded by white surf. It was beautiful.

When they reached Gozo, the German turned to hug the island's south-west coast, nestling against its towering cliffs in much the same way his pursuer had hugged the Dingli Cliffs less than a month previously. Jack wondered if he should climb and hope to ambush his opponent as he'd been ambushed. But no, the German had no reason to climb, change course, or do anything other than fly at full throttle for another 60 miles.

'Damn and blast!'

He was beaten. If nothing else, his fuel state made a

chase toward Sicily impossible. Reluctantly, he turned onto south and began a gentle climb toward Luqa.

When Jack reached G Shelter, Mal wasn't there.

'He landed at Takali,' Laddie said in answer to his query. 'Seems he was hit in the foot. They've carted him off to Imtarfa. Afraid that's all we have at the moment. How are you?'

'Fine, Laddie, thanks. Fine.'

Laddie didn't look convinced, but didn't push it.

'Okay. Go and give your report to Harry. We'll see how the rest of the afternoon pans out, but I think you might be on again if the need arises.'

The truth was Jack felt lousy. Two frantic flights so soon after days of eating even less than normal had really taken it out of him. And the loss of yet another wingman was a difficult cross to bear.

Had Mal been hit before he'd deserted him, or after? Okay, perhaps desertion was overly harsh. But perhaps he should have stayed with the young Australian.

Oh well, too late now.

He gave his report to Harry and found somewhere to sit.

That lunchtime, there'd been two new sergeant pilots on the bus. He'd walked for his first sortie before he'd had a chance to give them more than a cursory nod. Now, they were chatting to JC and Kim. Much as he felt like hiding away in a corner for a while, he decided to walk over and introduce himself.

Both Luke Elliott, a short, fair-haired American, and Newfy Brown, a tall, dark-haired, Canadian - presumably from Newfoundland - had flown in on the 29th. Once again, neither had much experience on the Spitfire, nor had they flown in the air defence role before.

Being hors de combat, Jack hadn't heard much about the final seven Spitfires from Eagle, other than that they'd arrived safely. But it sounded as if their transit had been a hairy old do.

'After Cap Bon, we were giving Pantelleria a wide berth,' Newfy said, with the air of a practised story-teller. 'But not wide enough it seems, because out of the murk a couple of thousand feet below appears a formation of CR42s. Now I know they're only biplanes, but with tobacco for ammunition, they looked pretty fucking intimidating, I can tell you.'

Jack smiled at the turn of phrase.

'Passed right underneath. I was bricking it. But if they saw us, they decided not to do anything about it. Just turned round and disappeared into the murk again.'

He looked at the young American for corroboration.

Luke obliged. 'Yeh, never saw 'em again. But I couldn't believe they hadn't radioed back for a squadron of 109s. I spent the whole leg to Linosa expecting trouble.'

Jack remembered how much the flashes of light in the distance had played on his imagination. 'Yes, I think we were all scared to death passing Pantelleria. But I think you're the only ones to see any actual bandits. Don't envy you that hour or so.'

He decided to change tack. 'And how's it been since you arrived?'

'Well,' Newfy jumped in, 'I've certainly eaten better.'

Their ironic smiles faded as the shelter shook, then again, and again, the tremors growing in frequency and intensity until they could also hear muffled booms. Dust fell from the shelter roof and people put on their tin hats.

'And I don't remember being bombed back in Kent,' the Canadian continued.

Experience told Jack that the bombs were, for the moment, dropping a fair way away. 'Yes, I'm afraid that's something else you'll have to get used to.'

The afternoon continued with much of the same, sporadic raids that did little more than heighten the tension in the shelter. The veterans - a category that Jack now accepted included him - were all too aware that others would be much closer to the action, sheltering in slit trenches at best, working in the open at worst.

He noticed Pete Brown sitting on his own, flinching with every tremor, no matter how distant. He wondered whether he should go over, but the decision was taken out of his hands when Laddie called the flight lieutenant, Mike, Zulu and Dave into a huddle.

Shortly after, Pete led the other three up the steps and away. Dave and the others looked fine, but Pete still looked pensive. Laddie watched them go, a concerned look on his face.

Jack realised he hadn't seen much of Pete, and they'd rarely flown together. On the ground, he kept himself to himself. Not always a bad sign, but sometimes…He decided to keep an eye on the young flight lieutenant.

The thought made him smile.

As a sergeant and flight sergeant on 646 in the summer of 1940, he'd been Muddy's right hand man. It hadn't been a matter of rank, but of character. He'd had the qualities and the capacity to fulfil that role. But he'd lost his way after his encounter with the 110 and Alex's death.

For whatever reason, that old character was back, and he was ready to contribute beyond the cockpit.

It sounded a bit conceited, but there it was. The CO and the flight commanders were often too busy with other responsibilities to keep a close eye on everyone. As unobtrusively as possible, he resolved to help them out.

Just before 6pm, the CO waved him over with Kim, Harv and Newfy. Jack was surprised the young Canadian had been summoned, but not as surprised as Newfy himself.

Eyes wide, he pointed to his chest, as if to say, 'Who, me?'

His expression mirroring the smiling faces around him, the CO crooked a finger and mouthed, 'Yes, you.'

It was a welcome moment of levity.

Newfy raised himself to his full six feet two inches, set his chin and marched over.

The CO nodded at him, and struck eye contact with each of the others. 'Woody wants us airborne in anticipation of the evening's raid.'

He pointed at a succession of pens on an airfield map. 'We'll go as Red Section; me; Sgt Kaminski, two; Flying Officer Williams, three; Pilot Officer Johnson, four; and Sergeant Brown, five. Scramble on two reds.'

Their pens were all down the strip. Jack was glad to see that his and Newfy's were next to one another.

Two red flares arced into the sky at 6.20pm. They were airborne two minutes later, Jack and Newfy to the left of the CO.

Newfy had recovered from his initial shock. But Jack had discovered that this would not only be the young man's first air defence sortie, but his first operational flight. Luckily, since the announcement that they were to join 249 rather than 126, Kim had taken both newcomers under his wing, so they'd been given a fair idea of the theory of flying over Malta. Now though, one was about to put it into practise.

Jack looked across. The way the Canadian filled the cockpit of his Spitfire reminded him of Alex. He reached down and stroked his calf – the first time for days.

'Stan, this is Woody. Seventy, I say again, seventy bandits approaching Gozo, angels one five and above. Climb to the south.'

The admonition to climb needed no repeating. With five against 70, height was likely to be their only advantage.

Would they ever have sufficient numbers to layer the defence of the Island rather than wait for the enemy to appear over their targets?

And how Newfy must feel at hearing the odds, Jack could only guess. The only indication of nerves was a tendency for him to ease closer, as if seeking the comfort of a tighter formation. Each time, Jack signalled him to move out, and each time he felt like a parent pushing a child away. Otherwise, the Canadian seemed to be coping, his head in constant motion, often a good indication that someone was on the ball.

Woody turned them back to the north as they passed over the south coast. Shortly after, the Valletta barrage began to pepper the sky.

'Stan, this is Woody, bandits approaching Valletta, angels one five.'

'Roger, Woody, tally ho, tens of the blighters. Tiger Red levelling angels one seven.'

'Roger Stan, good luck.'

Jack had also picked out the dark mass of German aircraft, stretching back to the north of the barrage. For once, they all seemed to be single-engined, those in the central phalanx noticeably larger than their escorts.

Stukas. About 50 of the bastards. The leaders were already peeling off and diving into the barrage.

Jack signalled Newfy and moved alongside the CO. Kim and Harv had done the same on the right. The CO looked to either side. Jack guessed they were about to head into the flak. Despite the obvious dangers, it seemed the best way to keep the 109s, many of whom were diving on them from above, at bay.

'Tiger Red, diving in, follow me.'

They hurtled towards the barrage and the diving Ju87s. Jack divided his attention between the enemy, the CO and his wingman, holding nicely to his left.

Suddenly, an image of Caroline came to him. She was sitting in the front room in Keston Avenue, sunlight shining through the window to spotlight her. It was a scene of serenity and peace that he so wanted to be part of.

The contrast as he entered the barrage could not have been greater. The very air heaved with the violence of tens, hundreds, of shell bursts; while the Stukas added their own menace, racks of bombs dangling beneath gull wings emblazoned with black crosses.

Jack had seen it all before, a picture of hell, a sign of man's insanity. But what would Newfy be making of it?

While the CO, Kim and Harv dived ahead, Jack eased left onto the tail of a pair of Stukas. The needle of his air speed indicator was sweeping past 420 mph, the altimeter unwinding rapidly. They probably had more than a 200-mph overtake on the bombers, rear guns now spitting tracer.

Return fire arced ahead of Newfy's Spitfire.

'Too soon,' Jack tutted, while understanding the young man's need to retaliate.

A second later, he was forced to recant as the Canadian's target exploded in a ball of lurid smoke and flame.

'Fuck me!'

He was so taken aback that he almost overshot his own objective. He'd squirted no more than a couple of seconds of cannon and machine gun fire before he flashed past the Stuka's startled pilot and gunner.

Newfy was still to his left and the other Spitfires were off to the right. Several more Stukas dived ahead of them, but Jack knew he couldn't afford to arrow down at his current rate. While the bombers would be able to pull out of their dives from as low as 3,000 feet, he and Newfy would be toast if they left it that late.

He heaved back on the stick, grunting against the airflow forces on the elevators and the onset of g. The nose of the Spitfire to his left also began to pitch.

'Good boy, Newfy, good boy.'

They flew clear of the barrage in a shallow descent passing 5,000 feet, St Julian's Bay to their front. Three thousand feet below, three Stukas also appeared, heading north east over the sea.

Jack eased the stick forward and rolled into a gentle right turn. Newfy held position and gave a confident thumbs-up as they levelled their wings behind the Stukas.

'Well done, Newfy.'

The young Canadian seemed a natural, much more

competent than Jack had been on his first foray over Dunkirk, or Malta come to that.

The Stukas were also diving, but the Spitfires still had a significant overtake. Jack quartered the airspace above. As yet, he could see no 109s. Off to his right, the other Spitfires were descending on their own gaggle of 87s.

Tracer flashed above his head, redirecting his attention to the front. The three rear gunners were firing, the middle one swinging his gun to shoot at each of the pursuing Spitfires in turn.

Jack focused on the Stuka to the right. He dived beneath its tail and levelled. Speed bleeding off slowly, he waited for the range to close. The pilot jinked madly, trying to give the rear gunner a view of his adversary, but Jack countered to stay in the blind spot beneath the tail.

At 100 yards, he pressed on the centre of the gun button and struggled to hold the gunsight steady against the vibration and recoil. His rounds smashed into the underbelly of the Stuka between the wings. A thin stream of white vapour appeared. He kept firing and his rounds kept thudding home.

Just as a collision seemed imminent, the Stuka rolled hard right. Jack passed its oil-streaked underside as the vapour darkened and ignited into a jet of flame.

He was at 1,000 feet, Newfy wide to his left, distancing himself from the other two Stukas, both turning left onto north in an attempt to make good their escape. Jack was considering how best to get back on their tails when, over his shoulder, he spotted two 109s diving toward his young wingman.

He pulled hard left and grunted into the radio, 'Newfy, two 109s, break left.'

The left wing of the Canadian's Spitfire arced downward. 'Roger, Jack.'

The voice betrayed not only the strain of speaking under g, but also the fear of pursuit. Its owner rolled out and, jinking madly, headed for the ground just to the north of St

223

Julian's Bay. The 109s swooped, turning in behind him.

Breathing heavily and sweating freely, Jack pulled as hard as he dare, playing the buffet and straining to maintain at least some vision. When he snapped to wings level, blood rushed to his head and cheeks and his eyes pricked with stars. The 109s were about 300 yards ahead.

It wouldn't be long before he was lost in their wake, so he eased onto the right hand 109, took a moment to adjust his aim, and fired. The rounds must either have scored hits or distracted the pilot because he rolled right.

The other German jinked to watch his companion who rolled to wings level and dived away north towards St Paul's Bay.

Jack sensed indecision in the remaining German pilot. He fired. His tracer sprayed harmlessly around the 109, but it too turned hard right.

'Yes!'

The sense of triumph was momentary. As he glanced inside to check the instruments, he noticed the needle of the oil temperature gauge rising toward 115 degrees, while that of the adjacent pressure gauge was falling – only slowly, but falling nonetheless.

'Damn!'

Unnoticed in all the excitement, he must have taken a hit in the oil cooler or tank from a Stuka. He needed to be on the ground, and preferably – he looked down on the patchwork of tiny fields - on an airfield.

Just inland of St Julian's Bay, a few miles to the north of Valletta.

'Takali then, Jack.'

Keeping an eye on the oil temperature, he eased left and into a climb, using the power he had while he had it.

He waited for a pause in the radio chatter. 'Woody, this is Jack, heading for Takali.'

Again, he was amazed that the controller both heard and found the time to reply to his message.

'Roger, Jack, I'll let them know.'

The only aircraft in sight were Stukas emerging from the barrage to his left and heading north to pass behind. They left clouds of smoke billowing above the harbours and surrounding areas.

Passing 2,000 feet, Jack could already see Takali, or the bald patch beneath the ridge that marked the airfield. It was about four miles ahead. No 109s were in sight, but that didn't mean they weren't out there. He hadn't seen the last one to nail him.

The oil temperature, although beyond max, was only nudging up, the pressure falling similarly unspectacularly. But he continued to aim for the overhead, keeping his options open until he was sure he could reach the airfield, at which point he might be able to cosset the engine and set himself up for an approach into the southerly wind.

Amazing how calm he felt.

And this time, the engine kept going. Approaching Takali at 4,000 feet, he eased the throttle back and lowered the nose to glide high downwind for an approach to the southerly runway. Even from height, he could tell how much work had been done on the airfield. Its surface was no longer pitted with holes, and the tell-tale rectangles of tens of new blast pens ringed the operating surface.

As he descended, lowering gear and flap and opening the canopy, it became apparent that most of the buildings were still derelict, although a few new ones seemed to have popped up here and there.

Most importantly, the anti aircraft gunners were holding their fire and no 109s were in evidence.

Again, he realised how calm he was. It was as if he was performing a practise approach with a student on the OTU. And his tic was a distant memory. The major threat was lethargy, or complacency.

'Come on, Jack,' he shouted in an effort to gee himself up again.

At about 300 feet on his curving approach, a green flare arced up from the left hand side of the strip.

Cleared to land.

As he arced over the boundary he could see hands and hats waving in the air. He waved back, before rounding out and floating for a perfect three-point touchdown on a surface remarkably free of craters – and red flags.

He let the Spitfire slow to walking speed before turning right to clear the strip, at which point he raised the flaps, set the radiator shutter to open and pulled the engine cut-out. As the propeller and the aircraft came to a stop in a cloud of fumes, he turned off the mag switches and fuel, applied the brakes and took a deep breath.

The engine smelled 'hot'. It had brought him back to the airfield, but at what cost?

Not the time to sit around and ruminate. He released the brakes again – so they could push the aircraft if it caught fire – patted the coaming, climbed out and waited for the vehicles bouncing across the airfield toward him.

'See you back at the Mess,' Laddie said.

Jack replaced the telephone in its cradle and sighed. They didn't want him back at Luqa. Perhaps he shouldn't have been surprised. It was well past seven and getting dark.

He wondered if Laddie knew that 249's next duty day would be at Takali, and that they had a brand new squadron ops room. A bit spartan - bare walls of roughly applied white plaster - but certainly an improvement on the tent.

While he waited for transport, an enthusiastic officer of engineers gave him a tour. The young lieutenant glowed with pride as he showed off the work undertaken by his troops. And Jack was genuinely impressed, especially as he knew the airfield had continued to suffer sporadic raids.

New slit trenches had been dug, ones with steps at either end that should stop him jarring his calf every time he jumped in. Their pens had also been strengthened, the fuel cans replaced or hidden within thick walls of stone topped with sandbags. And many more such shelters had been built around the perimeter. They'd even cut a few into the rock.

Finally, the Royal Engineer waved a hand over the airfield, proclaiming that the operating surfaces had been much improved, cleared of craters, aircraft wrecks and bombed out vehicles. He was delighted when Jack said he'd seen as much from the air.

And yet, as the Army officer finished, Jack couldn't help wondering how long the good work would last. The Germans were bound to return in strength when they realised the Spitfires were back.

He decided to keep such pessimistic thoughts to himself.

One thing that hadn't changed at Takali was the lack of transport. The lift he'd been promised failed to arrive.

At 8.30pm, he was nearing the top of the hill, panting with the exertion of his long walk. His eyes had become accustomed to, first the gathering gloom, then the dark. He was grateful for the relative cool of the night air. It beat climbing up in the heat of the day.

Before him, the ribbon of road running beneath the walls of Mdina glowed silver in the moonlight. Behind him, lay the plain, largely a black hole with a few pinpricks of light.

Occasionally, he'd heard aero engines and seen flashes from sticks of bombs, the echoing booms reaching his ears seconds later. It seemed to be single raiders, the location of the explosions random, peppering the plain or coming from behind the ridge to the south. On a couple of occasions, the Valletta searchlights had flicked on and there'd been a few flashes of flak, but all was silent now.

Then, he heard another engine. This one belonged to a vehicle labouring up the hill. When it appeared round the bend behind him, it revealed itself as a bus, and as it drew near, he could see it was full. Aircrew. Perhaps his own flight. He waved and stood to one side, waiting for it to stop and pick him up.

It didn't.

As it drew past and away, faces pressed close to the rear

227

window. He heard laughter and shouts. A voice with a Kiwi twang rose above the rest, 'See you later, Jack.'

He recognised a few of the smiling faces, including Laddie's.

You couldn't help but laugh. Nevertheless, just to play is part, he waved his fists and threw a couple of V signs.

Pilots!

When Jack reached the bar, A Flight were in fine spirits. He acknowledged a few waves, but didn't join in wholeheartedly until he confirmed that Newfy had reached Luqa intact.

'Sends his regards,' Harv shouted above the din. 'Said you swatted a couple of 109s that were bothering the pair of you.'

Jack nodded in acknowledgement.

'But otherwise,' Harv continued, 'it sounded as if he'd beaten off the might of the Luftwaffe single handed.'

'Yes,' Jack nodded again. 'I get the impression he's not going to suffer from under-confidence, or false modesty. Mind you, he did well. Did everybody else get back in one piece?'

'Can't you tell?' Harv said, waving his arm around the room.

After dinner, they gathered on the terrace. Jack had failed to find any more news on Mal Cotrell, his other source of concern. One of his tasks the next day would be to visit Imtarfa to see the young Australian.

He'd just secured another beer when Harry Boyd walked onto the terrace. He seemed delighted to be there, smiling and shaking hands with some of the pilots who went over to greet him.

A few minutes later, there was an emphatic banging. The chatter stopped and they turned toward the railings.

The CO put an empty pint pot on an adjacent table and stood back. 'Thank you everybody.'

He looked much less youthful than he had only a few weeks previously, his face gaunt and lined, eyes grey and sunken.

Partly diet, Jack guessed, but partly the pressure of leading a squadron on Malta. While the squadron leader usually flew with B Flight, he spent time at the airfield with both flights, which meant he worked longer days than anyone bar the engineers.

He ran a hand over his brylcreemed hair. 'No doubt you've all heard that we're moving back to Takali. 126 will fly the kites in and operate from there tomorrow. It's been transformed apparently.'

He looked at Jack, who nodded as faces turned towards him. Then, the CO mirrored Jack's own pessimism.

'Let's hopes the improvements survive until *we* get down there on Friday.'

This produced knowing snorts and grunts from several of the more sceptical among the company.

The CO smiled at the response. 'Anyway, moving on,' – he pointed to the group containing Harry – 'I'm delighted to announce that we now have our very own intelligence officer - Flying Officer Boyd.'

Harry, cheeks reddening, bowed his head and raised a recently-acquired beer in acknowledgement of the shouts of welcome.

The CO waited a few moments, before continuing. 'I'm particularly delighted because, as some of you will know, I've been keen for us to get a wider view of what's happening on the Island, if only to put our own efforts in context.

'So,' - he looked to Harry again – 'Flying Officer Boyd has *kindly agreed*,' – ironic cheers acknowledged that little choice would have been involved – 'has kindly agreed to give us frequent intelligence updates. We'll try and make it about the same time every evening, at least on the days we're flying, starting tonight. So,' – the CO extended an arm – 'over to Flying Officer Boyd.'

Smoothing his thin moustache and blushing even more deeply, the intelligence officer stepped forward. 'Thank you, sir.'

As he turned to face them, the night sky over Valletta broke into a rash of flashes. A chorus of gasps and pointing arms had Harry turning to see what was going on, just as more lurid flashes erupted at ground level. The respective crack and boom of anti-aircraft fire and explosions reached them a few seconds later.

Perhaps because he was no longer the sole call on their attention, Harry seemed to relax. He turned, patted his moustache again and set off in the assured fashion they'd become used to when he spoke in G Shelter.

'I thought I'd start by tying up some of the bigger stats. Not sure any of you have been around long enough to witness all of it, but Malta has been bombed every one of the last hundred and seventeen days...'

He stopped to acknowledge the few low whistles. Behind him, the sound and light show continued.

'Yes, for those that may not know, that's more than double the length of the blitz on London. Last month alone, there were two hundred and seventy raids, with over twelve hundred incursions by 88s, 87s and Jabos, not to mention their escorts.'

He stopped to acknowledge more low whistles, before continuing. 'Up to yesterday, you and 126 have managed to bag twenty for the loss of four in the air.'

Harry beamed, but most of the pilots, Jack included, looked less impressed. True, they were racking up successes, but the odds remained so overwhelming that the Hun were still pretty much bombing at will – and causing enormous damage, not least to aircraft on the ground - which Harry had obviously decided not to mention.

'On the ground,' – oh, here it comes, Jack thought. But the intelligence officer seemed determined to stick to the positive. 'The Army have laid twenty seven miles of dispersal track and runway; and, with your help, they've built fourteen bomber and one hundred and seventy fighter pens.'

Most of which seemed to have been flattened again, Jack thought, instantly admonishing himself. No-one could criticise the small number of troops on the Island for lack of effort, especially those who'd worked so hard at Takali.

Harry looked behind him. The raid on Valletta had finished. The world beyond the terrace was dark and silent.

He turned back. 'As for today, I'm afraid the harbour really copped it. The Navy lost two submarines and a minesweeper, with one more of each and three tugs damaged. And all the port facilities took another hammering.

'On a more positive note, although they only managed to unload about ten per cent of the cargo from Breconshire, Talabot and Pampas before they were sunk, they're still working to salvage more, and succeeding by all accounts, despite the raids.'

Jack wouldn't have wanted to be on any of the ships in the harbour, but especially not Talabot. Working atop all that ammunition was an experience he was only too happy to forego, raid or no raid.

'Closer to home,' Harry continued, 'between you and the AA gunners, we bagged twenty seven today, without loss.'

Once again, the decision to ignore damaged aircraft rankled with Jack. His own kite had been hit more than 20 times and was unlikely to be back on line for several days. Mal's had been the same. He'd seen it at Takali, holed like a pepper pot.

They'd started their shift with eight and even with others becoming serviceable during the afternoon, the attrition was such that only five had been available for the final sortie. And only four of these had landed back at Luqa. Jack had half a mind to ask how many were undamaged. Not many, he guessed.

He seemed to remember that during the Battle of Britain just one fighter squadron could go through 60 aircraft in a fortnight. Here, there were never more than a handful between two squadrons and 30 pilots. Without more deliveries, it wasn't hard to work out that the numbers available could go only one way, especially as the Hun was unlikely to back off any time soon.

He found that he'd missed Harry's concluding sentences, if there'd been any, and the CO was stepping forward again. After thanking the IntO, he seemed to mirror Jack's final thoughts.

'Not sure how many aircraft we'll have available on Friday, but let's be prepared for another busy day.'

Chapter 14 – Early April - Nibbled Away

The next afternoon, Thursday 2nd April, Jack and Mike walked over to Imtarfa. There, they joined JC and Kim, already standing at Mal's bedside halfway along a ward of 20 beds.

'You look to me as if you're malingering,' Mike threw at his fellow Antipodean.

And it was true. The young Australian was sitting up, smiling, his cheeks flushed with good health. The only thing that raised apprehension was the bulge of a frame holding the bedclothes clear of their friend's feet and lower legs.

'D'you know, apart from the fact that I'm short a couple of pinkies,' – he pointed to his right foot - 'you're spot on.'

They all winced at the brutality of the statement, although Jack was somehow relieved. He'd feared worse.

'Just a couple?' JC said.

'Yeh. Sorry to disappoint.'

'Not tiring you out, are they, Sergeant Cotrell?'

Jack thought he recognised the soft voice with its trace of accent.

'No, Sofija,' Mal said, a look of genuine delight spreading across his face.

A young nurse eased past them and gently lifted Mal's wrist.

'Hello, Nurse Dingli,' Jack said, with a hint of surprise.

The dark-haired young woman looked slimmer than when she'd stood by his bedside a few weeks ago. Obviously, the hospital staff were eating no better than anyone else.

'Hello, Flying Officer Williams,' she said, never taking her eyes off the watch supported in her other hand. 'How's the head?'

'Oh, not bad, thanks. How's the patient?'

She lowered watch and wrist and looked into Mal's eyes. 'Oh, he'll survive, I think.'

Then she turned to glower at the four pilots. When she

spoke, it was in a voice with a hard edge, like a schoolteacher's.

'As long as he gets enough rest.'

'Message received, Nurse,' Mike said with mock sheepishness. 'Loud and clear.'

'Good,' she flashed back at him, before returning her gaze to the patient, her voice softening again. 'No more than two minutes, now. I'll be back to check.'

'No worries, Sofija. I'll make sure they leave before Matron sees them.'

The pair exchanged another smile, and Nurse Dingli glided away.

'Sofija, ay,' JC whispered.

Jack joined in. 'I never got beyond Nurse Dingli.'

'That's because you're taken, Jack,' Mike said. 'Anyone can see that.'

Jack wondered whether it was that transparent, but decided not to chase the matter.

'Whereas,' Mike continued, 'our Mal is very much young, free and single.'

'If missing the odd digit,' Mal said, his face revealing the first signs of discomfort.

After a brief silence, Kim spoke for all of them. 'Well, I think you look bloody marvellous, and I suspect she does too.'

The words restored Mal's smile, and, unexpectedly, made him blush.

'It's her job to care,' he said defensively. 'Now bugger off, you lot, before she gives us all a good talking to.'

'Okay,' Mike said, 'we know when we're not wanted. But, before we go, what should we tell the grown-ups?'

'Well, I haven't seen the damage yet, but apparently the shell took the two littlest toes clean off my right foot. So clean, they say, that I should be up and about in a few days, and back to flying in a few weeks, maybe less.'

His expression became pained again. 'Not sure I believe it, but we'll see.'

He looked beyond them and smiled.

Jack turned to see Nurse Dingli stop several beds away and begin chatting to the heavily bandaged occupant.

'I'm sure they know what they're on about, Butt,' he said, turning back to his friend. 'Although if I was you,' – he nodded toward the young nurse – 'I'd stay here as long as I could.'

They all laughed and Mal blushed again.

'See you in a couple of days,' JC said.

They all uttered similar goodbyes and turned to leave.

Jack was suddenly struck by how unbelievable all this would have been to his younger self growing up in Barry. Here he was, part of a group of five men on a Mediterranean island, each thousands of miles from home: an Englishman, an American, an Australian, a New Zealander and a Welshman. It was like the start of a joke.

Nurse Dingli smiled as they passed. As they exited the ward, she was approaching Mal's bed.

Kim and JC walked off to try and catch a film in Rabat. Having discussed it beforehand, Jack and Mike decided to uphold 249 tradition by visiting some of the German patients.

An obliging sister showed them into a ward. It looked and smelled like the one they'd just left, but the atmosphere was very different.

For a start, apart from the odd shuffling and groaning sound, it was eerily silent, devoid of the banter between visitors and patients that had bubbled around Mal's ward. And the faces looked more pensive, perhaps betraying fears beyond their immediate medical problems. They all faced a transfer to Corradino Prison once they were well enough.

Those who'd spotted two 'British' pilots at the end of the ward looked at them, faces betraying, not hostility, but curiosity as to what their appearance could mean. One young man looked terrified, as if fearing they'd turned up to cart him away for interrogation, or worse.

Jack decided the visit was a mistake and was just about to say as much to Mike when another sister appeared.

'Follow me,' she said in a tone that brooked no argument.

Jack and Mike looked at one another, shrugged and did as they were told.

She stopped by the bed of a man with dressings encasing his right arm, upper chest and the side of his head and face to the right of his nose. Those areas of skin not hidden under dressings were speckled with gashes and nicks, the scabs of which looked several days old.

'Sergeant Fischer has the best English of those that are well enough to talk,' she said matter-of-factly. She turned about and cast the now familiar, 'No more than two minutes,' over her shoulder as she walked away.

Jack smiled down. The smile was not returned. He didn't want to stoop to stereotyping, but, if anything, the German looked surly, shifting the gaze of his one good eye between the two pilots. Jack wished more than ever that they'd turned round and walked out of the ward.

'As I told the man yesterday, sir, I have nothing to say.'

'No, no,' Jack said, 'this is a social visit.'

As if to emphasise the point, he produced two packets of cigarettes. He placed them on the bedside table and pointed round the room. 'For everybody.'

Some of the other patients raised their hands and smiled.

'Thank you, sir. I will make sure everyone gets their fair share.'

It was as far from cod German as you could imagine, closer to upper class English if anything, but very stiff and formal. Jack decided to see if a compliment would loosen things up a bit.

'You're English is very good, Sergeant. Better than mine, I think.'

The German seemed to relax a little. He obviously wasn't averse to flattery.

'Well thank you, sir. I studied at Imperial College before

the war.'

Jack judged him to be a similar age, no more than mid-20s, so it couldn't have been long before the war.

'No way,' Mike joined in, placing another two packets of cigarettes next to Jack's offering. 'Didn't end up bombing it, did ya?'

Jack winced, but the German seemed to take the question in his stride, although the seriousness of his answer indicated that he'd missed the joke.

'Well, no. I didn't fly missions over London. Ports and convoys, now that would be a different matter. I bombed many of those.'

He let the statement hang in the air. It would probably have been all right if he hadn't so obviously been enjoying the discomfort of his 'interrogators'.

Jack sensed Mike bristle. He tried to defuse the situation before the New Zealander dived in feet – or fists - first.

'And now Malta, ay,' Jack said, pointing at the dressings, 'where you seem to have ended up on the receiving end yourself, and soon to be a prisoner.'

'Oh, the wounds are not so bad, sir. And I don't expect to be a prisoner for long.'

'I shouldn't count on that, mate,' Mike jumped in, unable to keep the antagonism out of his voice.

The sister appeared at the end of the ward, looking impatient.

Jack laid a hand on his friend's arm. 'I'm sorry, but it looks as if we have to go. In the meantime, we wish you a speedy recovery.'

And a long incarceration, he thought.

'Thank you, sir,' the German smiled as they turned to walk away.

'Arrogant bastard,' Mike muttered when they'd gone no more than a few paces.

'Mm, not very likeable, was he' Jack replied.

He noticed the patients in the beds nearest the sergeant looking at their colleague as if in exasperation that he'd so obviously upset their visitors. A couple went as far as to smile warmly and wave farewell.

The two airmen followed the sister back toward the hospital entrance. Jack wondered whether they'd done something to set the brief meeting awry, or whether the German really was just an arrogant bastard. At least he'd be better prepared for his next visit, if he could find the resolve to make one.

The next day was Good Friday. It marked the start of an important weekend of religious devotion for the Islanders, but seemed not to make any difference to the conduct of the Germans. It soon became apparent that their blitz was to continue, and that the return of Spitfires to Takali had been noted.

Jack and Mike were woken at about 7.30 by the first raid of the day. Later, they discovered that 60 bombs had been dropped on the airfield, including one in the middle of the newly-repaired runway.

They watched a later raid from the terrace, tens of bombers diving in, this time seeming to concentrate on the gun emplacements and shelters ringing the airfield boundary, although there was little detail to be seen once the smoke from the first few bombs had drifted over the scene.

Before the drive down for their one o'clock start, they saw several more German formations fly overhead, and heard the rumble of distant explosions to the south, but they saw no reaction from Takali's fighters.

The reason became apparent when they arrived at the airfield. It was still out of action as a result of the first raid. At least this gave them a few minutes to admire their new dispersal hut, now, courtesy of B Flight, adorned with maps and a few more items of furniture.

The shortage of aircraft also became all-too apparent.

The seven kites flown to the Island on the 29th seemed to have made precious little difference. They'd proved too few even to replace those lost or damaged over the convoy. And there'd been other losses since, not least the previous day, when 126 had lost two in the air – one pilot killed and one hospitalized – and one had been destroyed in the workshops at Kalafrana.

When battle damage and 'routine' un-serviceability were added to the mix, they found they were starting the afternoon with only a handful of aircraft.

There was another unwelcome change. To date, sitting at cockpit readiness had been an infrequent event, always uncomfortable and, during a raid, bloody dangerous. But it had been decided that it was to be their new modus operandi.

Given the odds they faced, and the need to get to height as soon as possible, the change was hard to argue against, but with the temperature increasing every day – it had already reached the high 70s, early 80s - sitting in the cockpit was not a prospect to be relished, even if Laddie had promised to swap them over as often as he could.

Jack was one of the first to find out just how uncomfortable it could be.

Soon after an enormous explosion from a delayed action bomb, the airfield was declared fit for use. Ten minutes later Jack was in the cockpit of a Spitfire.

The temperature within the metal and perspex shroud must have been nearer 100 degrees than 80. Even dressed in only shirt and shorts, with the canopy drawn back and his leather helmet draped over the stick, he was soon sweating freely, which seemed to attract swarms of flies.

And, unlike the groundcrew who were so brown they seemed immune to such things, he could feel the sun burning his face and arms. He daren't fall prey to sunburn, or sunstroke. Next time, he'd have to concoct some sort of shade – something that could be whipped away when the call to scramble came.

Laddie was as good as his word. After 90 minutes, Mike

walked into the pen and took Jack's place. Jack went in search of Smudger.

Once more, the rigger was kneeling, arm lost up to the shoulder within a panel. Jack stood to one side until the young man turned his head, a look of intense concentration on his face. He spotted Jack, extricated his arm, spanner in hand, and broke into a smile that did more to raise the pilot's spirits than anything since his arrival on the Island.

'Hello, sir. How are you?'

'Very well, thank you, Smudger. What about you?'

Jack thought he looked pretty awful, thinner than ever, more haggard and lacking in sleep.

'Oh, not so bad, sir. Glad to see you're okay, though, after your prang.'

'Well, I wouldn't exactly call it a prang, but the kite was a bit of a mess.'

'Nothing new there then, sir.'

'No, I suppose not.'

They both laughed.

'How was Luqa?' Jack asked.

'Oh, not so bad, sir.'

This seemed to be the default reply to every question about his welfare.

'In fact, pretty good. Hangars, a proper cookhouse, and underground shelters.'

'Yes, we had one, an underground shelter that is. Seemed a lot safer than these.' Jack waved his arm in the general direction of the nearest slit trench.

'Tell me about it!' the young tradesmen shivered, his blue eyes taking a far away look.

'Couldn't have been much fun this morning,' Jack sympathised.

'You could say that, sir. Quite a welcome back. Hopefully, they'll give us a break now, although I'm not going to bet on it.'

Jack nodded and smiled. 'No, very wise,'

He decided to change tack. 'Anything from that

girlfriend yet?'

Immediately, he wished he'd chosen a different topic.

The airman nodded mournfully. 'No, sir. You?'

The return question rather knocked the wind out of Jack's sails. He realised he too was becoming anxious at the lack of correspondence.

'No, nothing. Not easy, is it?'

'I'd like to say you get used to it, sir. But you don't. The longer you go without hearing, the more you want a letter, but the more you dread what it might say.'

'Yes. And in my case it's only been three weeks,' Jack said.

He was beginning to realise how difficult mention of home could be, especially for someone who'd been without news for months. He tried to be a bit more upbeat, realising immediately how lame it sounded.

'Perhaps we'll both get something on the next flight in.'

'Perhaps, sir. Let's hope so anyway.'

Jack couldn't think of any topic guaranteed to raise their spirits, but he stuck with the familiar.

'How's life as a rigger, then?'

The reply was surprisingly frank.

'Pretty bloody difficult, sir.'

Jack left a space for Smudger to elaborate.

'Almost every kite getting airborne comes back full of holes, if they come back at all,' - an oblique reference to the previous days' losses that needed no elaboration. 'And the few extra spares we saved from the convoy are running out fast. We're already robbing again.'

The frustration in the airman's voice stung Jack, not least because he realised he could do nothing about it. No-one could. Presumably, a few spares would still arrive by air or submarine, but not enough to fix routine snags, let alone damage sustained in the air and on the ground. If things carried on as they were, they'd run out of airframes at some point, robbing or no robbing. They needed another convoy, and another delivery of Spitfires.

241

His face must have betrayed his thoughts.

'Just the way it is, sir. We've had plenty of time to get used to it.'

'It'd be bloody marvellous if something happened to change it though, wouldn't it.'

'Yes, but I'm not going to hold me breath for that either, sir.'

If we carry on, we'll both end up in the depths of despair, Jack thought. It was so hard to find anything positive in their predicament. And yet, none of them contemplated failure. As long as they could put anything into the air, they'd give the Hun a bloody nose.

'Well, I'm glad I've been able to cheer us both up, Smudger.'

They looked at one another and laughed again.

'It's a serviceman's right to whinge, sir.'

'Yes, and no-one's better at whinging than a couple of old riggers.'

Jack wasn't too embarrassed at claiming his heritage. *Once a rigger, always a rigger*, his mate Ginge had said.

'You're dead right there, sir.'

The conversation seemed to have reached as much of a high point as was possible under the circumstances.

'Oh well, I'll leave you to it again, Smudger. Good to see you though.'

'You too, sir. Take care.'

Jack waved and the rigger turned back to the Spitfire, kneeling and peering into the dark opening beneath the wing.

Jack did another stint on cockpit readiness but wasn't scrambled. Otherwise, the afternoon took on a pattern similar to that before they were exiled to Luqa. More heavy raids and sheltering in slit trenches. It was as if they'd never been away.

Soon, only those who had to were using the new squadron ops building – nicknamed the shed. It wasn't hardened, and it muted the whistle of bombs, often the first and only warning of an attack.

Most people preferred to rest under awnings in the open air, jumping up and shouting a warning through the shed door before haring for the nearest trench. Laddie, Harry and the ops and admin clerks would rush out, never far behind, but far enough when every second counted.

A raid in the late afternoon – mainly Stukas - destroyed yet another Spitfire and damaged three more. Another, in the early evening, – mainly 88s - made a mess of the airfield, putting it out of action again. Although no bombs seemed to fall within 100 yards of their shelters, it was another nerve-racking experience, putting them all on edge. Jack found himself longing for the relative safety of G Shelter.

A couple of Spitfires launched between raids and both returned.

Jack remained a spectator.

For reasons that no-one seemed able to explain, the squadrons swapped duty days at the weekend. So, having travelled up the hill at 8.30 on Friday evening, and following a few hours in bed with little sleep because of the incessant bombing, Jack found himself back on the bus at 4.30 the next morning, Saturday 4th April.

Luckily, all remained quiet for several hours, so in between bouts at cockpit readiness, he caught up on his sleep. Just after 11am, tens of 87s and 88s appeared. They watched them pass overhead, apparently bound for Valletta and its harbours. The noise of bombs and flak followed by the sight of smoke rising in the east confirmed their suspicions.

The bombers seemed increasingly to fly without escort. Presumably their confidence – arrogance even – was based on knowledge of how few RAF fighters were available, and the assumption that those there were would have to be husbanded. The defence of the Island was being left increasingly to the ack-ack gunners.

The canopy of smoke over Valletta made the drive back up the hill a sober affair. If only they had more kites.

When they flew, even when there were losses, they felt as if they'd given of their best. But when Woody held them back, however sensible the reasoning, it sapped their self-esteem.

After a meagre lunch, they witnessed more raids passing over the Palace. Only the final raid seemed to be opposed, four Spitfires launching to meet it at 6pm.

Late in the evening, B Flight returned in better spirits. Their four-ship had bagged three 88s for one slightly damaged, while the Hurricanes had hit a couple more.

Harry's intelligence brief was more sobering.

The Navy had lost a submarine and a previously damaged minesweeper, and HMS Penelope had suffered several hits and near misses, although her gunners had managed to down an 88. The harbour and surrounding settlements had sustained more damage and casualties, while one of the centrepieces of Valletta, St Paul's Cathedral, had suffered a direct hit.

Sporadic raids continued overnight.

Perhaps it was news of the cathedral in Valletta, or just the fact that it was Easter Sunday, but Jack decided to join Mike at mid-morning Mass in St Paul's Cathedral in Mdina.

Mike professed himself a churchgoer – if not a Catholic – but once he'd grown out of Sunday school and compulsory attendance with his parents, Jack had rarely attended his local chapel. Since joining the RAF, it had been a similar story. During his Halton days, he'd skipped as many church parades as he could get away with, and he'd rarely attended church voluntarily since.

The war had only confirmed his sense that if there was some higher plan, it was pretty bloody chaotic and cruel to those caught up in it.

And yet, once enclosed within the splendour of the

cathedral, the sights, smells and sounds of devotion swamped his senses. The ceremony itself was largely unintelligible, but he began to sense how the surroundings and the unfolding ritual could offer solace to those with faith.

Sitting towards the rear, he looked around, soaking up the atmosphere. Families made up the bulk of the large congregation. The men-folk of all ages wore black, the women, black dresses and headscarves, and the young girls, bright white dresses. Their chanting rose with the incense smoke to meet shafts of sunlight that highlighted the vibrant colours of the cathedral's architecture, art and decoration.

Jack found it moving, soothing even.

Every so often, he and Mike were slow to kneel, rise, stand or sit. At such times, Jack felt self-conscious, and infrequent eye contact confirmed that Mike felt the same. But mainly, both were lost in contemplation.

In Jack's case, his thoughts ranged from his early life in Barry, including his lack of gratitude at his mother's struggle to raise him following the death of his father, through his experiences to date in the RAF – Halton, flying training, Dunkirk, the Battle of Britain – to Caroline.

Mostly, he thought of Caroline.

It was funny, even when alone in his room in the Mess, he found it hard to conjure up and hang on to the essence of her for more than a few seconds before other thoughts or outside distractions intervened. But here, surrounded by hundreds of people, unfamiliar sights, sounds and smells, he had a clear and lasting image. He could smell, almost touch her. Her presence was achingly real.

If anything spiritual was happening that morning, that was it. A link, a feeling of proximity to Caroline. He wondered if anything similar was happening back in Keston.

As he'd suspected, the connection ended with the end of the ritual and the opening of the cathedral doors. Harsher light flooded in, sweeping away the sense of nestling in a cosy cocoon. As they filed out onto the square beneath the twin towers, he resolved to return. This would be his place of retreat.

He and Mike squinted at one another and nodded. They exchanged no words, but Jack knew that both of them had, in some way, been re-energised. How long such a feeling would last, who knew, but he at least felt better for it.

Toward the end of the mass, he'd sensed rather than heard explosions. Now, standing in the square, the sounds of conflict were unmistakable.

Valletta, Luqa, or both?

Jack hadn't noticed many other uniforms inside, but quite a few servicemen now exited the cathedral. The pilots gravitated toward one another until there was a group of about ten standing beyond the cathedral steps. Here they stood and chatted, acknowledging the well-wishes of passing Maltese.

Eventually, driven by thirst and hunger, they eased over to exit the square below the left hand tower and walked along narrow thoroughfares until they found a café atop the walls. Beckoned in by the smiling owner, they settled down for lunch. The man had obviously been hording provisions for Easter. It was another pleasant and unexpected surprise.

The sound of aero engines and explosions caused frequent, sober, pauses, but, in the main, Jack enjoyed several hours of laughter and unaccustomed good eating and drinking, bordering on gluttony. He consumed things he'd heard had been confined to the good old days before the blitz: olives and fresh bread - made with flour not ground potatoes – various cheeses, pastries stuffed with cheese and vegetables, more bread, delightful sticky sweet delicacies and bottle upon bottle of local wine.

Throughout, the moustachioed owner and his team of waiters treated them like VIPs, while tables of well-to-do local families encouraged them into frequent toasts, one initiated when the unmistakable sound of Merlin engines departing Takali caused a spontaneous cheer from diners and staff alike.

In the late afternoon, they threw what seemed far too little money onto the table and rose to depart. Jack and Mike decided to amble around the town, basking in the feeling of well-being caused by a full stomach.

They met few people, but in the distance they heard music and voices, often raised in song or cheering. The sounds became louder, until, turning a corner, they were swept up by a procession and jostled along the narrow, curving, streets. Such was the press that thoughts of stopping or backtracking were pointless, so they shrugged and went with the flow.

The music came from both ahead and behind, while above the bobbing heads 20 yards to their front, was what looked like the back of a veiled statue. It also bobbed along, and they followed. Only when the procession reached the square in front of the cathedral did they ease themselves to the side and join the spectators watching it pass.

It became apparent that the statue was one of many religious symbols on floats being pushed or borne along by the throng. The statues were of Christ, the Madonna and Child, or saints, but there were also religious paintings and ornate caskets of silver or gold. These, they were informed, contained sacred relics, parts of various saints – thumbs, wrists, skin and the like.

A bit gruesome to Jack's thinking, but not it seemed to the Maltese, who raised their voices in accompaniment to, or competition with, numerous bands that also filed past, playing their instruments with great gusto.

It was an incredible spectacle.

Throughout, the two pilots received handshakes and smiles. Given what the Islanders were going through, Jack found it incredible that they were thrown not one hostile glance. The only serious expressions were on the faces of older women, several of whom eyed them with pity. A couple even blessed them, something Jack found vaguely unsettling, akin to being given the last rites.

After about 30 minutes, what they assumed to be the head of the procession, a particularly impressive statue of the risen Christ, turned into the square. It seemed a good time to leave before the crush became even greater, so Jack and Mike pushed through to exit down the side of the cathedral again.

Although they'd been keen to escape the square, they were reluctant to return to the Palace, so they wondered the narrow alleys until thirst drove them into another surprisingly well provisioned café. A drink led into another meal, a hearty stew with more bread and wine.

The sounds of war sometimes intruded, but most of the time was spent chatting to the locals and laughing.

The sun had long sunk behind the buildings by the time they rose, said their farewells and set off to meander back. But, when they reached the square, such was the draw of the music, dancing and general enjoyment that they decided to stop again. And just as they'd resolved to leave with the falling of darkness, fireworks began to go off. So they remained, oohing and ahhing at explosions that, on this happy occasion, provoked laughter, not tears.

It was gone ten by the time Jack finally slipped between the sheets, tired and happy. He settled down, trying to hold on to that day's experiences and keep thoughts of the morrow at bay.

The four o'clock call came all too quickly and they walked out under a starless sky to board the bus.

Yet again, Jack didn't fly. None of them did. The cloudbase remained high but solid throughout the day, and the few engine sounds that reached them seemed to belong to small formations, mainly fighters. When larger formations passed through the overhead at about 6pm, explosions followed, and a few Hurricanes launched, but the handful of serviceable Spitfires remained unused.

They'd lugged a few sandbags, but mainly, it had been a day of wearying inactivity.

Chapter 15 – Tuesday 7th April – Down The Hole

Following another meagre breakfast, Jack, Laddie, Mike, Harv and Dave went to see Mal in Imtarfa. Zulu had another dose of the Dog. It seemed some were more susceptible than others. Jack hoped he wasn't one of them.

Yet again, Pete had turned down an invitation to spend time with his fellows. Jack wondered whether he should find an opportunity to see if Laddie shared his concern at the Englishman's growing isolation. Of course, Laddie might be oblivious, in which case Jack would have to decide whether to air his thoughts, or backtrack.

It was a tricky one. There was a thin line between intimating that someone was suffering from battle fatigue, and seeing them labelled LMF. Jack didn't want to infer the latter, not least because he'd seen no reason to do so.

When they reached the hospital, the NCOs – Kim, JC, Luke and Newfy – had also turned out, so they had to visit in shifts. Mal was recuperating well, and Nurse Dingli was still being attentive. Before she shooed them away, they'd managed to make her and Mal blush, and Jack sensed their relationship was blossoming more than they knew themselves.

Against their better judgement, Laddie had persuaded them to visit the German ward again. After a short wait, the sister allowed them to troop in en masse to dish out cigarettes. They also smuggled in a few bottles of beer.

Jack and Mike hadn't prejudiced the others against the arrogant so and so they'd met last time, but the pair made sure they steered clear of him. He looked just as grumpy, and it was noticeable that Harv didn't waste much time on him. The sooner Sergeant Fischer was in Corradino prison, the better, Jack thought.

His fellow countrymen seemed genuinely pleased to see them. There was even some good-natured banter with those that had some English. The two sides agreed to differ on the timing of the Germans' release. They remained convinced their countrymen would soon be in control of Malta.

Afterwards, they stood outside the hospital by a stone-rubble Austin Laddie had secured for the day from a friend, an Army major.

'Sorry, chaps,' he said to the NCOs, 'it's a bit of a squeeze with five. Not sure I can manage nine!'

'Oh, don't worry, sir,' JC replied on behalf of the others. 'Rank has its privileges and all that. We'll just have to bloody walk as usual.'

With that, the NCOs saluted, turned their backs and set off on Shanks's Pony, barracking the officers as they drove past.

Why on earth they were heading for Valletta Jack was at a loss to explain, even to himself. They could have driven to any of the Island's beauty spots, well beyond most reminders of the war, at least for a few hours. But, somehow, even after witnessing yet another raid during lunch, they'd been unanimous in their wish to see what had become of the city, its harbour and the ships.

There were hints during the drive, glimpses of water and wreckage, smoke blowing on the wind. The destruction in both Marsa and Floriana was much worse than on their last journey, almost a fortnight previously. Whole streets reduced to rubble, the upper storeys of more apartment blocks and shops displaying their contents to the world, not a window or wall intact. Nothing had been spared, not even the churches.

The Maltese worked among the rubble, shifting it with their hands, salvaging what they could. Every so often, there'd be a blanket, or a row of blankets, some with feet sticking out from beneath them, a shoe or shoes missing. On such occasions, the pilots looked at one another and shook their heads, reduced to respectful silence.

You had to admire the fortitude of people carrying on in the face of such carnage.

They found somewhere to park in front of the city walls and walked between the two great bastions onto the upper reaches of Kingsway near the Opera House. Here too, new piles of stone spewed onto the street. Laddie, who hadn't visited for several weeks, was taken aback at the destruction, and the stench of death that now pervaded the place.

They wandered along Kingsway and some of the adjoining, narrower, streets. Several times they had to backtrack, their way blocked by rubble or unexploded bombs. They witnessed harrowing sights and smells, and yet it was the more mundane vignettes that Jack found most affecting: families trying to get on with their lives, their shattered homes and possessions exposed to view from the street.

Even as he cursed himself for intruding on private tragedy, he found it impossible not to look. His self-disgust was fed with feelings of guilt. After all, shouldn't he be up there preventing such destruction?

Eventually, they headed for Upper Barrakka Gardens.

'Fuck me!'

Mike spoke for all of them. The words needed no elaboration or reply. In fact, no-one spoke a complete sentence for the several minutes during which they wandered about the Garden terrace. Sometimes, they pointed and added their own exclamations, but more often than not they stood and stared in silence, trying to make sense of the scene.

Littering Grand Harbour from the breakwater to their left, to the depths of Marsa Creek to their right, and all the creeks in between, were submerged, part submerged and listing wrecks, small and large, naval and civilian, Several were still ablaze, as was the seawater around them. Fire ships stood off, pumping water onto superstructures and into holds, at least one of which, they knew, still held ammunition.

Elsewhere, the mangled jibs of dockside and floating cranes leaned into the water alongside tumbled blocks of stone from bombed out quaysides and warehouses. Wherever there was an undamaged stretch of dock, ships, near-wrecks themselves, were moored alongside. Others were anchored as close to the wharves as possible. All bore the scars of bomb damage. The water was covered in a film of oil and dotted with flotsam.

And yet, little ships still plied this way and that, the boatmen at their oars busy carrying goods or ferrying people. Many passed close by the blazing hulks, even the Talabot, her bows still above the water at the mouth of Marsa Creek.

Did they know what was likely to happen if her cargo exploded?

How could they not? But whether they relied on religious faith or fatalism, Jack supposed life had to go on. If the ship went up, so be it.

He looked at his companions. If they had any sense, surely they'd be somewhere else.

'Well, blow me down. Look what the tides washed in!'

The familiar voice was so out of context that Jack struggled to place it. He turned.

Group Captain Woodhall stood with his hands on his hips, shaking his head and laughing.

'Hello, sir,' Laddie said with genuine enthusiasm as they all snapped to attention and saluted. 'What brings you above ground?'

It was a good question. Although there were other controllers, Jack had rarely, if ever, heard another voice on the R/T. He'd just assumed that Woody controlled singlehandedly from dawn to dusk.

The group captain returned their salutes. 'I do nip into the fresh air every now and then, if only to stop myself turning into a bat!'

It was their turn to laugh.

'I try and get out at least once a day, when there's a lull.'

He suddenly looked very tired. 'Not that there are many of those.'

After a short pause, he raised his right hand, gesturing with the stem of his pipe at the Harbour behind them. 'I don't usually make it this far, but I wanted to see what this morning's raid had done, especially to old Pepperpot over there.'

He pointed across to French Creek.

The pilots turned. Jack had found the whole scene so overwhelming that he'd failed to single out any ship for special scrutiny, except perhaps Talabot, because of her particular menace. But they'd all heard of HMS Penelope, the cruiser that had towed Breconshire into Marsaxlokk Bay. Harry's updates had detailed daily bomb damage, and the sterling defence of her gunners.

Looking over at the ship, it was all too easy to see how she'd gained her nickname. Her hull and superstructure were peppered with gashes and holes from direct hits and the shrapnel of near misses. Perhaps even more striking were the wooden beams protruding at odd angles from many of the holes near the waterline, presumably part of the effort to plug leaks.

It was a surprise to see her afloat at all. Harry had said she was in dry dock, and likely to stay there for some time.

'Not too bad,' they heard the group captain say.

They turned to face him again. Perhaps they all looked as surprised as Jack.

He gave them a wry smile. 'I have to tell you, I feared worse.'

Jack shook his head. It was hard to imagine a much more hellish scene.

The group captain breathed in deeply and stretched. 'Anyway, must be getting back,' he said. Then, as he brought his arms down, a thought seemed to strike him. 'But, as you're here, would you like to see down the hole?'

Tact and diplomacy dictated only one answer. But Jack sensed that Laddie's reply, an enthusiastic, 'Yes please, sir,' reflected the genuine feelings of the whole group.

Jack had often tried to visualise the place from which Woody's voice emanated, the nerve centre of air operations over and around Malta. Now he'd have the opportunity.

They followed the slight figure through the Gardens and round to the right, outside the fence. After zig-zagging down several ramps and goodness knows how many steps, they stopped by a door in a rock wall guarded by an imposing military policeman, pistol at his hip. He threw up a smart salute.

'I've brought a few visitors, Thompkins.'

'Very well, sir,' the corporal said, 'but I'd like to see some ID'.

The words carried not a hint of apology, and were backed up by a couple of gun barrels bristling from letterbox openings in a sandbagged guard post leaning against the wall a few yards behind the Redcap.

'Good man, Thompkins. Of course.'

The group captain gestured, and each of them flourished their IDs. The corporal perused each in turn.

'Very good, sir.'

He directed his words at the group captain, then unlocked and opened the door and stood aside, saluting as they passed. The door closed behind them.

The first thing Jack noticed was the immediate drop in temperature, from low 30s to something much cooler. It was a pleasant change.

The group captain was obviously used to this first impression. 'Cool in summer and relatively warm in winter,' he said, his voice somehow deadened and echoing at the same time, 'so not a bad working environment. By the way, we've come in through the back door, and I'd be grateful if you'd forget about it. It saves some of us time getting in and out, but probably best if not too many people know about it.'

He accepted their nods of agreement, before, with a,

'Follow me,' he set off.

They were in a well-engineered, whitewashed, rock tunnel, 20 or more feet wide and 15 tall. It was lit by lamps equally spaced on a black cable running along the ceiling. As they hugged the left wall, they began to pass compartments of stone to their right. They resembled cells or stables, complete with wooden doors and perspex windows. Most were small and decked out as offices, maps and charts on the walls and camp beds on the floors or leaning against walls.

The last few were larger and better furnished, more like apartments. The signs on the doors indicated why. They were for Vice Admiral Malta, General Officer Commanding, Air Officer Commanding and, finally, the Governor and Commander-in-Chief.

'The high-priced help spend a lot of time down here,' Woody said. 'But not today, it seems. All out on visits.' He smiled, before turning and walking deeper into the rock.

Jack, bringing up the rear, followed Laddie, Mike, Harv and Dave as the path began to descend into a narrower tunnel. After a short while, they emerged into a larger cavern.

Again, it was whitewashed and well lit, and as he moved forward to join the others, he realised they were on a viewing platform, looking down on to what he recognised immediately as an ops room. It was similar to, but unlike any other he'd been in.

They overlooked the plotting room floor with its table. To their right was a controllers' gallery, a stone balcony with a two-tier magistrates bench, behind which sat several officers and NCOs from each service.

On the wall to the pilots' left, opposite the gallery, were an ops room clock, maps and tote boards, detailing, by base and squadron, the assets available: bombers, fighters and recce aircraft; anti-aircraft assets, including ships and searchlight batteries; and army units.

The whitewash and bright lights combined to give it the

feel of an operating theatre.

Smaller tunnels ran off to left and right, and doors opened off the ops room and the controllers' gallery, presumably into other chambers and offices. The whole place was a complete honeycomb.

'Welcome to Fort Lascaris and the air ops room,' the group captain said, waving an arm over the scene. 'I'm sure you're all familiar with the set up, or at least something like it.'

Jack wasn't sure Harv and Dave would be, but they kept shtum, and he decided not to speak on their behalf.

'Good,' the group captain continued. 'As you can see, it's all quiet at the moment. Three Blenheims flew out for Egypt earlier, and there's one PR Spit out and about.'

Jack looked down on the table, similar to the ones in 11 Group, but with Malta centre and range circles radiating out over the sea to Sicily and half of Italy to the north and the coast of North Africa from Cape Bon in the west round to the south. There was one friendly plot over the toe of Italy, an arrow adjacent to it pointing north.

Around the table were a couple of men and half a dozen women, the latter dressed demurely in summer dresses, all with headsets and microphones, three holding croupiers' rakes.

Although there were no WAAFs on the Island, they'd often heard of the women on the staff of the headquarters, some local, but some the wives of soldiers, civil servants and diplomats who'd shunned the chance of evacuation. Apparently, very few were young, free and single, and those that were tended not to stay unattached for long.

Jack was finding it hard to take his eyes off them and realised the group captain was speaking.

'...probably looks closer from the air,' he said, pointing down, 'but even on the map, it looks barely more than spitting distance. Even if they form up over there, we get no more than twenty minutes' warning. But if the 109s come in at sea level, we get none at all, unless they pass close to a ship or an Observer Corps post. Gives us a real headache.'

And us, Jack thought, but he wasn't going to begrudge the controller the opportunity to outline some of his own difficulties.

'You can see from the boards that we're not blessed with assets either, and especially Spitfires.'

Jack strained to read the chalk figures on the daily state boards. Despite recent deliveries, it looked as if only ten Hurricanes and three Spits were serviceable.

It should have been a shock, but it wasn't.

Through enemy action or cannibalization, they'd lost 16 of the 31 Spitfires that had been delivered in the three operations since the 7th of March. Of the bakers' dozen that were unavailable, a few were probably undergoing routine servicing, but the others would undoubtedly be having snags or battle damage repaired.

Once again, the group captain seemed to divine their thoughts. 'I know I don't need to tell you, but every time you get airborne, you come back full of holes.'

Mike, ever the diplomat, voiced what they were all thinking. 'That's because there's ten Hun for every one of us, sir.'

'I know, Mike, I know.' It was said with sympathy. Woody took off his SD hat and ran a hand through his greying hair. 'All I can say for the moment is that the matter is receiving attention at the highest levels.'

'Well, sir, we'd all appreciate it if they could get their fuckin' fingers out.'

Jack wondered whether he should wince or laugh.

The group captain made the decision for him by nodding and chuckling. 'Quite right, young man, quite right. I'll pass the message on to the AOC next time I see him.'

Mike now looked a bit sheepish, which was the cue for the rest of them to laugh.

The group captain looked to the gallery, where someone was trying to gain his attention by waving a piece of paper.

'Excuse me a moment, chaps. I'll try and get back, but

there's not much more I can show you anyway. In the meantime, feel free to hang about and watch proceedings for a while.'

The group captain walked onto the gallery and, after a brief conversation, disappeared through a door to the rear. When, after a few minutes, he failed to return, they turned their attention to the ops room below.

Leaning over the balcony, they watched the odd hostile plot being placed on the table over Sicily, but none of these approached Malta before being raked off again.

Try as he might, Jack couldn't help watching the female plotters and their assistants. All were slim, attractive and in their mid-20s, he guessed. Four wore wedding rings. His companions were also admiring them, and he could tell that the women were used to the attention. Not that they courted it in any way. Quite the opposite. They never looked at or gave an indication that they were anything other than indifferent to their audience.

And also, try as he might, Jack was unable to prevent himself drifting into the odd erotic daydream, his conscience assuaged only by the fact that although the plotters were the catalyst, Caroline remained the sole object of his fantasies.

After about 20 minutes with little happening on the table, he was beginning to feel too voyeuristic. So he wasn't disappointed when Laddie coughed and said, 'Pleasant as this is, chaps, I think it's about time we were off.'

He was right. It was 5.30 and they didn't want to be weaving through craters and rubble after dark. But just then the group captain reappeared on the gallery and took a seat in the centre of the front row, vacated by a wing commander.

He pointed down at the table and shouted across, 'Might want to hang on a few moments, chaps.'

They looked down to see a plot being raked onto the table over the south-east coast of Sicily.

'We think this could be the evening raid, and I'd hate to think of you blundering about up there if it's headed this way.'

Jack couldn't have agreed more, especially when he squinted down on the plaque. It showed 100 plus, and the red course arrow corresponding to the red five minute sweep of the ops room clock pointed straight at Malta. Which part of Malta, of course, they wouldn't know for some time, but the RAF fighters would have to be launched soon if they were to make height and confront the raid.

As the minutes ticked by, the group captain chatted constantly to the Army and Navy officers to his left and right, but never once reached for the direct lines to the stations. You could see the anguish on his face.

To launch, or not to launch?

Jack didn't envy him the decision. Risk the few Hurricanes and Spitfires he had, or let the bombers through to be opposed only by flak? One of the determinants, impossible to know as yet, would be just how many 109s were hidden in the hostile plot.

As it moved south south-west, it split in two. One element, estimated to be 50 at 25,000 feet, pulled ahead as the course arrows changed from red, to yellow and to blue. It was nearing St Paul's Bay when he heard one of the plotters confirm that all 50 were 109s.

Jack thought the controller could have allowed himself a moment of self-congratulation for not sending his pilots into a trap, but he looked no less anguished.

The remaining plot, now estimated to be 100 at 15,000 feet was also nearing St Paul's Bay. Although nothing was said, the likelihood was that they were mainly bombers. One hundred and fifty German aircraft were roaming above the Island, so far unopposed.

There was a grim fascination in watching the situation unfold, waiting to see what target or targets would be hit. After a few tense minutes, Jack felt tremors, slight at first, but growing in frequency and intensity until he was sure he could hear muted explosions.

The vibration and noise increased. Nowhere near the intensity they'd experienced in G Shelter at Luqa or the slit trenches at Takali, but enough to make the walls shake. Finally, there could be no doubt that some of the explosions were right overhead, which meant that not only the harbour, but the city and its inhabitants were receiving another pummelling.

The group captain sat with his fists clenched. He acknowledged messages from either side, even cracked an unconvincing smile when a beaming Army officer leaned across, perhaps to tell of a bomber hit by flak. But, mostly, he looked sombre.

Once again, Jack began to feel like a voyeur, this time witnessing the pain of someone he knew and respected. He'd always felt that their flippant characterisation of controllers as unfeeling types sending pilots out on a whim was wide of the mark. Now, he knew it.

He also knew he'd much rather be in the air risking his own life than sending others into harm's way.

The bombing eventually stopped, or at least moved away. After several minutes, when all but a few plots were heading back for Sicily, an airman appeared.

'Group Captain's regards, sirs, but he says he's going to be tied up for quite a while. He thinks this may be the best time for you to get away, so he's asked me to show you out.'

The controller looked their way, smiled and waved. They waved back and turned to follow their guide.

As the back door was opened, Jack felt the increase in temperature, but also caught the whiff of explosives. Laddie acknowledged the salute of the policeman and they walked out into an atmosphere full of dust and smoke. Looking around, they regained the path and started to climb. Jack began to cough.

They were getting an inkling of what it was like to live

within the miasma they were used to seeing from the terrace.

At times, the smoke cleared enough to give a glimpse of the harbour, but not enough for them to assess the damage. That the city had suffered became more apparent as they regained the entrance to the Barrakka Gardens.

Within the limits of visibility, which often reduced to less than 20 yards, there was rubble everywhere, and the smoke, dust and stench of cordite had thickened to the point where they'd taken out handkerchiefs to cover their noses and dab their eyes, constantly assailed by ash and black smuts.

'I think we'll head straight for the car,' Laddie said, dowsing any thoughts of turning aside to look into the harbour again.

'Okay,' was the general refrain. Otherwise, they carried on in silence. More people began to appear, looking about them, trying to get their bearings. Most hurried on, presumably rushing home to see what damage had been done.

They stepped over and around mounds of stone debris from newly collapsed walls. The façade of a large palace to their right had collapsed. Smoke rose from within. But the worst shock was yet to come.

Fifty yards further on, the road was nearly blocked by a huge pile of stone. It had fallen from a building to the left of the street which seemed to be missing its roof.

It was the Opera House.

As they began to squeeze past the pile, the dust cleared enough to reveal that the route ahead was impassable, blocked by the remains of huge columns. They retraced their steps to walk round the back of the building, down its other side and into the very top of Kingsway.

A crowd had gathered. They stared into the broken heart of the Opera House. Many women sobbed openly, and even some of the men surreptitiously dabbed at their eyes and cheeks. Through the dust, they could just see the crimson and gold remains of the rear balconies and their upholstery. More fragments of crimson and gold peeped out below, and there was the odd glint of crystal glass. Everything else was buried in the debris beneath the remaining walls.

There was no urgency. The scale of the clearance effort was too monumental for the few onlookers to have any hope of making a difference, and there were no obvious casualties. Anyway, they all seemed to be in a state of shock.

After a few moments, the pilots turned their backs and made their way into Floriana.

Chapter 16 – Mid April – No Let-Up

The morning of Wednesday 8th April was one of immense frustration. Although the Maltese in Valletta the previous day had been unfailingly polite, Jack could tell they were desperate for the pilots – him - to act against the bombers pummelling their island to dust. You could see it in their eyes.

Out of the experience was born a simmering anger at not being able to get airborne and defend them. It was a long way from the fear of combat with which he'd arrived on the Island. And once again he was sure it was because his personal contribution was needed, vital even.

So, to sit inactive while yet more bombs fell on Valletta – not to mention Takali itself - was mortifying. Not one aircraft was available until mid-day, when three were declared serviceable. For the next hour, Jack sat in one, baking and uncomfortable, swatting away flies, eager to do his bit. But the call never came.

And then, to add insult to injury, as A flight drove away soon after 1pm, the three available Spitfires flew overhead, heading south.

That night, they heard from Larry Lloyd about B Flight's afternoon, and a lucky escape he'd witnessed.

Larry looked much better than the last time Jack had seen him, laid low by the Dog. Now, he stood in the bar, pint in hand, surrounded by most of the A Flight officers, plus a few of his own flight who either hadn't heard the full tale, or hadn't tired of it.

'Mid-afternoon,' Larry began in his cut glass accent, 'we launched against a raid of eighty big jobs plus escorts. There were three of us and nine Hurris, but we'd only made about eight thousand by the time the Hun began diving over the harbour. Nothing for it but to have at them, so we did just that, by which time the barrage had opened up.'

He took a swig of beer and wiped the corners of his

mouth delicately with ring finger and thumb.

'I was sitting to Nip's right glancing across, when all of a sudden his kite exploded – kaboom!'

An expressive hand gesture caused beer to slop over the rim of his glass. He grimaced, swapped hands and licked the beer off his fingers, before carrying on.

'It just blew up and broke apart. As I raced past, I actually saw Nip shoot into the air like a human cannonball.'

He paused briefly to let the picture sink in.

'I just assumed he was a goner. There seemed no way he could have survived. But just before we left the airfield we heard that he'd landed under his brolly in Floriana. Cut up and bruised, but very much alive when they carted him off to Imtarfa.

'Bloody miracle if you ask me.'

Jack had to agree. It was miraculous. But it also left them another aircraft down. A feeling of pessimism washed over him, a mood the IntO's evening briefing on the terrace did little to dispel.

Harry gestured toward the group of A Flight pilots. 'I think some of you witnessed the aftermath of yesterday's raids on Valletta - the destruction in the harbour and the loss of the Opera House.'

They nodded.

'Well, I'm afraid it was more of the same today. The whole harbour area took a real pasting, and Kingston was hit again. Larry told you about Nip Heppel, but weighed against the loss of his kite, between B Flight, the Hurris and the gunners, we bagged about a dozen.'

The young intelligence officer looked disappointed that the score failed to generate much enthusiasm. After a short pause, he continued.

'And finally, HMS Pepperpot has weighed anchor and is making a dash for Gibraltar.'

There were a few whistles of astonishment. No-one was more surprised than Jack. He couldn't believe something with so many holes could be considered seaworthy.

And as if her doubtful seaworthiness wasn't enough, Harry added a sinister postscript. 'Unfortunately, the Hun spotted her departing, so she can expect a rough passage. And because of the lack of kites, we can't provide her with top cover. I think all we can do is wish her God's speed.'

Jack was far from convinced that God would intervene on the cruiser's behalf, but he joined in the chorus of nods.

Thursday's rest day saw more heavy raids on the harbour and the airfields, including Takali, but also on the surrounding villages.

The Maltese had long been convinced the Germans were targeting their beloved churches. Late in the afternoon, further evidence was forthcoming when the huge dome of Mosta Church was pierced by a 500kg bomb – during a service. The bomb bounced off a wall, skidded along the floor and came to a standstill, all without inflicting so much as a scratch on any of the 300 astonished worshippers.

A passing member of 249's groundcrew witnessed the congregation making a quick exit. He then mucked in to help soldiers roll the bomb from the building and onto the back of a truck. For his pains, he was hit in the leg by a piece of shrapnel during another attack on the village.

Elsewhere on the Island, miracles were in short supply, with many civilian casualties, including 25 killed when two shelters in Valletta took direct hits.

The morning of Friday 10th April was another period of frustrating inaction. Jack boiled during two hour-long stints of cockpit readiness, but, once again, only B Flight saw any action when they launched to meet a late afternoon raid.

During the day, two Hurricanes were shot down, three crash landed and one was damaged, as was one of their Spitfires.

On Saturday, Jack and Mike managed to borrow a couple of

bikes and rode to the Dingli Cliffs and back. Occasionally, pedalling along dusty tracks in the middle of nowhere, they were able to savour a feeling of solitude and tranquillity. But the frequent sight and sound of distant bombing meant these didn't last long. German aircraft seemed to have complete control of the skies, roaming at will.

They arrived back at the Palace in time to witness a raid on Takali. Later, they found out it had damaged a further two Spitfires and a Hurricane. And HMS Kingston had finally received a mortal wound and rolled onto her side, adding another wreck to the harbour.

Increasingly, electricity and water supplies were disrupted, telephone lines were down and the Rediffusion system, so vital for getting messages around the Island, was out of commission. Thinking back, Jack couldn't recall hearing its tinny wail during the afternoon they'd spent in Valletta.

On Sunday 12th April, A Flight swapped to the afternoon shift.

After lunch and before driving to the airfield, they were told to report to the terrace. A few minutes later, AOC Malta appeared, accompanied by the AOC-in-C Middle East, Air Marshal Tedder. Apparently, he was there to see the plight of the Island and its defenders for himself.

No sooner had he started to shake a few hands than the sound of aero engines and gunfire drifted up from Takali. Opposed only by airfield gunners and small arms fire from soldiers and groundcrew, six 109s criss-crossed the airfield, strafing, raising clouds of dust and starting small fires.

After about five minutes, they climbed toward Mdina. Everyone on the terrace donned tin hats and watched the fighters approach. No-one flinched, but Jack could sense the doubt in the Air Marshal's mind.

Were they about to become a target?

He'd had the same thought. It wouldn't be the first time. But the 109s flashed overhead and made for Sicily, leaving an eerie silence in their wake.

Jack was delighted. If the air marshal needed a flavour of life on Malta, he'd just had it.

They heard later that the C-in-C was treated to similar demonstrations at every location he visited during the day. He was strafed at Hal Far, and witnessed the havoc wrought by another heavy bombing raid on Luqa. A Wellington burnt out before his very eyes, a graphic illustration of why offensive ops from Malta had all but ceased.

And as he watched everyone mucking in to fill holes and rebuild shelters, he was rumoured to have said, with great emotion, that he now understood *the spirit of Malta*.

They could only hope that his understanding translated into fresh resources.

Jack didn't fly; no-one on A Flight did. But they spent a fair amount of time in slit trenches as Takali was bombed several times. Between raids, the Army worked tirelessly to keep the airfield open. Another Spitfire was damaged.

249 Squadron spent most of Monday at St Paul's Bay, from where they saw little air activity. It was a quieter day over most of the Island. Notwithstanding this, Luqa was put out of action for a while by a well aimed bomb in the centre of the main runway. Takali was also heavily cratered.

Tuesday the 14th dawned cold and cloudy. For the first time in weeks, Jack huddled on the terrace in his blue jacket, caressing his tea. His eyelids drooped. He still found it impossible to sleep through the sound of guns and bombs, which meant he had precious little sleep most nights. If anything, his catnaps, which probably lasted no more than a few seconds, added to his tiredness. Just before 11am, he witnessed a raid on the airfield.

He assumed the three Spitfires he'd seen immediately afterwards had been sent after the raiders. But when A Flight arrived at the shed just before one o'clock, they discovered that the aircraft had actually been sent to escort a departing photo-recce Maryland. Inevitably, they'd been bounced, and although Ned Kelly had nailed one of the attackers, he'd been shot down, landing in the sea, from where he'd been picked up by a launch.

Two more Spitfires took off as the story was being related, this time to escort a returning Maryland. Both aircraft landed with several bullet holes. They'd met the twin-engined aircraft just as it was being set upon by a Schwarm of 109s, one of which the Spitfires sent into the sea. A section of Hurricanes then joined the party, and between them they damaged the other three Hun, which high-tailed it back to Sicily.

The story geed up the A Flight pilots, but they quickly realised that not many of them would have the chance to fly. Only two kites were serviceable, and these remained unused, even though there were several raids on the airfield, the final one blocking the runway.

That evening, Mal Cotrell reappeared in the mess after a few days at St Paul's Bay. He was walking remarkably well, with only the odd wince revealing that he might be in some discomfort. All questions about Nurse Dingli were deflected, but his blushes spoke volumes.

Soon, they were all in high spirits. A mail consignment had arrived. Jack devoured a fortnight's worth of letters from Caroline, beginning the day he'd left Gibraltar. Although they were nearly a month out of date and full of trivia, they made his heart leap.

For the next three days, a cold northerly wind brought low cloud and poor visibility. As a result, there was little enemy air activity, and the Spitfires remained on the ground. Whenever the opportunity arose, Jack read and re-read Caroline's letters.

He'd seen people in films sniffing such correspondence, and had always thought it a fanciful notion, something he would never contemplate. Now, however, he often put the paper of her letters to his nose. The scent, whether real or imagined, helped to clarify the image of her he'd been finding increasingly difficult to conjure.

The airfield was abuzz with activity.

The Army seemed to be everywhere, repairing airfield surfaces, building aircraft shelters and slit trenches, and laying new tracks.

On the RAF side, groundcrew took the chance to work on the remaining kites unhindered by constant raids, or pilots flying their charges off to an uncertain fate. Several times, Jack tracked down Smudger. Each time, he found the rigger and his fellow tradesmen battling against the lack of spares and equipment. Wrecks had already been stripped of anything useful, so, increasingly, they had to cannibalise damaged aircraft, effectively writing them off until new spares appeared.

There was little time for idle chatter, but Jack was relieved when Smudger confirmed that he too had received a fistful of letters, and that all was well at home – or had been a month earlier.

Station personnel worked with renewed purpose, fashioning accommodation from buildings that had been abandoned, salvaging and making furnishings to go in them and adding new facilities. Clusters of tents sprang up around the perimeter, as did new latrines and ablutions.

Apparently, there were similar levels of activity on all the airfields, and in surrounding villages, where more tents appeared close to buildings that had been commandeered to provide accommodation.

The pilots mucked in as required and ruminated on the reason for all the activity.

On Thursday, the grapevine began to hum with at least a hint of what was afoot.

One immediate outcome of the AOC-in-C's visit on the 12th had been the despatch of Jumbo Gracie to London to make the Island's case for more fighter reinforcements. No-one could think of a better, or at least a more forceful man for the job than OC 126. But they also wondered how long it would be before he punched some Air Ministry civil servant or staff officer he judged to be giving the issue less priority than it deserved.

Now, in less than a week, the wording of a signal he'd sent to Valletta had become the subject of widespread gossip. It seemed that *something big* was in the offing. It was hard to believe that even Jumbo could have had such an immediate effect, but the general assumption was that *something big* could only be another delivery of Spitfires.

That evening, on the terrace of the Mess, Woody Woodhall confirmed the rumour. A new consignment would arrive in the next few days.

'Until then,' he said, looking anything other than apologetic, 'I'm afraid you'll all be pitching in, whether it's your duty day or not, although those who should have been on stand-down needn't arrive until eight.'

He smiled at the grunts of mock gratitude.

'And while I'm at it,' he continued,' I might as well confirm two other stories, one good and one bad.'

Jack was certain he knew what the good news was, but he was mystified about the bad. Other faces betrayed the same puzzlement.

'Firstly, this morning's announcement in the Times of Malta is spot on. His Majesty the King has awarded Malta the George Cross.'

Jack hadn't doubted the veracity of the story, but now it had been confirmed by an even more unimpeachable source than the Island newspaper.

'That, I'm sure, comes as no surprise,' the group captain continued. 'But, the Governor is determined that the Islanders are left in no doubt that the medal is for them. Not for us, or the Navy, or the Army, but for the ordinary Maltese civilians.'

He looked at them with steely conviction. 'And I don't think there's a person in this room that would begrudge them the accolade.'

This time, the grunts were of assent, heartfelt and

sincere.

'Good, so please make sure you convey the Governor's message at every opportunity.'

He took a draw on his pipe, as if considering how to proceed.

'The news you may not have heard is less welcome. His Majesty's Submarine Upholder has been missing for three days. The assumption must be that she's lost with all hands.'

He looked over the faces.

Only the newer arrivals were unlikely to have heard of the boat and her captain.

'For those that may not know, she was the Tenth Submarine Flotilla's most successful boat, responsible for sending thousands of tons of supplies to the bottom, as well as a couple of U-boats. And with all hands means thirty officers and men, including her CO, Lieutenant Commander David Wanklyn, a VC holder and one of the most gallant and dedicated officers you could ever wish to meet.'

Jack knew him only by reputation, but it was quite a reputation. The Navy would be feeling a great hurt.

'Of course,' the group captain continued, 'it means the Island's offensive capability has taken another knock. Which is why it's vital that we do all we can to prepare for the arrival of these reinforcements. Only when they're operational will we be able to set about regaining control of the skies and re-starting the air offensive against Rommel's supply lines.'

It was a hope they all shared.

If almost everyone on the Island knew that a reinforcement of Spitfires was imminent, it was hard to believe that Kesselring didn't. But how would he react? The weather certainly wouldn't hinder any plans he might have. The wind had swung round to the south, and Saturday the 18th was a day of clear blue skies.

While 249 Squadron pilots toiled in the hot sun building

shelters, their counterparts on 126 took it in turns to fry in the cockpits of the few Spitfires available: three in the morning rising to four in the afternoon.

Meanwhile, waves of 88s and Stukas passed through the overhead. A few dived on Takali, but most carried on to other targets, including Luqa, from the direction of which a particularly loud explosion was heard in the late afternoon. A tall mushroom cloud rose over the airfield as more thumps and bangs reached their ears. They found out that evening that the commotion was the result a direct hit on an ammunition dump.

Despite, or perhaps because of the frequent raids, Woody held his fighters - Spitfires and Hurricanes - on the ground, presumably saving them for the protection of the Spitfire delivery, whenever that was to be.

In a graphic illustration of the Island's plight, after five days of almost uninterrupted effort by the groundcrew of two squadrons, only six Spitfires were serviceable on the 19th. Late in the day, 126 ferried three of these to Luqa, from where they would now be operating. The Hurricane force received a boost with the arrival at Hal Far of another six aircraft and pilots from Egypt.

Three large raids were mounted during the day, each meandering over a range of targets, including the airfields. 249 maintained cockpit readiness throughout, Jack's flight now back on the morning shift. Once again, no fighters were launched in anger, the attackers being confronted by flak alone.

Although there were frequent visits to shelters and slit trenches, activity on the airfield had, if anything, become even more frantic. And as the pilots were leaving in the late evening, they passed Bedford trucks and buses driving onto the station with fresh troops.

That night, after dinner, the officers were joined by the NCOs from Rabat. They were furnished with beer before they all climbed to the terrace. After a brief conversation with the CO, Harry stepped forward to brief them.

'I'm delighted to tell you that Operation Calendar should deliver about fifty...' – there were gasps.

Harry glanced at Squadron Leader Grant, his face creasing into a wide smile. 'Yes, *fifty* Spitfires, at around ten o'clock tomorrow morning.'

Unless the Royal Navy was risking three aircraft carriers in the Mediterranean, the most recent rumours must have been true. The Spitfires were to fly off an American carrier.

As if reading their minds, Harry continued. 'USS Wasp.'

Harv Johnson, Kim Kaminski and Luke Elliott looked especially pleased, smiling broadly at the nods of approval aimed their way.

'The plan is for half to land at Takali and half at Luqa, hence all the work on both airfields. And again, if all goes to plan, we hope to have as many as possible airborne within 90 minutes.'

'Better than the three friggin' days it took last time.'

The company broke into laughter at another of Mike's pithy one-liners.

Harry looked at the CO, as if offering him the opportunity to admonish the New Zealander, or at least call the room to order. But the squadron leader was laughing with the rest of them.

The IntO stroked his wispy moustache. 'Quite. Very true.' He waited a few moments, before continuing. 'And also, this time, it's formed squadrons that are flying in: 603 to Takali, 601 to Luqa.'

That made sense - if the squadrons were up to it, which they'd soon find out. Jack knew little of the recent pedigree of either squadron, although he'd heard of both.

601'County of London' Squadron had been the most famous of the Auxiliary Squadrons at the start of the war – known as *The Millionaires*. It had formed around a core of wealthy aristocrats and City types who wore non-standard uniform – royal blue ties and bright red jacket linings – and looked on regular and volunteer reserve pilots with disdain.

His own 646 Squadron had once been similar in composition and outlook. But such attitudes hadn't survived long during the Battle of Britain, when losses were high and replacement pilots came from a wide range of backgrounds and countries. Now, the auxiliary squadrons were barely indistinguishable from any other unit of the line, although the squadron bound for Takali, 603 'City of Edinburgh' Squadron, was commanded by a lord of the realm.

Apart from that, all Jack knew about them was that they'd forged a good reputation while operating out of Hornchurch during the Battle.

This time, when Harry looked to his right, the CO nodded his thanks and stepped forward. He stood, face sombre, striking swift eye contact with each of his pilots in turn. Jack straightened, sensing those round about him do the same.

'Right then, chaps. There it is. I don't need to tell you how important it is that all this goes smoothly. Eventually, the kites will be split equally between us and 603, the same going for 126 and 601 at Luqa. But, while the new arrivals settle in, we need to be prepared to shoulder the bulk of the burden, especially tomorrow.

'So, at least for the next few days, there'll be no more day-on day-off, or split shifts. It's going to be all hands to the pumps. We need to get as many kites as we can into the air as soon as we can. Let's see if we can't turn this ship around and start giving the Hun a bloody nose for a change.'

Now, the squadron leader paused, looking from man to man, as if gauging the tenor of his troops. As he'd spoken, Jack had felt not only a sense of heightened responsibility, but also a determination not to let down the CO, his fellow pilots and, more importantly, the Islanders.

Chapter 17 – Monday April 20th– New Hope

The sound was unmistakable. Merlins. Lots of them. Jack's heart raced. At last, they were getting the tools to do the job.

He looked at his watch: 10am. All around, pilots groaned as they lifted themselves from the chairs in which they'd been lounging, batting away flies. He smiled. Like a bunch of old men. But it was marvellous to be surrounded by so many, a whole squadron rather than a flight. More like the Battle of Britain.

For once, no-one was absent with the Dog, and even Mal had been declared fit. So they numbered 21, a few shy of a full complement as they'd received only two replacements following the loss of Pat Olsen, Pete Jones, Dougie Leggo and Kibec. Until the new airframes were ready though, they'd still have to fight for a mount. Takali could field only three serviceable kites.

They turned to look into the south-west. A few hundred feet above the ridge to the south of Mdina, a whole squadron of single-engine fighters was silhouetted against bright blue sky. They came on, looking and sounding magnificent. But…there was a caveat.

Buck was the first to speak. 'Must think they're at friggin' Hendon!'

Twelve Spitfires, four immaculate vics in tight line astern, approached the overhead, as if providing a fly past at a pre-war air show. Then and there, it would have been impressive. But here and now…?

Thank goodness the skies were free of 109s. They'd have had a field day.

The naivety of the tactics had taken the edge off Jack's initial excitement. It begged several questions. How long since 603 Squadron had been on the front line, and how experienced were its pilots?

At the least, a fair dollop of re-education looked on the cards.

Inexperience was also writ large in the tightness of the

formation landing on an unfamiliar dirt strip littered with craters, wrecks and unexploded bombs. The dust cloud kicked up by the first three Spitfires blinded those following closely behind. Several shot sideways out of the dust to rumble across the airfield. Jack winced as they passed perilously close to hazards of one sort or another.

A few minutes later, they'd reformed and, ungainly overload tanks nestling between their undercarriage legs, they taxied toward the blast pens around the western perimeter. Thinly spread, 249's airmen rushed to meet them. They'd secured a few extra tradesmen, but there were precious few on the Island. The sooner the new squadron's own groundcrew arrived, the better. It was another reason a convoy was desperately needed.

At least all the aircraft – Mk VCs, with two cannon and two machine guns on each wing – had been pre-fitted with Vokes filters. Their fuselages and upper surfaces had also been painted dark blue; blotchy and uneven, but an improvement on desert camouflage. It would do until someone found the time to apply a coat of blue-grey, if they ever bothered.

The Station Commander arrived and he and OC 249 walked into the pen that had swallowed up the formation leader. A few moments later, they emerged with a tall, dark-haired man in his mid to late 20s. It could only be OC 603, Squadron Leader Lord David Douglas Hamilton, the youngest of four aristocratic brothers, all RAF pilots who either were, or had been, squadron commanders.

Jack went to a pre-assigned pen to greet one of the new arrivals. He waited patiently while a sandy-haired pilot officer, Mae West over blue uniform jacket, unwound himself from the cockpit and stretched, then massaged his back and rubbed his backside.

Dinghy bottle, Jack thought.

He stepped forward but, with an apologetic wave, dropped from the wing and dashed over to the wall of the pen. After an emergency pee, he returned, smiling and holding out a hand, which Jack declined. They laughed, while completing their introductions. The youngster's name was Steve 'Danny' Danvers.

Then they laughed at the groundcrew. Once again, the ammunition boxes of all bar two of the machine guns had been filled with cigarettes, and retrieving these was taking priority over all other activities; although, to be fair, the cigarettes had to be out before the armourers could get to work.

Still shaking his head, Danny climbed up to retrieve his headset, parachute and a small kitbag, which Jack took before the young man jumped down again. They'd just walked out of the pen when the sound of more Merlins had them looking into the south-west. This time it was a formation of 11, the third element a pair rather than a vic.

'Must have lost one,' Danny said, squinting up with a pained expression.

'We were told to expect about fifty,' Jack said, not wishing to speculate on the many possibilities for disaster involved in a carrier launch and a four hour sea crossing.

'Should have been, but with fuel snags and the like, we were down to forty seven first thing this morning. Looks like forty six now – at best.'

Again, Jack saw no point in speculating, so they stood and watched another tight formation circuit and landing, all bar the leaders disappearing in a dust cloud as soon as they touched down.

'You'll learn to leave a bit more space when it's dusty like today,' Jack said, trying not to sound overly critical.

'Yes, it was a bit hairy,' Danny said, 'especially as I've only just got the hang of landing the damn thing anyway.'

That seemed to answer the question about experience for at least one of the new pilots. Jack decided not to press the issue, but held his arm out toward the shed, around which a larger than usual cluster of pilots was forming.

The next hour was very similar to that following his arrival just over six weeks earlier, only now, they were the ones trying to ease the new boys in and let them know the score, without overwhelming or scaring the life out of them.

There seemed to be no explanation for the missing man from the second formation, a young American NCO with a penchant for hypnotism. After a brief foray into cloud early in their transit, the leader of the third vic had found himself with only one wingman. No-one, not even those in the rear vic, had witnessed Sergeant Walcott's disappearance.

Perhaps he'd turned back with a problem and made landfall. The alternatives didn't bear thinking about, which didn't stop Jack imagining one: a lonely and lingering death bobbing about the ocean in a dinghy.

At least the Luftwaffe was playing ball. After a heavy raid on Valletta first thing, the skies had remained remarkably quiet. So they sat in the sun waiting for transport to drive the newcomers to the other side to complete arrival admin. Thereafter, the plan was to take them to the Xara Palace to settle in prior to a briefing that evening from the AOC.

Just before 11am, further formations of 12 and 11 respectively passed to the south, bound for Luqa. So, 46 it was.

Jack waved and the bus set off with a squeal of clashing gears. He walked into the shed and popped his head into the small office where Laddie, Buck and Flight Lieutenant Norm Macqueen, a stalwart of B Flight and a fellow Welshman, were squashed around a small table.

'They're off, Laddie,' he said.

'Thanks, Jack. Come on in and shut the door,'

Laddie waved him into the cramped space. There was no other chair, so Jack leaned against the door post.

That it was him rather than Pete Brown that had been called in was a bit of a mystery, especially as the flight lieutenant was sitting outside keeping himself to himself, as usual. Perhaps Laddie had concerns about him too. No way of knowing without asking, though. Anyway, Pete was out there and he was in here.

Laddie interrupted this jumble of thoughts. 'I've just been saying to the others,' he began, running a hand over his neatly brushed hair, 'it beggars belief. Half of 603 have less than twenty five hours on Spits. And,' his voice rose in incredulity, 'nine of them have never flown on ops. What experience there was, was posted away before they sent them here. Madness!'

Jack shook his head in concert with the others, and Laddie continued.

'I know their CO, and he's a cracking chap, but he'd be the first to admit that even he lacks operational pedigree. He was an instructor until he took command at Christmas, and it's only in the last month that he's flown a couple of ops over France.'

'Which is more than can be said of one of his senior flight lieutenants,' Buck jumped in. 'He came straight here from a desk.'

Jack now knew he was being taken into a special confidence. Laddie and Buck would never have spoken so bluntly about the new squadron's CO and one of his senior flight lieutenants in open forum.

Norm Macqueen was, like Jack, taking it all in, but, as yet, saying nothing.

Laddie sighed, before continuing in a more sanguine tone. 'Oh well. There it is. The bottom line is we'll just have to get on with it. OC 603 has agreed that the most sensible thing would be for them to fly with us for the first few sorties, at least until a nucleus of them learn the form.'

Jack got the impression Laddie was about to elaborate, and maybe explain why he and Norm were there. But Buck pointed past him through the glass top of the door.

'Chiefy's on his way, Laddie,' he said. 'And he doesn't look best pleased.'

Jack turned. The flight sergeant was stern of face, forage cap balanced precariously on the side of his head, defying gravity. He walked up to the door and knocked.

'Come in, Flight,' Laddie said.

The NCO opened the door. Jack had moved to one side, but there was still no room for him actually to *come in*, so he halted on the threshold and saluted.

'Sorry, sir, bad news I'm afraid.'

'Luckily we're used to that, Flight. What is it?'

'Not sure when I'm going to be able to give you the first kite, sir. Not in ninety minutes, that's for sure.'

It was already over an hour since the first formation had landed, but Laddie looked concerned rather than angry. They knew full well that if there was any way the groundcrew could produce the goods, they would.

'What's the problem?' he said.

'Well, to start with, sir, most of the radios are u/s. Some just haven't been set to the right frequencies, but others are just u/s. We'll probably have to rob some of our own kites to get them up and running.'

He paused, giving the flight commander chance to interject. Laddie remained silent, face still etched with concern.

'And then there's the guns, sir. I'm not sure most of 'em have been looked at since the kites were re-built and put on the carrier. Certainly haven't been cleaned or calibrated.'

He paused, twitching his smart pencil moustache, then continued. 'I won't bore you with the rest of the snags, sir, but working on them has taken men I need to do all the other things - remove the overload tanks, refuel and...'

The man could not have looked more contrite, as if taking personal responsibility for all the problems with which his troops were battling.

'Okay, Flight,' Laddie jumped in. 'We get the picture. We also know that it's not your fault.'

He looked at Jack and the other two. They nodded their assent.

The flight sergeant nodded back in gratitude. 'Thank you, sirs. All I can say is that we'll give you what we can as soon as we can.'

'Thanks, Flight. Just let us know when they come up.'

'Will do, sir.' He saluted, about turned and walked away.

Laddie watched him leave the building, then shook his head and turned to them. 'There's got to be a better way of doing this.'

At 12.30, Lascaris were on the blower to order maximum effort against a large plot forming up over Sicily. Maximum effort turned out to be just three VCs alongside the three VBs already declared. With 34 Spitfires now on the airfield, Woody must have thought it a pretty poor show.

Jack, at least, was delighted. He was amongst the six chosen to fly and found himself strapping into one of the VCs. There was something about four cannon thrusting forward of the wings that made him feel ready to face anything.

The wind was a brisk easterly, so it was a short taxy to the edge of the strip. He waited for the dust cloud to thin following the departure of Buck, Larry, Norm and the Rhodesian, Smitty Smyth. Then he nodded at JC, to his right, opened the throttle and led them both into the air.

It was nearly three weeks since he'd flown - another flight that had ended badly - and yet he felt no fear, only elation as he raised the undercarriage and turned hard right to cut the corner, climbing to the south. Tucked in beneath him, JC's Spitfire flashed above the fields, walls and buildings beyond the airfield boundary.

'Buck, this is Woody, twenty little jobs over Gozo, sweeping ahead.'

'Roger, Woody.'

Jack pictured the group captain, peering from the gallery onto the plotting table. One day, perhaps there'd be a way of giving them the same picture in their cockpits. Until then, they'd have to rely on the chain of RDF, Observer Corps, plotters and controller to relay information as best they could.

A minute or so later, Jack throttled back a smidge to sit about 300 yards behind Buck's finger 4, JC easing out to 100 yards. It was probably the clearest day on which he'd flown, not a cloud in the sky.

Framed against the deep blue, JC's machine, another VC, looked stunning, metal and perspex glinting in the sunlight. Jack had become so used to Vokes filters that they now seemed to intrude on the aircraft's clean lines not one jot. Even as he swivelled his head in a systematic search for enemy fighters, he found himself smiling.

He didn't want to analyse the absence of fear – and his tic - too closely lest it lead to a relapse. Better just to make the most of it.

'Buck, this is Woody, fifty big jobs plus escort, passing Comino, angels one seven.'

'Roger, Woody, Tiger Green coasting out, angels ten.'

'Roger, Buck, turning you in shortly. Eyes peeled for the free hunters.'

Jack dipped his left wing. Delimara Point and Marsaxlokk Bay were just behind, nothing but ocean to the front. They were passing 15,000 feet when Woody turned them about. In the turn, Jack looked down on Malta.

It seemed noticeably browner, dustier, than when he'd last flown. The airfields also seemed to stand out more clearly. It was partly familiarity, but partly that they'd had so much work done on them, so much soil turned and rock hewn to repair damage, lay new strips and build pens. Even Safi and the much smaller strip being constructed on the south-west coast at Krendi were clearly visible.

And of course, if *he* could see them so easily, so could the Germans. None was more than five miles apart, with the harbours, the only other targets of note, also within spitting distance. It was a tiny area on which to drop so many bombs, and over which to fight.

As usual, the Island disappeared as soon as he rolled out pointing north. In the distance, Sicily, but he looked at it for no more than a few moments before concentrating on the airspace around the aircraft to his front, and JC, now out to his left.

They were approaching Delimara again at 20,000 feet when a Rhodesian voice rasped, 'Bandits twelve o'clo...'

Jack saw only one 109, closing rapidly on the aircraft to the right of the finger 4. It fired. The Spitfire rolled left. Its right wingtip rose to strike the German, slicing his right wing clean off at the root. The remaining airframe veered toward Jack, flicking into a mad rotation and bursting into flame. Even as he gasped in horror, the flailing fireball flashed between him and JC.

Tracer arced in from the right. He rolled toward it. A dark shape passed behind. He rolled back to the left and pulled, straining against the g. JC was turning left beneath him. Far below, two aircraft were spinning toward the sea over Marsaxlokk Bay. Otherwise, nothing. The 109s and the remaining three aircraft of Green Section had disappeared.

Poor old Larry.

'Buck, big jobs over Takali, angels one seven.'

'Roger, Woody. Larry's going down over Delimara.'

'Woody, Larry here...'- the voice was breathy, scared – 'heading for Takali.'

Jack was astonished. How...?

'Roger, Larry. I'll tell them to expect you.'

Jack whispered, 'Good luck,' while rolling right to chase the invisible Buck, Norm and Smitty toward Takali. JC appeared on his left again. They exchanged nods and a thumbs-up.

The airfield was beneath a blossoming barrage. The gunners were rumoured to be rationed to 15 shells a day, but it didn't look like it. Human nature, Jack thought. Why save ammunition for an uncertain future when bombers were actually diving on you?

'Woody, Buck, tally-ho, big jobs over Takali, diving in.'

Jack jinked right then left for a better look. Behind him, the Luqa and Hal Far barrages had opened up. Ahead, bomber after bomber – 88s and 87s - was diving on Takali.

A line of explosions crossed the airfield, like splashes on a puddle.

He decided to maintain height for the moment, making for a point above the tail end of the bomber stream. His headset was alive with noise, Hurricanes from Hal Far adding to the calls from, Woody, Buck and Co. Then, he spotted a pair of 109's.

'JC, 109s twelve o'clock, one mile.'

He had no idea whether his friend had heard the message over the other chatter. The Messerschmitts were easing from a shallow dive so the closing speed was probably well over 700 miles an hour. They were already within 1000 yards.

Jack pressed the centre of the gun switch as tracer set out from the 109 to his front. His Spitfire shuddered with the recoil. But his nose also yawed violently right. The left wing arced upward, sending his rounds hopelessly off target.

The yaw stopped as soon as he released the rocker switch. He rolled left again. The violent swing had surprised him, but it may also have saved his life. After it, he'd seen neither tracer nor 109.

The Hispano cannons in his left wing must have jammed. Others had had similar trouble, traced to faulty ammunition, but this was the first time it had caught him out. Or was it just the lack of testing the flight sergeant had mentioned. No time for deeper analysis. He just needed to bear it in mind.

All these thoughts bubbled as he manoeuvred to look for the 109s, and JC. His relief at the absence of German fighters dissipated when he spotted his friend's Spitfire, sitting about 100 yards to his left. He eased toward it, eying a jagged hole behind its canopy arch with foreboding.

Movement. A flush of relief.

JC was dabbing his face with a gloved hand. Both were red with blood. As soon as he saw Jack, the Yorkshireman gave an emphatic, if bloody, thumbs-up and waved him away.

Jack did as bidden, turning away and taking the opportunity to look down. They were above Takali, and the bombers. He reversed the turn, levelled the wings and took one last glance at his wingman. JC nodded.

'Rolling right, JC.'

He moved the stick crisply right, his stomach flipping as he rolled past the inverted and increased the back pressure to dive on two vics of 88s about 2,000 feet below.

'Woody, Tiger Green five and six diving in above Takali, angels one nine.'

'Roger, Jack…'

His cheeks flushed as he unloaded the g to point his reflector sight at the rear left 88, then pulled to put it out of sight beneath his aircraft's nose. JC was already firing at a bomber to the right.

Jack counted, 'One… and two…and.'

For some reason, his mind refused to work out how to counteract the swing if he fired his cannon, so he pressed the bottom of the rocker switch and eased the stick forward. The machine gun tracer was racing away before the bomber inched into view. The rounds raked its top surfaces. He kept firing until he was diving on its tailplane, so close he could see its rivets and panel fastenings.

A moment's heart-stopping doubt, then he flashed behind the rudder, his airframe shuddering in the slipstream.

Too bloody close, Jack! Too bloody close.

He continued his dive, JC doing the same 200 yards to his right. What it was like in that cockpit with a 420 mile an hour gale ripping in he dreaded to think.

They were closing on the barrage, but also the bombers diving into it. A quick look round. Two 109s high in his 8 o'clock. Far enough away to ignore for the moment. He refocused on an 87, one of several now being rocked by shell bursts.

Jack was breathing heavily, pulse racing, but his primary emotion was still excitement. The thrill of the chase. Even without two of his four cannon, he still had the firepower to stop some of the bastards dropping their bombs on target, and maybe regaining Sicily.

They were closing fast on the gull-wing bombers, and from an ideal position shielded from the gunner in the rear of the cockpit. No sooner had Jack entered the barrage himself than he was pulling hard against the airflow to raise his Spitfire's nose toward the Stuka's belly. He edged the reflector sight up, waiting for the right deflection.

'Hold it...hold it. Now!'

With the gunsight a tad ahead of the bomber's nose, he fired, pushing on left rudder to counteract the yaw induced by the jammed cannon. His tracer hosed away, and Jack played the rudder until his fire raked over and around the 87's underside. The cannon rounds broke off chunks and left holes. Closing quickly on the tail, he stopped firing, counteracting the reverse swing, and raced past, into the arc of the bomber's rear machine gun.

Jack half-rolled to look *down* on the bomber. As he dived onward, already rolling right, there was no sign of the gunner, and the pilot slumped, unmoving.

Jack jinked to check the airspace around him. An 87 high to his right was smoking. JC was about 400 yards away among the flak, already chasing down another line of bombers. The 109s were still half a mile away. Jack eased right to join his companion in the hunt.

Rods of light shot overhead. Rear right. He rolled hard and pulled, straining to hold his head up and maintain vision while looking over his shoulder. Another pair of 109s. Perhaps they'd been shielded by the smoking bomber.

Their tracer passed behind, and they soon followed. Jack rolled left, expecting them to be manoeuvring for either him or JC. But no, they'd continued their arrow-like trajectory out of the barrage.

The left hand Rotte was still stalking, though, and his manoeuvring had allowed them to close.

'JC, two Snappers' – a reversion to Battle of Britain

language he failed to notice – 'left, seven o'clock, eight hundred yards.'

Below, his wingman twitched left. At the same time, the two 109s, much closer to Jack, turned right, their noses pitching up. Good for JC, but not for him.

Jack pulled to the buffet and relaxed a smidge to maintain it while arcing over the top in a barrel roll around the two Messerschmitts. They passed beneath, both pilots looking up. He finished the second half of the barrel to roll out 200 yards behind them, delighted and surprised at the success of the manoeuvre. He'd lost speed and they were travelling much faster, pulling away, but he sent machine gun rounds after each in turn.

They didn't attempt to re-engage or chase after JC, but flew on out of the barrage.

Jack rolled left and pulled down, groaning, sweat pouring from his aching body. Seven thousand feet. Time to engage at least one more of the Stuka's below. Not so ideally placed this time, looking down on his target's upper surfaces, and its gunner. He dived for a point ahead of it.

At 400 yards, its machine gun sparked. The pinpricks of light elongated and fanned out, as if from the vanishing point in a painting. Jack's stomach tightened in his first conscious recognition of fear that morning. He hadn't even registered the shell bursts all around him during the last 5,000 feet of descent.

Now, he resisted the temptation to duck as the tracer grew and flashed past. At 200 yards, still pointing just ahead of the bomber, he fired, counteracting the swing and pulling to straddle it from nose to tail. Once again, he saw sparks before the Stuka disappeared beneath his Spitfire's nose.

This time, he flew out of the barrage to the south of Takali. Immediately, he spotted two 88s off to his right, slightly below and about a mile away. They were heading north towards Mdina, presumably having just bombed the airfield. Jack turned hard right in pursuit.

They were climbing and the residual speed from his dive gave him a good overtake. He continued his descent, aiming to slide directly behind and sneak up from beneath the right hand bomber, trusting that the gunners would find him harder to spot against a background of broken terrain than against the sky.

Just north of Mdina, he'd passed 2,000 feet and was preparing to zoom up and attack, when the guns of the left hand bomber began firing.

So much for sneaking up!

The lower rear gunner of his target joined in. The tracer was too close for comfort. Jack was sweating, and not just because of the temperature in the greenhouse of his cockpit. He gritted his teeth and pushed on the throttle.

At 300 yards, he could wait no longer. He pushed gun button and left rudder, bracing against the vibration and swing. The machine guns gave out almost immediately, but the right cannon continued to pump.

Tracer suddenly appeared over his left shoulder. Even with the thumping recoil of his cannon, he felt impacts.

'Fool!'

He rolled hard left and pulled down, the g increasing until his vision darkened from light grey towards black. Fearing unconsciousness, he relaxed the back pressure a little, straining to look over his shoulder for his attacker, shrouded within a grey veil studded with stars. It seemed to have disappeared.

Pulse racing, breath coming in rasps, Jack unloaded the g, weaved and dived for the dry stone walls, cheeks flushing with the return of blood to his head.

Whatever transpired, he deserved all he got. He'd allowed himself to become fixated on the 88s. Goodness knew how long it had been since he'd looked about him. Perhaps he needed to feel more fear, not less, at least enough to keep him on his toes.

He levelled a few hundred feet above the ridge to the south of Mdina and made a more systematic scan of the sky.

Nothing until he looked toward Takali. There, smoke pillars rose and a few shells still burst, low down in the immediate overhead. Several fighters raced through and around the smoke, chasing and being chased.

Jack looked toward Luqa and then Hal Far. Smoke rose above both. Would either be any safer? Probably not.

'Better the devil you know, Jack.'

He climbed to the south and levelled at 500 feet before turning back toward Takali. A couple of 109s were climbing away to the north, chased by shell bursts. But at least two others still orbited at about 3,000 feet. Two Hurricanes maintained a weaving vigil 2,000 feet below them.

The thickest smoke billowed into the west from north of the easterly strip. It looked to be free of craters, so, keeping an eye on the 109s, Jack set himself up for a curving approach.

Against all the omens, he completed an uneventful landing.

Taxying in, he passed a dust-covered Spitfire resting on its belly within 100 yards of the shed. It was missing about two or three feet of its right wingtip.

'Larry's,' Mike said as Jack walked towards him a few minutes later, hitching a thumb at the wreck.

Jack halted next to the Kiwi. 'Thought it might be,' he said. 'Lucky boy.'

'Don't say that to him,' Mike whispered, pointing to a group of B Flight pilots sitting in the shade of the shed. 'He's only just stopped shaking.'

'Not surprised,' Jack said.

Mike pointed at the Spitfire. 'Not from the wingtip. Says he doesn't remember much about that...'

Jack interrupted. 'I do though. Happened right in front of me. But go on.'

'Says all he remembers is waking up in a spin. Recovers from that, and then gets chased all the way here by a couple of 109s and forced into a downwind landing. Touches down, but long. And then he discovers, *No Brakes!* Has to raise the gear to stop himself demolishing the shed. And then, to add insult to injury, he has to jump out and run for cover, chased by another couple of 109s. Not a happy lawyer.'

'I can imagine,' Jack said, smiling at Mike's rendition of the saga.

'Your kite didn't look too healthy either, Jack.'

Jack considered himself extremely lucky to have got away with no more than a dozen holes in his rear fuselage.

'Could have been worse,' he said. 'Speaking of which, how's JC?'

'Could have been worse,' Mike batted back. 'Much worse, from the amount of blood. But it seems it's just a nasty gash. Should get away with no more than a few stitches, but they carted him off to Imtarfa just in case.'

Jack felt a surge of relief. 'Thanks.' He pointed at the shed. 'Better go and give my report to Harry.'

As he walked toward the building, he stroked his own recently-acquired scar.

The first raid of the day could also have been worse. Although the airfield was peppered with new craters, there was remarkably little damage to the strips. A Blenheim had burnt out and a Hurricane had been damaged, as had four Spitfires, one of the new ones seriously. But none had so far been destroyed, which must have been the aim of the attack.

Of course, another four, including the three VCs, had been damaged in the air, Larry's being the worst, maybe a write-off. JC's needed no more than a new – or cannibalised – canopy, while the other two seemed to have only superficial wounds that Smudger and his fellow riggers would eventually patch up.

At least a few of the new Spitfires were beginning to come on line.

The rest of the afternoon was remarkably quiet. It was a

tense, brooding, silence, though.

'I don't like it,' Buck said, looking up into the cloudless sky. 'Something's brewing.'

The sun beat down mercilessly, and those who weren't sweltering at cockpit readiness clustered in the shade of the shed, swatting flies.

The annoying pests made even a quick nap impossible.

No matter how hard they tried, few were able to ignore the buzzing, or the tickle of tiny feet on any portion of exposed skin. And even these hardy folk eventually succumbed to the fear that one of the creatures crawling on them could be a mosquito or, worse still, a sand fly, the bite from which could lead to a nasty sore and a fever.

Fly swatting had become the major sport.

Jack often found himself smiling as those around him clapped or flapped their hands at the air, or slapped at their faces, necks or bare legs. And whenever a hand or bundle of paper showed a squashed insect, there'd be a whoop of triumph. The bloody evidence would be shoved under the nose of each neighbour in turn until someone gave in and muttered, 'confirmed'.

The one exception to all this was Pete Brown.

He sat slightly apart, motionless, apparently friendless. His aloofness garnered no hostility, nor was it a matter of comment. People had just taken to letting him be.

For the umpteenth time, Jack looked across. Of course, the inscrutability could be hiding inner serenity, a man at peace with the world and his part in it. But Jack suspected otherwise. The receding hairline didn't help, but the 22-year-old seemed to have aged more than most. And caught in unguarded moments, Jack thought his eyes had a faraway, increasingly haunted, look.

They'd never been friends, but at least on Eagle they'd had the odd chat, and Pete hadn't been quite so stand-offish. Something was wrong. Jack was sure of it. And yet, he remained reluctant merely to go over. If the man had had a particular friend, he could have sent him to winkle out the truth. It was what he used to do back at Biggin. But Pete didn't seem to have anyone to whom he was close.

Perhaps someone unfettered by British - and RAF - reserve would have just strolled over and asked what was wrong. But Jack couldn't. He needed an excuse, a smokescreen.

An hour or so later, heading for the shed from an uncomfortably hot stint on cockpit readiness, he decided to take his chance and stop by Pete's chair.

'Hello, Pete, how's things?'

The young pilot looked up. 'Fine, thanks, Jack.'

The lightness of his words was not reflected in his grey eyes. These remained cold, unsmiling.

'You?'

'Not too bad, thanks, now I'm out of that bloody cockpit.'

'Yes. Getting more unpleasant by the day, isn't it?'

Again, the words were light and conversational, but the delivery was too flat, as if the speaker was merely going through the motions. There was no law against it, and it would have been a tremendous surprise if he'd opened up in the way Dave Campbell had, but Jack remained worried.

For the moment though, he was also stumped. 'Oh well, better report in' he said, setting off with a waving salute. 'Stay cool.'

'You too, Jack.'

If he wanted to find out what was really going on with Pete, he'd have to gird himself to take a more direct approach. Still contemplating the issue, he passed the main group, now swelled by a handful of the new pilots. He checked in with Laddie and Harry before stepping back into the sunlight to join them.

The newcomers had witnessed the early afternoon raid from the terrace and decided to come down to see the aftermath. Jack hoped they didn't regret their decision, but they seemed happy enough for the moment, being entertained by Dave, Harv, Newfy and Mal. The latter was just about to take off his boot to show his war wound when Laddie appeared from the shed.

'Woody says something's brewing. He's launching a pair to cover the airfield until we see how things develop.'

The flight commander re-entered the building.

A few minutes later, Mike and Zulu taxied past, waving at Jack and the other pilots lounging in their chairs. And as the two Spitfires roared down the strip in a cloud of dust, the CO and Laddie walked out with parachutes and helmets. Grim-faced, they made for the pens.

Jack watched them go, then sank back to swat flies and wait to see what unfolded. Approaching 5.15, two red Very flares arced through the air. Less than two minutes later, a further four Spitfires taxied past and took off, the sound of their Merlins fading as the dust of their departure dispersed on the breeze.

Buck and Norm had been on cockpit readiness and were now airborne with the CO and Laddie. Jack waited to see if Pete, the remaining flight lieutenant and deputy flight commander, would make a move to find out what was going on. After several minutes with no sign of action, he decided to take the initiative and headed into the shed.

Pencil in hand, Harry was leaning over a map on a table against the side wall. 'Looks like a big raid,' the intelligence officer said without looking up. He then pre-empted Jack's follow-up question. 'And the six that have gone are all that are serviceable.'

This time he straightened, turned to look at Jack and smiled. 'Six more are airborne from Luqa, and I'll let you know if any more come on line.'

All his immediate questions answered, Jack settled for a quick, 'Thank you, Harry.'

As he turned to leave, the IntO leaned back over the map.

Jack rejoined the others, passed on the news and eased back into his chair. Once more, it was eerily quiet – Mike and Zulu had failed to return to the overhead. But the silence didn't last long.

From the north and west came a drone that rose in volume. They looked at one another nervously. It was a lot of engines. The first sighting was of about twenty 109s at 10,000 feet, followed after a short while by tens of Ju88s and 87s, escorted by more 109s, all at or above about 15,000 feet. The lead 109s split into fours, heading off in several directions and descending.

Sirens wailed and the pilots trotted over to stand by the slit trenches, the new boys looking particularly pensive. Eight of the 109s descended toward the airfield, but passed overhead, seemingly bound for Luqa.

What would the bombers do?

The screech of bombs provided the answer. The guns crashed out before the first impacts, and Jack and his fellow pilots ran down or jumped into the trenches. He soon discovered that his new sangfroid in the air didn't extend to being bombed on the ground. His reaction to this bombardment was as bad as it had been to most of the others.

Worse.

The heavy raids a month earlier hadn't included Stukas. Jack had been on the airfield when a few had attacked before, but perhaps he'd been far enough away to escape the full horror of their onslaught. Today, the western boundary was very much on the receiving end.

On the few occasions he dared look up, the sight of the 87s swooping down and releasing their bombs ratcheted up his terror to new levels. And the scream of their Jericho Trumpet sirens threatened to unhinge him. Even with his hands over his ears amid the most intense ack-ack fire and explosions, they were still audible. The sound seemed to shut off all hope of escape - or survival.

With the 88s joining in, the raid was as least as heavy as those in March. The ground heaved and debris rained down. Jack rolled into a ball, praying that none of the near misses turned into direct hits. He lost track of time as he bounced around, grimacing in the face of the incessant vibration and racket, pummelled by successive pressure waves and debris.

After a lifetime of torment, the ground stopped shaking and the noise abated. When no more stones had spattered him for a while, Jack raised his head and coughed on the dusty air. He groaned as he raised himself up.

The sight was all too familiar. Tin-helmeted figures covered in dust straightened and looked around, eyes wide, spitting and racked with frequent coughing fits. Perhaps the old hands would recover more quickly, but at that moment, all, new and old looked equally startled, stretching, rubbing aches, discovering and dabbing at cuts.

Jack craned his neck to look above ground. The smoke and dust were dispersing to reveal another all-too-familiar scene of desolation.

Fifteen minutes later, the AOC appeared. Perhaps fortuitously, he'd been held up short of the airfield when splinters from a wayward bomb had punctured a tyre on his staff car. Now, face etched with concern, he was being directed toward the pens holding the new Spitfires, above a couple of which rose ominous pillars of bubbling black smoke.

Pete had retrieved his upturned seat, sat in it and showed no sign of taking a lead. So, after eying an ominous crack running from the corner of its door to its flat roof, Jack entered the shed. The duty clerk was righting a table and Harry was trying to re-hang a notice-board. Jack grabbed a corner and they both peered behind it to lower its brackets over nails sticking from the wall.

'Thanks,' Harry half shouted. They were all still a little deaf.

He patted down his uniform from chest to thigh, raising a cloud of dust, which he then waved away from his face. 'If mother could see me now,' he said.

'Probably a blessing that she can't, Harry,' Jack bellowed back. 'I think the state of your uniform would be the least of her worries.'

Harry cast his dark eyes over the shambolic office. 'You're right there,' he said, before turning and clearing his throat loudly enough for Jack to hear.

He refrained from spitting on the floor and turned back toward Jack. 'Sorry, but I've nothing much to tell you at the moment. Like the AOC,' – he pointed out of the door – 'I suspect the airfield may be out of action for a while, days even. But the phones are down, so I'll have to wait for news from the far side before I can confirm anything. As for closer to hand,' – he gestured to the door again – 'you know as much as me, which is not a lot.'

Jack felt sorry for the young man, reduced to the same state of ignorance as the rest of them, and forced to tell the AOC as much.

'Okay, Harry, I'll get out of your hair.'

After relaying the information – or lack of it – Jack decided to walk over to the pens. The AOC's entourage, including the flight sergeant, were walking along the line. Jack headed for the pen they'd just exited. As he entered, standing in front of the right wing of the resident Spitfire, was Smudger.

'Not a happy air marshal, sir,' the rigger said, wiping his hands on a grubby piece of cloth tucked into the waistband of his KD shorts.

'No. He didn't look too chipper. Something the flight sergeant said?'

'Everything the flight sergeant said, sir. *Everything.*'

Jack raised an eyebrow.

'Well, he was none too happy when he heard about the radios, but when he saw the state of the cannon, I thought he was going to burst a blood vessel.'

Smudger gestured at the wing and Jack leant down to peer into one of the two cannon. He couldn't see far into the dark pipe, but the sunlight fell on bits of grit and an area of rust just inside the 20mm opening.

Jack whistled. 'Two of mine jammed on the last sortie.

Not surprised if they were like this.'

'Don't think we'd have let you take off with them looking like this, sir.'

Jack smiled at the gentle admonition. 'Sorry, I know that. But they should never have been delivered in this state.'

'The AOC's point exactly, sir' the airman said. 'I think somebody's going to get a piece of his mind before the day's out.'

'You're not wrong there, Smudger. And quite right too!'

Not wanting to take up too much more of his friend's time, Jack gestured over his shoulder out of the pen. 'Any idea on the score yet?'

'Two destroyed and three damaged, the flight sergeant told the AOC, sir.'

Jack nodded. 'Mmm. Thought it might have been worse.'

As soon as he'd said it, he wished he hadn't. Three damaged mightn't sound many, but add the four damaged in the first raid, those damaged in the air, the legacy of unserviceable kites, and the new ones still to be made battle-worthy, and you had more than enough to keep five times as many groundcrew occupied.

'Probably enough for you to be going on with though, ay, Smudger?' was the best Jack could come up with. He winced at its inadequacy.

'Probably, sir.'

The young rigger did his best to raise a smile, but he looked unbelievably tired. Jack felt the deepest sympathy for him, and the rest of the groundcrew. Their burden just kept on growing.

Most of the pilots were bussed off to Mdina to hear the AOC's call to arms. Jack was one of four chosen to remain, just in case the airfield could be cleared in time to get them airborne against any new threat.

As he sat with Mal, Newfy and Luke Elliott in the

gathering dusk, the news, relayed by Harry, became grimmer. The CO and the other 249 pilots had all landed safely at Luqa, but two of the six 126 pilots launched from that airfield had been lost, while another had been on final approach when a bomb exploded beneath him. He and the remains of his Spitfire had been blown hundreds of feet into the air. Somehow, he'd managed to bale out, but very low. Unsurprisingly, he was in Imtarfa, with no word on his injuries as yet.

And the news at Takali also seemed to darken by the hour. For a start, there was another raid. It seemed less accurate than those earlier in the day, and no further aircraft were damaged. But it caused yet another delay in the repair work being undertaken by the groundcrew.

And although the airfield also seemed to escape comparatively lightly, it had become clear that many of the Spitfires, serviceable and unserviceable alike were trapped in their pens by tons of debris or cratered taxyways. The Army and civilian work parties were too thinly stretched to do much about it, struggling as they were to get the rest of the airfield back in business.

At 11 o'clock that morning, the Island had suddenly had 60 Spitfires. It had seemed an embarrassment of riches. Now, Jack doubted if more than a handful were serviceable at either airfield, and those at Takali were trapped, unusable, even if a strip could be cleared.

By 8.30pm, when Harry came to say they'd been stood down, it was dark. Their mood was pretty low.

'No transport, I'm afraid,' he said, adding to the gloom, before lowering himself into a chair.

With the light leaking from the shed door extinguished, the only illumination came from the faint glow above several pens, and from clusters of lights scattered across the airfield. Beneath these the Army toiled, producing the only sounds to rival chirruping cicadas - the clink of spade or pickaxe on rock.

'The heaviest day's bombing of the war so far,' Harry

said eventually, drawing Jack's eyes back to the group. His colleagues remained invisible, lost behind spots the lights had imprinted on his retinas.

There was no comment, but Harry continued. 'Two hundred and seventy bombers and two hundred and twenty fighters the Observer Corps counted.'

Now they'd been stood down, it seemed as if they were too dish-ragged even to engage in conversation. After all, they'd been up since 4.30am. But Jack felt sorry for the young intelligence officer, earnestly relaying the information he'd just been given to a wall of silence.

'Hopefully, a lot less returned to Sicily,' he said, raising himself from his chair with a loud sigh and turning on the rest. 'Come on you lot, or we'll still be here when the sun comes up. And look on the bright side; at least we'll have missed the AOC's pep talk.'

Chapter 18 – Tuesday April 21st – Spitchered

The small group gathered around Mike included JC, a line of ugly stitches holding together a jagged gash above his right eye. Jack was glad to see him, but doubted he'd be flying. The New Zealander was regaling those that had been absent with the story of the AOC's talk.

'Suddenly, there's the whistle of bombs.' Mike makes a screeching sound. 'Half the blokes in the hall dive under tables or cringe against walls. The AOC looks down his nose at them, snorts and carries on as if nothing's happening.'

Doing his best to look and sound like the AOC, he continued. 'After this war, whenever the name of Malta is mentioned, you will be able to say with pride, *I was there.*'

He looked around, as if awaiting a round of applause. Getting none, he proceeded, in broad Kiwi.

'Anyway, all hell breaks loose. Must have been at least a two thousand pounder. Blew in the shutters, knocked over the chairs, rattled the chandeliers. It was all you could do to stay on your feet.

'But talk about finishing a speech with a bang. The old man couldn't have timed it better if he'd scripted it. Even if he did end up looking like a music hall comedian, wobbling about with his cigarette bent at ninety degrees.'

Mike duly wobbled, obviously pleased to receive the odd titter of laughter this time. 'Just remember,' he said, adopting the AOC's stentorian tones again, 'whenever Malta is mentioned, you can say, *I was bally well there.*'

Laddie appeared behind him, immaculately groomed and sporting a royal blue cravat. 'Okay, Mike. As you're here, cockpit readiness, number two to the CO.'

That raised a hoot and a round of applause, Mike responding with a good natured V sign directed at his audience.

'You too, Jack, on my wing. OC 603 and John

Buckstone' – one of the new squadron's flight commanders – 'will be five and six. Ten minutes,' he concluded.

No-one had expected Takali to be open. But, although nine Spitfires were still trapped in their pens, the Army had pulled a blinder, clearing a route to the main east/west strip and the strip itself. The aircraft situation was less good. Of the 50 or so still in one piece, only 27 were available, the bulk at Luqa, where eight of the Takali strength still sat.

They didn't actually launch for another hour, which meant Jack experienced another first: being bombed while at cockpit readiness.

He'd barely strapped in when his starter crew began pointing at the sky. Over his left shoulder, tens of bombers and their escorts were approaching. His fingers hovered over the switches, expecting the Very signal at any second, but it never appeared. Instead, the bombers came on until he could see red flags rising over nearby buildings and gun emplacements, and hear the wail of a siren, muffled by the earpieces of his headset.

Sitting in the centre of the pen, Jack felt a bit like a sacrificial goat tethered to a stake. He saw no point in the two bare-chested airmen he'd come to know as Taff and Nobby sharing the same level of vulnerability. He waved them away.

Even when he'd gained their undivided attention, they seemed reluctant to move. He reinforced his next gesture with words of encouragement.

'Fuck off and find some shelter.'

That seemed to work. Nobby and Taff both jogged over to the back left corner of the pen and huddled under the corrugated iron roof of a small sandbag refuge. Not as secure as a slit trench, but better than standing in the middle of the pen.

No bombs fell as the bombers – all 88s as far as he could tell - streamed through the overhead. It began to look as if they were bound for other targets. But even as the leading elements split and began descending towards Valletta and Luqa, two sections about turned and dived toward Takali.

And still the Very signal didn't come.

Surely it was better for them to be airborne than sit around waiting to be hit?

Perhaps he'd missed the signal, or the others had taxied past. For a moment, he seriously considered starting and taxying off on his own.

The barrage opened up and the moment of madness passed. He'd merely have been caught in the open. As if to drive the point home, a fountain of dirt appeared above the parapet to his front right. It was followed by others, marching across the airfield – the other side of the airfield as far as he could tell.

Smoke billowed as the tremors rocked his Spitfire on its olios. Jack's bowels grumbled and he felt the blood draining from his cheeks.

More shocks, but not too close. The first bomber emerged above the smoke, levelling from its dive at about 4,000 feet and heading west. A second followed as the tremors continued. Both were surrounded by ack-ack, but remained unscathed.

Jack had counted four 88s before another fountain of dirt rose ahead of the smoke. Successive explosions strode diagonally across his front, the impacts now visible down the side of his engine cowling through the opening of the pen. Each rocked his Spitfire more forcefully. The last two bombs hit the ground in just about the dead centre of the airfield. He pulled the canopy shut before the pressure waves passed over him. The noise became even more muffled, the sight even more surreal, viewed from within his perspex bubble.

A fifth, sixth and seventh 88 passed overhead, their bombs seemingly confined to the far south-east, within the existing smoke. He waited for the eighth.

'Come on, you bastard, come on.'

Tremors.

That wasn't what I meant, Jack thought.

In the area visible down the side of his cowling, an explosion kicked up the dirt ahead of the smoke. More followed, this time heading toward his pen.

Forgetting where he was for the moment, he made to turn and run. The grip of his harness gave the rush of adrenalin no release. It brought a feeling of entrapment not unlike when the pen wall had fallen on him and the CO. He struggled for breath, mesmerised as the dirt pillars and accompanying mushroom clouds approached. His Spitfire rocked wildly and debris spattered the closed canopy and airframe with muffled thuds and clangs. He closed his eyes.

The impacts stopped. He opened his eyes. The canopy was speckled with dust, grit and pebble-sized stones. The nearest smoke looked to be a few hundred yards ahead of the pen.

The Spitfire rocked and his heart raced. But it was Nobby and Taff jumping up. They appeared to either side of his canopy, trying to clear the surface as quickly as possible without scratching it. It was almost comical, but the task was deadly serious. If he was to spot enemy aircraft, the perspex had to be blemish free. He sat back and watched as cloths came out and it was polished.

Seemingly content, they swept over the engine cowling, taking much less care.

Jack slid the canopy back. 'Thanks,' he shouted.

They acknowledged with smiles, then dipped to sweep at those parts of the wings they could reach. In the next few minutes, they cleared the rest of the debris from the Spitfire's wings, fuselage and tailplane.

One minute, OC 603 and John Buckstone were there, the next, they were gone.

As they'd initiated a dive onto 88s heading for the coast after attacking Luqa, the pair had looked to be in good order, tucked in behind the rest of Tiger Red with ideal lateral spacing. But the next time Jack looked back, they'd disappeared from view.

Thereafter, it was the usual confusing mêlée but, unusually, the four 249 Squadron pilots had managed to regroup for the recovery and land in one piece, despite the attentions of 109s dodging in and out of the flak.

Jack and Laddie claimed the probable destruction of an 88, the Welshman having caused flame to belch from its left engine while the Englishman put the right out of action. It seemed inconceivable that the bomber could make it back to Sicily, although they'd had to pull away before the kill could be confirmed.

The 603 Squadron pair had also found their way back. During a short debrief in the shed, they admitted that the speed of events had been so far beyond their previous experience that they'd been unable to keep up. They'd fallen straight from the fray and failed to close with any of the enemy formations they'd spotted afterwards.

It had been a salutary lesson, but one from which Jack was confident they'd profit. He'd been impressed by the noble lord's humility and lack of bluster in the face of what could have been seen as a humiliating debut. It augured well for the future.

Stan Grant softened the blow by stating that staying in contact during an action and regrouping afterwards were fine in theory, but rarely happened in practise. Jack nodded in agreement.

He left the shed and was heading over to join the rest lounging in the shade of an awning, when he spotted half a dozen 603 Squadron pilots, including Danny Danvers, approaching from his right. Something about their demeanour made him stop.

Their blues were coated in Maltese dust, but not enough to account for their ashen complexions. They looked like a bunch of frightened schoolboys.

'Everything all right, Danny?' Jack asked, knowing it wasn't.

The group stopped and the tall youngster walked

towards him.

'Just had a bit of a shock, Jack, that's all.'

The others shuffled impatiently, like children forced to wait while their parents chatted to someone.

'Carry on, you lot. I'll catch up in a minute.'

They made off for the shed, looking relieved to have been dismissed. Danny took off his Service Dress cap and wiped a hand through his hair. He suddenly reminded Jack of Alex. He even had a similar accent, although perhaps Bristol rather than Shropshire.

'We've just walked down from Mdina,' he began, pointing up the hill toward the bastions.

'A raid started when we were halfway down, so we crouched in a ditch. We'd just set out again when a Hurricane appeared. He was trying to evade two 109s. But they got him, in the fuel tank judging by the flames streaming back over the cockpit. Looked like he was toast, but he managed to get out. Just above us – at about a thousand feet. We let out such a cheer.'

The young man looked at, or rather through, Jack.

'But when his brolly came out, it just candled. Flapped uselessly above him. We watched him fall, arms and legs...'

He closed his eyes and shook his head.

'I thought I could hear the screams...' He looked at Jack, head still shaking. 'Or perhaps I just imagined it. Anyway, he smashed into the ground a few hundred yards from us.'

The pilot wiped his palms down his jacket over his hips, before examining them. 'We should have gone over. But there was no way he could have survived, and...Well, we didn't.'

'Good job, too' Jack said, laying a hand briefly on the taller man's shoulder. 'It wouldn't have done any good.'

'You may be right,' Danny said, looking far from convinced. 'We directed a group of Pongoes to where he'd fallen.'

Taking a deep breath, he drew himself up. 'Not a great

way to start the day, but onward and upward, I suppose. I better join the others.'

'Okay,' - Jack hesitated for the briefest moment before using the nickname he'd just heard – 'Danny. But trust me, there was nothing you could have done.'

With a thin-lipped nod, the young man turned and walked away.

Jack watched him go. What a thing to witness less than 24 hours after you'd arrived, and before you'd even been into combat yourself. It highlighted another serious problem, though.

Back home, parachutes were kept in sterile conditions, hung in purpose built towers, examined and packed with great care. At all the bases on Malta, the parachute bays had long gone, and the flimsy canopies and cords were stored wherever could be found, sometimes in the open. Evidence was mounting that many were faulty, damaged in raids, either before or after they'd been packed.

It was another risk he tried not to think about.

The next warning of a large plot approaching from Sicily came soon after noon. This time, eight Spitfires were launched as soon as the news was received.

Jack watched them climb away, the dust of their departure drifting west on the breeze. A few minutes later, the sirens began to wail and flags were hoisted. Laddie, Harry and the intelligence and ops clerks ran out of the shed. Jack followed them to one of the nearby slit trenches and ran down the steps. There they stood, gazing anxiously into the west and north-west.

When the sound of engines reached them, it was not the usual even drone, but the rising and falling note of aircraft in combat. Confirmation came when the first bombers appeared to the north-west, not in the tight formations to which they'd become accustomed, but singly or in pairs, diving and corkscrewing, surrounded by smaller silhouettes manoeuvring over a wide expanse of sky.

Jack, surrounded by smiling faces, felt his own cheeks flush in elation. For once, they seemed to be disrupting the bombers forward of their targets.

The elation was short-lived.

More engines. This time, they belonged to a formation of 87s approaching, unmolested, from the west. As the droning rose to drown the sound of combat, most in the shelter shifted their gaze. Jack scanned the north-west a while longer, concerned that the bombers there were re-grouping.

A roar. He turned to see arms pointing. Four 109s screamed in from the south, a few hundred feet above the pens lining the western perimeter.

Jabos!

The first released its bomb. As if in slow motion, the projectile dropped behind the fighter-bomber before beginning to arc downwards. It fell straight into a pen.

A bright flash. Debris flew upwards on the leading edge of a fireball of burning fuel. The characteristic bubbling cloud of orange and black followed. A pressure wave and thunderclap dulled Jack's hearing.

For some reason, he didn't duck, but watched the other three Jabos drop their bombs. These seemed to explode in unison, one close to the pen in which Jack had been talking to Smudger the day before.

Whether this had any bearing on his actions, he was unable to say. All he knew was that as the dust cleared and groundcrew began to rush in with buckets, he knew he had to join them. He ran up the shelter steps, grabbed a fire bucket from the shade of the shed and headed over.

The belated bark of the Bofors guns was barely audible as he neared the opening of the pen...

Muffled voices. Jack opened his eyes. He was in the shade of the shed. Laddie and Mike were nearby, chatting. Beyond them, smoke rose from a couple of pens. The Kiwi looked at him and smiled. He touched Laddie on the forearm. The flight commander turned and also smiled.

'Welcome back,' he said.

'From where?' Jack replied, trying to raise himself on one elbow.

His *bed* wobbled and he looked down. He was lying along the seats of four office chairs, a rolled up jacket under his head.

'Out there.' Laddie pointed towards the pens.

Jack pushed himself up to sit on one of the chairs. His head felt muzzy and he ached a bit. Otherwise, he seemed unhurt. But even he realised there was a gap in his memory.

'What happened?' he asked, rubbing a hand across the back of his neck.

'We were hoping you could tell us, old chap,' Laddie said, sitting on the chair next to him.

Jack flexed his shoulders. 'I remember running towards the pen, then…Well, nothing.'

Mike lowered his towering frame onto one knee. 'No-one noticed you'd disappeared until the raid stopped. Then Harry looked around and said he was sure you'd followed him into the trench. By the time we climbed out to look for you, the groundcrew were carrying you over.'

Laddie took over. 'They'd been forced to shelter in the pen with the burning Spitfire. Not a comfortable place to be. But the bombs were falling so close, they couldn't risk moving. It only lasted a few minutes, though. And when they came out, there you were, fast asleep.'

Mike again. 'That was about fifteen minutes ago. Harry called the medics, but they've got a lot on their plates, I guess.'

Jack began to stand. Both pilots made to help, but he flapped them away. Once upright, he gave his limbs a shake. Apart from the usual twinge in his calf, he felt fine. Even his head had cleared.

'Well, sorry to disappoint,' he said, 'but I feel fine.'

'Mmm!' Laddie looked unsure. 'Have a cup of tea and see how you are in half an hour.'

'You mean, if I survive the tea?' Jack shot back.

They all laughed.

'Okay,' said Laddie. 'Skip the tea and come and tell me how you are in half an hour anyway.'

He turned and walked round the corner of the shed.

Jack and Mike looked at one another.

'You have to admit, Jack, it is pretty miraculous.'

Jack held up his arms and inspected them, then looked down at his legs. His right side was more than usually dusty, but there were no scuffs on his uniform, or bumps or scrapes on his skin.

'Well don't ask me. Must have been one of the shock waves or something.'

A few minutes later, he had a visitor. Mike eased to one side as Jack put on his hat and he and Smudger exchanged salutes.

'Can't hang about, sir. Two spitchered and one damaged. We're salvaging what we can, but I wondered how damaged you are.'

'Not sure how, Smudger, but not at all. Thanks for the concern, but you don't have to rob any parts for me – not yet anyway.'

'Hopefully never, sir,' the rigger said, reddening slightly as he said it. 'Anyway, best be getting back. The flight sergeant said to say thanks for trying to help.'

He saluted.

'Tell him, thanks,' Jack said as he returned the salute, 'but I think I'll leave you to it next time.'

The airman smiled and turned to trot away.

Mike came closer. He nodded toward the pens.

'You've became quite a celebrity over there, you know. Dashing to help them during a raid. Even if it did all turn to worms.'

Jack wasn't sure whether to believe his friend or not.

All eight Spitfires returned safely. The pilots, led by Buck, walked towards the shed, the old hands smiling and reliving the battle with their hands. The two 603 pilots looked more sober, dazed even, but at least they'd survived.

It was more than could be said for some of their peers at Luqa.

During the afternoon, they heard that two pilots from 601, including their CO, John Bisdee, had been lost into the sea, while another had crash-landed at Hal Far, his fate unknown.

The air above Malta was a harsh classroom, and not everyone was granted the time to learn their lessons.

The Lascaris ops room ordered another scramble at four. A few minutes later, Jack and Mal were reunited as a pair, flying as Yellow 3 and 4, alongside Laddie and Mike. Ahead was a Red section of five kites, led by the CO and including another couple of 603 pilots.

That the groundcrew had been able to provide nine aircraft when some in the previous formation had been damaged was another glowing testament to their efforts. And from Jack's point of view, flying among eight other Spitfires was a major step forward. He felt another lift in his spirits.

They climbed to the south.

'Stan, this is Woody. Total one twenty, I say again, one twenty bandits, passing Comino in waves, angels one four to one six. Includes forty little jobs up to angels two five.'

'Roger, Woody, Tiger passing angels ten.'

The CO didn't sound perturbed. Neither was Jack.

The odds may be four to one in fighters and ten to one in total, but they were better than usual. Plus, there were nine of them, and he was flying a Mk VC again.

He looked at Mal, holding 100 yards to his right. The youngster gave a thumbs-up. He'd been fine on the ground, happy even, buoyed by his relationship with Sofija, Nurse Dingli, as Jack continued to call her, much to the Australian's amusement. But getting airborne against such odds after three weeks couldn't be easy.

Let him survive, Jack thought. If there is a God, please let him survive.

They climbed southwards for another couple of minutes before Woody turned them about. They'd made height, but the pay-off was that they wouldn't reach the bombers before they hit their targets.

'Woody, Tiger vectoring north, passing angels one eight.'

'Roger, Stan. Little jobs in your...'

'Tiger, tally-ho, twelve o'clock low, diving in.'

The noses of Red section dipped before the CO had finished speaking. Yellow section followed, Jack and Mal now to the left of Laddie and Mike. Malta appeared. They were passing over the south coast. As hard as he looked, Jack couldn't spot the bandits against the background of rocky terrain, shadows and the Takali barrage.

Tracer sparked from two of the lead Spitfires, and then Jack had them. Eight 109s 2,000 feet below, heading south south-west. Tiger were diving from the Germans' ten o'clock, closing fast. All five of Yellow section fired at the lead pairs, who'd yet to react.

Jack eased left and he and Mel headed for the furthest pair, arrowing down from their upper left quarter. As the penny finally dropped, the 109s broke into pairs, Jack and Mal's targets rolling right. This reduced them to a side view, but Jack adjusted the deflection, braced the stick and pressed the centre of the rocker switch. Cannon and machine gun rounds clattered out – with no stoppages. His chosen 109 flew into the stream of tracer. He kept firing, raking it from spinner to tailplane, then flashed behind, sure of hits but not the damage inflicted.

On another day he'd have pulled round to re-engage, but...

'Tiger Red and Yellow, Takali!'

The CO was obviously on the same page. Hitting the bombers was their primary aim, and the barrage pointed to where they were needed.

Mal was still to the left, silhouetted against the horizon to the south-west of the Island. They turned 30 degrees right onto north.

A few miles ahead, the sky above Takali was dark with ack-ack. More worryingly, the ground was obscured by clouds of smoke. Even as they approached, these expanded, thickened and rose ever higher.

Too late to stop the bombing, but they might yet exact revenge.

'Tiger lead, Yellow 4, nine o'clock low, dozen big jobs diving for Dingli, angels twelve.'

'Woody, tally-ho dozen big jobs running away, Tiger diving in.'

'Roger, Stan.'

Mal hadn't mentioned the escort of half a dozen 109s diving above and behind their charges. Jack turned hard, passing behind Mal to end up on his left as they gave chase.

He could see Laddie and Mike beyond Mal, but not the CO and Red section, although they were obviously close enough to see the 88s. Surprisingly, the 109s seemed to be matching the speed of the bombers, probably no more than 250 miles per hour. The Spitfires were already exceeding 420, so had a massive overtake.

Jack shook his body and flexed his hands. A slight tightening in the stomach, but no real fear. Closing fast. A last look round. Five Spitfires high in his four o'clock, also diving in. His stomach flipped with elation at the sight.

Tracer set out from the rear upper guns of a couple of bombers. The 109s broke outwards. Jack ignored them. A problem for later.

He picked an 88 to the rear left. Five hundred yards. Tracer hosed toward him from its rear upper gun. He fought the urge to duck, or at least retaliate. Three hundred. Impacts? Two. Fire!

He fought to keep the reflector sight centred as his rounds smashed into the 88's rear fuselage, then its left tailplane, ripping off great chunks of metal. One jagged shard shot past no more than inches above his canopy. Too late, he flinched. And then, he was through the slipstream, looking up.

No sign of his target, but a bomber on the far right was ablaze. To his left, a pair of 109s, reversing their turns. Above, another line of bombers, the lower rear guns spitting tracer. To his right, Mal and a confusion of manoeuvring shapes.

Jack gritted his teeth and pulled. Almost immediately, his vision dimmed. He grunted and strained, forearms burning as he heaved the nose through the horizon, relaxing only as he pointed at dark shapes ahead. His cheeks flushed and his vision cleared. All around, bulbs of hot metal grew and flashed past.

He fought to control his heart-rate and breathing.

The left hand 88 was no more than 300 yards ahead, its gunner still firing, and getting more accurate by the second. Meanwhile, the 109s to the left were steaming in.

'Mal, 109s left eight o'clock high.'

No reply he could pick out from the other noise in his headset.

At 200 yards, Jack felt he could wait no longer. He fired cannon only, fighting to keep the reflector sight somewhere near the bombers mid-section as the recoil threatened to throw him off.

A quick glance left.

Even as he rolled that way, tracer flashed in. The resulting rush of adrenalin caused him to pull straight into the heavy buffet. Before he could react, the left wing tucked under and he was upside down.

'Whoa!'

The world continued to rotate. Blue, brown, blue…

Instinctively, he centralised the controls. The Spitfire kept spinning, its nose dropping.

Had he left it too late to catch the spin before it developed? And would he have enough height to recover if he had?

He was about to apply full counter-spin rudder when, with a jolt, the rotation stopped.

Thank fuck for that. But what about the Messerschmitts?

Breathing heavily and drenched in sweat, he manoeuvred to scan the sky.

Nothing.

He was at 6,000 feet over Hal Far, itself showing signs of recent bombing. Luqa, Valletta and Takali were also easy to spot, all three capped with smoke plumes, like erupting volcanoes. Takali had the doubtful distinction of being the most active.

Feeling a tad light-headed and nauseous, Jack set heading just to the west of the Takali plume and began a descent. Chatter in his headset mentioned 109s making a nuisance over the airfield. Then, he noticed that his right wing bore a couple of neat holes outboard of the machine guns.

Surely he'd have known if a control run had been hit. He rolled left and right. No restrictions, just added work for Smudger and his fellow riggers.

Jack approached the overhead at 4,000 feet. A Spitfire appeared from behind the smoke less than 1,000 yards away, heading right to left. A 109 followed, then, to its right rear, another. The leading 109 fired and the Spitfire turned hard right, away from Jack, but into the path of the second German. The first 109 also rolled right.

Through sheer good fortune, Jack found himself in the ideal position, the lead 109 flying into his gunsight, belly-up, at a range of a few hundred yards. He pushed on throttle and gun switch simultaneously. The rounds hit home and the 109 emitted the merest zephyr of dark smoke from beneath its engine cowling, then exploded.

Jack was into the fireball before he could react. He flinched, both at the heat, and at the prospect of collision with a large chunk of wreckage. And then he was on the other side – glancing half right into the startled eyes of the pilot of the second 109.

Jack pulled, his head dropping towards his chest with the g.

He zoomed upwards, feeling drained, struggling to lift his head. The Messerschmitt was still out there. He rolled left into a wingover and looked back.

The Spitfire was descending Mdina hill in a curving approach to the easterly strip. The 109 – or maybe another - was in a diving turn from the west to intercept it. Jack tightened his wingover to arc down in an attempt to save the Spitfire pilot's bacon.

It would be touch and go, the 109 aiming for a point in space the unsuspecting Spitfire would arrive at in about five seconds.

'Too far and too late, Jack.'

He fired anyway, hoping to distract the German if nothing else. As the tracer appeared ahead of it, the 109s nose lifted.

'Yes!'

Unfortunately, the Spitfire pilot had also been distracted. His kite's stub exhausts flamed as he applied power and overshot from an approach he really needed to complete.

You couldn't have everything.

The 109 arced up to pass about 50 feet beneath Jack, who rolled and pulled into a climbing left turn. He strained to keep the blackness at bay, groaning with the effort of controlling limbs weighing six times normal. When he unloaded and his vision cleared, he quartered the sky.

A 109 in his ten o'clock seemed to be sneaking away. He was tempted to give chase, but two more orbited a couple of thousand feet above. They were buffeted by ack-ack but still posed a threat to him and the three Spitfires he'd spotted in the circuit below. He decided to stay and keep an eye on them, at least until the others landed.

'Tiger, this is Jack, providing top cover above Takali, angels three.'

'Roger, Jack.'

Jack recognised Buck's voice and expected to hear nothing more. But the Canadian continued.

'Shouldn't be long, but if Red 5 doesn't land this time, *I'm* going to shoot the fucker down.'

Since the Point De Vue bombing, Buck had become much more up-tight and prone to angry outbursts. But this had Jack laughing out loud, his tension easing with each roll of his shoulders. The barb was only partly in jest, though, and he wouldn't want to be in Red 5's shoes when Buck caught up with him.

Jack looked up again. The 109s were nowhere in sight. Buck's Spitfire touched down and he made his own uneventful approach and landing.

The airfield was a mess again, barely open for business. If the wind shifted, they'd struggle to find a take-off run free of craters or other obstructions. The Army were going to have another busy night - as were the groundcrew.

The last raid had seen two more Spitfires destroyed and four damaged. And Jack's wasn't the only one to suffer in the air.

As he walked towards the shed, everyone, old hands and new, looked stunned, jittery even. But miraculously, there'd been no casualties.

Tired as he was, Jack was glad he'd been in the air.

Harry's briefing on the terrace that night produced a couple of pieces of good news, both from Luqa. The 601 Squadron pilot who'd crashed at Hal Far was unhurt, and their CO was alive. He'd spent six hours paddling ashore.

The rest of the address was more depressing.

Harry confirmed that Luqa had still lost two pilots and three Spitfires in the day's battles, with several more damaged, both in the air and on the ground. And no less than five Wellingtons had been destroyed during the day's raids, with another two severely damaged.

And finally, rations were to be cut again. This news elicited a groan from the audience. It was a real blow to morale.

Others were suffering more, but Jack always felt hungry, especially as he lay in bed listening to the distant thump of exploding bombs and anti-aircraft fire. From tomorrow, the pangs of hunger would be even worse.

On the plus side, he seemed to have suffered no ill effects from his short period of unconsciousness.

Chapter 19 – Wednesday April 22nd – The Lowest Ebb

'*Seventeen*!'

'Fraid so,' Harry said.

It seemed incredible. Less than 48 hours after the number had soared to 60, they were down to just 17 serviceable Spitfires. Some of the remainder were recoverable, but some were touch and go, while ten had been spitchered - gone.

The young IntO stood before the side wall of the shed. Behind him the sky was showing the first hint of dawn. To his front were nearly 40 pilots of 249 and 603 Squadrons. Most stood, but several sat on the few undamaged chairs or the ground. There was much shivering and yawning.

Harry continued. 'And believe me, it's something of a minor miracle we've got that many. Until an hour or so ago, it was seven.'

He paused as the pilots, Jack among them, looked at one another and shook their heads in disbelief.

'Well that's alright then,' Harv piped up from a seat at the front. 'Seventeen between four squadrons. That's, ooh, let me see, four and a quarter each - or would be if most weren't at fuckin' Luqa. Should have stayed in bed.'

'Glad you didn't though, Pilot Officer Johnson.'

Laddie stepped out of the gloom.

Jack smiled as Harv cringed. The flight commander had a habit of turning up when anyone – usually the fair-haired American or Mike – was shooting their mouth off.

He smiled down at Harv. 'Even if I can't find you a cockpit, I'm sure the Army'll be glad of your assistance.'

Harv wasn't the only one to spend the next few hours toiling in a way he could never have conceived before leaving the British Isles.

Interrupted only by a breakfast of urn-stewed tea and curled up bully beef sandwiches delivered on a gharry, the majority of them spent the next few hours throwing rocks clear of the track running along the front of the pens. It was back-breaking work.

At about 9.15, Buck led off three of the new boys.

At 9.30, the work party ran for the shelters and cowered under the first raid of the day. When the all clear sounded, they emerged to find much of their work undone, the tracks once more covered in debris. They set to again, heartened only by the sight of all four Spitfires returning.

About 30 minutes later, Buck led off another formation, this time of seven: two B Flight stalwarts, Norm and Larry, and four more new boys from 603. Shortly after their departure, the sirens wailed and Takali suffered another, longer, pounding from a large force of 88s bombing from about 15,000 feet. The centre of the airfield was soon shrouded in smoke and dust, but none of the bombs came closer, so Jack spent most of the time looking over the parapet of the trench. As the bombers departed and the dust cleared, he could see several fires around the north-eastern perimeter.

This time, the pilots returned to their labouring work assuming the airfield to be out of action, at least in the short term. So they were surprised to see the Spitfires return. Or at least, six of them.

Jack looked up, taking the opportunity to straighten his back and stretch his aching limbs. One of the kites sat at about 3,000 feet providing top cover, and the first three found a safe landing run into the strong south-westerly wind. But the fourth always looked to be in trouble.

'He's going too long,' Mal said.

'And too fast,' Mike added.

Both were right. The Spitfire was way beyond the middle of the airfield before its wheels were anywhere near the ground.

'Time to go round, Buddy,' Harv shouted.

But, until it disappeared behind the wall of an adjacent pen, the Spitfire continued to sink toward the dusty earth.

At the sound of a muffled crump, heads dipped between shoulder blades and faces grimaced.

Immediately, the sound of the fifth aircraft's throttle closing had their heads turning back to the north-east. They watched it float, touch down and begin its landing run.

'Oh no.' Harv's voice rose in exasperation. 'You're kidding!'

It had tipped forward into what Jack could only assume was a fresh crater. When the dust cleared, only the rear fuselage and tail were visible, pointing up at an angle of 45 degrees.

If they hadn't already been in such dire straits, it might have been funny. But to lose two aircraft to such avoidable accidents seemed criminal, no matter what the mix of adrenalin and inexperience.

The roar of a Merlin drew their eyes heavenward again. The sixth Spitfire was heading into the south-east, no doubt bound for Luqa, which is probably where they should have gone in the first place.

The sound had just about faded, when a new roar rushed upon them.

'109s!' Dave shouted, pointing north-west.

Four of the single-engined fighters shot over the perimeter no higher than 50 feet. Their noses sparked and dust spurts raced across the airfield. Soldiers trapped on the airfield jumped into craters they'd only recently vacated after the previous raid. The pilots ran for the slit trenches.

Jack thought of the two pilots who'd just crash landed. If they'd survived and were able to move, he hoped they managed to find shelter.

For the next ten minutes, the Messerschmitts criss-crossed the airfield, firing at everything that moved, and many things that didn't. The barrage of flak and small arms fire was intense, but it didn't prevent them pressing home attack after attack. Several times, cannon fire thudded around the pilots' trench.

When the guns fell silent and they climbed above

ground, Jack cast his eyes over his colleagues. They looked all in. Shoulders sagged and some looked worryingly strained, as if their nerves were being stretched ever closer to some undefined limit.

And yet, it was only just past 11am. The way things were going, few were likely to get airborne, which meant spending another nine hours on the airfield.

Who knew how many more raids there'd be in that time?

Flying had its own dangers, but most, like him would far rather have faced these than sit on the ground being bombed and strafed.

Pete Brown looked especially tense and thin-lipped, huddled beneath his tin hat. He avoided eye contact and spoke to no-one. Jack thought about going over, but he didn't want to provoke a complete collapse, at least not in public. It had got to the point where he was going to have to do something, though.

With a sigh, he reached down, picked up a rock and heaved it clear of the track.

Laddie waved them in for a tea break. As they approached the shed, Jack spotted Norm and Larry sitting in the shade drinking tea. Twenty yards further on, the 603 Squadron pilots, who'd been working a few hundred yards to the north, stopped and gathered round three of their own, sitting in the shade of a stumpy tree.

'Just in case there's any doubt in your minds,' Larry began, shifting to a stage whisper, 'we were two of the three that landed successfully.' He flicked a finger between him and Norm.

'Never doubted it for a minute,' Mike whispered back.

Larry pointed at the other group, still keeping his voice low. 'Bloody miracle both of them are okay, but their kites are a state.'

There was a short pause. Jack looked over and tried to work out which of the three seated pilots were responsible for the crash landings.

'Who was providing top cover?' Mike asked, as Pete Brown walked straight past and into the shed.

'Buck,' Norm said.

There was a surge of relief at hearing the Canadian flight commander's name.

'The missing man is one of their young Americans,' Norm continued, pointing at the 603 Squadron party, now joined by their squadron commander. 'Last seen chasing an 88 out to sea.'

The break was likely to be a short one, so, immediate curiosity sated, they filed over to the urn for their tea.

When, 15 minutes later, they returned to the pens, Pete Brown was absent. Every now and then, Jack looked toward the shed, but the flight lieutenant failed to re-emerge. It was strange the way the two of them had reacted to the stresses of life on Malta. As Jack's mental state had improved, Pete's had deteriorated.

Noon approached, the temperature increased and they were plagued by ever-larger swarms of flies. Concern for his colleague waned, replaced with a focus on his own discomfort, aches and pains. Increasingly, he straightened and stretched, his groans growing ever louder.

'Thought you'd have been used to it, Jack,' Larry Lloyd piped up.

Jack raised a questioning eyebrow and the Englishman, adopting a cod Welsh accent, delivered his punch line. 'From being down the mines.'

Jack shook his head, and the ex-lawyer smiled, looking pleased with himself.

'Yes, Larry, every Welshman's a miner, just as every Englishman's an *upper class twit*.'

'Now then, children,' Mike interjected, 'if you can't play nicely, I'll take your rocks away.'

All three laughed and took the opportunity to stretch some more.

Larry looked at his hands. 'If I ever get back into a courtroom, I promise I'll never ask a judge to sentence someone to forced labour, whatever their crime.'

The exchange was light-hearted, but feeling the aches in his muscles and joints, Jack thanked his lucky stars that he hadn't had to go down the pit, or follow his dad into the docks. On the other hand, he thought, as the sirens began to wail and they scanned the sky, he might have been safer in any of those back-breaking occupations than here in Malta.

It was 88s, 15 of them.

This time, bombs crashed on and around their dispersal area. Jack curled up, consumed by terror. After another age, the bombers moved away. He stirred, feeling numb with fear and fatigue. Eventually, he dusted himself off and climbed out of the trench.

They'd received at least a taste of the destruction meted out to other parts of the airfield earlier in the day. The operating surfaces they'd spent all morning clearing were not only covered in fresh debris, but also pitted with craters. Several blast pens had received near misses, damaging walls and the resident aircraft.

Jack looked around at his fellow pilots. All were caked in dust, moving among the destruction like figures in a silent movie. Some betrayed their inner turmoil, some inner strength. He knew neither group was likely to give up.

And so, they spent the afternoon doing what they'd spent most of the morning doing. At least the rocks they shifted could now be used to fill in craters and repair blast pens close at hand. Within these, the groundcrew worked on the Spitfires, healing scars caused by bomb fragments and fractured stone.

There were a few false alarms, and the sight and sound of formations passing through or close to the overhead always set Jack on edge. You just never knew if they were going to release a rain of bombs. Just after 5pm, a formation of about a dozen 88s approached. This time, the sirens were followed by screeches, explosions and the crash of guns.

The raid was the least accurate of the day, with more bombs falling outside the airfield boundary than within it.

As it was happening, several more formations passed to the east.

Was there no limit to the number of bombers Kesselring could send over?

Seemingly not. No sooner had the all clear sounded than the sirens warbled another warning. And this time, the bombers had regained their former accuracy, hitting the north-eastern corner of the airfield especially hard.

It was the second time that day they'd plastered that area. Perhaps they still believed it contained underground hangars. Whatever the reason, Jack was grateful, even if not all the bombs fell there. During a long and sustained bombardment, several sticks fell close enough to his trench to make it a tense and uncomfortable 15 minutes.

When the dust cleared, flames rose above several blast pens and the air was full of the stench of burning fuel.

They huddled by the shed. The Flight Sergeant came across to inform the squadron commanders that three more Spitfires were burning out. Jack looked around at the destruction and the world-weary expressions of those moving about among it. He wasn't sure how much more they or the airfield could endure.

But the day wasn't over.

At 6pm, four Messerschmitts strafed the tented villages recently erected around the perimeter. At least this time they saw one of the fighters hit by small arms fire. Streaming vapour, it climbed to no more than 200 feet and headed into the north-west. As it disappeared from sight, its engine began to cough.

That evening, they heard that the machine gunner had been none other than the Station Commander, Wing Commander Satchell, firing from the roof of the caves. He'd also claimed hits on two 88s and another couple of Messerschmitts.

He wasn't the only one achieving some success. Apparently, the anti-aircraft gunners were scoring steadily and, in the last two days, the Spitfires had claimed 16, although they'd also lost five pilots and their aircraft. The fifth was Frank Jemmett, a newly-arrived pilot on 601 Squadron flying his first operational mission.

Having been attacked by two 109s, he'd crash-landed near Rabat. The aircraft caught fire and a group of soldiers rushed up, but they couldn't undo his seat harness. It was a passing pilot from his own squadron that eventually released him, but he died from his injuries soon after arriving at Imtarfa.

There was an ugly rumour circulating that he hadn't been able to bale out because his parachute had been stolen.

The story put the seal on a dreadful day.

Chapter 20 - Late April – And There's More

Thursday dawned with leaden skies and a cold south-westerly wind raking the airfield. Once again, as the sun rose, the pilots of two squadrons sat around, shivering under jackets and coats.

Pete Brown wasn't among them.

'Left on a Hudson last night,' Laddie whispered in answer to Jack's gentle enquiry.

'Gone to an instructor post back in England.'

No more was said, but Jack had no doubt someone had acted to allow a brave man who'd simply reached the limit of his endurance to leave the Island with his reputation intact. He also had no doubt that Laddie had been behind the move.

Jack nodded his gratitude. The flight commander rose from his chair and patted him on the shoulder as he walked toward the shed.

Jack stretched and looked over the faces of those around him. Most had their eyes closed, trying to sleep, or just to shut out the day. Those with their eyes open stared ahead, lost in some reverie. They looked tired and tense, waiting. But none quite had the haunted look of a Pete Brown. Not even Dave Campbell. After his initial crisis of confidence, the young Scot seemed to go from strength to strength. He and Harv were whispering, smiling and nudging one another like naughty schoolboys plotting some practical joke.

As yet, there were no serviceable Spitfires at Takali.

When the squadron and flight commanders emerged from the shed it was to detail them to work parties rather than cockpits. The apologetic tone of the executives did little to assuage the frustration of pilots who, despite the odds, and their own fears, just wanted to get into the air.

As they worked, the clouds began to break. There were

frequent sightings of enemy aircraft and the sound of bombing was heard to the east and south. Until 1035, Takali was subject only to false alarms. But then the airfield was bombed by tens of 88s and 87s.

In the brief moments when he felt able to look up, Jack spotted a couple of Spitfires and a Hurricane jinking among the bombers and their escorts. He witnessed one success, by the anti-aircraft gunners, who sent an 88 diving away to the east trailing black smoke. The cost, yet more buildings and operating surfaces damaged, and a Spitfire in a pen close to Jack's trench spitchered.

During a break between raids, he walked along the line of pens. As more were built, rock and stone had begun to run out, so they'd had to make more use of earth-filled fuel cans again. They reflected the sunlight, making the pens visible for miles, and when hit, they produced vicious shards of silver shrapnel. Many of these sat, glinting, among the rocks and shattered stone blocks in and around damaged pens. Inevitably, some of the resident aircraft had also been dented or pierced. These were being worked on by hunched figures in KD.

The more Jack saw and heard of the groundcrew, the more he sympathised with their plight. They were working themselves into the ground, trying to maintain twice the normal quota of aircraft with little sleep, and less food. He was reduced to eating half a round of bread and jam for breakfast, some bully beef and a slice of bread for lunch and the same with an extra slice of bread for dinner. It was hard to believe the groundcrew were being fed any better.

He kept an eye open for Smudger. When he spotted him, the rigger was on a set of steps leaning over the leading edge of one of the new Spitfires. So absorbed did the young man seem that Jack debated whether he should disturb him. But he decided to go ahead, drawn by friendship and an irrational sense of responsibility.

Rather than startle with a shout, he walked toward the wingtip. Smudger turned his head and shoulders at his approach. It was Jack that was startled. He barely suppressed a gasp.

Even in a world where everyone was tired and under-nourished, the young tradesman looked awful. Sunken eyes stared out of grey/brown sockets above cheeks that were more than usually hollowed and jaundiced, while the limbs emerging from his KD shirt and shorts were stick-like. And then, Smudger coughed, a dry, hacking, cough that caused his features to crumple in pain.

'Hello, sir,' he rasped, grimacing and coughing again.

'Hello, Smudger,' Jack replied, unable to maintain even a forced joviality. 'You sound awful.'

'Just a cough, sir. Lot of it about.'

'Even so, perhaps you ought to see the Docs,' Jack persisted, the concern evident in his voice. Perhaps too evident.

The slight edginess in Smudger's reply confirmed this. 'Thanks, sir, but there's too much on.'

Jack realised he couldn't just barge in and become paternal, and certainly not if he wanted their relationship to remain on its current footing, which he did.

'Okay, Smudger. But it can't be easy at the moment.'

Smudger turned, sat on the top of the steps, ruffled his sandy hair and gave an apologetic smile. 'You could say that, sir. None of the new blokes have worked on Spitfires before, and no sooner do we get a kite ready than this happens.'

He waved an arm over the Spitfire, its wing peppered with jagged gashes and holes. The sight seemed to re-focus him. He shook his head and sighed.

'Sorry, sir. Got to get back to it.'

The rigger was so enslaved to the pressure of work that even a brief rest was unthinkable.

'Okay, Smudger, but you look after yourself now.'

'Okay, sir. You too.'

Jack turned his back, feeling guiltier than ever. Smudger faced a Herculean task that seemed close to breaking him.

In fact, it didn't seem too dramatic to say that the rigger's determination not to let anyone down was likely to kill him.

Jack wasn't in any position to keep an eye on him, but he resolved to have a quiet word with the flight sergeant.

When he did so during another break, it only added to his guilt. Chiefy, normally the most resilient of men, was also visibly bowed by the weight of his responsibilities. Jack hated giving the poor man one more thing to worry about. But what else could he do?

Just before lunch, another formation of 88s targeted Takali. This time, the centre and southern sections of the airfield bore the brunt.

During a lull, Jack looked over the lip of a slit trench. A few hundred yards away, a couple of soldiers jumped up out of the ground and began to run. They'd taken no more than a few steps when the earth to their right heaved and they disappeared behind – within - a hailstorm of earth and rocks.

Jack grimaced, shutting his eyes and feeling sick. When he steeled himself to look again, the smoke and dust were blowing away to the north, but there was no sign of the soldiers.

How could there be?

Whether a lone bomb had dropped from the sky after hanging up on its bomber, or a delayed action device had chosen that moment to explode, was immaterial. It had blown two men to smithereens. Many other troops working on the airfield had been killed or injured, but these were the first such deaths Jack had witnessed. He hoped they'd be the last.

Later, they heard that two members of the Manchester Regiment were missing presumed dead. In this case, Jack knew what the classification meant: no identifiable remains had been found.

At 4pm, 60 bombers plus escorts passed through the

overhead. While most carried on toward Valletta, ten turned about and circled Takali. The pilots ran into a nearby shelter, then looked up and waited for the whistle of bombs.

The bombers continued to circle. If the pounding in Jack's chest and the fearful expressions of his fellow pilots were anything to go by, the delay - because surely it was just a delay – was doing little more than ratcheting up the tension. And when the bombs began to fall, it seemed to matter not one jot that there were ten rather than 60 bombers. The bombardment was just as timeless and unhinging.

It left another Spitfire destroyed and three seriously damaged.

Afterwards, the pilots toiled away, lugging rocks, for another three hours. They saw scores of enemy aircraft and heard bomb and ack-ack reports all around, but the only further raid on Takali was by a Schwarm of 109 Jabos. These dropped four more bombs on the north-east quadrant.

When the light failed and they trooped onto the transport for the journey to Mdina, it was all Jack could do to clamber onto the bus. He groaned as he sat down and every time the vehicle jolted, ie, every couple of seconds.

After a dinner that replaced few of the calories they'd expended, they trudged up to the terrace for Harry's intelligence update. Both COs were also there. They'd been down the hole in Valletta most of the day, so their uniforms were clean, their eyes and cheeks bright, and their countenances youthful. By contrast, Harry and the pilots were coated in a layer of dust that made them look prematurely old and grey.

As a hush descended, OC 249 stepped forward. 'Apologies to Harry,' he began, nodding at the young intelligence officer, 'but for once, I think I may know more than him.'

Harry smiled and held a hand out to indicate that he was happy to relinquish the floor.

'We were all grateful for the delivery of the new

Spitfires,' Squadron Leader Grant continued. 'But you won't need me to tell you that, after barely three days, we seem to be back at square one.

'In that time, the Hun have dropped nearly four hundred tons of bombs on Takali, and over a hundred on Luqa. Between the two airfields, we've lost nine in the air and thirteen on the ground, including another one at Luqa this evening. Add to these, twenty nine damaged by the bombing, thirteen seriously, plus others damaged in the air, and you can see why none of us are getting much flying, despite the best efforts of the groundcrew.'

Jack was trying to keep track of the maths, subtracting from 60. Without knowing the state of the *less damaged*, it was hard to come up with a precise number of serviceable kites, but it couldn't be more than a couple of handfuls.

And, although none of them would have dreamed of blaming the groundcrew for the dearth of aircraft, Jack was pleased to hear the CO acknowledge as much.

'The reason I'm telling you this,' the squadron leader continued, 'is that the AOC has used these figures in a signal to the CinC pleading for more Spitfires. Whether he's successful or not, only time will tell, but I can assure you that it won't be for the want of trying.'

He looked around, his eyes passing from face to face.

'Any questions?'

What was there to ask? They were in dire straits – there were fresh rumours of invasion forces massing on Sicily – but they now knew the high-priced help in Cairo were aware of the problem in the starkest terms.

Faced with a resigned silence, Squadron Leader Grant said, 'Righto then, carry on.' He waved Laddie and Buck over.

The junior pilots looked at one another and blew out their cheeks. Three days earlier, it seemed their prayers had been answered. But within hours, their optimism had been crushed. Now, unless the great men acted on the information they'd been given, and swiftly, it was hard to see a light at the end of the tunnel.

Talking in hushed tones, some of the pilots continued to sup their beer, or returned to the bar for refills. But most, grim-faced, shuffled off the terrace, bound for their rooms.

Jack joined them. What was he going to tell Caroline in tonight's letter?

Friday morning dawned with Jack suffering another attack of The Dog. Not as bad as the first, but bad enough to confine him to the Palace. On the occasions he caught his reflection in one of the washroom mirrors, he hardly recognised himself, so thin and drawn had he become. And as he sat on or retched into the toilet, he marvelled at his body's capacity to produce something out of nothing. The Doc called by, once again offering little beyond tea and sympathy.

In between fitful naps and visits to the cracker box, Jack lay clutching his stomach and listening to the sounds of combat. He tried to imagine what could be happening outside his window. Impossible, of course, but of one thing he was certain: neither the Island nor Takali were receiving any respite.

Mike confirmed as much when he returned in the evening, although he said that the bombers seemed to have re-directed some of their effort toward the harbours, not that they'd noticed much difference at Takali.

Yet again, most of the small number of Spitfire sorties had been flown from Luqa. They'd achieved some success, but a pilot from 126 had been forced into a crash landing, and a flight commander from 601 had stalled onto the airfield as he'd attempted to evade a 109. Both pilots were okay, but another two Spitfires had gone, while another was damaged during a bombing raid in which a Wellington and two Hurricanes were also destroyed.

Takali had been hit several times. Another Spitfire had been spitchered, and one severely damaged when Dave Campbell crash landed after suffering an engine failure after take off. Jack was relieved to hear that the Scot was okay, as was Larry Lloyd, who landed safely after his kite was damaged in combat. The Takali pilots had also had some success, as had the gunners, who continued to do well after the re-supply of shells from the convoy.

Mike unfolded more of the same on Saturday night. Luqa had been hit especially hard, losing another Spitfire and its pilot, shot down by four 109s. Takali had finally begun to launch more aircraft, including a four-ship led by Buck that had not only shot down several Hun, but also protected a pair of Hurricanes low on fuel as they landed at Hal Far. Elsewhere, 42 British and Maltese soldiers had been killed in various locations on the Island, some when a barrack hospital had been hit.

Bombing could be heard all that night, and Jack for one found it impossible to sleep.

By Sunday evening, he began to feel a little better, but not well enough to make dinner or the briefing on the terrace.

Mike confirmed Jack's impression that the morning had been quiet, and that the Hun had made up for it in the afternoon and evening. On the plus side, as well as letting Jack get some much-needed rest, the slight lull had given the groundcrew time to repair more kites. This had allowed the squadrons to achieve more successes. Mike himself had shot down an 88.

The rest of the news was bad.

Valletta telephone exchange had been knocked out and they'd lost contact with Lascaris for a couple of hours. In the air, a Canadian NCO from 603 was forced to bale out. Following yet another parachute malfunction, he'd hit the ground hard. He'd been taken to Imtarfa in a bad way. And Luke Elliot's kite was hit by 109s that went on to strafe the airfield as he crash landed. The young American escaped with cannon splinters in his leg and neck. Unlike the Canadian, he was expected to be out of action for no more than a few days.

On Monday, Jack was up and about, if reluctant to stray too far from the ablutions. Climbing up to the terrace mid-morning, he discovered that the cloud of the last few days had cleared and the wind had gone round to the south. It was pleasantly warm – and quiet. But not for long.

Soon after 11am, over thirty 88s and about 20 Stukas plus escorts passed overhead. Shortly after, smoke rose over Valletta and the surrounding area, followed closely by the sound of explosions and ack-ack. Twenty minutes later, the performance was repeated over Luqa. Takali was next, dived on, either by the original Stukas, or another formation of similar size.

No fighters rose to meet them.

Lunch caused a relapse and a return to his room via the cracker box, so he missed sight of the Italian bombers and fighters joining the assault, something the pilots had long been awaiting. He also ate dinner, but thought it prudent to return to his room straight after. This meal stayed down and he was soon asleep, waking in the early hours when he heard Mike stirring.

It had been his best night's sleep for weeks.

On the spur of the moment, Jack dressed and joined his fellow pilots on the bus. Apart from a nod of acknowledgement from Laddie and a brief bantering welcome from Harv, the journey was completed in silence.

He'd only been absent for four days, but he'd forgotten how depressing the jolting drive in the chilly pre-dawn was. Most of his fellow pilots were so huddled up as to appear as little more than piles of rags, and the faces of those he could see were thin and grey, even before they'd received their daily coating of dust.

As hazardous as flying over Malta was, Jack was sure they'd be more animated if they were spending more time in the air. After all, it was what they were there to do, what they expected. Not days of labouring amid the heat and the flies, or sheltering in a slit trench waiting for death or disfigurement.

It was this that was taking such a heavy toll, he thought, alongside the lack of food and sleep.

When Harry, almost invisible in the gloom outside the shed, briefed them, it became apparent they were likely to spend another day with little flying. Few Spitfires were serviceable. Most of the pilots looked crestfallen, condemned to another day hauling rocks. Jack, on the other hand, felt only relief.

He certainly couldn't fart with confidence.

The day dawned hazy beneath a layer of high cloud covering seven tenths of the sky. The first bombers appeared soon after 8am, and Jack heard the sound of bombing to the east. At the same time, three pilots from 603, including Danny Danvers, strode past, looks of grim determination on their young faces.

They seemed much more confident than when he'd last seen them, just a few days earlier. At 8.30, they taxied past and sped off like old hands. About 40 minutes later, they were back, their kites seemingly undamaged, a welcome change for pilots and groundcrew alike.

When Jack went over to speak to Danny a little later, the young man said they'd had some success. But he'd also witnessed another drama involving a pilot forced to abandon a blazing Hurricane.

This time though, the problem wasn't a parachute failing to deploy, but deploying too soon, before the pilot had even exited the cockpit. As a result, it had snagged over the stricken aircraft's tailplane. The last glimpse Danny had was of the pilot, arms and legs flailing, being dragged to his death.

Unlike the raw emotion with which he'd related a similar story only a week earlier, the young man unfolded events matter-of-factly. At least outwardly, he'd developed the hard skin necessary to cope with such experiences. As Jack knew only too well, it was either that, or crack up.

They parted having agreed to view the episode as a

salutary lesson in parachute handling - which it was.

Still weakened by the effects of the Dog, Jack did his best to help various work parties. The lunchtime raid was late, but no less effective for that. It left more damage to runways, shelters and pens, and another spitchered Spitfire. Two further raids in the evening damaged buildings and two more Spitfires.

As he lay in his bed that night, Jack felt lucky to have survived, both the day's raids and his second bout of dysentery.

Wednesday 29th April dawned with full cloud cover, but too high to cause any disruption to enemy operations. That said, it was a day of smaller raids, and most were in the direction of Valletta and Luqa. Takali wasn't hit until just after 7pm, and by just three bombers that caused little more than superficial damage.

That night's intelligence briefing raised the prospect of something other than normal fare. For a start, the NCOs were present, and as Harry took centre stage, the two squadron commanders standing off to the right were accompanied by Group Captain Woodhall. His presence usually meant something major in the offing.

For once, there were no fireworks to accompany the briefings, the darkness beyond the railings broken only by the odd light breaking the blackout, or by stars unveiled briefly by the scurrying clouds.

The IntO began by confirming that the only Spitfires to launch had been from Luqa, where one had landed wheels up after being hit by a Messerschmitt, and another had been damaged in a raid. He also confirmed that the Italians had appeared again, with two incursions by formations of Cant Z1007bis bombers supported by Macchi MC202s.

Jack thought back to the recognition pictures he'd studied on Eagle. The Cant had twin tail fins like a Dornier 17, but otherwise looked like a sleek Junkers 52, one engine on each wing and one in the nose. The Macchi was sleek and long nosed, with the cockpit well back, like the racing planes of the 1930s.

Harry went on to confirm that Valletta had received another pasting. He painted a grim picture of the capital and its inhabitants, suffering from frequent cuts in power and water, not to mention continuing shortages of food and accommodation. So many buildings had now been destroyed that most streets were blocked, with no prospect of the rubble being shifted in the short term.

Jack found it all too easy to imagine the scene, and the smell.

Harry's youthful features took on what they'd come to call his *bad news face.*

'I'm afraid there's been another result of the bombing. It's been some while since we've been able to provide effective air cover for the harbours. As a result, a few days ago it was decided that the 10th Submarine Flotilla would move to Alexandria. The first boats have already left, and one, *Urge,* met and engaged an Italian convoy. Unfortunately, she was attacked by its air escort and sunk. Lost with all hands.'

He let them digest the news. *Urge* had been approaching the legendary status of *Upholder,* her loss another sad blow for the Navy, and for the Island.

After a suitable pause, he turned toward the group of senior officers and nodded. Group Captain Woodhall stepped forward.

The stern expression on the group captain's face was so at odds with his usual persona that Jack stiffened, sensing those around him do the same.

'Evening, chaps,' the group captain began. 'You'll be all too aware of the high hopes we had when the Spitfires were delivered on the 20th. And you don't need me to tell you that those hopes were pretty much snuffed out in the first forty eight hours. Since then, through a combination of continuing losses and the need to husband resources, you've been getting precious little flying. Much like the period before the delivery.'

After a wry smile, he produced his pipe from behind his back and took a slow, deliberate, draw, then a couple of quicker puffs with a hand over the bowl. When he lifted his fingers, it was to reveal a red glow. He lowered the pipe and blew out a long, thin, stream of blue smoke. The action seemed to calm, not only him, but the whole room.

'You also know that we've been trying to make the powers that be realise our predicament. And, at last, it seems that our voices have been heard.'

The group captain raised a hand to hush the ripple of murmurs.

'Now, why am I telling you this?'

Jack had asked himself the same question.

'Well frankly,' the group captain continued, 'because there's no way I can keep what I'm going to tell you next secret.'

He paused to take another draw on his pipe.

'In a few hours, OC 249 and others who've already been informed will leave for Gibraltar.'

He paused, smiling and looking back at the squadron commanders as another murmur of surprise rippled round the room. Jack looked at Mike, who arched his lips and shrugged. The group captain gave a little cough.

'Now, this will lead to much speculation, I know. All I can tell you is that there is nothing sinister behind it, and that they will be back, although I can't say when.'

He waited for more murmuring to subside. When he spoke again, it was in an authoritative tone backed up by a prodding motion with the stem of his pipe.

'I don't need to tell you the importance of your speculation going no further than this room. The Island will be abuzz with rumour soon enough, but if I hear that any of you were responsible, I'll have your guts for garters. Understood?'

There was a muted mumble.

'*Understood?*' the group captain repeated more

forcefully.

'Yes, sir.'

This time, the chorus was more emphatic. The controller seemed content.

'All right then. Carry on.'

He turned and strolled over to the two squadron leaders, leaving a babble of excited chatter.

Jack knew what his money was on. He was just about to tell Mike when his name was called. It was Laddie. Jack shrugged at his friend and walked over to the flight commander.

Early next morning, after weeks of sitting outside the shed, Jack found himself sitting in it, occupying the little office reserved for 249 Squadron executives.

He was acting Flight Commander A.

Opposite him sat the acting squadron commander, Norm Macqueen, and next to him, acting Flight Commander B, Larry Lloyd.

Jack felt shell-shocked. From their expressions, so did the other two.

Accompanying Squadron Leader Grant on the Hudson that had left for Gibraltar soon after midnight had been his two flight commanders, plus Mike and Zulu du Toit.

Mike had been sworn to secrecy, but Jack was still miffed that his friend hadn't let him in on the plan before Woody and Laddie had spilled the beans, even pretending to know nothing as the briefing was unfolding. And the New Zealander had left without confirming what they all suspected, that they were off to lead in another reinforcement of Spitfires.

Well, all being well, they'd be over halfway to the bright lights of Gibraltar now, while Norm, Jack and Larry sat trying to come to grips with events.

'Apart from the fact that we're now in these hot seats,' Norm said, in what Jack called his *posh* Welsh accent, 'I'm not sure a lot's changed. There still aren't any aircraft —

three at the last count – and the CO said not to worry about paperwork, although we might pick up a few more letters to censor.'

Jack had always been horrified at the admin burden Muddy had shouldered at Biggin Hill during the Battle of Britain, both as a flight commander and a squadron commander. And he'd had an adjutant to share the load! Here, one of the things that had never arrived was a squadron adjutant, although the station one sometimes showed his face. But even so, now he thought about it, Jack couldn't remember the CO, Laddie or Buck seeming to be snowed under with paperwork. Perhaps it was being overseas, or, more likely, being bombed so regularly that made admin disappear, or at least take a low priority.

Either way, Laddie had said pretty much the same to Jack: shouldn't be too much admin, and if there is, ignore it. Jack was only too happy to comply.

'And to be selfish about it,' Norm continued, 'despite what Harry's just told us, with five pilots gone, there should be a bit more flying for the rest of us.'

As soon as they'd entered the shed that morning, Harry had briefed them and the 603 Squadron execs that invasion forces were continuing to mass in southern Italy, where gliders were being held at railheads ready for delivery to Sicily. He'd also passed on that the AOC was determined to retain at least some Spitfires to deter Kesselring from mounting an airborne invasion, or to shoot down as many gliders as possible if deterrence failed. That would further limit their flying, especially in the afternoons.

Jack couldn't help thinking that if they couldn't deter the bombers, they were unlikely to deter an invasion force. And attrition would continue to reduce their numbers. Even now, they'd be lucky to generate more than half a dozen kites at each airfield. So much for Norm's idea of more flying!

He kept his thoughts to himself, not least because he didn't want to undermine his new squadron commander in their first few minutes together. Norm was just trying to be positive.

Luckily, the day began quietly, and the new 249 Squadron execs were able to chat with Squadron Leader Lord Douglas Hamilton and his flight commanders. Nominally, each squadron had its own aircraft, but they'd developed a give and take system whereby they tended to fly whatever was available turn and turn about. Norm was more than happy for this to continue under his watch.

So, when the first call to scramble came at 11am, it was OC 603 and three of his pilots that were sitting at readiness in the blistering heat. They blasted off, returning 25 minutes later accompanied by a pack of marauding 109s. These harried the Spitfires as they tried to land, until one of the Messerschmitts suddenly flew into the ground on the north of the airfield, at which point, the remaining Germans lost interest and departed. Jack could only think that the pilot had been hit by small arms fire.

When the 603 pilots returned to the shed, they were far from happy. They'd had some success against a formation of about twenty 88s attacking Luqa, but not as much as they might have done had the cannon of all four not jammed.

If it wasn't one thing, it was another! And as if the groundcrew didn't have enough to contend with, they now had to renew their efforts to identify faulty ammunition.

While the Spitfires had been airborne, Jack had taken the opportunity to talk to the flight sergeant about Smudger.

'Sent him to the medical centre, sir,' the NCO said, when Jack caught up with him walking between pens.

'The MO sent him to Imtarfa,' he continued, striding out so that Jack had to almost jog to keep up. 'Exhaustion and malnutrition. Probably keep him in for a few days, they said. Feed him up.'

They reached the next pen and the flight sergeant turned in. 'Kept your name out of it, sir,' he shouted over his shoulder before he disappeared within the sandbag walls.

Jack shouted his thanks and turned about, unsure

whether to be happy or even more worried. At least his friend wasn't suffering from some of the things he'd feared, such as tuberculosis or jaundice. But he was unwell enough to merit a hospital stay.

Must try and make time for a visit, he thought.

In the afternoon, Norm led off Larry and a couple of other B Flight pilots against a reported plot of Italian bombers and their escorts, but they failed to make an interception. Later, they heard that Luqa had been bombed with the loss of a Spitfire.

In the late afternoon, they heard of another change at Takali. 249's first CO on the Island, Wing Commander Bull Turner, had left for a well deserved rest, replaced as OC Takali Wing by the newly promoted Wing Commander Jumbo Gracie. Jack couldn't help thinking that Jumbo would roust things up a bit when he got his feet under the table.

It didn't take long.

About 15 minutes after they'd heard the news, Norm and OC 603 were called to a meeting. They returned to say that, among other things, Jumbo had authorised all airmen who wished to do so to draw rifles from the armoury so they could fire at enemy aircraft that came within range.

Jack thought it was a good idea on several levels. Not only would it make it hotter for the Hun, and especially the 109s during their strafing runs, but, thinking back to his experience of firing the machine guns with OC 249, it would boost morale, making those who took up the offer feel they were fighting back – whether they hit anything or not.

Jumbo had also ordered an increase in the number of blast pens being built. And they were to include a new feature, a short wall angling out from one front corner to give added protection to the opening. And just in case that wasn't enough, he wanted new walls added to existing pens, tens of them.

Flying or not, life on the airfield was not going to get any easier.

Chapter 21 – Early May – Hanging On

Soon after 7am on the first day of the new month, Jack was airborne, the first time for 10 days. He felt mildly guilty, having abused his new status to snaffle a kite and accompany an air test. Only mildly, though. It had been too long.

The other Spitfire was piloted by Danny Danvers, newly transferred to Jack's flight from 603, an attempt to even the numbers, at least until those in Gibraltar returned.

Danny had just successfully tested a newly-robbed and fitted flap motor, flap and aileron, when they were contacted by Woody. He directed them to circle over the Dingli Cliffs and look out for a Schwarm of 109s seen sneaking past Gozo at low level. No sooner had the two Spitfires reached the coast at 8,000 feet than Jack caught a shimmer of movement over the sea a few miles to the north.

He scanned the area, initially seeing nothing but blue green water and a few white caps. Then, there they were, blurs disrupting the pattern of the waves rather than aircraft. But he had no doubt it was them.

His pulse surged and he felt his cheeks flush. At last, a chance to avenge days of sitting in a trench while Takali was being pummelled.

'Tally ho, Woody, four little jobs approaching Dingli from the north. Going in.'

'Good luck, Jack. Eight more little jobs two minutes behind. Woody out.'

Jack looked to his right at Danny, sitting tall in the cockpit. On receipt of an emphatic thumbs-up, he pushed the nose forward and dived into the north-west, paralleling the coast. He hoped they'd be difficult to spot against the background of high grey cloud. Their speed built quickly and his controls grew ever stiffer.

Ahead were two pairs of 109s, the first in wide line abreast close to the craggy coastline, the second a few hundred yards further back and out. He and Danny had height and speed, but that didn't guarantee a successful bounce. It was up to him to turn them in at just the right time. Too soon and they'd end up ahead of the 109s, sky-lined sitting ducks. Too late, and despite the impressive overtake, they'd never catch the blighters.

It would have to be the trusty TLAR method again.

Under the cloud, the colours of the craggy terrain were muted, more grey than cream or gold. Somehow it made the turquoise and white collision of sea on coast especially vivid, and beautiful.

At 3,000 feet, the 109s disappeared beneath his Spitfire's nose. Jack rolled into a descending left turn, trusting that Danny had learned enough about crossovers not to hit him.

After 90 degrees, they were descending through 2,000 feet and all was looking good. The leading 109s had appeared low in Jack's ten o'clock, just ahead of his wing, and Danny was in his seven o'clock beneath his tailplane, still turning hard to end up on his left.

As the turn progressed, Jack eased their descent, fighting the airflow forces to raise the nose, beneath which the 109s disappeared again. But when he rolled out and pushed the nose forward, there they were, skimming the waves 1,000 feet below, still in their pairs to the right of the Dingli Cliffs. He sensed they were heading for Hal Far or Kalafrana.

To his left, Danny was rock steady. The similarity with Alex suddenly struck again. Jack resolved to do all he could to bring the young man home. Danny glanced right and they exchanged a thumbs-up.

With the 109s only about 200 feet above the waves, it would be all too easy to flash past them and into the sea, so Jack reduced their rate of descent further. The Messerschmitts' were foreshortened, growing with their approach until he could clearly see the black crosses on their wings.

Tracer flashed toward the left Messerschmitt of the rear pair. The right one twitched. Jack fired. As his airframe shuddered, cannon and machine gun rounds smashed into the 109. Bits rose into the air, its nose dipped and Jack flashed a few feet above.

He pulled hard left, grunting at the first high g of the sortie. Danny was also turning and easing up from the waves, now less than 100 feet below. Jack couldn't see his wingman's first target, but the remaining two were clearly visible, flying straight on as if nothing had happened.

Perhaps their pilots were mesmerised by the creamy cliffs towering above them, but they gave no indication that they'd seen the approaching Spitfires.

Danny snapped to wings level and tracer shot from his shuddering wings. Jack smashed the stick to the right, unloaded the g to point ahead of the nearest Messerschmitt. Its pilot looked right as Danny passed behind him.

'Too late, Butt,' Jack shouted as he too fired.

His Spitfire juddered and smoked. Tracer snaked ahead of his target, which flew into it. He kept firing, his rounds flashing around the 109 from nose to tail. It rolled right. As he stopped firing, Danny's 109 was also turning right, its pilot looking up at him.

No sign of Danny. The cliffs suddenly filled Jack's field of view. Heart racing, he pulled up and left, straining against the g and the grey mist. Below, a brief glimpse of another Spitfire, elliptical wingtips leaving trails of grey as its pilot too pulled in a frantic effort to avoid the creamy limestone wall.

For a few heart-stopping moments, it seemed as if neither of them would make it. Jack was turning as hard as he could and still bellying into the rock face. He looked at the sea below and flinched in expectation of a rending crash. And then, grass and bushes raced past a few feet beneath his left wingtip. He'd shot over the cliff top.

Could Danny have been so lucky?

He kept turning and looked down. And there, by some miracle, was the other Spitfire, busy chasing one of the surviving Messerschmitts out to sea. Danny's eagerness to

346

prevent the escape of an adversary was laudable, but it was a tactic fraught with danger, especially as they knew more 109s were on the way.

Much as he hated to dent the young man's enthusiasm, Jack couldn't allow him to fly on into a potential ambush.

'Knock it off, Danny, knock it off.'

After a short delay, came the reply. 'Roger Jack, wilco.'

Jack smiled. Sounded a bit like a five-year old reluctantly obeying his mother's call in for tea. They returned to the airfield, reaching their pens just as a Schwarm of 109s carried out a strafing run. Once in the shed, they submitted claims for three damaged.

Before he left the building, Danny hesitated and turned to catch Jack just before he ducked into his new office.

'Sorry about back there, Jack. Rush of blood to the head.'

Jack smiled and patted the taller man on the shoulder. 'Don't mention it, Danny. It's all too easy to get caught up in the heat of the moment - and you did bloody well.'

Danny nodded his fair head and turned away.

Jack watched him go, relieved to have got them both back in one piece.

The rest of the morning and early afternoon were remarkably quiet, and it was 5pm before OC 603 led three of his pilots into the air. One failed to return, his aircraft last seen several miles out to sea chasing a 109.

During that evening's intelligence briefing, Harry informed them that April had been the heaviest month of bombing so far, with almost 7,000 tons of bombs dropped on the Island; remarkable, when you realised that greater London was hit by only 18,000 tons during the whole of the Blitz. Takali alone had been hit by more than 800 tons. Three hundred and forty civilians and more than 200 servicemen had been killed.

Harry tried to temper these grim statistics with the news that the fighter force had destroyed 53 German aircraft, while the anti-aircraft gunners had shot down 102, a number Jack couldn't help feeling was too good to be true.

But overall, perhaps there were some grounds for optimism. On arrival, they'd been told they faced 600 enemy bombers and fighters. Since then, they'd destroyed at least a quarter, which might just explain the reappearance of the Italians. They were hurting the Hun, when they could get at him.

If only the rumours of a fresh delivery of Spitfires turned out to be true. They might yet turn the tide.

The next two days failed to dent Jack's optimism completely. Raids continued, but at Takali at least, they seemed lighter than those of the previous month, with the emphasis shifting from day to night bombing. It disrupted their sleep, but also seemed to indicate that the Hun was finding daytime raiding too costly? The Italians were also appearing in greater numbers, although Jack had yet to fly against them.

Indeed, he had yet to fly again. There were still no spares with which to repair aircraft damaged the previous month, so there were never more than a handful of aircraft available. And when it was 249's turn to fly, there were still two flights to satisfy, each with 9 pilots.

On the Sunday, Jack found time to visit Smudger in Imtarfa. His friend lay toward the far end of a ward of 30 men. Their appearance was a shock. Cadaverous faces, tanned, yet sallow, contrasting starkly with the white sheets and pillowcases. Although most were in their late teens or early 20s, they looked twice that age.

At least Smudger seemed to be benefitting from his rest. His cheeks had some colour, and he was visibly less stressed. He'd been told he'd picked up an infection, which they were treating, but Jack still thought it was sleep and food that were doing the trick. Hopefully, they'd give him a little longer to recover before sending him back to work.

Woody held them back again for most of Monday 4th May. When he eventually called on 249 in the late afternoon, Norm led off three B Flight pilots: Larry Lloyd, Smitty Smyth and an inexperienced American, Fred Almos. Jack and the remainder of the squadron sat outside the shed and watched them go.

Thirty minutes later, they heard the sound of Merlins to the north-west. Two Spitfires in echelon at about 1,000 feet. Beyond them, Jack noticed movement. Two more fighters were diving in.

Spitfires? Hurricanes?

'109's', someone shouted.

'Watch out, you two. Watch out!'

They'd voiced Jack's thoughts. He had a terrible sense of foreboding.

The two Spitfires, now in the overhead, flew on, oblivious. The 109s bottomed out and began to zoom up and close from about 500 yards. The first spat tracer.

Rat-a-tat-tat!

The sound came to them as both tracer and 109 shot beneath the lead Spitfire. The wings of both British fighters twitched, but the second 109 was already firing. This time, the tracer smashed into the first Spitfire amidships, beneath the cockpit.

Brrrrr - Rat-a-tat-a-tat.

The second 109 flashed past, climbing and turning back into the north-west after its leader. The lead Spitfire rocked, emitting a thin stream of vapour. But then it steadied.

Jack and his fellow pilots shielded their eyes as it headed into the east, its companion moving into tighter formation. At about the right point to start an approach to the westerly runway, they began a gentle descending turn. But the lead Spitfire, now following its wingman in echelon right, had begun to leave a trail of dark mist.

Come on, come on. Jack willed its pilot to make the runway.

At about 400 feet on the curved approach, its nose

dropped.

'Oh no!' someone gasped.

'Come on. Pull up,' another encouraged.

But the Spitfire's nose continued to dip and it dived straight into the ground close to Naxxar. A plume of smoke rose above the rocky ground.

The remaining Spitfire overshot and flew overhead before turning back into the east. As it tracked downwind, another pair landed. And shortly after it touched down, another four joined the circuit. They too landed without incident.

As the seven Spitfires approached the pens, there was only one, unvoiced, question etched on every face.

Who had they just seen die?

Norm. It had been Norm. Their tall, inspiring, acting CO, a Malta ace, was dead.

While the other three B Flight pilots spoke to Harry, Jack shepherded Fred Almos into the 249 office and shut the door.

'I should have been watching his tail,' the dark-haired American said, his hands shaking, his youthful features crumpling in sorrow.

'And he yours,' Jack said.

Perhaps Fred had been too close to scan the air behind his leader adequately, but Jack's point was also valid.

'When I spotted the 109,' Fred continued with an accent Jack couldn't place beyond southern States, 'I shouted. But he'd been having trouble with his radio all trip, and I don't think he heard me.'

'Look, Fred,' Jack said, fixing the American's brown eyes, 'You couldn't have done anything. And once he'd been hit, you did all you could to get him down.'

The youngster looked at Jack. He sighed. His shoulders seemed to relax and the shaking subsided.

'Yes. He did seem to follow for a while, even into the turn. But I could tell he was struggling. And then his head just lolled forward and...well, you saw. Probably better than me.'

'Yes. We saw,' Jack said. He fixed the American again. 'But I mean it, there was nothing you could have done.'

The young pilot shook his head in gratitude. 'Thanks, Jack.'

He turned, opened the door, stepped out into the main body of the shed and joined the others, huddled around Harry's desk. Larry turned to greet him with a sympathetic nod.

Jack sighed, and looked at the CO's chair. Who was going to fill it?

Jack followed the AOC over to the rest of the group, standing in the centre of the railings, overlooking the plain as the light faded on another bloody day. Facing him, were all the Spitfire and Hurricane squadron and flight commanders from Luqa, Hal Far and Takali, men he'd always looked up to and respected. He felt shell shocked.

Lord David Douglas Hamilton smiled and extended a hand. 'Congratulations, Jack.'

The others echoed the sentiment, and as OC 603 relinquished his hand, Larry stepped forward to shake it. This eased Jack's most pressing concern, that his friend might resent the AOC's choice. Then Woody emerged, smiling, from the centre of the knot of officers.

Jack guessed the group captain had told the rest as the air marshal was telling him. He still couldn't believe it. Two months earlier, he'd been a flight sergeant. Now he was an acting flight lieutenant *and* an acting squadron commander.

'Better have these,' Woody said, holding out two sets of flight lieutenant shoulder slides. 'Otherwise, you're improperly dressed.'

'Yes, Flight Lieutenant Williams, you better take them.'

At the sound of the deep baritone, they turned their attention back to the AOC.

'Because I'm afraid you're not going to have time to go

351

to the tailors.'

The air marshal took a sip of gin and cleared his throat.

'Firstly, I'm happy to confirm the rumours of another reinforcement. On Saturday, up to 67 Spitfires are due to fly in from Wasp and Eagle.'

He paused a moment, letting them absorb his words.

'Yes, spiffing news, isn't it? But it is just five days away, and you don't need me to tell you that there is a lot to do before they arrive.'

He nodded toward two of the party. 'In a minute, Group Captain Woodhall and Wing Commander Gracie will go into more detail about what I expect, what we have to do to ensure we don't lose three quarters of the new kites before they bally well get into the air.'

A slight exaggeration, Jack thought, but he knew what the AOC meant. They couldn't afford a repeat of April's botched reinforcement. Heads cocked at the sound of aero engines in the night sky.

The air marshal looked up before casting his eyes around the group and continuing. 'I am counting on you all to make sure that everything is in place before Saturday.'

His face became stern. 'Is that clear?'

'Yes, sir.'

He seemed content with the chorus of replies. 'Good. Let us make sure Saturday is the day we turn the tables and start sticking it to the Hun.'

He drained his gin and put the glass on a nearby table.

'Oh, and Flight Lieutenant Williams, better not get too used to your new status. Squadron Leader Grant is leading in the reinforcements, and he will undoubtedly want his squadron back.'

As Jack's cheeks reddened and the others laughed, the AOC picked up his hat and swagger stick from the table. He angled the stick towards his forelock and said, 'Carry on,' then turned and walked toward the stairs. Without breaking stride or looking back, he waved the stick to acknowledge the click of heels as the group came to attention.

Group Captain Woodhall stepped forward to take the AOC's place. Behind them, booms crashed out. Instinctively, they turned to see flashes of flame erupting in and around Valletta. The group captain coughed and they turned back to face him, doing their best to ignore the frequent explosions and the accompanying ack-ack barrage.

'I know you've been frustrated at being held on the ground,' he began. 'And especially when the few kites we have are sitting there, ready to be used. But I'm sure you're also aware of the invasion forces massing in southern Italy and Sicily, many of them potentially arriving by parachute or in gliders.'

He pulled his pipe from his KD jacket pocket and looked at it, rolling it in his hand and poking a finger into the bowl. After a few moments he raised his eyes again.

'The AOC and I are treading a very thin line between meeting enough raids to show the Hun we're ready for them, and retaining sufficient strength to give them a bloody nose if they do decide to invade.'

He washed the fingers of his left hand over his forehead, down his cheek and onto his chin. The poor man looked so tired. Jack really felt for him.

'Hopefully, they won't come before Saturday,' he continued, 'at which point, as the AOC puts it, we can start *sticking* it to them. To avoid a repeat of April's débâcle, I want as many aircraft as we can muster airborne to protect the delivery, and every new aircraft that arrives is to be airborne within thirty minutes.'

In answer to sceptical murmurs and raised eyebrows, the Controller continued.

'Yes, thirty minutes, less if we can crack it. This time,' he paused to gesture towards Wing Commander Gracie, 'if OC Takali Wing got his message across in Whitehall, which I have no doubt he did, the kites should be Malta ready - pre-painted, weapons calibrated, radios set. And the pilots should all be combat veterans, rather than cannon fodder from the OTUs.

'So there should be no excuses. It will be up to us,' - he prodded toward them with the stem of his pipe – 'to *you* and your chaps, to get the overload tanks off, turn the kites round and get them airborne again - pronto.'

Jack breathed in and blew out his cheeks, a gesture echoed in one form or another by others in the group.

'Yes, a tall order, I know. But OC Takali Wing will now outline how he proposes we do it.'

The group captain had barely finished the sentence before Jumbo stepped – almost leaped - forward, pink gin in one hand, trademark long cigarette holder and exotic cigarette in the other.

'Thank you, sir,' he said, placing the gin on the nearby table and turning his large frame to fix them with a steely, almost demonic, gaze.

'Right chaps, by Saturday, when the new kites arrive, all three airfields will have more than enough pens to receive them.'

Jack didn't doubt it. Harry had told them over 350 had been built on and around the airfields, although not all were for fighters.

'Each kite will be numbered and, on landing, its pilot will expect to be met and directed to a pen bearing the same number. If their kite is damaged or unserviceable, they'll have been briefed to taxy to pens in the rear, where tradesmen will be waiting.'

The wing commander was enjoying unveiling his plans, leaning his broad shoulders forward and waving his cigarette in his enthusiasm.

'By Saturday, each pen will have a second slit trench stocked with fuel, ammunition and the like. While the groundcrew are doing their stuff, you and your chaps will relieve the delivery pilots and launch as soon as possible. Thereafter, you'll fly as often as necessary to keep the Hun off.'

He looked toward the Hurricane squadron and flight commanders, who'd gravitated toward one another.

354

'I suspect that Hal Far at least will be short of Spitfire-qualified pilots, but we've decided that experience of Malta rather than type will be more important on the day, so some of your chaps will have to learn on the job.'

While the group as a whole digested the information, and mulled over the task facing them, Jumbo took a draw on his cigarette and a swig of his gin.

Manpower was Jack's biggest worry. Their groundcrew were already stretched to breaking point. It was hard to see how they could meet so many aircraft and have a reserve to fix those taxying to the rear. And most pens had only one trench, so there was more digging to be done, most of it by hand. Who was going to do that?

Even as he wondered whether to raise the issue, Squadron Leader Bisdee, the CO of 601 Squadron, newly-returned from convalescing at St Paul's Bay, piped up.

'Of course, we'll all do our best, sir. But what about groundcrew? I don't think we've got enough to turn round that many aircraft in three *hours*, let alone thirty minutes.'

For a moment, Jumbo Gracie's lips thinned and his eyes flashed with anger, or was it pain? Whichever it was, he soon regained his composure.

His reply, 'We're working on it,' betrayed a level of uncertainty missing from the rest of the briefing.

OC 601 had obviously hit a raw nerve, airing perhaps the one problem that couldn't be solved through sheer, dogged, hard work.

Group Captain Woodhall, who'd been busy re-charging and lighting his pipe, made to step forward, but Jumbo gestured a plea to be allowed to stay centre stage. The Controller relaxed, as did Jumbo, barrel chest rising as he took a deep breath.

'Sorry, John. You can probably tell that that's the one problem we haven't been able to solve – yet. But, all I can say is, you put in place what you need, and we' – he held out a hand toward Woody, who nodded – 'and we'll continue to work on the manpower problem. Okay?'

OC 601 nodded, the gesture speaking for all those present.

'Good,' the wing commander continued. 'Now, I'd like you to brief your chaps tomorrow morning, with the usual warning to keep it under their hats.'

The group captain stepped forward to stand next to the wing commander.

'So, a busy few days ahead,' – he looked across at Jumbo – 'for all of us.'

Turning back to the group, he clapped his hands round the bowl of his pipe and smiled, signalling a lightening of mood.

'But, in the meantime, I think it's up to the new OC 249 to buy us all a beer, don't you?'

Leaving the noise of bombs and anti-aircraft fire behind, Jack led them down the stairs to the bar, where he was soon surrounded by people, many of whom he barely knew, all smiling and shaking his hand.

For Jack at least, three of the next four days were surprisingly quiet. 249 flew only three small formations and he remained on the ground, feeling he had to let others fly.

Luqa lost another Spitfire on the 6th – its pilot ending up in Imtarfa with shrapnel wounds and burns. So, by the 7th, they were down to no more than six serviceable Spitfires on the whole island. Following a delivery of pilots and airframes from Alexandria, the Hurricanes were a little better off, but even they could muster only a dozen kites.

There was still no paperwork on his desk, which was just as well because he wouldn't have known where to start without an Adj. So, when not attending meetings on the other side of the airfield or in Valletta, he walked around, briefing the troops and offering encouragement. It seemed to him that Chiefy and his two flight commanders, Larry and – much to the young American's surprise – Harv, did all the real work.

And much to his surprise, Jack enjoyed most of the

meetings, especially those in Valletta. It was good to hear things from the horse's mouth, rather than second hand, or through the rumour mill. Unlike his first visit to Lascaris with Woody, he entered via the front door, accessed through a series of short tunnels and man-made canyons beneath the Bastions. At least it spared him sight of the ruined city, not that the destruction on the approach through Marsa and Floriana wasn't sobering enough.

Manpower wasn't the only problem discussed at these meetings. Another was the supply of ammunition. The squadrons – and the gunners - had been told to use as much as necessary to defend the airfields and the new kites. But there'd been no major delivery beyond the rounds salvaged from Convoy MW10. These weren't going to last long if there was no constraint on their use, perhaps not much beyond the weekend.

The high-priced help seemed less worried than their subordinates. Amid an air of mystery, they stated that the matter was in hand, before moving swiftly on to discuss less intractable problems, such as tactics. These were summed up succinctly in every meeting chaired by the AOC.

Kill the Hun.

Friday the 8th May saw a return to bigger and more effective raids, akin to those in April. They assumed Kesselring was trying to disrupt the forthcoming delivery. Takali was being strafed even as Jack was driven away to another meeting beneath Valletta. Two of his aircraft roared overhead, taking off in pursuit of the attackers. He wished them a silent, good luck.

Once sitting round a table at Lascaris, he discovered there'd been a change of Governor.

The previous evening, a Sunderland had flown into Kalafrana carrying the now ex-Governor of Gibraltar, General Lord Gort VC. After a brief ceremony during an air raid, Lieutenant-General Dobbie and his family had flown out on the same aircraft.

It was said the changeover had been necessitated by old Dobbie's ill health. But inevitably, speculation was rife, most concluding that he'd run out of steam, and that Lord Gort was there to gee up the defences in preparation for the reinforcement.

Whatever the reasons, the new Governor was rumoured to be carrying the Island's George Cross. And with his arrival, previously intractable problems seemed to melt away.

More soldiers were allocated to each airfield and the rate of activity increased. Troops began to complete trenches the air and groundcrew had been working on only when they had a spare moment. The long term problem of who would service and repair so many new aircraft remained unresolved, but the shortage of manpower for Saturday was to be addressed with a radical, yet surprisingly simple, solution.

Each pen would be allocated a team of soldiers to help the groundcrew with refuelling, re-arming and any other task they could manage.

Jack returned to Takali in the early evening. He found it had suffered several raids during the day. However, most of the damage was superficial and the Army teams were already much in evidence. For the first time, he began to believe they could really accomplish their task. And when he briefed soldiers, groundcrew and aircrew, including the, mainly American, pilots of 126 Squadron, he could tell that they too were buoyed by the plans for the next day.

Before, morale had been high, but fuelled by black humour in the face of a seemingly impossible task. Now everyone dared hope for success.

Nothing cheered Jack more than the sight of Chiefy, smiling for the first time in days, the years dropping off him in the process.

Chapter 22: Saturday 9th May – Light At the End of the Tunnel

'Listen!'

Since they'd arrived at the airfield at 5am, there'd been plenty of noise. Army engineers and labourers had raced to dig and stockpile the final slit trenches; groundcrew had hammered away getting as many aircraft as possible serviceable; Hun recce aircraft had snooped around; and German and Italian bombers had passed overhead on the way to attack Valletta, from where the sound of explosions and flak had drifted over.

But, in the 20 minutes since six Spitfires crewed by 603 Squadron had scrambled, it had been remarkably quiet.

Until now - 10.30am.

There was no mistaking the drone of aero engines. Lots of them. Jack was convinced they were Merlins. He and his fellow guides rose from the dusty earth next to the runway intersection. For the last 30 minutes, they'd been lying down, trying to look inconspicuous as the temperature rose and the flies swarmed.

'There!' another guide shouted, pointing north.

Four fighters appeared out of the haze beyond the Mosta Dome. Another four followed. No tight vics this time. The widely spaced finger 4s were staggered in extended trail. By the time a third and fourth section appeared, any doubt that Jack's ears had deceived him fell away.

Spitfires.

His heart soared. All 16 of the first batch from Wasp had made it. If the rest of the operation was going to plan, two more formations from the American carrier should be heading for Hal Far and Luqa, while smaller flights from Eagle were destined for Takali and Luqa. That meant some of the guides standing around him would have to be patient.

He didn't envy them. Under clear skies, it was only ever going to get hotter, especially as the brisk southerly wind seemed to have come from a furnace, serving only to add to their discomfort by coating them with dust. They were also very exposed, no matter how closely they hugged the earth.

The Spitfires were setting up for straight in approaches to the southerly runway. Above and slightly behind, about a dozen Hurricanes had also appeared to provide top cover.

Jack was the only pilot among the guides, there to meet the first kite down, which, unless things had gone awry, should contain Squadron Leader Grant.

The queue of approaching Spitfires stretched into the middle distance. The first was just touching down when two dark shapes broke in from the east. They flew straight toward the middle of the queue.

'109s,' Jack shouted in unison with several other voices. Tracer filled the sky around a Spitfire wallowing at about 400 feet with its wheels and flaps down.

How many had enough fuel to evade the attackers? Most were probably on the vapours, committed to their approaches, no matter how dangerous. Very few had manoeuvred out of the stream.

More 109s appeared, some with flaps and wheels down in an attempt to confuse the defenders. The Hurricanes dived. One, wings sparking, latched onto a 109. The German broke away and climbed into the north-west, trailing vapour. The anti-aircraft gunners joined in, focusing fire on a small area of sky just to the north of the airfield.

Jack felt a tap on his arm. 'Sir.'

He'd become mesmerised by the mêlée. Close at hand, a Spitfire had turned right onto the east/west strip and was coming to a halt before him. In front of its yellow, blue, white and red roundel was the letter C, behind it, the number 1. And sitting in the cockpit, looking back, oxygen mask hanging down was a smiling Stan Grant.

Jack was no longer OC 249, although he wondered if the CO even knew about Norm Macqueen. A conversation for another time.

'Thanks, Corporal,' Jack acknowledged and ran towards the Spitfire.

Nearing the wing root, he leaned into the slipstream and heaved himself onto the wing, noting that only one cannon protruded from its leading edge. Weight saving. A hand appeared through the open cockpit door and he shook it, returning the nods of his CO. He pointed straight ahead.

The squadron commander opened the throttle. Jack turned his head to shield his eyes from the dust and debris flying back in the slipstream, then hung on to canopy arch and canopy as the Spitfire lurched forward.

When they'd settled into a steady pace, weaving from side to side, the CO pointed at Jack's rank slides and shout-mouthed 'Congratulations.' Jack nodded in acknowledgement, sensing the squadron leader knew at least some of what had happened in his absence. Good.

Most of the time, they looked to the north, into a confusion of Spitfires, 109s, Hurricanes and flak. Only when they neared the end of the strip did the gunfire stop. What looked to be the last 109 was being chased toward Mdina, and the Spitfires that had overshot were sorting themselves out for their approaches.

Jack tapped the CO on the shoulder and signalled left. The squadron leader nodded and turned them along the line of pens, each with a knot of airmen and soldiers standing outside. They waved as the Spitfire passed.

Five along, they came to a pen with a large white sign on its angled front wall: C1. The CO knew the form. Even before the airmen had grabbed his wingtips, he'd angled his tail toward the entrance and come to a halt. And the propeller had churned and popped to a standstill before Jack jumped to the ground.

The CO echoed the call of 'Brakes off,' and Jack leant against the tailplane as others leaned on the wings and the kite began to roll backwards. With other Spitfires taxying past, they manoeuvred theirs through the entrance and into the centre of the enclosure. Chocks were put in place and another call of brakes off was repeated from the cockpit.

Jack turned from the tailplane. For a few moments, the

361

only sound within the high-walled enclosure was the ticking of engine components cooling. It was as if everyone had taken a deep breath before the off. The airmen looked determined, the soldiers nervous, their senses working overtime, trying to assimilate the unfamiliar sights, sounds and smells of such an alien environment.

And then, a pair of airmen dived under the fuselage to remove the overload tanks. Others, leading or directing soldiers, stooped under or climbed onto the wings, preparing to re-arm and refuel the aircraft occupying centre stage.

The pen was suddenly awash with sound: tools on metal as panels were removed and fuel cans opened, raised voices, some giving orders, some acknowledging, others seeking clarification or consent.

After taking in the tableau for a few moments, Jack was just about to launch himself onto the wing when a large man in pristine KD stepped in front of him. With a mighty groan, the figure began heaving himself up. Jack stepped forward with half a mind to giving Air Vice-Marshal Hugh Pughe Lloyd a helping shove. The great man must have gleaned his intent.

'Don't you dare, young man,' he said as he raised himself to his full height, turned his head and shoulders and looked down. 'There's life in the old dog yet.'

He flashed a smile, dispelling Jack's concern that he might be in for a mighty bollocking. Then, the AOC turned his attention to the cockpit. He started by touching the tip of his swagger stick against the peak of a cap bearing a double row of scrambled egg.

'Don't want to keep you, Stan, but just wanted to tell you how much we've been looking forward to your arrival. You made a spiffing sight as you came in. Well done.'

He patted the squadron leader on the shoulder.

Jack was surprised to see OC 249's cheeks redden as he replied, 'Thank you, sir.'

'That's alright, my boy,' the air marshal said with a

tenderness that wasn't part of his usual repertoire.

The next words, though, were in the usual booming baritone. 'Now, bally well get up there and kill the Hun.'

The squadron leader looked back with a broad smile. 'Wilco, sir.'

This time, when he reached the rear of the wing, the AOC stooped and held out a hand. Jack took it and helped the older, weightier, man step down, with another groan. The AOC pushed a hand into his lower back and turned toward the cockpit.

'By the way, OC 249, you need to watch out.' He pointed at Jack. 'This young man made a top-hole squadron commander.'

With that he walked round the wing, dodging piles of cigarette and tobacco boxes and made for the exit, touching the peak of his hat with his stick again as he disappeared from view.

Jack shook his head and climbed onto the wing. Squadron Leader Grant would be remaining in his cockpit, as would the other Malta veterans leading in the reinforcements. Their experience was needed, although Jack didn't envy them another few hours sitting on a dinghy bottle. He knelt next to the cockpit door.

'Thanks, Jack, and well done.'

It was Jack's turn to blush. 'Thanks, sir.'

That was it. The last few days were consigned to history.

'Now get out of the way, will you,' the squadron leader said, his face taking on a pained expression. 'I'm dying for a pee.'

Jack stepped down as his CO unstrapped, fairly sprang from the cockpit and walked briskly to the rear corner of the pen. Despite the fatigue of his long transit, he looked healthier than anyone Jack had seen for weeks. Amazing what ten days of proper food and undisturbed sleep could do.

The pen was alive with noise and motion. The overload tank was off and the armourers were already closing up panels. A fitter tinkered under the engine cowling, while a rigger walked round tapping and peering at the airframe.

A soldier holding a fuel can stood forward of the wing root, while a second standing atop the wing poured the contents of a can through a makeshift funnel into a filler point in front of the cockpit. After a few moments, he shook the can and threw it down to a third soldier who took it and placed it among a growing pile against the pen wall, before walking to a slit trench and pulling out another. Meanwhile the second soldier had taken the can from the first and begun pouring.

When the CO returned, he climbed onto the wing, leaned into the cockpit and passed down a hat and small bag. By the time Jack had passed it into the safe keeping of an airman, the squadron commander had already settled back into the cockpit.

Jack knelt by the open door. 'The only real change since you left, sir, has been the reappearance of the Italians – Cant's and Macchi 202s mainly. Otherwise, it's much as you left it.'

'Thanks, Jack.'

Jack felt as if there should be more to say. But there really wasn't.

The CO obviously felt the same. After a short pause, he shrugged and said, 'Well, I guess that's that then. See you when I get back.'

'Wilco, sir. See you later.'

Still feeling awkward, Jack stood and jumped down from the wing. An airman was already handing the CO his straps and the kite looked just about ready to go. Couldn't have been more than ten minutes, Jack thought as he waved his goodbye and walked toward the opening.

He was destined for an aircraft in the second batch, number 20. Before then, he had to check that all was going well.

As he rounded the wall, a Spitfire trundled past, one of several still taxying north or south to their designated pens.

A dust-covered guide clung to each. One kite was nearing the end of the east-west strip. Behind it, the airfield and the air above were empty, a plume of red dust drifting into the north from the runway intersection.

He looked into the second pen, where the groundcrew also seemed to be wrapping up. In the cockpit of the resident Spitfire was the bulky frame of Jumbo Gracie. The wing commander had been determined to be among the first airborne. Jack waited to see if he was waved in, but the helmeted figure merely gave a smile and a thumbs-up, so he ducked out and walked on to the next pen.

Exiting the fifth, he bumped into Chiefy. The flight sergeant was walking in the opposite direction, clipboard in hand. He threw up a smart salute.

Jack, without his hat, acknowledged with a formal nod. 'Thanks, Chiefy,' he said cheerily. 'Seems to be going swimmingly so far, don't you think?'

'Yes, sir,' the flight sergeant replied. 'We do seem to be beating the 30-minute target at the moment.'

The words were uttered with the wariness of a man more used to disaster than success.

'Well don't knock it, Chiefy. It's a long time since anything went well.'

The flight sergeant's thin features finally cracked into a smile. 'You're right, sir. About bloody time though, isn't it?'

'Yes it is.'

'Anyway,' the flight sergeant said with an air of finality, 'if you don't mind, sir, I'm off to check the pens to the north.'

'No, off you go, Chiefy. I'll carry on with these.' Jack pointed along the line of southerly pens.

The flight sergeant saluted again and set off at a brisk walk.

As Jack left the last occupied pen, two red flares rose into the sky. It was 10.53, just 20 minutes since he'd helped push the first arrival back. Batting away flies, he leaned against a sandbag wall to watch events unfold.

Two minutes later, OC 249 led 11 Spitfires VCs into the air. Jumbo Gracie was among them. Even he'd have to admit it was a remarkable achievement. And from what Jack had seen, the remaining five should also be ready well within 30 minutes.

He'd barely reached the shed when another eight Spitfires appeared in the overhead. It had to be their second batch. The knot of guides stood and pointed, no doubt as relieved as they were excited. They'd soon be able to leave their exposed position.

Jack dashed into the shed to bring Harry up to speed, then made for pen C20.

Only one thing nagged. Very few of the eight pilots he'd visited seemed to fit the mould of the battle-hardened combat veterans they'd been promised.

The dark-haired young pilot officer that stepped out of Spitfire C20 didn't either.

Oh well, no time to worry about it now. Jack had time to offer only a quick handshake and welcome to Malta before the newcomer, dressed, like most of the others, in blue uniform, ran to the corner of the pen. Jack waited patiently, watching groundcrew and soldiers removing bottle after bottle of Coca-Cola from the wings.

Coca-Cola!

Tens of glass bottles were appearing. Tobacco might leave you defenceless, but at least it saved weight. Jack marvelled the kite had made it into the air at all.

'Couldn't imagine life without it.' The accent was American.

Jack turned. 'I can see!' he said, smiling and shaking his head.

The young pilot climbed up and retrieved his headset, a crumpled hat and a small bag. He had a quick double take at the soldier pouring fuel into the tank, then turned and jumped down.

'Nothing to report' he said. 'She was sweet as a nut.'

'Thanks,' Jack replied, grateful for the succinct report. 'Someone'll point you at the shed. Harry the IntO will sort you out when you get there.'

'Okay. Good luck.' The American touched his forelock, turned and walked round the wing, picking up a bottle of Coca Cola on the way.

Twenty minutes later, Jack found himself taxying toward the southerly strip, from which the last five Spitfires of the first batch were just getting airborne. And remarkably, he was leading all eight Spitfires from the second batch. They were piloted by Dave Campbell, Kim Kaminski, Mal Cotrell and four 126 Squadron pilots. Barring last minute glitches, all 24 new arrivals at Takali would make it into the air within 30 minutes of landing.

He lined up and waited a few moments for his wingmen and those behind to slot in, by which time the dust of the earlier departures had dispersed. With a nod of the head, he opened his throttle, keeping straight using brakes to fight the torque as the speed increased and his rudder gained authority. Fumes filled his nostrils and the sweet roar of the Merlin his headset.

In next to no time he raised the tail and the aircraft skipped off the rough surface and into the air. His heart skipped with it. Who knew what the next hour held, but at that moment, with the dusty ground and dry stone walls racing past, he couldn't have been happier.

He raised the undercarriage and looked left to Dave and right to Kim and Mal, all easing away into finger 4. Canting his head fully back, he could just see two other Spitfires separating from their shadows.

'Woody, Tiger Yellow airborne.'

'Roger, Jack, tens of big and little jobs approaching Hal Far angels twelve and below.'

'Roger, Woody, Hal Far.'

Jack climbed them just to the east of south. As they approached Luqa, the slant visibility into sun was too poor to see much beyond Safi. But looking up into the blue to his front, he spotted the bombers.

'Woody, Jack, a dozen 88s and five Cants plus escorts passing abeam Luqa southbound.'

'Roger, Jack, buster for Hal Far. Little jobs making a nuisance of themselves.'

Jack had briefly considered heading for the bombers. The Controller's words killed the idea. He levelled at 5,000 feet.

'Wilco, Woody, Hal Far it is.'

Approaching Safi, Hal Far came into sight, or rather, short-lived globes of orange lit the haze where it should be. The bombs were already falling. As they flew on, the flashes were joined by the glint of buildings speckling the haze and then the silhouettes of fighters darting in and around a fearsome ack-ack barrage.

'Woody, Jack. Tally-ho ten or more 109s attacking Hal Far.'

'Roger, Jack, have at them.'

The turn of phrase brought a smile to Jack's lips. 'Wilco, Woody.'

He looked to left and right. 'Tiger Yellow, follow me.'

Jack pushed the nose forward. His wingmen followed, as did the four 126 pilots, easing their charges to the right. When the small coastal airfield was in clear sight, the scene was apocalyptic. To either side of the strip, explosions sent up great fountains of dirt and mushrooms of smoke. Pillars of smoke from earlier bombs rose ever higher.

Amid the mayhem, Spitfires were taxying, landing and trying to land. German fighters, ignoring the ack-ack, strafed those on the ground and harassed those on approach.

Hal Far was barely big enough for Spitfires at the best of times. Today, it would be a minor miracle if any, even those that avoided 109s and bombs, got down in one piece.

Jack's eyes suddenly lit on a Spitfire racing across the

grass to the side of the strip, against the stream of landing aircraft.

What was it doing? Trying to take off downwind?

If so, it was about to run out of airfield. Even as he thought it, the Spitfire clipped a pen and cart-wheeled into the surrounding countryside at the head of a jet of lurid flame.

Jack winced. His cockpit fell into shadow. Fool. He'd been distracted too long. His breath caught and his pulse raced as the oil-streaked belly of a 109 arced down no more than 50 yards ahead. From his right, beads of light raced toward it.

Kim.

Galvanised into action, Jack pressed the centre of the rocker switch. His tracer joined that already slamming into the 109's undersides. It sank from view, black smoke belching from beneath its cockpit. Jack's Spitfire rocked as it passed through the turbulent slipstream.

With 1,000 yards to go to the dense smoke over the centre of the airfield, he carried out a belated lookout scan. Dave to his left, Kim, Mel and the others strung out to his right, but already turning away or climbing. Ahead, Spitfires that had overshot, 109s chasing them into the barrage and, below, a trio of Spitfires, strung out on the approach.

He was about to pull up for the 109s when he realised the middle aircraft with its wheels down was a Messerschmitt. At about 300 feet, it was closing on the unsuspecting Spitfire on short finals.

Before Jack could jink towards it, the 109 was silhouetted by a sun-like flare that darkened into a black cloud. The fighter shuddered and flick-rolled right, most of its right wing missing. Spiralling madly, it dropped away, disappearing beneath Jack's engine cowling. A bright yellow flash lit the darkest recesses of his cockpit. It was followed by a shock wave that buffeted him and his Spitfire.

One up to the gunners.

Re-focusing on the 109s above, he strained against the onset of g, then pulled up and left. The sky was alive with red ack-ack tracer, explosions, balls of black smoke and manoeuvring aircraft. A 109 passed no more than 20 yards ahead. Moments later, he ducked as another shadow dimmed the sunlight entering his cockpit. A Spitfire wing sliced past a couple of feet above his head.

Pulse racing, he kept pulling into a tight wingover, finally looking down from about 2,500 feet on a 109 pulling onto the tail of a Spitfire flying downwind 1500 feet below. On the way down, Jack pushed and rolled hard left, coordinating with a bootful of rudder. He followed the swift rotation of ground and sky before snapping to wings level a few hundred yards above and behind his prey.

The 109 fired at the Spitfire, which was struggling to jink at low speed. Jack pulled on the stick, edging his reflector sight ahead of the 109's nose.

'There.'

He fired guns and cannon, watching his tracer set out amidst the usual judder, clatter and hiss. The 109 flew into the stream, shuddered and rolled left, its nose dropping.

Jack continued to pull, easing right to pass abeam the Spitfire. He lowered his left wing just long enough to receive a grateful thumbs-up from its pilot as he sped past. Continuing his climb, he jinked right and left to quarter the airspace above Hal Far.

The barrage had shifted its focus to the north-west, and the air above the airfield belonged to the Spitfires. Several were still manoeuvring briskly, but like him, he guessed, failing to find any targets. A couple were on short finals and the one he'd passed was dipping into its finals turn. It seemed to be the last of the new arrivals.

On this occasion at least, they seemed to have been able to match the 109s. It felt good. But the bombers had wreaked a terrible revenge. The landing Spitfires disappeared into a shroud of smoke that now covered most of the airfield and drifted high into the north.

Jack thought of giving chase to the bombers.

'Woody, this is Jack, new arrivals down and raiders heading north-west.'

'Roger, Jack. New party over Valletta angels five. Care to join in?'

'Wilco, Woody. Break. Tiger Yellow one orbit above Hal Far, angels three.'

When Yellow Section reached Valletta, the party was over, the 109s long gone, or so far ahead as to make a chase toward Sicily futile.

They landed at Takali. Jack was pushed back into his pen and the airmen and soldiers had him ready to go again in 15 minutes. Re-fuelled and re-armed, he sat and waited for a runner to appear with fresh orders.

As noon came and went, the temperature in the pen rose into the high 80s, in the cockpit even higher. Flies swarmed over everything. They seemed especially drawn to the flesh of his arms, neck and legs, their numbers increasing as he sweated and squirmed, until the confined space seemed black with their bloated bodies. Between the prickle of sweat and the tickle of flies, relaxation was impossible.

He'd taken to carrying a large, folded, map. Originally intended as a fan and a sunshade, it spent equal amounts of time being used as a fly swat. And when it failed to provide relief in either role, Jack squirmed and swore in frustration, which, of course, only made things worse.

After about an hour of slow torture, an airman dashed into the pen. Two minutes later, Jack led Dave, Kim and Mel into the air.

Woody vectored them after an 88 and two escorts passing east abeam Gozo at 25,000 feet heading north. Jack guessed the 88 was a recce aircraft sneaking back to Sicily, perhaps with information on the whereabouts of the new Spitfires. If so, the Ops Room would be very keen to prevent its film reaching the German intelligence staffs.

He climbed his section in pursuit, scanning the sky

ahead as Woody counted down the range. But even when they should have been right on top of the bandits, there was no sign of them in the vast ocean of blue sky. Long after the 88 would have reached its destination, they set up a patrol line at 30,000 feet, five miles to the south of Sicily.

At first, the view of the Island, and especially the snow-capped crater of Etna 50 miles to the north, had captivated Jack. It was hard to believe such a beautiful island could be the source of the vicious attacks on Malta, barely visible beneath a crown of scattered cumulus 60 miles to the south.

During their frequent turns, he looked down, hoping to spot a raid setting out, or fighters climbing to attack them. But soon, he was distracted by a more immediate concern.

It had been a long time since he'd been so high, or so far. At first, the cooler air in the climb had been welcome. But now, with the canopy growing ferns of frost, he was shivering uncontrollably, and his hands and toes had gone beyond cold to numb.

Over northern Europe, they endured the cold, but usually, they were dressed for it. At ground level on Malta, wearing anything more than the standard rig of short sleeve KD shirt and shorts was unthinkable. You'd fry. But up here, such flimsy attire was totally inadequate. They'd have to come up with a compromise.

Jack was particularly worried about his fingers. They'd turned from pink to white, as if the very blood was freezing. He sensed he may be only minutes from frostbite. To add insult to injury, at least one large raiding party had slipped past unseen. He'd heard Woody announcing its approach to Malta, and then directing several callsigns toward it.

He decided it was time to head for home. After informing Woody, he led his section in a steady descent southward. The ecstatic signals from Dave, Kim and Mal indicated that they were equally relieved be going down.

And then, his digits began to thaw.

The pain in fingers and toes intensified until it was excruciating, much worse than the childhood memory of warming before the fire after a snowball fight. But by the time he coasted in to the north of St Paul's Bay, colour and feeling were restored, and he'd long stopped shivering.

Passing 18,000 feet, they were still well above the pencil-sharp horizon line formed by the top of the haze layer. Into-sun, the slant visibility was again limited, but Jack could see the ground clearly. And then, he spotted movement. Stukas.

'Woody, Jack, tally-ho, four Stukas heading north over St Paul's Bay, angels 12. Diving in.'

'Roger, Jack, good luck.'

Jack turned 90 right, searching for escorts. Satisfied there were none he could see, he turned right through a further 110 degrees, putting the sun behind them and lowered the nose to dive more steeply.

By now, the Stukas were a few miles ahead, but he knew he'd have no trouble chasing them down. Overshooting was a greater concern, so he eased his throttle back.

The other three Spitfires, Dave to his right, Kim and Mal to his left, had edged forward to sit, rock steady, in line abreast. They were diving out of the sun at approaching 400 miles per hour, passing 15,000 feet and closing quickly. So far, the rear gunners had failed to spot them.

Jack looked at his fuel gauge. Ten gallons. The others would probably have less. This would have to be a classic fighter bounce.

'Tiger Yellow, one pass and away.'

He acknowledged the thumbs-up from each cockpit.

Their overtake was such that, as Jack opened the throttle again, the final two thousand feet took no more than a few seconds. One by one, the other three began firing, eliciting a ragged response from the rear gunners. At 500 yards to his chosen Stuka, the range diminishing rapidly, Jack pressed the gun switch.

His tracer sparked around the bomber. Before he could ascertain whether he'd hit it, he flashed behind and beneath. Heart in mouth, he looked to either side. The others were there, Spitfires arrowing down through the rusty haze, seemingly unscathed. A surge of exhilaration and relief coursed through him. He relished it for no more than a few moments before leading a spiralling descent towards Takali.

Jack was nearly abeam his pen when the three airmen and three soldiers approaching him began running and looking up, their faces etched with concern, if not downright fear. Only when his propeller stopped did he hear sirens wailing and the crack of the first anti-aircraft shells being fired. He unstrapped and made to jump from the cockpit, but the airmen and soldiers leant against his wings and pushed. Humbled by their example, he stayed put.

Just before the front wall of the pen obscured his view, he saw an 88 pulling from its dive and the splash of the first explosion in mid airfield. He made to rise from his seat again, but his chaperones stayed at their posts until he was safely within the four walls. Only then did they run for the slit trench. Jack, shrugging off the usual stiffness in his calf, was about four yards behind.

Despite the earth tremors and shock waves, once in the trench, Jack turned and watched the smoke rising above the angled entrance wall. The explosions were getting closer, a fact that became all too clear when stones began to rain down. Without a tin helmet, Jack knelt and covered up.

The booms became louder until a massive crack and accompanying shock wave deafened him. The ground heaved and larger stones pummelled his back. Paralysed with fear, he waited for the next impact.

Thankfully, it never came.

The rain of debris stopped, and although Jack could still feel tremors and shock waves, they were much reduced in intensity. He began to unwind, coughing to clear a throat lined with grit. He opened his eyes to visibility of no more than a few yards in swirling red dust. Around him, the airmen and soldiers were also rising, stretching and coughing, wide eyes peering into the mist.

Jack was suddenly more keenly aware of his rank than at any other time since he'd been commissioned. He moved around the trench, helping those slower to rise to their feet, checking through expression and gesture that everyone was all right. Nods of gratitude were his only reward. It was enough.

Figures appeared out of the dust and lined the rim of the trench. One was Chiefy. His expression of concern melted into relief as their eyes met. He held out a hand and Jack grabbed it as he picked his way up the rock-strewn steps. Once above ground, he moved aside to let the others up.

The left wall of the pen bulged inwards and a few cans had been dislodged, but it was still intact. The ground was strewn with clods of earth and stones. Unfortunately, so was his Spitfire. Some of the debris had left sizeable dents and gashes, enough, he was sure, to make it unserviceable for a while. But Chiefy still looked relieved, so Jack guessed it could have been worse.

Conversation proved impossible, so he retrieved his parachute and headset, waved and mouthed a farewell and walked out of the pen. Twenty yards to his left, midway between his sanctuary and the next, was a large, smoking crater, the last in a line that, 50 yards apart, disappeared into the dust and smoke obscuring the centre of the airfield.

Thirty minutes later, hearing on the mend, he sat in a battered wicker chair in the shade of an awning draped from the shed. Mal, sitting a few feet away on a wooden crate, was in the same boat, his Spitfire also damaged in the last raid. A large formation had taxied and taken off while they'd been sitting there, and a few aircraft had returned.

Jack watched the Australian gurning and massaging his ears.

He moved his own lower jaw from side to side, before enquiring, 'How's Nurse Dingli?'

The youngster blushed. 'Very well thank you, Jack.'

Mal paused, as if considering whether to add something,

then continued, 'Going to see her parents the next time we both have a day off.'

He looked sheepish, as if expecting cold water to be thrown on the idea, or to have a joke made of it.

Jack wondered briefly whether Mal realised the meeting would put the relationship on a formal footing, at least in the eyes of Sofija's parents. But it had always been more than a dalliance, with serious intent on both sides.

He settled for a quick, 'Let's hope that's not too long.'

Mal smiled and leaned back. 'No, let's hope not.'

Both went quiet, Mal no doubt thinking of Sofija, while Jack thought of Caroline. Unlike during the Battle of Britain and operations over France, there was little time for day-dreaming in the air over Malta. Concentration on the job in hand was total, anything less likely to be lethal.

But since receiving her letters, when not in the air, he often pictured Caroline around the house in Keston, or working in the NAAFI at Biggin Hill. And since the first batch, he'd had a few more, although none less than three weeks old, and he hadn't received one for a week now.

Hearing restored, he thought he better go and find Harry. Before they'd given up trying to converse straight after the raid, Jack had gathered that Laddie, Buck and Zulu were still in Gibraltar, due to lead in a further delivery from Eagle in about a week's time.

Now, he wondered whether that meant he was still a flight commander. Once in the shed, Harry seemed to assume he was and set out on what turned out to be quite a lengthy update.

It seemed the first fight over Valletta had occurred because the leader of the last formation bound for Luqa, none other than Mike Daly, had tried to join a formation of 109s he mis-idented as part of their escort. Mike had had a large piece blown out of his Spitfire and had crash-landed at Luqa. The rest of the formation had landed safely.

Given that there'd been no loss of life, Jack allowed himself a smile. The story was likely to run and run, and

Mike was going to take a lot of stick. He knew the Kiwi had a thick skin, but even so…

The news from Hal Far was less good. The Spitfire Jack had seen crash was also being flown by a formation leader, an Australian named Ray Sly. The 109s had attacked just as he reached the end of his landing run, so it was assumed he'd tried to get airborne again to help those with less fuel. Unfortunately, he'd failed to notice how tight the airfield was, especially for a Spitfire running before a tailwind.

Having witnessed the crash, Jack found it little short of miraculous that the Australian had been pulled from the wreckage alive, if in a bad way. He was less surprised to hear that Hal Far was out of action.

There was more bad news at Takali. 603 flight commander, John Buckstone, had been shot down as they tried to protect the first formation coasting in. He'd followed a 109 into the sea. And one of the first 11 to launch, Arcy Milburn from B Flight, had also been lost when bounced by four 109s as he approached Takali after the fight over Valletta. He'd crashed near Safi.

As to the new arrivals, as far as they knew, only three aircraft had been unserviceable before departure. So 64 aircraft had launched: three formations from Wasp and two from Eagle.

One of the second formation from Wasp had plunged off the end of the flight deck to be run over and cut in two by the bows of the carrier. Of the pilot, a Canadian by the name of Sherrington, there'd been no sign.

And there was still no news of one of the third batch from Wasp, another Canadian, Jerry Smith, who'd found his overload tank wouldn't feed and decided to turn back to attempt a landing on the carrier. Whether he'd succeeded, failed or been shot down by the Americans before he could endanger their flight deck, no-one knew.

En-route, two Spitfires had disappeared, meaning 60 had arrived over the Island. Harry wasn't sure how many Spitfire squadrons there were now: presumably five, 249,

601, 603, 126 and 185, newly converted from Hurricanes. Neither was he sure how many would operate from Takali when things settled down. Hopefully, 126 would return to Luqa, leaving 249 and 603 with 12 kites each, at least until attrition took its toll. There was still a glut of pilots, if not groundcrew.

Jack couldn't imagine there was much more for the IntO to add, but even if there had been, the sirens called an end to his update.

A tight vic of five Italian Cant bombers had flown through the overhead at about 15,000 feet. They'd been escorted by 12 MC202s in four similarly-tight vics. Why they still flew in this parade-ground fashion when their German allies were so tactically aware was a mystery.

Jack had still to fly against the 202s, but their behaviour in combat was also meant to be strange. It seemed that when evading, they favoured straightforward, smooth, looping and rolling manoeuvres, as if performing an aerobatic sequence. It made them easy meat, and they didn't seem to learn.

It was a different kettle of fish when they were doing the chasing, apparently. Then, they'd be tenacious, jinking and countering every move attempted by their prey, no matter how eccentric. But even then, they appeared reluctant to make the kill, as if the chase was everything. There were even instances of them drawing alongside a well-beaten opponent, saluting and flying away without firing a shot.

Opinion on the reason for the strange behaviour was divided. Some though it was a code of chivalry belonging to a different age, while others maintained that it demonstrated the Italians' reluctance to fight alongside and for the Germans.

Jack wasn't sure about the latter. There were enough instances of them going for the kill to convince him that he should do the same if he ever came up against them.

No bombs fell, and when the all-clear sounded, Jack was directed to a pen to relieve an American pilot from 126 Squadron. The young man, still twitching with adrenalin, said his was one of tens of Spitfires that had met the Italians over Valletta, giving them a thorough mauling. Those with fuel and ammunition had set off to chase the survivors back to Sicily, another indication of the change in Woody's tactics.

The Spitfire was turned round in double quick time, and Jack hadn't sat for long when a message was rushed in. He started up and taxied out to lead Mal and Dave into the air behind eight kites from 603 Squadron. Woody directed them to climb into the south, ready to turn back on a force of 88s and 109s coasting in over Gozo at 15,000 feet. Another formation of Spitfires was climbing out of Luqa, and Hurricanes had also managed to get out of Hal Far.

Jack watched the sun sinking toward the south-west, where it suffused the haze with a fiery glow like the steel furnaces of his native south Wales. The canopies of the eight Spitfires ahead flashed with colour as they manoeuvred. To his left, Mal's canopy shone like flame. To the right, Dave's kite was little more than a dark silhouette.

It was another of those occasions when Jack felt blessed to be a pilot. Few earthbound mortals would have such a view that evening. And when they climbed out of the haze, his heart soared further as the lead aircraft took on the salmon tints of the sky. Inevitably, it wasn't long before the war intervened.

'Big and little jobs passing St Paul's Bay. Looks like Takali.'

But as they rolled out pointing north, the scene to his low left was equally stunning in its own way, the dark canopy of smoke above Takali glittering with pinpoints of light. No-one could accuse the gunners of not doing all in their power to protect the new Spitfires. It was only to be hoped they had some ammo left for the morrow.

Jack spotted ten Hurricanes, which led his eyes to the

bombers. Both formations were nearing the overhead from different directions. He was about to press the transmit button when the noses of the aircraft ahead dipped and OC 603 called tally-ho.

If the noble Lord had seen any 109s, Jack still couldn't. Some sixth sense persuaded him to maintain height for the time being. Vindication for his insubordination came much quicker than he could have imagined.

Eight 109s were diving out of the east to turn onto the tails of the 603 Spitfires. Now Jack acted.

He pushed the stick forward and transmitted, 'Viken, Jack, eight little jobs turning into your six from high in your eight o'clock.'

'Roger, Jack, Viken looking.'

The eight Spitfires jinked, the rear quartet most emphatically - self-preservation, Jack thought. But then all eight pulled round to the right, presumably having decided the Hun were too close to ignore.

The eight 109s had rolled out in Jack's 12 o'clock, about 800 yards ahead. Now, they turned to follow the eight Spitfires. Jack looked to his wingmen. Both were rock steady, diving alongside. He was determined not to be caught out himself, so he quartered the sky. All clear.

The Germans had lost some speed in the turn, but they were still closing on their prey. Below, the Hurricanes were attacking the 88s, which were beginning to peel off and dive into the barrage.

Just as Jack thought he was close enough to have a crack at his first 109, the 603 Spitfires broke in every direction. The 109s did the same.

'Bugger!'

He considered diving straight through the mêlée into the bombers, but he couldn't leave 603 to their own devices.

'Tiger, stick with the little jobs.'

A quick glance to either side revealed Dave and Mal breaking away after their own adversaries. Jack took a moment to identify the 109 offering the greatest threat.

Dead ahead, one was pulling up behind a looping Spitfire.

'Righto, Butt,' Jack grunted, pulling his nose ahead of the 109, which was approaching the vertical.

Jack's airframe buffeted. A high speed stall! Before he flicked into a spin, he released some of the back pressure, losing some of his overtake in the process. He and the German fired at the same time. The 109's tracer flailed behind its target, but Jack's played over the Messerschmitt from nose to tail, sparking on the airframe and flinging debris into the airflow.

He flashed through the slipstream and rolled left into a wingover, already searching for new targets. Below him, another 109 was easing onto the tail of a diving Spitfire. Stomach lurching and eyesight speckling with stars, Jack rolled under and pushed to dive in pursuit.

The Spitfire was jinking gamely, but so predictably that the German was closing. It could only be a matter of seconds before he was able to fire. Jack was still 500 yards back; nevertheless, he sent a stream of machine gun and cannon tracer snaking toward the 109. It missed, but led the 109 to break right, giving up the pursuit.

Making a split-second decision, Jack rolled right to chase it down. They were close to the top of the barrage. He fired and the 109 rolled left and pulled into a tight descending turn. Jack followed, straining and pulling to about 6g. As the speed washed off, his airframe reached the buffet and he relaxed the back pressure to maintain it.

Both aircraft spiralled down, turning at their maximum possible rate. In theory, the Spitfire could just out-turn the 109, but this pilot was good, and they seemed to be evenly matched. As they descended, Jack looked across the circle at the German, looking up at him. All around, anti-aircraft shell bursts, some close enough to make both airframes jump. Every so often, a bomber or fighter entered Jack's eye-line, but he maintained focus on the 109.

Suddenly, they were out of the barrage, spiralling down in clear air, neither gaining, neither falling back. Jack's arms ached. He was breathing hard and grunting to counteract the g, and he was coated in sweat. But, weakened as he was by hunger, he daren't relax. This, he sensed, was a gladiatorial combat, a fight to the death.

The dusty horizon was up round his ears before Jack glanced down to discover they were at little more than 1,000 feet, just to the north-west of Mdina. Every few seconds, sight of the Takali barrage arced past beyond his adversary's 109. German fighters and bombers emerged, some heading unchallenged for Sicily, some jinking to escape the attentions of a pursuing Spitfire or Hurricane.

Jack daren't break away to join the wider hunt. If he did, he sensed he'd be dead meat, falling to a fellow combat veteran, a pilot at least equal, perhaps superior, to him. Anyway, things were about to come to a head, and to his advantage if he stayed alert.

Soon, they'd both have to level or fly into the ground. And at some point before or soon after that, the German would have to head for home, if only for lack of fuel.

They'd been drifting north on the breeze and were approaching the rugged north-east coast. The sustained g had finally taken its toll. Jack felt so weak that he didn't think he could maintain his turn for much longer. But it was the ground that forced the issue.

Two hundred feet or so above the dusty scrubland, the German suddenly rolled out and set off into the north-west. Jack sighed with relief as he released the back pressure and followed suit. But the relaxation was a double edged sword. His hands and arms were so fatigued he doubted his ability to make them do his bidding, and the blood returning to his head momentarily studded his vision with so many stars he was blind.

Perhaps the German had suffered the same effects, because when Jack's vision cleared, the 109 was no more than 200 yards ahead, and still flying straight and level. It wouldn't do so for long. He gritted his teeth, eased the reflector sight over the 109's tail and pressed the centre of the rocker switch.

The violence of the firing rattled him back to life, and he watched the tracer rush away. It sparked around the 109, which now started to jink and dip into the contours. Jack followed, countering every swerve and maintaining pressure on the gun switch. A few seconds in, the machine guns stopped, but the cannon continued to pop away.

Suddenly, a strip of metal flew up from the 109's left wingtip. It rolled rapidly left. Somehow, the pilot stopped the roll and seemed to be correcting it, but not quickly enough. His wingtip hit the top of a small hillock. Breaking apart, the 109 cart-wheeled through the air.

Jack pulled up and right to avoid the debris and shot out over the coast. When he reversed the turn to look down, an avalanche of rock and dust was cascading down a low cliff. Beyond it, for several hundred yards, patches of boiling white water disrupted the otherwise smooth blue surface of the sea.

Jack circled several times, during which a wing, most of the tail assembly and several other, less easily-identifiable, pieces of aircraft rose to the surface - but not the fuselage, a life raft, or a pilot bobbing in his life preserver.

He supposed he should have felt at least a glimmer of triumphalism, but he was too tired, too numb with the exertion of the last – how long had it been? – ten minutes, to feel any such emotion. If anything, he felt a twinge of sadness at the demise of a pilot with whom he might have had much in common.

It was in this subdued mood that he climbed over the coast and returned to Takali.

Standing toward the back of the terrace, Jack played little attention to the AOC's rousing address to the packed audience of new pilots. Of more interest had been Woody's summary of the day's events.

He confirmed that 60 Spitfires had made the Island. There was still no news of the two pilots that had disappeared en route, but, Jerry Smith, the one whose overload tank had failed had managed to land back on the US carrier. That news caused a murmur of excitement and delight. Jerry was either very clever or very lucky, or probably a bit of both; he'd certainly earn himself a few beers on the back of the story.

Five Spitfires and four pilots had been lost. It came as no surprise that Ray Sly, the Australian Jack had seen crash so spectacularly at Hal Far, had succumbed to his injuries. One kite had been damaged in the air, and six on the ground, a remarkably low number in comparison with those lost and damaged without getting airborne in mid-April; although, tomorrow was another day.

After the AOC left, Jack stayed in the bar for a beer with Mike, who was taking his newfound notoriety on the chin. Just before he left, he spotted the CO and Woody in earnest conversation. Perhaps he was being paranoid, but he was sure they were casting furtive looks in his direction. As he left the room, they both raised their glasses to him and smiled.

Chapter 23 – Sunday 10th May – A Glorious Day – With A Twist

Jack had wondered whether the CO and Woody's little chat the previous night had been about Mike replacing him as a flight commander. So, when Squadron Leader Grant called him and Larry into the shed the next morning, he feared the worst. But the CO - looking smart, well-fed and rested – merely said he intended to retain them both until Laddie and Buck returned, sometime in the next week or so.

Jack had the impression the CO wanted to say something else to him, but with Larry there and people beginning to rush about as if there was some flap in the offing, the brief meeting came to an abrupt end. Shortly after, Larry rushed from the shed. And a few minutes after that, he led three other B Flight pilots down the strip and into the air.

At 6.30am, when Harry briefed them under a lightening sky, the source of the excitement became clear.

The young intelligence officer couldn't have looked more different from when they'd first seen him in G shelter, six weeks earlier. Gone was the sheen of health and cleanliness, replaced by a sallow, gaunt and careworn appearance that mirrored that of the vast majority of the pilots in front of him – 249 and 603 had received few of the replacements, most going to 126, 185 and 601.

He looked as if he'd been up all night, and perhaps he had. His eyes were sunk within dark grey sockets underscored with drooping bags, and his cheeks and chin were covered in a downy stubble. The only feature that seemed to have benefitted from his brief time on Malta was his moustache, now a solid black bar worthy of the name.

He stroked it and set off, voice still managing to convey the boyish enthusiasm to which they'd become accustomed.

'Morning, everyone.'

'Morning, Harry.'

The grunted response had indeed become a tradition, enjoyed by the pilots as much as Harry.

'I'm delighted to be able to start with some good news for a change.'

Foregoing their usual display of studied indifference, many of the pilots hauled themselves up and leaned forward. Even Jack, standing to one side with the other execs, responded to the change in mood, drawing himself upright.

Harry was pleased with the effect. 'Good,' he beamed. 'Well, I'm delighted to announce that just over an hour ago, the fast minelayer, HMS Welshman, made it through to Grand Harbour with a cargo of food, medicine, aircraft spares and anti-aircraft ammunition.'

He paused to let a murmur of approval run round the assembled company.

'And perhaps, most importantly,' at this, he nodded toward the rear of the group, 'among her passengers were more than 100 aircraft tradesmen.'

Everyone, Jack included, turned round to see the flight sergeant's eyes open wide with astonishment. After waiting a few moments, as if half expecting it to be some cruel joke, he lowered his head, put a hand over his eyes and blew out the most tremendous sigh.

Jack thought the man might actually burst into tears of joy and relief.

'Those for Takali should be arriving shortly, Chiefy,' Harry continued.

The flight sergeant struck eye contact with the CO, nodded and doubled away to the rear, presumably to pass on the news and make arrangements for the reception of the unexpected boost in manpower.

The pilots looked at one another, nodding and murmuring their own appreciation of the news.

'Okay,' Harry shouted, drawing their attention to the front again.

'It would be wishful thinking to imagine the Hun doesn't know about Welshman, which means that, what with yesterday's deliveries and all, they're spoilt for targets. But, for the next few hours at least, the consensus is that they'll concentrate on trying to prevent the unloading of the ship.

'So, when they come, we expect them to come mob-handed.'

Jack smiled as he sensed Harry building up to a Churchillian finale. He wasn't disappointed.

'But, for once,' the IntO continued, thrusting out his youthful jaw, 'we can counter with force.'

After a short pause, came the final flourish, 'And we will.'

A few of the veterans burst into applause, while Harv and Mike shouted, 'Bravo!' Others joined in, calling, 'More.'

Harry blushed, looking mildly confused. His attempts at such rhetoric were usually greeted with stony silence or a few world-weary groans.

OC 249 stepped forward and gestured for calm. 'Well, it's good to see what a few new kites can do for morale,' he said, looking at Harry and smiling.

'But Harry's right. We're probably never going to have a better opportunity to give the Hun a bloody nose. Let's make the most of it.'

And then, nothing happened. Or very little.

Larry's section returned from chasing a recce 88 and its escorts back to Sicily. The Hun had flown over the harbours, presumably trying to spot Welshman. But all Larry had been able to see was an other-worldly green/grey fog drifting north from the Three Cities' shoreline to obscure Grand Harbour, all but the highest points of Valletta, and much of the ground to the north.

He was sure that when the 88's photographs were developed, the smokescreen – which Welshman must have brought herself - would confirm the minelayer's arrival, but not her exact location.

About 9am, four 603 Spitfires raced off. They returned with a similar story: a recce 88 scuttling away to the north with photographs of nothing more than smoke.

And then, just before 10am, there was a general call to cockpit readiness.

It was another clear day. The temperature was nudging 80 degrees, the haze was beginning to shimmer and the flies were swarming in earnest. As Jack walked into his allocated pen, resigned to another unspecified period of slow torture, he received an unexpected boost to his spirits.

'Smudger!'

'Sir. Good to see you,' the young airmen beamed, rising from his seat on the trolleyac.

'You too,' Jack said. 'And looking so much better than when we last met.'

It was true. Although it would be pushing it to say Smudger's face glowed with good health and vitality, it had lost some of its more haggard, jaundiced, look.

'That wouldn't be difficult, would it, sir?'

'No, it wouldn't.'

And then Jack noticed two tiny chevrons on his friend's shoulder.

Smiling broadly, he pointed at them. 'And I see congratulations are in order.'

Smudger looked bashful. 'Thanks, sir. No-one more surprised than me. Only acting, though,' he emphasised, as if not wishing to over-egg the achievement. 'And I'm not sure how long I'll get to keep them now this lot's arrived.'

He nodded at a bulky young man in sweat-stained blues standing on the wing.

'Don't do yourself down, Smudger,' Jack retorted. 'Chiefy'll need some experienced NCOs, if only to show this lot the ropes. I wouldn't be surprised if you don't keep those longer than you think.'

They stood and looked at one another. Their lives were very different, they rarely met, and yet Jack felt he had more in common, and a closer bond, with Smudger than many of his fellow pilots.

'Anyway, the war beckons,' he said, 'best get back to it.'

They nodded and Jack walked round and clambered onto the wing root. While he positioned his parachute and headset, checked the oxygen, brake pressures and trim, he chatted to the new man, a fitter from RAF Turnhouse, struggling with the temperature change between Scotland and Malta.

Smudger joined them on the wing and helped strap Jack in. Jack thanked them and they returned to their start-up positions, Smudger at the trolleyac, the fitter to the front left. And there they waited, all three getting progressively hotter and more agitated by the flies.

At 10.50, a messenger rushed in. Jack was to be number two in a 5-ship led by the CO.

As soon as they took to the air, Jack sensed he was about to be involved in something extraordinary.

For a start, there was so much friendly chatter on the R/T that the CO had found it hard to get a word in. There were already excited calls of tally-ho against 87s, 88s and their escorts over Grand harbour.

The visuals were pretty amazing as well. The Valletta barrage had always impressed, but looking left as they climbed into the south, he could hardly believe the intensity of flak. Tens of shell-bursts a second flashed within a dark cloud stretching from near the surface to about 7,000 feet. Below, completely obscuring the surface, sat a swirling greenish fog that fitted the description of Welshman's smokescreen.

Above the barrage, tens of aircraft wheeled and dived, but mainly dived, forming long chains, most with a bomber or section of bombers at the head. Some kites within each chain already trailed smoke as, one by one, they swooped into the barrage. Lower still, aircraft spat out of the cloud, several being chased, some smoking.

It was a mesmerising sight.

'Come on, Jack. Work to do.'

They'd launched a few minutes behind eight kites from

603 and were at 7,000 feet before the Controller, having acknowledged several more formations diving into the mêlée, found time to speak to them.

'Tiger, Woody, time to join the party. More gatecrashers arriving all the time.'

'Wilco, Woody, Tiger turning about.'

Jack had already noticed the reversion to callsigns rather than names. With so many units now airborne at the same time, it would be a necessity, which didn't stop Jack feeling a hint of nostalgia for the old intimacy.

More chatter brought him back to the present. It seemed that after a late start the Hun were sparing no effort. But if they'd hoped to catch Welshman before she was unloaded, they were already too late. Before they'd walked, Harry had delighted in telling them that, unlike the ships in March, the minelayer had been emptied in less than three hours.

Another minor victory, although it would be little consolation to the civilians bearing the brunt of the bombing, Jack thought, as bomber after bomber disappeared into the swirling grey mist.

Steady on north, climbing through 10,000 feet, the CO brought them into wide line abreast. Jack had Danny Danvers to his right, while Mal and Luke were to the CO's left. Jack scanned the sky.

The last of a stream of Stukas a few thousand feet below were commencing their dives. The head of the column was being assailed by Spitfires, probably 603 Squadron. They, in turn, were about to receive the attentions of a posse of 109s. Five thousand feet above, eight more 109s circled.

Even as Jack reported the bandits to the CO, he sensed he'd be ignored. He was right. Tiger Blue were about to become the top layer of meat in a multi-layered sandwich.

'Woody, Tiger diving in over Valletta, angels one two.'

Jack followed the CO into the dive. Once established, they closed rapidly on the final section of three 87s, now 2-3,000 feet below. He eased for the right hand bomber, keeping an eye on Danny, who was doing the same. He also glanced above to where the 109s were now arrowing down, but still a few thousand feet above.

'Too late,' Jack muttered.

He looked to the front just as streams of tracer set out from all three 87s. Balls of light arced towards him. He knew he should have been fearful – a few weeks earlier he'd have been terrified – but now, looking down on tens of aircraft manoeuvring against a background of sparkling flak, he felt only excitement.

Danny was firing, but Jack waited until the 87's wingtips sat within his reflector sight. Only then did he press the gun button centrally, sending his own tracer against the flow coming the other way. As he fought to maintain aim on his target, his rounds danced over and around it. Shards of perspex rose into the airflow. The return fire ceased as the 87 disappeared beneath his nose and he dived deeper into the battle.

All around, bombers were dropping their bombs, or more accurately, jettisoning them because there was no way they could see where Welshman was within the smokescreen. If she was hit, Jack thought, it would be extreme good or bad luck, depending on which side you were on.

Danny Danvers had eased right, the CO left. Jack went with Danny. He found himself looking down on a 109 chasing a Spitfire. He checked the airspace around him. It was full of aircraft hurtling this way and that, but nothing seemed to offer an immediate threat, so he rolled left and pulled inside the arc of the 109. It began to fire at the jinking Spitfire.

A square wingtip with a black cross appeared only yards ahead. Before Jack could react, it disappeared again, leaving a knot of fear in his stomach. Re-focusing, he pulled his Spitfire's nose ahead of the 109 and fired blind. As he eased the back pressure, his tracer wobbled drunkenly across the space between them and played over the German fighter as it came into sight. It rolled hard right away from the

Spitfire.

'Yes!' Jack hissed as he entered the barrage.

He rolled right and pulled, looking for new targets. Among the diving aircraft, ack-ack tracer climbed and burst. One red hot cylinder exploded beneath an 88, snapping its tail section, sending it and the fuselage tumbling end over end. Jack grimaced and focused on another 88 a few hundred yards away. A shimmer in the corner of his right eye turned into a Spitfire. It dived down at 45 degrees, passing no more than 50 yards ahead of him.

Another spasm of fear. It turned to paralysis as he looked right to see a 109 almost on top of him, tracer setting out from its sparking nose. It shot above his canopy.

By the time he snapped his eyes to the front again, he was within 100 yards of the 88 and too high to engage. He rolled left to pass above, looking down into the startled eyes of its rear upper gunner. And then, he was in clear air at about 5,000 feet. Way below, aircraft burst out of the barrage to snake away at low level. In almost every case, a few moments later, a Spitfire or Hurricane burst out in pursuit.

Jack decided to stay high for the moment. He continued rolling left through the inverted until, right wing low, he pulled round to re-enter the smoke. Almost immediately, he wished he hadn't. Arcing down from high to his left were several 109s. Grunting against the g, he pulled up and left toward them.

A bright flash to his right. He and his Spitfire lurched as if kicked by a giant boot. His head hit the canopy. He winced in pain, expecting to be torn apart by shrapnel from the exploding shell or his disintegrating airframe. When neither seemed to happen, he opened his eyes.

His world was rolling rapidly left. He heaved the stick right. Dark shapes flashed to either side. The rotation stopped and he centralised the stick. Initially, the smoke made orientation difficult, or was it the bang on the head?

When he'd eventually gathered enough sensory cues, he

realised he was inverted, pointing up at about 80 degrees and running out of airspeed - fast.

Despite the urgent thrumming of the Merlin, it was eerily quiet. Jack's fuddled brain struggled to come up with a course of action. Then, from somewhere in the dim, distant, reaches of memory, came the voice of his first instructor, Chalkie White.

'Don't try and fly your way out. Just hold on to everything.'

Jack clamped his hands round the spade grip and braced his feet on the rudder pedals.

Almost immediately, he felt the beginning of a tail-slide. The nose bobbed as if the Spitfire was deciding whether to pitch forward or fall onto its back.

Jack's stomach was already in his mouth. Now, he held his breath. After an agonising few moments, the nose fell forward, arcing swiftly down. He clamped the controls even harder. Just in time. The airflow forces tried to wrench them from his hands. For a few seconds, he hung against his straps, looking straight down, his Spitfire swinging like a pendulum. Then, it arrowed vertically down.

Back in control now – mentally and physically – Jack eased the throttle back and, as the speed increased, played the buffet to ease out of his precipitous dive. The whole episode had taken no more than a few seconds. It had seemed a lifetime.

'Thanks, Chalkie,' he muttered as he looked about.

His estimate of 3,000 feet was confirmed by a quick peek at the altimeter. He was back in the middle of the sandwich, action taking place all around him. Then he spotted a nasty gash in his right wingtip, jagged spikes of aluminium ringing an irregular tear.

Was that enough to call it a day, he thought, as he eased the throttle forward again?

Perhaps, but she was handling okay, and the rest of the airframe looked intact. And then, down to his left, he saw a 109 with a thin stream of vapour funnelling back from its engine cowling.

That was it. He rolled left and pushed the nose forward. The other aircraft manoeuvring nearby, mainly fighters, seemed to be caught up in their own battles. He guessed this 109 was trying to slip away.

They flew out of the barrage over the sea to the north-east of Valletta. The 109 began a lazy left turn, the vapour stream thickening. Jack was closing so fast there seemed little doubt his adversary was losing power. He continued to turn while steepening his dive to arc into the German's low six o'clock.

His control inputs were automatic. But his mind began a feverish debate.

The 109 offered no further threat. Its pilot was merely trying to coax his crippled fighter home. He may even be injured. At the least, he was likely to be plagued by fear, facing a transit of enemy airspace and a 60 mile sea crossing with a suspect engine.

Shouldn't Jack seek a more dangerous, a more worthy prey?

He rolled out at 1500 feet in the ideal position, 200 yards behind and 50 below the Messerschmitt. The vapour had darkened. It pulsed, spitting out sooty smoke rings.

In the moments remaining, Jack remembered similar moral questions during the Battle of Britain. The answer was the same as then, the same as when he was caught fighting in the playground as a five year old. It came to him as he pressed the gun button.

They started it.

His cannon shells slammed into the 109's lower fuselage. As he slid swiftly past on its right, he fancied he saw a glint of flame. He pulled hard right, grunting at the g. Reaching the buffet, he relaxed a smidge to play it. Halfway round, he forced his tired neck muscles to give him a view of his opponent.

Lurid flames played along the 109's lower fuselage.

Fuel tank, Jack thought, as tongues reached up to lick the

angular canopy. The 109 rolled right to reveal a glow inside the cockpit. The pilot twitched as if sitting on hot coals, his hands up, frantically trying to open or smash through the perspex.

The image was fleeting, but seared on Jack's retina as he continued the turn. When he rolled out, the fuselage of the 109 was completely wreathed in flame. It descended in a tight spiral. He watched it go, imagining what it must be like in that cockpit: the unbearable heat, the sight and smell of burning flesh, the agony. He grimaced, striving to erase the images as the blazing 109 smashed into the sea in a shower of spray one mile to the east of Sliema.

Feeling drained, physically and mentally, Jack made an orbit, during which the water boiled but nothing beyond a few dark specks appeared on the surface. A belated lookout scan revealed other aircraft, but nothing close enough to cause concern.

If his ammunition wasn't spent, he was. He set heading for Takali, passing abeam Valletta, which was still shrouded by the smokescreen. The greenish mist had drifted far enough north to obscure most of Sliema before it dissipated on the breeze. Above it, the sky was filled with tell-tale signs of further destruction, pillars of smoke rising to form a larger pall funnelling away into the north.

If Welshman had survived, it would be at the cost of the civilian population.

Jack shook his head and sighed. So much death and destruction, in the air and on the ground.

When Jack rolled off his headset, he realised he had no recollection of how he'd made his way from north of Sliema to his allocated pen.

'All right, sir?'

Smudger's voice broke the spell. Jack shook his head and looked up. The newly-promoted airman smiled down, waiting for Jack to hand him his straps. Somehow, sight of him had banished the dark thoughts. So complete was the transformation that Jack's reply was jokey in tone.

'Yes, fine now, Corporal Smith. Don't know what came over me.'

He handed up his straps.

'Nothing to do with that, was it, sir?' Smudger asked, pointing at the jagged hole in the wingtip.

'Might have been, I suppose. Sorry to bring more work – on your first day back as well.'

'Suppose I'll cope, sir. But you're sure it's not me. This kept happening last time I was your rigger.'

Jack felt another lift at the term, *your rigger*. Perhaps there were now enough groundcrew for them to have their own. And if Smudger really was to be his rigger, he couldn't be happier.

He heaved himself up and stepped left onto the wing. 'Well, we'll just have to see if we can both do better this time, won't we?'

'Yes, sir. But I'm afraid you won't be seeing this one for the rest of the day.'

'I guessed not. But I'm sure you'll find me another.'

Jack looked up as he said it. A couple of Messerschmitts flashed overhead, chased by ack-ack bursts. Instinctively, he and Smudger ducked.

'I think I'm probably going to need one,' Jack said as he straightened.

Smudger's eyes followed the retreating 109s. 'Yes. I think you probably are, sir.'

The 109s weren't going to give up their dominance without a fight, Jack thought. He'd been right to prevent one of them making it back to Sicily. Despite the horror of the young German's death, it had to be done.

He pulled his parachute out of the seat, grabbed his headset and turned to jump down from the wing.

After reporting to Harry, Jack stayed in the shed with the CO, Larry and the 603 execs. OC 603 was fuming, having just had his cannon jam when in prime position for a kill.

Faulty ammunition was still a major irritant.

While other pilots filed their returns, Jack joined the CO and Larry in their small office. There was little to say. Although there were now more aircraft, they were still going to be launching flights rather than squadrons. So, on 249 at least, the plan was to have the flights alternate between periods of cockpit readiness.

The CO put his head down to look through some paperwork – probably something I should have done, Jack thought – and the shed began to fill with airmen updating maps and returns under the direction of Harry and his clerks. Jack and Larry retreated to join the rest of the pilots outside in the shade.

Before they left though, Harry informed them that the first raid had been met by 37 Spitfires and 13 Hurricanes, and that, between them, 249 and 603 had claimed five destroyed, two probables and eight damaged. In addition, the Welshman was still intact.

Out in the fresh air, those that had flown were in high spirits, chattering animatedly, hands replaying the combat for an eager audience of those yet to fly. Jack and Larry looked at one another and smiled.

Jack was especially amused by Luke Elliott. Perhaps understandably, the young American NCO had been nervy and subdued since his brush with death in late April. But now, out of the shadow of Newfy, who was confined to bed with a nasty case of the Dog, he was regaling Harv and Dave with his exploits, interweaving his hands like a hardened veteran.

Jack struck eye contact with Dave, who raised his eyebrows and nodded at Luke. Jack nodded in return. Since that day outside G Shelter, the Scot had seemed to go from strength to strength. Perhaps all he'd needed was to voice his fears, and to hear that they were shared by someone more experienced than himself. Whatever the reason, beyond nods and glances, the episode had never been mentioned again.

The stories of combat continued, and if the claims were to be believed, and the other two airfields had been as successful, they'd really given the raiders a bloody nose. And perhaps they had, because there were no further alarms until 2pm, when the CO and Larry led off most of B Flight.

They returned with tales of joining Spitfires from Luqa and Hal Far to see off a force of 88s and their escorts who were making another attempt on Welshman. Once again, they lodged several claims, and only one of the Takali aircraft had been damaged.

By the late afternoon, Jack was on his third stint of readiness, sweltering in a fly-infested cockpit. Smudger and a new fitter, LAC Paddy Rice, shared some of his discomfort, although, as the sun sank a little, Jack made them step into the lengthening shadow of the pen wall.

Paddy, a willowy Londoner who'd arrived on Welshman less than 12 hours before, looked particularly uncomfortable in his hairy blue trousers. He'd removed his blue shirt for a while, but Smudger had made him put it back on when his shoulders and arms began to redden. Now, the freckly youngster's light blue shirt had large dark patches expanding from his armpits and over much of his back and chest.

Sunburn was a rite of passage for most of those new to the Island. The soldiers and groundcrew just put up with it until their skin gained the texture of tanned leather. Jack, like most of the pilots, was more careful, put off by the agony of wearing harnesses over sore shoulders. Not that everyone was that sensible. In the early days, many Hurricane pilots were rumoured to have flown without shoulder straps. A few of these were said to have met grisly ends, hitting the ground while still trying to don their parachutes.

Jack was fanning himself with his map when one of the ops clerks ran in. It was 5.50. He hoped the message meant either a stand down or a scramble, anything to get out of the cramped cockpit.

It was instructions to scramble, plus the order of battle. A few moments after the messenger jumped from the wing, Jack started his Merlin, relishing the buffeting from the cool, fume-laden, propeller slipstream. Smudger and Paddy guided him through the front of the pen and stayed at his wingtips as he waited for the CO to taxy past, leading Mike, Kim and Luke, who all gave cheery waves.

The messenger had said ten from 603 would follow, and beyond Harv, Mal and Dave, patiently waiting for him to edge out, Jack could see more Spitfires emerging from pens further along the line. Feeling a surge of emotion at the sight of so many, he added a growl of power and waved a farewell to Smudger and Paddy as he pulled forward to follow Luke.

It was the first time Jack had seen Italian kites close up. Five thousand feet below, five Cant Z.1007bis bombers were surrounded by 20 Macchi MC202 fighters and ten Hurricanes.

Jack looked again. Hurricanes!

It was uncanny. Recognition posters highlighted the similarity between Sidney Cam's fighter and the Reggiane Re 2001, but it still came as a shock to see them in the flesh. He hoped no real Hurricanes appeared in the next ten minutes or so. If they did, he couldn't guarantee they wouldn't get a squirt from his guns.

Woody had put them in the ideal place, above and behind the Italian formation as it approached the Valletta barrage from the north-west. Other squadrons were being vectored onto a follow-on force of Hun aircraft approaching from the north.

'Woody, Tiger diving in.'

'Roger, Stan, good luck.'

The lead section dipped into the dive. Jack counted to five as he quartered the sky and looked to either side at his wingmen. No enemy in sight, so he pushed the stick forward. He had no doubt two sections of 603 Spitfires would do the same about ten seconds later.

Beneath him, the CO dived straight for the five Cants, still in their tight vic. Jack followed, waiting every moment for the Italian fighters to react. But, either the section leaders hadn't spotted them, or they were maintaining their ludicrously tight vics in the deluded belief that such a tactic would give the bombers greater protection. Either way, he wasn't complaining.

'Your funeral,' he muttered.

The words had hardly left his lips when tracer from the lead Spitfires raced towards the bombers. A flash to the right of the formation caught Jack's eye. The initial starburst dimmed to reveal the left engine of the right hand bomber glowing with a fiendish intensity. From its fiery heart, a fan of flame flared back in the airflow, licking inward toward the fuselage, no more than a few feet away.

Still, the Italian bombers maintained formation.

You had to admire their courage and discipline, if not their combat nous.

Jack re-focused on the lead bomber as the CO's section all found gaps through which to descend. The Italian fighters finally began to react, turning to chase down the attackers, but still in their vics.

Tracer flashed from the Cant's upper gunners, eliciting an immediate response from Jack's wingmen. He felt his stomach tighten, but held his fire.

Even as time careered forward, he noticed how Harv, Mal and Dave's fire hosed harmlessly ahead of or behind their targets. At the same time, and by a mechanism he still didn't really understand, he calculated his own deflection. Without conscious commands, his hands and feet moved to position the gunsight half an aircraft length ahead of the bomber – and he waited.

Until…'Now!'

He pressed the centre of the rocker switch. Again, as his airframe reared and bucked with the vicious recoil, his hands and feet moved automatically to keep the sight centred. His tracer had set out into clear air, but now the Cant flew into his fire, the first rounds sparking on the nacelle of the radial engine in the monster's nose.

'Fuck me!'

The bomber burst into a rapidly expanding cloud of orange and black. Huge chunks of wreckage flashed all around. Jack entered the fireball, wincing in expectation of a nasty end. But somehow, his Spitfire emerged in one piece, leaving him breathing heavily and flushed from the heat of the fireball.

Before he had time to check on the progress of his wingmen, tracer arced in from the right. Impacts.

'Shit!'

He pulled right, grunting against the sudden onset of 5g, straining to retain vision as the grey shroud descended. Three shapes flashed past, one overhead and one to either side. Ahead, another three, Macchis, a tight vic in upper plan view, as if displaying at Hendon.

Jack fired as he pulled, raking them nose to tail before passing behind. He snapped to wings level and jinked to look around.

To his front, nothing. Above, three bombers, one smoking, bombs falling from their open bomb bays. These threatened to hit Spitfires diving between them. Behind and beneath, a confusing ball of combat, mostly just above another intense barrage. Some aircraft sank into the gun-smoke, from which flashes of orange erupted.

Jack rolled left and pulled, reversing to roll out on the tail of three Reggiane's. As he sank beneath them, he took an extra moment to check their wing insignia - three strange black prongs within a circle. Even after looking at wrecks on the ground, they still had no idea what the symbols were: the silhouettes of three torture devices, or maybe three Thompson submachine guns.

Very fascist anyway, and definitely not to be seen on Hurricanes.

Ideally placed 100 yards behind and below the left hand fighter, he pressed the gun button. In quick succession, the four machine guns gave out, but the two cannon continued to pump away. His shells rammed home, raising sparks.

A trail of dark smoke appeared from the Reggiane's left wing root and it rolled hard left. Jack pulled right and gave the remaining two Eyeties a few shells before he passed behind them. To his right, another Macchi was chasing down a Spitfire.

Jack pushed on the throttle, jinked right, rolled left and pulled hard. In no time, he reached the buffet and relaxed to maintain it, holding 120 degrees of bank and grunting as he pulled over, looking down on Spitfire and Macchi. The Macchi closed, easing into a firing position.

Jack realised that if he was to save the RAF pilot, once again he was going to have to take a tricky deflection shot. Setting his jaw, he played the buffet, eking out the maximum rate of pitch, arcing his Spitfire's nose over the Macchi until it had disappeared. He pulled the sight halfway toward the Spitfire, then pressed the bottom of the rocker switch.

The recoil as his cannon shells raced away forced him into the heavy buffet and his left wing dropped, tucking him upside down in an instant. He centralised the controls. His Spitfire completed two complete rolls before the rotations stopped and he sank into the barrage.

He was sweating freely, breathing heavily. The misty air crackled with fury. He seemed to be in the centre of a 100-yard diameter bubble, shells bursting all round its circumference. And the bubble seemed to move with him. His Spitfire lurched with the shockwaves, throwing him from side to side of the cockpit.

Why no shells exploded closer, or why he hadn't been hit by hurtling shell-cases, he had no idea. But it was only a matter of time.

A Stuka dived into the smoke ahead of him.

Where had that come from?

It didn't matter. There it was. Jack rolled hard left and pulled. Again, he reached the buffet relatively quickly. Playing it, he arced over to sit high in the bomber's 12 o'clock as they both dived. Tracer set out from its upper gun. Sparks played on his propeller and he flinched, dipping his head.

Regaining control, he steadied the gunsight over the bomber's nose and pressed the gun button. His tracer flashed into that coming the other way. The return fire stopped as an explosion ripped away the bomber's left wing outboard of the gull-wing fold. This time, Jack knew it was ack-ack.

As the bomber began to topple left, he eased right and out of the barrage.

Two 109s in his high three o'clock. Their noses sparked. Jack rolled toward them and pulled, the tracer passing behind. Before he'd even regained level flight, and long before he had a chance to fire, they also passed behind. But he could see others above, several within striking distance.

Heavily outnumbered and with no more than a few seconds' ammunition remaining, he was in a bind. Four 109s turned toward him.

'Shit!'

Jack pushed the nose forward again, rolled hard left and pulled, straining to look up as he turned back toward the barrage. He didn't want to re-enter it, and if they'd leave him alone, or were after other targets, he wouldn't. But no, as they came into sight, all four were still arrowing toward him. There seemed little doubt he was their prey.

He rolled out. Above, the noses of the lead 109s sparked and tracer set out. Ahead, the smoke was thicker than ever. He pushed on the throttle and speared into it. Immediately, he was surrounded by flashes and dark balls of soot. His Spitfire began to bounce in the disturbed air.

He was tempted to close his eyes and give in to fate. But, gritting his teeth, he looked around. No sign of the 109s, but several Stukas were being chased down by Spitfires. Grand

Harbour was still obscured by an effective smokescreen. A flash of light within it dimmed to an orange glow, from which circular ripples pulsed out.

And then, he was clear. Three thousand feet above Marsa Racetrack. No sign of any other aircraft, just the smokescreen drifting to shroud the surface north of Valletta. Finding himself in philosophical mood, Jack headed for Takali.

He couldn't imagine experiencing a more intense, what, ten or fifteen minutes. And somehow, he sensed that he probably wouldn't, not on Malta anyway. If even a fraction of the other Spitfires and ack-ack gunners had achieved the successes he'd witnessed, the enemy, German and Italian, must have been routed. And for the second day in succession.

Something told him it was a turning point. For the first time since arriving on the Island, he felt there'd been a genuine shift in the tide.

Smudger gave his pilot an admonishing look and shook his head.

'Could have been worse, Smudger,' Jack said, as he looked at the jagged holes in his tailplane and fin.

'I'm sure it could have, sir,' the rigger replied, 'but patching those up'll still keep me up way past my bedtime. If you keep this up, I think I might have to ask for a transfer.'

Jack felt a genuine twinge of guilt at the reality behind Smudger's light-hearted words. The damage was repairable, and probably by the morning, but it really would mean another late finish for the rigger.

And yet, as he glanced at the new engine fitter beetling away under the cowling, he sensed there was room for even the groundcrew to be optimistic. More manpower. More supplies. He decided not to overplay his new-found enthusiasm, though.

'Point taken, Smudger. I'll try and do better next time.'

'Thank you, sir.'

They smiled and Jack noticed that Paddy was now leaning on the leading edge of the wing, listening to their conversation.

'And how're you feeling, LAC Rice?'

'Not too bad, sir. Glad to be off that bloody ship at least.'

'I bet,' Jack said. 'Although I think you'll miss the food.'

'Couldn't keep it down anyway, sir, so anything that stays in me stomach'll be a bonus.'

'Ah, so not a sailor then?'

'No, sir. No way. Can't understand anybody wanting to join the Navy.'

Jack thought back to launching from Eagle, and fighting over the March convoy.

'You and me both, Paddy, you and me both.'

After a brief pause, Jack brought the brief confab to a close. 'Anyway, best be getting on.'

He looked up at the sky. 'Hopefully, that'll be it for today. If not, I'll see you both later.'

'Okay, sir,' Smudger replied. 'Have a good night.'

'You too,' Jack said and walked away.

As he neared the shed, Jack realised he wasn't the only one to feel more optimistic.

Up until two days ago, and especially at this time of day, the pilots would have been lounging around in silent, weary, contemplation, no doubt feeling sorry for themselves and their plight. Now, they were all up and moving, smiling, clapping one another on the back and chattering excitedly.

Those that hadn't contributed directly to the day's successes had witnessed them. They all agreed that the enemy had suffered a terrible reverse, while, at Takali at least, there hadn't been a single loss. And so far, there hadn't been a single raid on the airfield, either.

There had been humour, before. Of course there had. But

it had mainly been of the black variety, a defence mechanism. This was joy. You could see it on the faces of Larry and Mike, Harv and Mal, JC, Kim, Dave, Danny and Luke.

Jack's hard-headed, pragmatic, side nagged him not to get too caught up in the euphoria, sensing an element of hysteria in the mix. After all, there'd be plenty more challenges, losses and disappointments. But as he joined the rest, he decided to try and sideline such thoughts and go with the flow.

Clutching their beers, Mike and Jack reached the top of the staircase and stepped onto the noisy terrace. Mike raised his voice over the general hubbub to carry on relating his story. But Jack had ceased to hear.

Group Captain Woodhall was with the CO again. Both were looking at him, just as they had been the previous evening. But whereas then there'd been an element of uncertainty in their expressions, now they looked as if a decision had been made. They were all smiles, and yet Jack sensed he was about to be told something he might not wish to hear.

Possibilities flashed through his mind. His mother? Caroline?

The controller waved him over.

The engines droned and the metal tube rocked from side to side. Jack leant back and tried to catch up with events.

Apart from the headlines - Welshman departing and spectacular success in the air – most of the briefing on the terrace had washed over him. Even the parts relating to him had unfolded as if he'd been in a dream. He'd acknowledged the cheers and applause at the announcement of his DFC. But he'd probably looked as surprised as the rest at the news that he was leaving the Island that night. Even though he'd been told a few minutes earlier, it was as if he didn't really believe it until it became public.

The rocking stopped momentarily. Jack's eyes struggled to see anything in the dark belly of the Hudson. Only the odd glint from eyes and faces confirmed that several other people sat opposite him. The engines wound up and the airframe shuddered.

He'd been able to say goodbye to most of the pilots, but not to Laddie, to whom he owed so much, or to Buck. And of course he hadn't been able to see Smudger. Mike had promised to wish his rigger all the very best, but Jack couldn't help feeling guilty for deserting him again, albeit in less dramatic fashion than at Biggin Hill. Now there seemed some hope of victory on Malta, he hoped the young man wouldn't be too long getting home to his girlfriend.

And as for him..?

He held onto his seat and braced as the brakes released and the Hudson began to lurch down Luqa's main runway. He should have been over the moon. Leaving Malta, not only to be a flight commander, but to serve under a squadron commander he already knew and respected: Piers White, the young man who'd made such a positive impression during their few weeks together in the summer of 1940.

The Hudson lumbered into the air. The ride became only slightly smoother as the airframe continued to try and rattle itself to pieces.

Working for Piers had all the makings of a dream posting.

And yet?

He closed his eyes and willed the Hudson to turn right, to head for good old Blighty, for Caroline. But no, there was to be no last minute reprieve. The twin-engined bomber-cum-transport aircraft turned left. Finally, he was forced to accept it.

He was bound for Egypt.

Epilogue

Delays introducing the Spitfire to North Africa meant that Jack spent several months on the ground in Cairo and Alexandria before taking up the promised flight commander post.

Meanwhile, back in Malta, despite several close calls, all his friends survived. Most of the pilots left the Island somewhere between early June and late July. The vast majority returned to the British Isles, but a few, including Mike Daly, left for Egypt. Before he left, Mal Cotrell married Sofija Dingli. Smudger remained on the Island until well into 1944.

Of the real characters, Hugh Pughe Lloyd rose to the rank of Air Chief Marshal and was AOC-in-C Bomber Command between 1950 and 1953. He died in 1981. Woody Woodhall left the Island on 15th July 1942. He retired from the RAF in 1945 and died in New Zealand in 1968. Laddie Lucas went on to command 249 Squadron and several others, retiring as a wing commander. After the war, he became a journalist and an MP. He died in 1998. Buck McNair remained in the Royal Canadian Air Force, commanding several squadrons and wings, and rising to the rank of group captain. He died in 1971.

Historical Note

The travails of the Maltese began with the Italian declaration of war on 10th June 1940. There was an air raid the very next day and the Maltese began to suffer the hardship, death and destruction that, in varying degrees of severity, would be with them for the next two and a half years.

Given the acknowledged strategic importance of the Island, efforts at air defence had always seemed half-hearted – from the Gladiators, Faith, Hope and Charity, through a dogged persistence in retaining Hurricanes as the fighter of choice, even as it became increasingly obvious that they were outclassed by the 109F.

Hitler was little better. If he'd heeded the advice of Rommel and invaded the Island at its lowest ebb in early 1942, North Africa and the oilfields of the Middle East might have fallen to the Nazis. As it was, starting with the delivery on 9th May, the Spitfire pilots regained control of the air, allowing Malta's offensive forces drastically to reduce the tonnage of supplies reaching North Africa. It was this that made Montgomery's victory at El Alamein in October/November 1942 possible.

The Luftwaffe continued to pound away, but more and more Spitfires were delivered (213 between June and October 1942) and the Germans never regained their former ascendancy.

The Islanders suffered throughout. Only two ships made it through in June, and only five from Operation Pedestal in August, although even this seemed miraculous, with the tanker Ohio inching into Grand Harbour lashed between two destroyers, a wrecked Stuka adorning her mangled superstructure. The siege was finally lifted with the arrival of convoys in November and December 1942, although the hardships continued long after that.

The last, ineffective, blitz took place in October 1942, and the Island went on to be the stepping stone for the assault on southern Europe beginning in July 1943.

King George VI visited Malta in June 1943, Churchill in November and President Roosevelt in December. The President ended an address at Luqa with the words, 'Malta stood alone but unafraid in the centre of the sea, one tiny bright flame in the darkness – a beacon of hope for the clearer days that have come.'

There have been many political changes since these momentous events. But, as its flag testifies, Malta remains proud to be known as The George Cross Island.

Author's Note

For many reasons, I found Wings Over Malta a much more challenging project than my Battle of Britain book, Wings Over Summer. The major problem seemed to be how to meld the fictional with the historic.

While the Battle of Britain was fought over a relatively short timescale, it was a large battle with many participants. It seemed relatively easy to slip a mythical squadron and its characters into the skies over England.

In contrast, the air war over Malta was fought over a long period, but with a much smaller cast of squadrons and characters. From the outset, I felt I had to include at least some of the genuine participants, and to do so without doing them an injustice.

As with the Battle of Britain, I decided to cover only a relatively short but critical period of the battle, from the day of the first Spitfire delivery from HMS Eagle in early March, to the day following the second large delivery from USS Wasp two months later. By this time, although the battle had some way to run, the Spitfire pilots were well on the way to regaining control of the skies over the Island.

Once again, the book is based as much as possible on the daily pattern of activity on and above Malta. I received much help on a research visit to the Island, notably from the Director of the Malta Aviation Museum, Ray Polidano, and from a guide at the Lascaris War Rooms, Wayne Saillard.

My other major research tools were the books: First Light, by Geoffrey Wellum (which provided the spark); Malta, the Spitfire Year, 1942, by Christopher Shores and Brian Cull with Nicola Malizia; Malta Spitfire Aces, by Steve Nichols; Malta, The Thorn in Rommel's Side, by Laddie Lucas; The Air Battle For Malta, by Lord James Douglas-Hamilton; Malta Spitfire Pilot, by Denis Barnham; and Fortress Malta, by James Holland. In addition, I found the website, maltagc.wordpress.com extremely useful.

Special thanks go to Martin Butler for the maps and the

cover design, based on the image, Spitfire Flypast, by Paulo Camera; to members of the Tiny Writers of Penarth, who listened to and commented on my monthly readings; and to my wife for her patience and her proof reading.

As in Wings Over Summer, I chose to concentrate almost exclusively on the Spitfire pilots and their groundcrew, which means the heroism of others has gone largely unmentioned.

While on a few occasions I claimed artistic license to manipulate the facts, there is no doubt that I will also have made many mistakes; for these, I can only apologise.

You can find out more about my writing from my website: http://www.ronpowell.co.uk.

And if you enjoyed Wings Over Malta, please try my Battle of Britain novel, Wings Over Summer, and my memoir, Shropshire Blue, A Shropshire Lad in the RAF.

Mediterranean Map

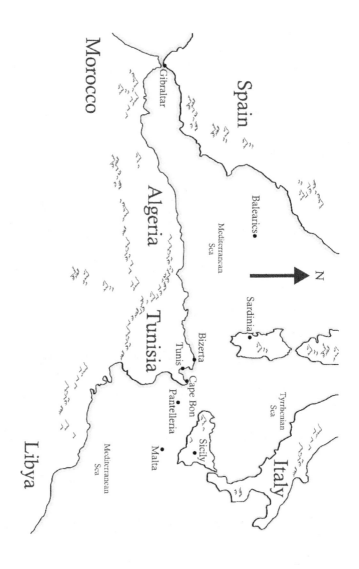

Malta Map

Gozo

Comino

N

Ghajn
Tufficha

St. Paul's Bay

Imtarfa•
Mdina•   •Mosta
•Rabat   •Ta Qali   Sliema•
         •Attard   Valletta
                  Floriana•
Dingli   •Grand
Cliffs   Harbour
         Luqa • Marsa•   Three
                              Cities
              Safi•

Mediterranean
Sea

Hal Far•

•Filfla   Marsaxlokk
                          Bay

                    Delimara Point
              Kalafrana

Glossary and Abbreviations

Ack-ack: Anti-aircraft fire.

Angels: codeword preceding height in thousands of feet (eg, angels one five = 15,000 feet).

AOC Malta: - Air Officer Commanding Malta - the officer commanding Malta's air assets.

AOC-in-C Middle East: - Air Officer Commanding-in-Chief Middle East– The officer commanding the Middle East's air assets.

Bandit: enemy aircraft.

Buster: full throttle.

Clock Code: the pilot imagines himself sitting at the centre of a clock face, with twelve o'clock dead ahead and three o'clock ninety degrees right, etc. He reports sightings accordingly (eg, bandits ten o'clock high = enemy aircraft 60 degrees left of the nose and above the horizon).

CO: Commanding Officer.

DFC: - Distinguished Flying Cross - medal awarded to officers in recognition of gallantry in the air.

DFM: - Distinguished Flying Medal - equivalent of the DFC awarded to ranks other than officers.

Echelon: Each successive wingman sits alongside the tailplane of the aircraft in front, so the formation flows diagonally from the leader.

Finger Four: Based on the Luftwaffe's Schwarm, the RAF formation that superseded the Vic. The four aircraft position as if on the fingertips of a flat hand, the two pairs quartering the airspace around them.

Flak: Anti-aircraft fire.

Flap: A commotion or disturbance, as in, 'there's a bit of a flap on.'

Flaps: Surfaces on the inboard rear of each wing, lowered on final approach to increase lift, allowing a lower nose attitude and a higher stalling speed.

Flight: 249 Squadron comprises two flights of eight aircraft - A and B.

g: the effect of gravity on pilots in a manoeuvre, making them feel heavier or lighter. Pulling 3g makes them feel three times their normal weight and drags blood from their brains, while pushing to 0g makes them feel weightless.

George Cross: Highest civilian award for gallantry.

GOC Malta: General Officer Commanding Malta – the officer commanding the Army on Malta.

Jabo: Fighter bomber version of Messerschmitt bf109.

KD: - Khaki Dress – Uniform to be worn overseas between certain dates, say 1st April to 30th September. Included more formal attire, but, by day, likely to be khaki shirt, shorts and long socks.

IntO: Intelligence Officer.

Line Abreast: a formation in which aircraft fly side by side, their wingtips generally no more than a few yards apart.

Line Astern: a formation in which aircraft fly one behind the other, generally no more than a few yards apart.

LMF: Lacking Moral Fibre, the term for cowardice. Bomber aircrew were more likely to be given the label and treated harshly than fighter pilots.

MT: - Mechanical Transport - an RAF station's fleet of vehicles.

MO: Medical Officer.

NCO: non-commissioned officer.

OTU: Operational Training Unit.

Pair: Formation of two aircraft flying a couple of hundred yards apart, each pilot looking primarily inward to quarter the airspace around the other.

Pancake: return to base and land.

RDF: Radio Direction Finding - the early name for Radar.

R/T: Radio Telephony – radio conversations between different stations: ie, aircraft and controller.

Roger: message heard and understood.

Rotte: Pair of German aircraft.

SAC: Senior Aircraftman.

Schwarm: Formation of four German aircraft.

Section: 249 Squadron's two flights each have two sections of four aircraft (eg A Flight comprises Red and Yellow Sections and B Flight, Green and Blue).

Sitrep: Situation report.

SOPs: Standard Operating Procedures.

Swagger Stick: Short stick – about the size of a riding crop – made of rattan and carried by some officers. Some still carried them when I joined the Royal Air Force in 1973, but I don't think I saw them after the 1970s.

TLAR: That looks about right. Jack's method of estimating when to do things.

Trolleyac: Trolley Accumulator – small, two-wheeled, trolley containing batteries, from which, via a long black lead plugged in beneath the engine cowling, electrical power was provided to an aircraft on the ground.

u/s: Unserviceable.

UXB: Unexploded bomb.

VC: Victoria Cross - Highest military award for gallantry.

VHF: Very High Frequency radio.

Vic: a formation like an arrowhead with wingmen fanning back either side of the leader, each sitting to the side of the tailplane of the aircraft ahead.

Vector: codeword preceding the course to steer in degrees (eg vector zero nine zero = steer a course of 090 degrees).

WAAF: member of the Women's Auxiliary Air Force - pronounced Waff.

Wilco: I will comply with your instructions.

Made in the USA
Coppell, TX
11 September 2020